TORMENT

The Inferno Trilogy
Book Two

TORMENT

A. R. Nicole

Torment: Book Two of the Inferno Trilogy
Copyright © 2019 by A. R. Nicole

Published by

PINECONE PUBLISHING

PineConePublishing.com
ARNicole.com
AR@ARNicole.com
Follow on Twitter @ARNicoleBooks, Pinterest, Facebook
and Instagram: books.arnicole

Cover and Interior Design: Nick Zelinger, NZGraphics.com
Editor: Barb Wilson, EditPartner.com
Book Shepherd: Judith Briles, TheBookShepherd.com

ISBN: 978-1-7320699-2-3 (print)
ISBN: 978-1-7320699-3-0 (e-book)
Library of Congress Control Number: 2018964394

First Edition

Printed in the United States of America

For my sister, Elise.
No matter how far apart we are,
you are always here with me.
You show the world what it means
to be a beautiful person.
Every single day.

Books by A. R. Nicole

The Inferno Trilogy
Book One: Descent (2018)
Book Two: Torment (Spring 2019)
Book Three: Ascent (Summer 2019)

**Watch for The Aftershock Series
Coming in 2020**

BOOK TWO

TORMENT

PROLOGUE

It has started.

It started with one. Now there are five. There will be even more.

The descent has started. It cannot stop. There is no turning back. Down, down, down I go…

And there, in the deepest pit, I will reap my reward.

He laughed into the darkness. The darkness did not echo back.

They have no idea what's coming.

1

THE SOUND OF leather gloves hitting hundred-pound heavy bags was usually therapeutic. Whenever the running and the scotch didn't take the edge off the job, he'd turn his mind off here. The physical release was always painful, but it was welcome.

He knew he would hurt like hell in the morning. It didn't matter. His knuckles were bleeding, his arms were begging for a break, and he didn't stop. He couldn't stop.

It's not working.

He hadn't been able to calm down since the morning. Nolan had driven him home in silence and dumped him at the front door without a second glance. He'd spent hours endlessly pacing around his apartment, playing the scene over and over in his head. Each time it ended with her icy expression and her roommate's parting words.

"I should've let her beat the living shit out of you, you asshole."

After three hours of wearing a track in the carpet, he'd gone for a run. Two hours later, frustrated and cursing, he'd thrown his bag into his car and headed to the gym. His usual sparring partner wasn't around, so he'd picked a bag in the back corner and gone at it. Hard.

Ryder wiped the sweat off of his face. Every goddamned time his eyes shut…

Fuck.

He hit the bag harder.

The gym was busy, so it took a few minutes to find him. He was kicking the crap out of a heavy bag, and from the looks of it, he'd been at it for a while. Harrison stood back and watched him swing wildly, picking up his pace until he missed the bag altogether and lurched forward into the wall. The older detective chuckled under his breath and sauntered over toward the sweating, swearing heap in the corner.

"You know, the whole point is to actually hit the bag, Gabe."

Ryder looked up, surprised to find his former partner looming over him. He wearily pushed to his feet.

"What…what're you doing here, Logan?" he asked, steadying the bag and getting ready for another set.

"Why does anybody come to the gym?" he replied.

"Not for the reasons I do."

"Clearly. The run didn't do it for you today?" He nodded, moving to stand behind the bag and hold it still.

Ryder didn't argue or tell him to move. He just started hitting the bag.

"So," Logan said in between hits, "you wanna talk about it?"

"About what?"

"You know what. The scene you made this morning."

Ryder put his head down and focused on the black bag in front of him. That earned him a slap on the side of the head. He ripped his eyes up and glared. "Hey! What the fuck?"

Harrison smirked. "Eyes up, dummy. You know you don't box like that. Did I teach you nothing?"

"Don't fucking hit me in the head again," he spat.

"Don't let yourself get hit."

"If you came here to try to piss me off, it's working."

"Great. Maybe you'll get pissed enough to tell me what the hell happened today."

Ryder stopped mid-swing.

Logan noticed his facial expression change. His eyes closed, then tore open just as fast. Logan's forehead wrinkled. Gabriel looked like he was going to be sick.

What the hell is up with him?

"Look, finish whatever you're doing here and meet me on the mat. You could use some agility work," Logan said, grabbing his gym bag and heading off toward the locker room.

He emerged several minutes later and found Ryder still going hard on the same bag. Logan stepped behind him and grabbed his right arm as he brought it back, locking it in place.

"Enough. I said get to the mat. Now."

Ryder glared at him but nodded, grabbed his towel, and followed him to the center of the gym. A large area had been cleared out to let fighters train out in the open. Logan grabbed two small sparring pads, one for each hand, and put them on. Ryder slipped his hands out of his boxing gloves and rewrapped his hands up to the wrists. It didn't take long.

"C'mon, rookie. Start easy. Transition when you're ready." Logan grinned, holding out his hands.

Ryder started in, alternating jabs. Harrison moved backward, slowly, in a circle, forcing the younger man to move his feet to keep the pads within striking distance. After a few minutes, he started moving the pads themselves, forcing Ryder to concentrate even harder.

Logan kept the pace slow. He wanted something more out of this session besides sore wrists and a pissed-off partner.

"You didn't answer me."

Hit. Hit.

"About what?"

Hit. Slide to the right. *Hit.*

"About what the hell happened today."

Hit. Hit. Alternate. *Hit.*

"I don't want to talk about it."

Hit. Hit.

"Did your mind just short-circuit?"

Hit. Alternate. *Hit. Hit.*

"I said…"

"Or have you decided bullying young girls is your thing now?"

Hit. Hit. Hit. Ryder picked up the pace. "Shut the fuck up."

Hit.

"No. I'm curious," Harrison said, advancing forward, sarcasm dripping off his lips. "Just how did you think that would go?"

Hit. Hit.

"Drop it, Logan."

Hit. Hit. Alternate. *Hit.*

"She didn't deserve that attack, Gabe, and you fucking know it."

Ryder stopped in his tracks. Harrison powered forward, shoving him back with the pads. Ryder regained his footing quickly and squared up. He wasn't about to be dropped on his ass twice in one day.

"Did you think it would be fun? Bullying her into a half-assed confession?"

Hit. Hit. Hit. Faster.

"No."

Hit.

"Did you ever think to yourself 'hey, I'm acting like a complete nutjob'?"

Harrison took a swipe at Ryder's head with the pad, which he dodged.

Hit. Hit.

"If you'd have told us what the hell you were thinking, I wouldn't have let you fucking near her."

Hit. Pause. *Hit.*

"Did you even give a damn about what you were doing to her? Did you see her face, Ryder?"

Hit. Hit. Alternate. *Hit. Hit.*

Gabriel picked up his pace again, and Logan compensated accordingly, still advancing. "Shut up."

"No. Fucking answer me."

Ryder's eyes blazed. Harrison just smirked and lowered his voice.

"So, you did it to, what, get your rocks off watching her cry? Was that fun for you, Gabe? She's prettier than your usual playthings."

Gabriel froze, glaring at his former partner. He tightened his fists. Logan wriggled his hands free from the pads. Ryder growled and lunged forward, his right fist intended for Harrison's face.

At the last second, Logan dodged and threw him to the floor, the pads unceremoniously tossed to the side. He grabbed Ryder's right arm and wrenched it behind his back, then put a knee to the back of his neck.

Gabriel struggled until he felt the pressure against his spine, then went limp to signal defeat. Logan had made his point. He didn't need a broken neck on top of it.

When he was sure the fight was out of him, Logan released his hold and let him roll onto his back. Gabriel sat up, draped his arms over his bent knees, and hung his head between them.

"Tell me this," Logan said, sitting down beside him. "And don't bullshit me. Do you honestly believe she's responsible? That she's pulling strings to have these people killed?"

Ryder shook his head.

"Then why the fuck did you accuse her like that?" he asked, sighing. "Gabe, you didn't just politely ask if she had anything to do with this shit. You hung her out to rot. Jesus."

Ryder mumbled under his breath. The older man smiled and nodded.

"That's what I thought. C'mon. You've beaten yourself up enough for one day."

Logan hauled Ryder to his feet. They walked back to the locker room in silence, showered, changed, and headed outside. The afternoon sun was up and, despite the low reading on the thermometer, it still felt warm outside.

Ryder threw his gym bag in his car, and Harrison did the same. The younger detective opened his driver side door, his biceps screaming in protest.

"Nope."

Logan shoved the door closed before Ryder had a chance to even consider sitting down. He walked off down the sidewalk without looking back. Ryder followed, head down. He knew better than to argue.

They ended up at a coffee shop two blocks down from the gym. They both knew it well. Logan grabbed a table by the window while Ryder paid for the coffee. He gave his former partner a minute to compose himself.

"So, explain something to me."

"I thought we were done talking," came the exhausted reply.

"We're done fighting, dumbass, not talking."

Ryder sighed and closed his eyes, then instantly opened them again.

Every time.

Logan was smirking at him when he looked up. "All right. Where were we? Oh yeah, the part where you start talking."

"What do you want me to say?"

"I want you to tell me what the hell snapped in you this morning. Nolan was right about you taking the news about Carrol badly, but holy shit."

"I, I..." he stuttered, staring into his coffee, "I don't know. You saw how he treated her on Friday. What he called her. Then he turns up dead with his tongue cut out on Sunday morning? It fit."

"And so clearly she murdered him," Logan said sarcastically.

"She's connected to all of them, Logan, not just Carrol. She has ties to all of them."

"And since when does that mean she's a criminal mastermind? Not to mention it seems like she's really protective of your first vic, that Oakes girl. You've got a nasty bruise on your face to prove it. Why would she kill her?"

"I don't have an answer for that. She's the one that doesn't fit."

"Carter?"

"Oakes. I can't make her murder fit with the others. The other victims had something wrong with them. Some kind of vice. For all we can tell, Lisa Oakes was a good person. But she kicked this whole thing off."

"And again, how does this mean young Dr. Carter's to blame?"

Ryder dropped his head into his hands and sighed. "Do you have a better idea, Logan?"

"You just said you don't believe she did this."

"I don't."

"But you're going after her anyway. That makes perfect fucking sense."

"She fits. I just need time…"

"No, she doesn't, Gabe. And you know it."

They sat in silence for a few minutes. Logan was just about to open his mouth when Ryder's face cleared. "She's the link."

He waited, and when his partner didn't elaborate, he pushed. "Yeah, you've said that…"

"I accused her because I didn't see any other options. Any… any other way this made sense."

"But you do now?"

"Maybe."

Harrison leaned back in his chair enough to take the front two legs off of the floor. "All right. I'll humor you. Start talking."

2

GRAYSON SPENT THE better part of her Sunday trying to keep control of herself. She attempted to smile at regular intervals and participate in small talk, but it was no use. She felt awful, and it showed. By noon, she'd completely given up the masquerade. She was miserable.

Noah had shown up at the house after he'd finished rounding at the hospital, and he'd spent the day trying to keep her spirits up. He had even brought groceries to cook a proper dinner. She never came right out and told him what had happened, but she had the feeling Babs had given him a play-by-play. He fussed over her more than usual, and both he and Barbara tried to keep the conversation as far away from the hospital and cops as possible.

Grayson waited until early evening, when Babs had gone upstairs to take a shower, to say anything. She was sitting on the couch with Noah when the time hit.

"You two can stop walking on eggshells around me, you know," she said softly.

Noah smiled at her and turned the TV volume down. "We're driving you nuts, aren't we, lovie?"

She nodded. "Kind of."

Noah flinched. "I'm sorry."

"Don't be. I appreciate it, I do. But it's getting a bit, um, unnecessary. We all know what happened this morning. Not talking about it isn't going to make it disappear."

Noah rested his arm on the back of the couch. "I heard you kicked his butt."

Grayson smiled shyly and diverted her eyes to the floor. "I wouldn't say that. He just wasn't expecting me to do anything like that. It caught him off guard."

"Neither was Babs. She told me she nearly peed her pants when you slapped him."

"It wasn't my finest hour, Noah." She shook her head. "I shouldn't have done that."

I actually HIT him. I attacked another person. Good God, what's wrong with me?

"It still would've been great to see," he said, his smile fading. "Do you think they're serious? About coming after you for all this?"

She hugged her knees to her chest. "I don't know, Noah. I know I didn't do any of this, but what does that prove?"

"If those idiots believe that, they need to reassign the case."

"I did a bit of digging right after Lisa's funeral." She shrugged. "Those detectives are some of the best in the department, Ryder included."

"What is his problem?"

"Who?"

Noah scooted closer on the couch. "You know who, Gray. Ryder. One minute, I think he's making eyes at you, and the next he barges into your house and talks to you like you're the scum of the planet."

"I told you that you were blowing things out of proportion," she scolded.

"I'm usually so good at picking up on that kind of thing," he moaned.

"I'll forgive you this once." She grinned at her friend.

She didn't dare mention that since Halloween, she'd started to think the same thing. Just for one quick, fleeting moment, she'd let herself believe. Not anymore.

Noah sighed and nodded. "Thanks. Are you going to be okay?"

"We'll see. Probably. I just need a few days to get my head around the fact that I'm being accused of murder."

"Shouldn't they have arrested you or something?"

"How should I know? All of my police knowledge comes from watching *Law and Order* reruns."

Noah smiled at her, then opened up his arms. She gladly settled into his side and threw a blanket over her legs. They flipped channels until they found a movie they could both agree on and watched in amicable silence until Babs came back downstairs. Her hair was wet, thrown back in a towel and twisted in that way that only women seem to know how to do.

"I swear, you two are going to give me diabetes," she said, rolling her eyes and sitting down on the side chair.

"What?"

"This…" she motioned with her hand moving in between the two of them. "This…sickeningly sweet display. Ugh. It's like biting into a sugar cube," she said, feigning annoyance.

"We'll keep that in mind," Grayson replied.

"So, J.B., what're we planning for our girl?" Babs asked, looking at Noah.

He wrinkled his forehead at her, confused.

"She's calling you James Bond right now, J.B. for short," Grayson explained.

"Original," he returned sarcastically.

"Don't be too harsh. She was strongly influenced by mimosas," Grayson chided.

"Well?" Babs pressed.

"It's a surprise." He winked.

"You really don't have to do anything," Grayson started in protest.

"Nope. Stop right there. You've had a shitty few days. Maybe the week gets better; maybe it doesn't. But I wanna take you out for a fun night. A real grown-up night out. No costumes. Babs is coming, too. Just deal with it."

"You know I don't like big surprises," she moaned. "I don't have time to…"

"Stop being so difficult. We'll take care of everything. You just have to show your pretty face." Noah winked.

Barbara nodded enthusiastically from her chair.

Grayson leaned back on the couch and sighed. She was going out next Friday whether she liked it or not.

3

THE START OF the week didn't bring any surprises. Rounding. Operative cases. Consults. Bland hospital food. Repeat. Listening to the rumor mill about Dr. Carrol. Attempting to avoid it. Failing miserably. Repeat.

It was now officially November, and that meant Thompson had gone back to the emergency medicine department where he belonged. His replacement was nearly an exact carbon copy, however, and Grayson was seriously considering calling him "Thompson Two." He was just as slow and just as timid.

Oh well.

On Wednesday afternoon, midway through a pelvic ring reconstruction with a particularly cantankerous attending, her pager went off. She didn't think twice about it. It had been going off all morning. Why should it stop during a critical part of the case?

She kept her focus on the surgical field while noticing in her peripheral vision that the circulating nurse had grabbed the stupid black box and was getting on the phone. Five minutes later, the nurse was still on the phone, attempting to explain yet again that Grayson wasn't able to break scrub at the moment.

"What the hell is going on over there?" Dr. Finney bellowed.

The nurse put the receiver to her shoulder.

"It's the department secretary. Apparently, there are two detectives at her desk asking for Dr. Carter."

Grayson stiffened but tried not to show her panic in her face. As long as she could keep her eyes from bugging out of her head, she could hide her fear behind her surgical mask.

Breathe, breathe. In and out. Breathe.

"Expecting someone, Carter?" Finney spat.

"No, sir."

He looked up and over her shoulder to the circulating nurse. "Tell that ridiculous woman that Carter is staying here. She can take a damn message. She's a secretary. That's her entire job!" he bellowed.

Grayson craned her neck around and nodded her agreement to the nurse, who in turn raised the receiver back to her ear.

"No message, Dr. Carter. They said it wasn't important."

"Okay, thanks." She did her best to keep the tremor out of her voice.

"If you're done chatting, Carter, I'd like to finish sometime this week…"

Finney glared at her over his wire-rimmed glasses.

"Sorry, sir," she replied, moving her retractors into the proper position.

4

THIS HAS TO be the week from hell.

Ryder closed his eyes against the strong fluorescent lights in the squad room and rubbed his temples. His headaches were getting worse.

The captain wouldn't get off of his back about their lack of progress finding a suspect. He knew the pressure wasn't McCallister's fault, not directly. He was getting pressure from the media, the chief of detectives, the mayor, and now Dr. Carrol's widow. The psychotic harpy was on track to sue everyone from the janitor to the President of the United States over her husband's death. Nolan and Harrison were keeping as much of the fallout from hitting him as possible, which made sure his guilt was at an all-time high. And of course, there was...

Shit.

He glanced at the black overcoat thrown over the back of his desk chair. It had been delivered by courier Monday morning. There was a perfectly folded white linen pocket square in the right pocket.

Goddamn it.

Logan and Blake had gone to the hospital yesterday. Grayson had refused to talk to them. Ryder appreciated the effort since they'd actually gone on his behalf. At the end of the day, he was the one who had made such a royal fucking mess of things. He hadn't slept. Nolan was damn near force-feeding him. The caffeine in his morning coffee wasn't cutting it anymore. Neither was the scotch when he got home at night.

A soft knock on the interview room door startled Ryder out of his head.

"Easy." Nolan smiled, holding up a white paper bag. "It's just lunch."

"Not hungry," he replied.

"I didn't say it was for you," he said, sitting down.

"Really?" Gabriel smirked. He was almost disappointed. "That's a first."

"No, of course not, ass. You're eating lunch today. Deal with it."

Blake took two sandwiches and two bags of chips out of the bag, passing one set over to his partner.

"Where's Harrison?"

"Taking a nap in the crib. We're wearing the old guy out," he replied, taking a bite.

Ryder just stared at his meal, picking at the plastic.

"Don't make me get the captain to make you eat," Blake threatened. He knew Ryder hated that tone, and sure enough, he picked up the sandwich without hesitating.

"You come up with any more ideas?"

"The same ones I told you at the beginning of the week."

"Remind me."

Ryder rolled his eyes. Logan was rubbing off on his partner. It was becoming annoying.

"My assumption that Gray... Dr. Carter is at the center of these murders hasn't changed."

"So, she's why these doctors are dying. Great."

"Yes, but not as I originally thought. I got stuck on her..."

"Yeah, no shit," Blake mumbled into his sandwich.

Ryder shot him a glare. "...and I didn't step back. She didn't kill these people. But she's the reason someone is killing these doctors."

"You've lost me," Nolan said, mid-bite. "You told me she's not pulling the strings."

"Whoever is killing these people is doing it because they're related to her somehow. I can't figure out what has them targeted. If it's just because they've had contact with her or if it's something more."

"And the church thing?"

He shook his head. "I'm not sure yet."

"So, we've eliminated one suspect. Kind of."

Ryder nodded and took a bite of his sandwich, suddenly realizing it had been a long time since he had properly eaten. He was halfway through his meal before he noticed Blake had stopped eating. The color had completely drained away from his partner's face.

"What's wrong?"

Blake stuttered and cleared his throat repeatedly. "Uh, well... umm...I...so, these people are all connected to Dr. Carter somehow..."

"We've just been over this."

"Maybe this is a stupid question then, but..." he trailed off, then thought better of it and asked anyway. "Gabe, what's stopping him or her or them or whoever from...from going after Grayson?"

The room went dead silent. You could have heard a pin drop. When he didn't get a response, Nolan looked up across the table. His partner was white. The blood had drained from his face, and his eyes were fixated on the shining steel in front of him.

Before Blake could say anything, Ryder was sprinting down the hallway toward the elevators.

5

NOAH MASON HAD had a rather rough day. Thursday morning had brought an onslaught of extremely sick patients into the hospital. His interns were still finding their feet, and on top of all of his usual duties, he'd had to double-check their work all day.

He gratefully breathed in the evening air as he walked out to his car. The nights were getting much longer, and the air was definitely cooler, but he didn't care. He was just happy to be outside of the hospital.

He hit his key fob as he approached his car, absently noting that Grayson's car wasn't in its designated spot. Hopefully, she was already at home. He'd been tasked with picking up dinner on his way down to see her. She was still a wreck after Sunday, even though she refused to openly show it.

He hurt for her.

Noah dropped his bag into the back seat, pushing a few books onto the floor to make room for the impending to-go bags. He stood up and carefully extracted himself from the car.

Detective Ryder was waiting for him.

"Fecking hell!" He startled, moving backward.

"Dr. Mason." Gabriel nodded by way of greeting. He kept his hands shoved deep in the pockets of his overcoat.

"Detective Ryder," Mason replied sharply, immediately turning his back.

"I need to talk to you."

"Fuck off, detective," he said without turning around. "I don't have anything to say to you."

Noah started to open his driver's side door, but Ryder slammed it shut and held it closed.

"What the fuck..." he spat, spinning around.

Noah was about to start telling the detective off, but the look on the man's face stopped him. Something was wrong.

"You don't have to say a damned thing to me. Just listen," Ryder hissed. His voice was pressured.

Noah inwardly shuddered. Eventually, he relaxed against the side of the car. "I'll give you five minutes."

"More than enough," he mumbled. He removed his arm from the car door and started pacing. "She won't talk to me."

"Excuse me?"

"Grays...I mean, Dr. Carter."

"Can you blame her? You treated her like shit on Sunday, from what I hear."

Ryder didn't argue, which surprised Noah, but he did grimace. It was almost as if remembering the day caused him physical pain. When the detective didn't continue, Noah jumped in. "You tried talking to her?"

He nodded.

"Today."

"She slapped you again, did she?" Noah grinned.

"No, but I wouldn't have blamed her if she had. I didn't get close. Her department ran interference."

"Good."

Ryder nodded again.

Noah huffed. "So, what do you want from me? I'm not going to let you bloody near her."

"I know that," Ryder said, now pacing frantically behind the car. "I'm not asking...I..." he paused. "I need her to be safe."

Noah shoved himself up from the side of the car, suddenly on alert. "She's in danger?"

"I don't know for sure."

"But she might be," he pressed.

Ryder nodded.

Noah weighed his options, grinding his teeth. "As much as I want to kick your arse, detective, I'm listening. Just stop..." he motioned toward his pacing, "...doing whatever the bloody hell that is."

Ryder stopped and leaned up against the trunk of Noah's car. "I was a fucking idiot. It was the first connection between them all that I could make. I was wrong to accuse her. But I can't prove that she's not next on the list."

Ryder subconsciously pleaded with the young doctor in front of him to understand. By the look on Mason's face, he did.

"So, now what?"

"I need to see her."

Noah vehemently shook his head. "I won't do that to her."

"Mason..." Ryder warned.

"The answer is no." Noah's voice was firm.

"I can't protect her if..."

Mason held up his hands. "You have no clue what you did to her on Sunday. And you know just as well as I do that you don't have to do anything personally here. Send someone else to talk to her. One of your partners, maybe."

Gabriel shook his head. "No, it has to be me."

"Oh, please." Noah rolled his eyes dramatically.

"Goddamn it..."

"Fine, explain it then," Noah said.

"Because she's my responsibility to protect, goddamn it!" he roared, slamming his hand down on the trunk of a neighboring car.

Noah jumped back, completely startled by the outburst. It was a miracle there wasn't a large dent in the body of the poor sedan.

He studied the detective for a moment. There were bags under his eyes. He looked pale. He hadn't shaved. It looked like he hadn't been sleeping, let alone taking care of himself. Noah noted the broken skin and bruises on his hands. He'd been in a fight with something.

Or someone.

"Okay, you have your reasons to be around her. I have mine for keeping you away from her. But if she's in danger, I want her protected," he relented. Noah ran a hand through his hair and paused. "Figure out a way to make this Grayson's decision. I'm not forcing either of our positions on her."

Ryder nodded.

"Either way, I'm still taking her out tomorrow..." Noah muttered under his breath.

"What was that?" Ryder asked coolly.

"No...nothing," Mason stuttered, looking wide-eyed at the detective.

How in the bloody hell did he hear me?

"Where?"

"I'm not..."

"Goddamn it, Mason..."

Noah held up his hands again. "Her decision, remember? If she stupidly lets you anywhere near her, I'll tell you when and where. But this is a night for her, to undo the shit you put her through. So, no screwing it up. Good enough?"

"Good enough." Ryder nodded. He took the binder out from underneath his arm, opened it on the trunk of Noah's car, and took a pen from his coat pocket.

6

GRAYSON AND BARBARA were sitting on the couch in the living room when Noah opened the front door. He was late, which was unusual.

"You're late! I'm starving over here!" Babs exclaimed, jumping up to grab the bags of food.

"Sorry," he mumbled.

"Let me get these dished out. You both stay here. Noah, your money is on the table," she said, practically running off into the kitchen.

He nodded, grabbing the bills and stuffing them into his wallet. Grayson noticed he was on edge.

"Hey, you okay? You look like you've seen a ghost," she teased.

"Um, I need to talk to you about something."

Her smile faded. "What?"

He sat down on the couch.

"Have they tried to contact you? The cops?"

She nodded. "Yeah, at the hospital. Most of the time I've been able to dodge them since I've been in the OR. Somebody showed up yesterday and then again today at the department office, but we had a trauma patient waiting in the ER. I got out of it. Why?"

He sighed. "Gray, I need you to keep an open mind here, okay?"

"Okay…" She narrowed her eyes at him.

"I talked to Detective Ryder today…"

"You *what?* And you said what, exactly?" she shrieked, immediately standing up from the couch.

"Be quiet and sit down. This isn't something your roommate needs to hear," he hissed, glancing toward the kitchen. "He cornered me in the parking lot. They know you didn't kill those people. I'm not sure what the hell happened here on Sunday. I don't think *he* knows what happened. But you should see him, Gray. He looks like shit."

"He does?"

Noah nodded, hastily digging into his coat pocket. "We talked. About you. Look, I...I told him it wasn't my place to just let him come back here. Truthfully, I'd prefer to forget the man exists. But what he said worried me. For you. So, this was the compromise," he said, pulling an envelope out of his coat. "You decide, love. Read it. Burn it. I don't know what it says, and I don't care," he said, pressing it into her hands. "Please don't be angry with me. But what he said just..."

She held up her hand to silence him. "I trust you," she said, hiding it in the front pocket of her hoodie just as Babs returned with dinner.

Grayson spent the next hour with one hand stuck into the front pocket of her hoodie, fingering the letter that she had hidden there.

What in the hell am I supposed to do with this?

The man who had written it had barged into her house and accused her of murder. She still couldn't get the things he'd said to her in the kitchen out of her head. But Noah had been the one to bring it into the house, and if whatever Detective Ryder had said had agitated him that much...

Babs was halfway through a bottle of chardonnay and babbling on about her upcoming charity gala when Grayson decided she couldn't take it anymore. Clutching the letter for dear life, she grabbed a blanket off the couch and quickly walked out onto the front patio. She sat down on one of the rocking chairs and pulled the blanket over her lap. Sucking in a deep breath, she finally looked at it.

Her name was written across the ivory envelope in a masculine, albeit elegant, script. She popped the seam and pulled out a single piece of ivory card stock. Same handwriting. Grayson pulled her feet up underneath her and started reading.

Dr. Carter-

Before I begin, please forgive Dr. Mason. I gave him no choice in this, despite what he may have told you.

There is no way for me to apologize for my actions on Sunday. I have no reasonable excuse for them. I'm sorry for any suffering I caused you. If I could take back every word I said to you, I would.

I believe you are at the center of all this, and I am incredibly concerned for your safety. I don't know what's driving this, or who, and the danger is escalating. I don't want to see you hurt.

Grayson, I know that I have lost your trust. I know you no longer wish for me to say your name. I have to live with that. Please don't endanger your life out of spite for me. Let me do my job and protect your life with mine. You have my word that once I close this case, you will never have to see me again.

Please, let me keep you safe.

-Gabriel M. Ryder

Grayson read the letter through three times before she looked up. The street was completely quiet. Even the birds were asleep. She turned the card stock over in her hands. It was heavy, expensive. A monogram was subtly embossed on the lower right corner.

Keep me safe? Protect my life with his? What on earth?

She wrapped the blanket tighter around her legs. It wasn't particularly cold outside for a Colorado November, but Grayson suddenly felt like she couldn't get warm. She closed her eyes against the cold. The thought of having to have anything to do with him again was terrifying, but if he was right…

She jumped when she heard the front door close. Noah settled back on the porch railing opposite her, his arms crossed over his chest. He eyed her suspiciously. "You read it."

She nodded.

"And?"

"Here." She handed the letter over. He read it through twice, eyebrows raised. When he finished, he sucked in a large breath and whistled through his teeth. "Wow."

"Wow, what?"

"You read this, right?" he chuckled, waving the paper back and forth.

"Yeah."

"The last paragraph, too?"

"Noah…" she sighed.

"Look, lovie," he said, sitting down in the other rocking chair, "I don't know about you, but that last bit is as close to a love letter as you get nowadays."

Grayson dropped her eyes to her lap and blushed. "So, you think I should…"

"I don't think anything. What you do with this…," he said, waving the card stock again before handing it back to her, "is entirely up to you."

"Am I supposed to...?"

"There is no supposed to."

"I don't know if I can face him, Noah."

God, that makes me sound like a weak, whiny baby.

"No one said you have to."

"Stop it!" she hissed, standing up from her chair. "You're not helping! I just...I don't...Argh!"

She stormed over to the opposite side of the porch and looked out into the black night sky. Noah took the cue and, without a word, went back inside the house.

Grayson stayed outside for quite some time, leaning her head on the side of the house to think. After a while, the temperature dropped below freezing, and even the fleece blanket wasn't enough to keep her warm. She bundled herself up and walked back inside the house, intentionally avoiding the living room. Noah was asleep on the couch in front of the TV. Barbara had gone to bed.

She made her way slowly up the stairs to her bedroom. After changing into black jersey pajama bottoms and a gray tank, she grabbed the letter off of her dresser and curled up on her window seat. She read through the letter again, twice, and let her eyes drift out over the street. A black SUV was parked across the street, just beyond the street light.

Was that there the whole time I was outside?

She didn't recognize it but thought nothing of it. People were always parking different cars along her street. Her eyelids grew heavier and heavier. When the words on the page in front of her began to blur together, she knew it was getting late. The street below was still quiet. No one else was awake.

Time for bed.

She was about to call it a night and go to bed when the driver's door on the SUV popped open, and a dark figure stepped out onto the street. It rested back against the hood of the truck and looked up at her house. Right at her bedroom window. Grayson froze, pressing her back up against the side wall. She held her breath.

Someone is watching me.

The high beams from a passing car gave her a lightning-fast glimpse of the figure's face. Grayson bolted from the window and down the stairs, grabbing the discarded blanket at the front door. She threw the fabric around her shoulders and launched herself out the door to the top of the porch steps, trying her best to see across the street in the darkness. She waited in utter silence. The street was quiet again.

Stupid girl. You were seeing things. Also, probably not the best idea to bolt outside if somebody is stalking you…idiot.

She sighed and reluctantly turned to go back inside the house.

"You shouldn't be out here," came a low voice from beyond the bushes.

She froze and gripped the edges of the blanket. "I could say the same thing about you, detective," she said softly.

He came into view, walking slowly but deliberately up the front path. He was dressed in black. All black. Grayson recognized the coat he was wearing. She had recently returned it. And Noah had been right. He looked rough. His hair was unkempt; he hadn't shaved. His five o'clock shadow had been around for days. He just looked…tired, like the fight had been knocked out of him. He stopped at the bottom of the stairs and looked up at her, hesitating.

"I'm…I'm sorry if I frightened you."

"Frightened me?"

"You spotted the SUV from your room," he said, motioning toward her bedroom window. "When you saw someone get out, you came outside."

"I came down because I thought I saw *you*, detective, not because I thought you were an intruder."

She walked over to the side of the porch and hopped up on the porch railing, wrapping the blanket tightly around her shoulders. When she looked up, he'd come up the stairs and was leaning against one of the porch columns, looking at her.

"What are you doing here? It's almost midnight."

Gabriel's eyes dropped to the concrete. His face fell. "He didn't give it to you," he whispered, shaking his head.

"Of course he did," she soothed, "But it doesn't answer my question."

The relief that flashed across his face made her chest tighten. Grayson fought the urge to reach out to him.

You're still mad at him, damn it. Pull yourself together.

Gabriel cautiously crossed the porch and stood in front of her.

"Your protection is my responsibility, doctor. That includes when you're sleeping."

"My protection is my own responsibility, detective. Not yours. I don't need you staking out my house."

His face fell further. "So, you don't want me here."

That's right. I don't...right?

"I...I didn't...I don't...," she stammered. *Shit.*

Grayson glued her eyes to the concrete. The wind kicked up, and she shivered involuntarily. It was getting colder. Yet again, the blanket wasn't enough.

She startled when she felt something warm drape across her shoulders, but when she took the fabric in between her fingers, she knew what it was. She looked up to find him standing very close, his fingers gripping the collar of the overcoat he'd wrapped around her. He was left in black dress pants and a T-shirt.

"No, you'll be cold..." she protested, wiggling out from underneath it.

"I couldn't care less," he said, tightening his hold on the coat to keep her still.

"Well, I do," she replied, sliding down from the railing. "If you insist on being stubborn..." she trailed off, throwing the blanket around his shoulders and bringing the two edges together at his chest.

Ryder stood absolutely rigid and stared down at her. For a split second, he almost looked like he hadn't any idea what to do.

Grayson jumped back up on the porch railing and pulled the coat tightly around her shoulders. Her head cocked to one side as she scanned his face, looking for any reason to be afraid of him. She found none.

"So, you're worried about me?"

He nodded.

"About my safety. Not about me being a serial killer?"

Ryder's eyes shot up to meet hers. Her face was cool and collected, without any hint of a smile.

"Y...yes," he stammered.

Grayson's eyes fell. She shook her head. "Do you have any idea what you did to me?" she whispered.

Ryder groaned and dropped his head into his right hand.

She doesn't forgive me. Shit.

He didn't know what to say to her. He'd tried in the letter. It hadn't worked. How else could he explain what had happened? How desperate he'd been to make a connection...

any connection…between the victims. How he'd clung to the first idiotic thing that had popped into his head. How he regretted every word that had come out of his mouth that morning.

Gabriel rubbed his fingers across his forehead. The blanket fell away, unheeded, from his right shoulder. He barely registered the bite of the cold against his skin. A disembodied force pulled him forward, and he obeyed. The front of his thighs hit the porch railing. His shoulders fell. Soft fingers pulled his hand away from his face, and he felt the blanket drape back around him.

He looked up, eyes wide. Grayson was holding the blanket closed around him, and her eyes had softened. "Good," she said. "Don't do it again."

He sighed in relief. She wasn't letting him off the hook, but at least she wasn't going to slap him again. Gabriel fought off the desperate urge to rest his forehead against hers. Instead, he reached up and rubbed his left cheek. Grayson noticed the light bruise underneath his eye.

"Did it hurt?" she asked.

He nodded. "Remind me to not make you angry again."

"Don't give me a reason to be," she fired back.

"I didn't mean to suggest…" *Shit. This went downhill quickly.*

She stopped him by holding up a hand. "I don't want to fight, detective. I want you to go home."

"What?" He looked around the porch in a panic. "Why?"

"Because you're exhausted," she explained, her voice soft and calming. "I can see it. You can't tell me you've been sleeping."

"I'm fine," he grumbled.

"No, you're not," she replied sternly, raising a hand to touch the bruise on his face.

The warmth of her hand was too much to resist. He leaned into her touch without thinking.

Jesus, I'm tired. I have no self-control. And I don't give a shit.

"If I am supposed to trust you to protect me," she began, "then I have to trust that you're up to it. Being exhausted, malnourished, and on the verge of collapse isn't exactly helping your argument, detective."

Gabriel opened his mouth to protest but slammed it shut just as quickly. He couldn't argue with her. Especially since it sounded like she was going to give him what he wanted. So instead, he kept quiet and focused on the feeling of her hand on his face. He closed his eyes and leaned in.

"Besides, if patterns repeat themselves, I'll be in danger on Saturday night or early Sunday, right?"

He wrinkled his forehead, then nodded.

I knew it. Smart girl.

"So, go home and go to sleep. Then come protect me when I actually need protecting."

"I'm not taking any chances with you," he replied quietly.

"I'm not giving you a choice here," she countered. "If this is so important to you, for whatever reason, then do it right. You're useless to me as a corpse."

He smiled at her. *Checkmate.*

"All right."

Grayson smiled back at him, then eased herself down off the ledge. "I should be going to bed."

He nodded and stepped aside. She started to remove his coat. He reached out and stopped her. "What have I told you about the coat?"

"I returned it," she replied.

"I noticed," he smiled. "Now, so have I."

She looked up at him, her eyes wide and searching. Something flashed across her face, for only a moment, before she turned away. He couldn't identify it.

Since when can't I fucking figure out a simple facial expression? What the hell is wrong with me?

Grayson walked inside the house without another word, and he heard her lock the door. He took the blanket off of his shoulders, neatly folding it over the back of one of the rocking chairs. He walked down the steps and out to the SUV, stopping abruptly at the driver's side door as he patted down his pockets for the keys.

Shit.

They were in the left pocket of his coat. He looked back at the house.

I'm not waking her up to get the goddamned keys. I'll walk.

A metallic tinkling sound came from the asphalt near his feet. He looked down and saw his key ring glinting against the blacktop. He bent down, picked it up, and looked across the street.

Grayson was watching him from her open bedroom window, his coat still draped around her shoulders.

7

FRIDAY WAS A relatively easy day at the hospital, and Grayson was able to start her drive home before the evening traffic jam hit. She rolled the windows down and shook her hair out of the ponytail. The breeze felt great whipping through her honey-brown strands.

She'd been completely on edge since last night. Part of her still wanted to kick Gabriel out of her life, permanently. The other half was almost desperate to see him back on her front porch again. Between Noah's constant mothering and Ryder's insistence on keeping her under surveillance, she felt stifled. If she hadn't had responsibilities at work today, she would have seriously considered running off to a secluded mountain cabin for the weekend.

As for her fate tonight, she wasn't particularly sure she was up for one of Noah's grand schemes. A night out, a real night out, for him was never simple. There was always a grand plan. And that grand plan never went according to plan.

The lights were on in the house when she pulled into the alleyway. As usual, Barbara had beaten her home. She wasn't milling around in the kitchen, and she wasn't sitting around on the couch, so Grayson assumed she was upstairs getting herself ready. She dropped her bag and coat by the front door and started up the stairs. A crashing thud from her roommate's bedroom had her taking the last few stairs two at a time. She hit the landing and knocked sharply on the door.

"Barbara? Are you okay? Babs?"

A few choice words filtered underneath the door before it opened.

"I'm fine. C'mon in, hon," she said, moving out of the way and heading back toward her bathroom. She was dressed in a pair of terry shorts and a tank top, her hair half up in curlers. There were no fewer than ten different dresses strewn out over her bed.

"Um, okay. What happened?"

"Oh, I was trying on a pair of heels and fell into the wall. They're gorgeous but way too high."

"Then why did you buy them?" Grayson asked, sitting down on the bed in the one spot not covered by clothing.

"Because they're gorgeous," she replied.

"Oh, of course," she replied, rolling her eyes.

Babs stepped in front of her mirror, meticulously rolling her hair into the final few curlers. "So, are you excited for tonight?"

"I don't know if I'm up for this, Babs."

"Wrong answer, sweetie, 'cause we're going out Noah Mason-style."

"That's my point," she sighed. "Where exactly are we going?"

"It's a surprise."

"Babs…"

"You'll love it. Trust me." She winked.

"I take it I can't wear jeans?" Grayson asked, eyeing the outfits Babs had strewn out on the furniture.

"No, you can't wear jeans! You can't wear pants of any kind! Dress and heels, Gray."

"How much time do I have?"

"A little over an hour and a half. Don't worry. I'll be in to help."

Grayson stood up from the bed. She was suddenly exhausted. "Go easy tonight. This isn't Halloween."

"I'll show restraint." Babs rolled her eyes, watching her roommate head out the door.

Grayson let out a long sigh as she opened her closet doors. She eyed her meager supply of dresses skeptically. Most of them had been chosen for their ease of washing and work-appropriateness.

Compared to what Barbara had laid out on her bed, nothing in her closet was going to cut it. She briefly took the dress she had worn to Lisa's funeral out and looked at it on the hanger. Almost immediately, she shoved it into the back of the closet. It was going to be awhile before she could put that dress on again. The rest were very basic, black or gray or brown, and none of them remotely looked like something to wear on a fancy night out.

Crap. Well, it looks like I'm wearing pants whether Babs likes it or not.

She took off her scrubs and shuffled into the bathroom, turning on the shower and letting it get hot before she stepped in. The warm water felt great against the chill in the air. She had the time, so she took a long, leisurely shower, letting her muscles relax under the hot water. She washed her hair, shaved, and spent a ridiculous amount of time rubbing sugar scrub onto her skin. It was one of the only girly indulgences she let herself have, and after this past week, she was going to take advantage of it. The mix felt wonderful on her skin, and it was always incredibly smooth afterward. Babs said it made her glow.

Maybe that'll offset the pants at dinner.

When the water turned cool, she frantically rinsed off. Grayson threw her hair up into a towel and slathered herself in her favorite lotion, the one that had just the slightest hint of orchids and musk. It took the place of wearing any perfume.

She grabbed her robe from the hook on the door and tightened it securely around her waist, then took her hair down and dried it in record time.

Grayson was three steps into her bedroom before she realized that Babs had taken up residence on her bed, a rather large white box by her side. She looked ridiculous, with her short shorts and her hair wrapped up in curlers, grinning from ear to ear.

"Hi." She smiled, broad and wide.

"Um, hi?" Grayson parroted back.

"So, what have you decided you're wearing tonight?"

She sighed and looked back at her partly open closet. "I don't know. I think it's going to have to be pants, Babs."

That comment earned her a scowl.

"I'm serious," she continued. "Look, I have the dress I wore to the funeral, which I refuse to wear anytime soon. The rest are all for work. You can't tell me you'd prefer me in one of these," she said, pulling one of the other dresses out sideways on its hanger.

"Yeah, you're right. I don't want to see you in any of that," Babs replied, wrinkling her nose. "But you're not wearing pants."

"I literally have nothing else to wear. And don't start trying to tell me I can wear something of yours, because we are a good three sizes apart. I've never been a zero."

"We are not three sizes apart. Don't be stupid. But I wasn't going to suggest that, either." Barbara looked over toward the white box and then back at Grayson, who motioned toward it.

"Am I supposed to know what that is?"

"No, but it's for you." Her roommate grinned and held it out to her. "Open it."

"Why would I open that? It's not mine." She stubbornly shook her head.

"Because it *is* yours. God, you can be stubborn!" Barbara smirked and pushed the box at her roommate, who promptly sat down on the bed next to it.

"Now, don't be mad..." she said as Grayson started opening the first side of the box.

Of course, that stopped her from continuing. "Why would I be mad? No wait, let me rephrase that. *Should* I be mad?"

"No, but I can see you getting all worked up over this."

When she didn't continue opening the box, Babs huffed under her breath.

"You've had a shitty few weeks, okay? And Sunday was just...awful. And we wanted to do something fun for you. I knew you wouldn't have time for anything. It...it just got taken care of, okay? Please, just humor me," she begged.

Grayson wrinkled her forehead, but she went back to opening the box. She lifted the lid off, dropping it on the floor, and was met with a sea of light pink tissue paper. The gold sticker holding the pieces together bore the logo of one of the boutiques they had visited in Cherry Creek. She shot her roommate another suspicious look but broke through the seal. When she peeled the tissue paper back, she gasped.

"Oh my God..." she whispered.

Staring her in the face was a swathe of beautiful, incredibly intricate material.

Babs squealed and jumped off of the bed, clapping her hands together. She grabbed the dress and gently lifted it out of the box, holding it up in the light. She took it to the closet and hung it up on a hanger, hooking it over the side of the door so they could both see it from across the room.

"What do you think?" she asked excitedly.

Grayson couldn't answer her. The dress was beautiful. A sea of small green flowers and leaves was delicately laid on top of a base of warm nude tulle and lace. It had a high boat neck collar, and the sleeves came just to the wrists. She couldn't see the back. From a distance, it looked like the deep green vines were floating on bare skin. She felt a poke at her ribcage and found Barbara had resumed her position on the bed.

"C'mon! There's more in there!"

Grayson dug further into the box to find a pair of nude sky-high pumps and a sparkling, delicate set of gold earrings. She stared at them for a moment before placing them back in the box.

"I can't wear these."

Her roommate's face fell. "What? Why not?"

"Because I can't afford them, for one. Look where they came from, Babs. These were not cheap."

"Don't worry about it." She waved half-heartedly in the air.

"Don't tell me that! There's no way you can afford this, and that goes double for Noah. Just take it back, please," she sighed, shaking her head.

"No."

Babs' tone caught Grayson by surprise. "Excuse me?"

"I said no. I'm not taking anything back. Forget how this got here. Stop over-analyzing everything. For once, you are going to look and feel like a million bucks, and there's no way in hell you're leaving this house in anything but this dress. Now..."

She stood up and grabbed the back of the desk chair, hauling it into the bathroom.

"...get in here and sit down. There's hair and makeup to do."

"You know I don't have anything to wear underneath that, right? And I'm not going naked."

"There's a box underneath the bed."

"What?"

Sure enough, there was a smaller white box hidden at the foot of the bed. She ripped it open and pulled out the contents. "Oh, my…"

Babs tapped on the chair in front of her. "Get over here, Gray."

She didn't argue.

8

SEVERAL HOURS LATER, Grayson was sitting at a cozy table, Noah to her right and Barbara to her left, laughing harder than she had in quite some time. Noah was reminiscing about his first time skiing, and the intentionally over-dramatized pain in his face as he described every fall he took during the course of a week was becoming too much to bear. It felt good to be at ease again, even if she did feel half-naked.

After spending half an hour on failed attempts to figure out why Babs had gone shopping for her and exactly how she'd managed to pay for it, Grayson had resigned herself to her fate. Barbara had pulled her hair up. What started out as a braid curled in on itself, dissappearing behind the sleek wrap of a French twist. She'd thankfully gone easy on the makeup, keeping her eyes bright and her lips blush pink.

The undergarments fit, but there was very little to them. It had taken a minute to figure out exactly how the thigh-high stockings fit into the garter belt. Grayson had managed, after a few choice curse words and a quick Google search. When she was finally fully dressed, shoes and jewelry and all, she'd taken a quick glance in her full-length mirror. She hadn't recognized herself. She looked sophisticated and elegant and…half-naked.

"Babs, I can't wear this…" she'd whispered.

"What on earth are you talking about? You look incredible! Do you not see yourself?"

"I'm naked."

"You're not naked," she'd replied, rolling her eyes. "It's the fabric. It matches your skin tone. You have layers of fabric here, okay? They're just thin. You're not naked. You have at least three times the material on than I do."

Grayson had looked at her roommate, who was wearing a tight purple dress that ended a few inches above her knees and equally purple heels.

"See?" she'd emphasized, spinning around in a circle in the middle of their living room. "You're fine, hon. In fact, you're a lot better than fine. Just embrace the fact that you look incredible and go with it. Here, this is on loan from me."

She'd pressed a black clutch into her hands and sauntered off without another word. A moment later, Noah was at the door, ushering them both into a waiting town car and off toward downtown.

They'd arrived under the covered awning of one of the fanciest restaurants in the city. They were surrounded by pro-football players, CEOs, and trust-fund heirs. Grayson had turned more than a few heads when she'd walked in, not that she'd noticed. The trio had chatted away in between the salad and the main course, sipping wine that Grayson knew none of them could afford. Still, it was wonderful.

When Barbara had excused herself to answer a phone call from work, Noah grabbed her hand under the table and squeezed. "You having a good time, love?"

"Of course," she smiled. "How on earth did you arrange all of this?"

"I…um…called in a favor…"

"What favor?"

"Don't worry about it," he mumbled evasively.

"Well, thank you for dinner. And for this," she motioned toward her dress.

"I didn't have a thing to do with that, love," he mumbled into his wine glass. "Or dinner."

"But Babs said…"

Noah nodded. "I know what she said. Ditto from me. Enjoy it." He squeezed her hand again as Barbara returned to the table. "Everything okay?" he asked her.

"Oh, of course. Just my boss checking in before the weekend. He's a nice guy, but he always has the worst timing." She started back in on her salmon, and Noah focused back on his steak.

Grayson looked at her scallops, and suddenly she felt ill. She took a few deep breaths, trying to settle her stomach, but the feeling didn't go away. She closed her eyes. That just made her head spin.

Babs looked up from her meal, mid-bite, and frowned. She put her fork down, threw her napkin on the table, and stood. "I'm off to the powder room. Gray? C'mon, we girls need to go in pairs."

She held out her hand and Grayson grabbed it without a word. Barbara steered her through the door and onto an ottoman in the corner. She precariously bent down in front of her. Then, thinking better of it, she just plopped down onto the floor.

"You've gone white. What's going on?"

"I don't know," she replied honestly. "All of a sudden, I just felt sick. Like…like something was really wrong. I couldn't make the feeling go away."

"Do we need to take you home?"

Grayson shook her head, embarrassed. "No."

The blonde looked up at her roommate skeptically. Grayson waved her off, still taking measured, deep breaths. "No, really, I'm fine now. I…I just needed to get out of that room for a minute. Whatever it was, it's gone."

It's not gone. What the hell is going on? This isn't right. I shouldn't be here. This isn't me at all.

"Okay," Babs replied warily.

Grayson stood and walked over to look at herself in one of the mirrors.

Jesus, I look like that?

"You don't have a hair out of place, sweetie," Babs said, walking up behind her.

"Neither do you."

"Eh, I should've done something different with mine. Oh well. I'll live." She shrugged. "C'mon. Noah's probably worried about you."

"You both need to stop worrying about me," she admonished.

"Give me a reason to stop, and I will, Gray," she muttered before following her roommate out toward their table.

Noah stood when they came back, holding out each of their chairs. "You all right?" he whispered in Grayson's ear.

She nodded in response.

"Okay."

They finished their meal at a leisurely pace. Their waiter eventually came back with questions about coffee and dessert. Before either woman could politely decline, Noah shook his head and asked for the bill.

"We're eating dessert someplace else," he explained casually.

"I'm too full for dessert, Mason," Babs moaned.

"You may not be after what I have planned. I didn't say we were eating it just this second," he replied, winking.

"That wink is never good," Grayson whispered to her roommate.

"You never know. Maybe tonight is the exception." She shrugged in reply.

Grayson looked from Barbara to Noah, who was scribbling his signature on the bottom of a receipt.

"You two are in cahoots with each other, aren't you?" she asked, narrowing her eyes at them.

"Maybe," Noah smiled back, standing up from his chair.

She looked at her roommate. "Traitor," she hissed.

"I like to think of it as highly secretive teamwork," she replied, sliding out of her chair.

"I'm in so much trouble here."

Noah just chuckled and pulled her chair out. "Get up, love," he whispered in her ear. "You're going to love this next place."

She followed Barbara out of the restaurant, completely resigned to her fate.

Noah followed behind them, eyeing up the other patrons as they left. Grayson was definitely turning heads, and she had absolutely no idea. He grinned, satisfied with Phase One.

9

THE PETAL CLUB was a boutique members-only establishment hidden in the middle of downtown Denver. To the untrained eye, it looked like any other hole-in-the-wall basement-level bar tucked away underneath an office building. There was no line outside. No velvet ropes. If you weren't actively looking for it, you'd walk right by it. Rumor had it the membership waiting list was over five years long, and it took a pretty penny just to keep one's place in line. Only the elite of Denver society were given access…which is why Grayson froze when Noah headed down the stairs toward the nondescript black door.

"C'mon, love," he said, holding the door open.

"I'll wait out here for you to get thrown out, thanks," she said sarcastically.

"Don't be ridiculous. We have a table waiting. Now, come on," he repeated. Noah walked back up the stairs and tugged on her arm. She didn't move. "If you don't start moving, I'm going to pick you up and haul you in there on my shoulder," he warned. His eyes were full of spunk, fueled by alcohol. He was serious.

Grayson forced her feet to move and precariously made her way down the cobblestone steps in her heels. She rolled her eyes at herself.

I've had a death grip on handrails all evening.

They walked into the dark entryway, which was draped from floor to ceiling in sumptuous red velvet and made their way through two larger wooden doors. A young man dressed in black stood behind a small lectern at the edge of a descending stairwell.

"Can I help you?" he asked calmly.

Grayson stood rooted to her spot by the doors, certain they were going to be thrown out, her heart pounding in her chest. Noah took a business card out of his suit jacket pocket and handed it over. "We're expected."

The young man nodded. Somehow, the small white card was all he needed. He leaned forward and had a brief, hushed discussion with Noah, who nodded and beckoned both women forward into the lobby.

"If you would like for me to take your coats, ladies," the young man offered.

They both nodded and handed them over. The young man added Noah's overcoat to the pile and disappeared behind a well-hidden side door. He emerged a quick moment later and gestured toward the staircase.

"Please, follow me."

Barbara immediately started after him. Noah fell into step next to Grayson. She eyed him suspiciously as he wrapped his arm around hers.

"Just go with it," he smiled, rolling his eyes at her. "Have some fun."

The staircase wrapped around to the left and descended abruptly into the Petal Club's great room. Grayson pulled Noah to a stop for a moment when the full expanse of the club came into view.

Wow.

It was beautiful. The massive room was filled with rich warm wood, copper ceilings, and marble floors. Gold accents trimmed the corners of the doors and the vast bar that took up the back wall. Intimate tables for two with white tablecloths and votive candles were tucked into dark corners. Semi-circular booths upholstered in dark brown, well-worn leather lined the rest of the wall space. The light from the overhead chandeliers was low, supplemented by masses of pillar candles and mirrored glass hurricanes.

The center of the room was dominated by a dance floor. Several couples were already taking advantage of the music drifting over from the band playing on the small stage at the right. The staff were plentiful but faded completely into the surroundings, all clothed in black with slicked-back hair and black starched aprons.

"Excited now?" Noah whispered in her ear.

All Grayson could do was nod and smile.

"Good."

He nudged her forward and she continued down the stairs after Babs, who had followed the host to one of the booths. The young man handed over two leather-bound books, one the wine and cocktail list, the other the extensive evening menu. Barbara grabbed the first and Noah the second. Grayson didn't mind; she simply took in her surroundings.

There was a middle-aged couple directly across the floor from them, trying to argue without attracting attention to themselves and failing miserably. Next to them was an elderly couple, clearly out on a date. He had on a sharp suit. She had on a dress and a coordinating set of pearls. They just sat giggling at each other over coffee. She recognized more than one famous face in the crowd. Which begged the question…

"All right, Noah, out with it. How did you do this?"

He shrugged, never looking up from the menu. "I just did."

"I want a real answer, Mason."

"You're not getting one," he said simply.

"Why the hell not?"

"Because I said so, that's why. It's part of the cahoots."

"Fine," she scowled, scooting out of the booth.

"Where are you going?" Babs asked, peering over the wine list.

"To get a drink," she muttered, grabbing her clutch from the table and storming toward the back of the club.

Noah shrugged at Babs and went back to looking at the menu. "Let her go."

Grayson walked as quickly and as gracefully as she could manage, sliding into the first open barstool she found. Within seconds, one of the bartenders set a cocktail napkin in front of her. It was red with the club's name scrawled across the middle in gold letters.

"What'll it be, doc?" a familiar deep voice asked.

Grayson raised her eyes to find Kyle, one of the bartenders from the Duck and Coach, grinning back at her.

"Kyle?" she asked, baffled.

She blinked rapidly, once and then again, just to be sure he didn't suddenly disappear into thin air.

"Yeah, it's me," he assured her, chuckling deep down in his chest.

"What're you doing working here?"

"I pick up shifts on the weekends when I don't have time blocked out at the D&C. It pays well, and it's a different clientele. Keeps my life interesting," he admitted.

"It's good to see you," she said.

He nodded his agreement. "I hardly recognized you. You're a long way from scrubs and a North Face jacket. Do a twirl for me."

She smiled, stood up, and spun herself around in a circle.

"You clean up well, doc," he mused as she sat back down.

"I don't look naked, do I?" she asked.

He laughed. "Ha! No, you don't. You look pretty incredible, actually. You can wear that to the bar anytime."

"I don't think this is D&C attire, Kyle."

"Suit yourself. I don't think too many people would complain," he shrugged. "So, what'll it be tonight?"

She narrowed her eyes. "Um, well…I…I hadn't really thought about it."

"You want me to make you something?"

"Out of thin air? Can you do that?"

He grinned. "Sure. Look what I have to work with," he said, motioning to the bottles displayed behind him. "You have a kind of drink in mind?"

"Something soft," she replied after a moment.

"Okay, I can work with that. Anything you don't like?"

"That gin that tastes like a Christmas tree," she said, wrinkling her nose.

He smiled wide. "Give me a couple of minutes."

She nodded as he moved away. She rested her elbow on the bar and watched the reflections of the club in the mirror. Whatever strings Noah had miraculously pulled to get them into this place, she owed him. It was beautiful.

For the first time that night, she felt like she wasn't the least bit overdressed.

10

HE'D BEEN SITTING at the bar, halfway through his second glass of scotch, when the hair on the back of his neck had stood up on end.

She's here.

He looked up into the mirrored glass behind the bar and instantly picked her out at the top of the stairs. She was clinging onto Mason. And smiling. His fingers went white around the glass in his right hand. He hissed under his breath and turned on the barstool. Any other night, he wouldn't have thought twice about a woman coming down the stairs at the Petal Club in a nice dress, but tonight…

Holy fucking hell.

Ryder barely managed to keep himself in check as she descended the stairs, following Barbara Parker to his usual table. She slid into one end, to Mason's right, and lost herself looking around the club. Her eyes eventually started to drift toward the bar.

Shit.

He spun around rapidly on the barstool and dropped his head. He sat incredibly still, willing her eyes away from the back of the club.

She can't know I'm here. That's the arrangement.

Gabriel took a deep breath and a long drink of his scotch, then looked up into the mirror behind the bar. She wasn't at the table. Instead, she was walking briskly toward the bar. He would have registered the panic rising in his chest if it hadn't been for the distraction of her dress. It looked like she was covered in emerald green vines and little else. She was draped in fabric and looked naked at the same damned time. His black coat would cover her completely. He shook his head viciously.

Fucking hell, Ryder, focus! You're not here to ogle her. Enough.

She chose a chair several seats to his left, far enough away to keep him out of her peripheral vision but not far enough to keep her out of his. She immediately struck up a conversation with the bartender. He made her smile. She leaned in closer to talk to him. Ryder scowled at them both.

She knows him.

She slid off her barstool and spun around. He swallowed hard. The back of her dress was cut into a very, very low V, which stopped at the small of her back. The soft curve of her spine was accentuated by the flowing lines of the vines and flowers that curved around the edges of the fabric. Anyone and everyone could see her.

He growled and downed the rest of his scotch, signaling for another. He kept her in his peripheral vision, watching her chat with the burly bartender. She smiled at him before he moved away and started grabbing bottles from the wall.

Tequila.

So, he'd guessed right at Mick's last week.

He swirled the scotch in his glass idly, watching Grayson from the corner of his eye. The bartender set a drink in front of her and winked at her. Gabriel nearly snapped the glass in his hand. She took a sip and closed her eyes, clearly pleased. While her eyes were closed, he dropped his own to the polished wood of the bar and attempted to steady his breathing.

When he looked up, he couldn't see her. Noah Mason was blocking his view.

Noah sidled up to the bar and tapped twice on her right shoulder. "You calmed down?"

Grayson ignored him and stared into her drink. He sat down in the seat to her right. "Why are you having such a hard time with this?"

"Because as wonderful as this is, Noah, I can't afford what comes in the morning. This is too much."

He smiled. "Sweetheart, none of us can afford this, and none of us are footing the bill. So please, stop ruining your own night by overanalyzing. Let it go."

Grayson shot him a suspicious glance over her right shoulder and opened her mouth to fire back, but she stopped herself short.

Stop imagining things, idiot. He's not here.

"Now, are you going to come dance with me or am I going to have to haul Barbara out onto the floor?"

"You know I don't dance, Noah."

"Of course you do."

"No, I don't," she countered, turning her attention back to the drink in her hand. "Not in public."

Noah, in turn, quickly pulled it out of her grasp. "You do this, and I'll ask the big lug out. Deal?"

Her eyes shot up.

"Got your attention now, don't I?" he smirked.

"Yes."

"Good. Now get up." He stood and held his hand out to her, and she followed, resting her left hand on top of his right.

"Go easy," she warned.

"Where's the fun in that?" He smirked as he led her out into the middle of the floor. More than one set of eyes followed them.

The club was crowded. Couples were dancing along to some of Dean Martin's snappier songs, spinning and twirling around the floor as safely as the alcohol and stilettos would allow. Mason knew what he was doing, he'd give him that. The young Brit knew how to lead a woman around the dance floor.

Ryder kept a close eye on the pair, mostly on her. She started rigidly, not used to the floor or her partner. But soon enough, Noah was steadily leading her around. People were clearing out of the way to take a better look at them. Mason eventually dropped his hand to the small of her back, forcing Ryder to growl possessively into his glass. Grayson smiled, laughing as he dipped and spun her around. His scowl deepened.

What the fuck is wrong with me?

Several songs in, Barbara Parker appeared, stealing Noah for herself. Gabriel expected Grayson to go back to the booth they had reserved.

Instead, she made her way back to the bar, smiling at the burly bartender when he appeared with another ruby red tequila-laced cocktail. She sat by herself for several moments, savoring her drink and watching the crowd reflected in the mirror behind the bar.

Ryder didn't immediately react when someone claimed the barstool next to her. The club was busy. Seating was at a premium.

But his right hand balled into a tight fist when he noticed the occupant angle himself in Grayson's direction. Pressed suit, expensive watch, cologne even he could smell four seats over.

This guy was trouble.

11

GRAYSON WAS COMFORTABLY chatting away with Kyle when she registered someone take the seat to her left. She didn't make much note of it, at least until the overpowering wave of cologne hit her. She stumbled over her words momentarily, attempting to stifle the cough threatening to get the fumes out of her lungs. She took a sip of her drink to try to get the taste of it out of her mouth.

Kyle attempted not to laugh and placed a cocktail napkin down in front of the new arrival. Grayson went back to watching the club in the mirrored glass. Unfortunately, her peace was broken when she heard "and one for the lady" drift from the same direction as the wretched smell.

Grayson looked up and saw the questioning look on Kyle's face. She hesitantly turned to look at the man who had sat down next to her. He was younger, well dressed and, though not her type, reasonably attractive. But he was already smiling at her a little too much, angling to show off the gold watch on his left wrist. Everything about him screamed trying too hard, and it was instantly off-putting.

"Thanks, but I'm good here," she said, tipping her head toward her nearly full glass.

"Aw, come on." The man grinned, leaning closer to her on the bar. "Be nice and let me buy a pretty girl a drink."

"There are plenty of those here. Go take your pick," she replied, motioning out toward the rest of the club.

"I took my pick already."

She leaned back in her chair, attempting to put at least a little space between them. "Regrettably, I'm not up for auction," she replied sarcastically. "Spend your money somewhere else."

Grayson turned back toward the bar, irritated. She completely missed the smile fade from the man's face. She saw him stand up out of the corner of her eye and assumed he'd gotten the hint.

What a creep.

She looked up, desperate to calm herself down and resume her people-watching in the mirror. Instead, without warning, the same man slammed into her left side and bent down to whisper in her ear, caging her into the bar with his outstretched arms.

"Now look here, you're going to act like a good little girl and do what I tell you…" he began, his voice low.

Her eyes shot wide. She could smell the alcohol, mixed in with the overwhelming stench of his cologne. Kyle started toward her like he was going to come over the bar and punch the man in his face. Almost as quickly, he stopped in his tracks.

She sucked in a panicked breath.

Oh no, please tell me Kyle isn't afraid of this jerk.

Grayson took another deep, shaking breath, preparing to try to talk the drunken playboy down. She had to say something, anything, to get him to back up. She never got the chance.

It all happened so fast. She felt, rather than saw, someone quickly come up on her right side and shove the pretty boy away from her.

"Hey!" he whined, stumbling backward.

A hand rested on the back of the barstool, the fingers making minimal but deliberate contact with the exposed skin of her back. As her unwanted suitor tried to regain his footing, Grayson twisted in her chair.

Detective Ryder was standing over her. His face was tense and rigid. His breathing was ragged. He was focused on the other man and his eyes were blazing with a fury that frightened her.

"Gabriel?" she whispered.

When his eyes briefly looked down to meet hers, the fire instantly softened. The deep blue color returned. He ran his fingers across her exposed skin. Grayson shook under his touch. He smiled at her, only for a moment, before refocusing on the young man desperately gripping the edge of the bar.

"I think it's best if you move on," he said icily.

"Fuck that," the man spat. "I saw her first."

"I doubt that," he replied coolly, placing his hand possessively on Grayson's right shoulder. "And she very clearly told you to get lost. I would do what she says."

The drunkard decided that simply ignoring Ryder was the way to go and put a smile back on his face. He oozed his way back toward her along the bar, clinging on tightly for balance.

"C'mon, baby," he purred, slurring his words. "You know I can make you feel better than he can..." he grinned, circling his hand over her wrist.

Grayson's eyes instantly snapped up from her lap. Before anyone had taken a breath, she'd slid off of her chair, grabbed the man's wrist with her free hand, and twisted around behind him. She locked his shoulder and elbow out straight, and he went down on his knees. The man was either too stunned or too drunk to cry out in pain. He tried to stand up, but Grayson simply jerked his arm up toward the ceiling. He fell back down again, cursing under his breath and whimpering.

Ryder stepped up behind her, tensed and ready to intervene. There was no need. She didn't need the help.

From the back of the bar, three large men dressed in black appeared and positioned themselves around the patrons. The leader, a man in his mid-forties with a shaved head, sized Grayson up with a proud smirk on his face.

"If you're finished with him, miss, we'll take him for a walk," he said, unable to hide the amusement in his voice.

She nodded and let go. The two other men hauled the playboy to his feet. Despite the large amount of alcohol obviously in his system, he looked stone-cold sober.

Grayson looked him directly in the face, her eyes cold. "The next time a woman tells you no, pay attention," she said softly. "You're lucky you still have your arm attached. I take them off for a living."

The man's eyes widened in shock, and the three bouncers hauled him quickly through a back door out of the club. Grayson smoothed a stray hair back into place behind her ear, then sat back down at the bar. For all her cool exterior, her heart was beating wildly out of her chest. She desperately tried to get the tremor in her hands under control. She took a brief sip of her cocktail.

The sound of barely stifled laughter had her looking up at Kyle's amused face. "Holy crap, doc, what the hell was that?"

She just shrugged and drained what was left in her glass.

"No, seriously," he said, setting to work making her another cocktail, "that was fantastic. I've wanted to deck that guy for almost a year. He sprawled out on the floor like a fish."

"That's not the first time someone's grabbed me like that," she mumbled vaguely. "I had to learn how to…uh…get out of it."

"Well, all I know is, I wish I'd had a camera," he said, straining the cocktail from the shaker into a fresh glass.

She quirked her eyebrow up at him. "A camera? Why?"

"Honestly? You, all made up in that dress, bringing that jackass to his knees like it was nothing? That's a Kodak moment if I've ever seen one." He set the glass in front of her. "On the house," he added, winking and walking down the bar toward a pair of new arrivals.

Grayson smiled after him, then closed her eyes and shook her head.

Of course, my night gets capped off by some drunken jerk I have to put on the floor. Just like any other night in the ER.

She took a sip of her new cocktail, which was much stronger than the previous two, and sighed. It took several moments for her to realize that someone was still standing over her right shoulder. She twisted backward and found Gabriel still standing protectively by her side, the shock and pride written all over his face.

Now that she didn't have some jackass to fend off, Grayson took the time to look him up and down. He definitely looked like he belonged in a place like the Petal Club. Dark blue tailored suit, black shirt, and a very familiar white linen pocket square. He was immaculate, with that same bad-boy air that he'd had on Halloween.

I can't keep my head straight around him. He touches my skin for two seconds and I'm a mess. And why the hell is he staring at me?

"Are you coming or going, detective?" she asked, in a much more sultry tone than she had intended. *Whoa, slow down on the tequila, Gray.*

Ryder sat down on the barstool next to hers and motioned to Kyle for another drink. When the brooding detective didn't answer her, Grayson hastily switched topics, her cheeks flaming. "Thank you, by the way."

"For what?" he asked as Kyle pushed a glass of amber liquid in front of him.

"For helping. With that. With him," she nodded toward the vacant chair.

"I didn't do anything," he shrugged, taking a drink. "You took the guy down yourself. I…I wasn't fast enough," he added, wrinkling his forehead in frustration.

Grayson narrowed her eyes at him, watching his fingers go white wrapped around his glass.

Wait, is he upset? What on earth?

It took a moment, but it dawned on her. "You wanted to deck him, didn't you?" she asked softly.

"I wouldn't have turned the opportunity down, no," he replied honestly.

"Can't you get into trouble for that?"

"Not if it's done protecting someone else. I still might…" he drifted off, his eyes landing on the back door the playboy had been hauled out of.

"Well, it was still reassuring you were there," she said. "Speaking of which, why are you here?"

He shrugged. "Why are you?" he countered.

"Noah's idea. A night out after a particularly crappy week. He's…" she turned in her chair slightly and looked out into the crowd, "…out there somewhere with Barbara."

"The Petal Club is quite a night out," Ryder said cautiously.

"You have no idea," she said, rolling her eyes. "We had dinner at Gustavo's before we came here. Oh, and this," she motioned to her dress, "just happened to show up while I was in the shower today. It's more than a couple month's salary. I swear, if I didn't know better, I'd think there were little mice behind all of this."

He wrinkled his forehead a bit and smiled at her. "Mice?"

"Mice," she nodded, then seeing his discomfort added, "like in Cinderella. The mice make the dress…. At least I think they do. Oh, never mind. It's the fairy godmother. Damn."

He chuckled.

"You're laughing at me, detective," she observed calmly.

"No, I would never," he replied, trying to stop himself and failing miserably.

"Yes, you are! You," she replied, playfully pointing a finger at him, "have a terrible poker face when you've been drinking."

"I have a terrible poker face when I'm sober," he countered.

"So, answer the question. What are you doing here?"

He fell silent and didn't answer her for a few minutes. "Where should I be on a Friday night?" he finally asked.

"I'd imagine somewhere without a strict dress code and a five-year waiting list for membership, for starters," she replied smartly.

"You never know."

"Stop avoiding," she replied, emboldened by the alcohol running through her bloodstream. "It's an easy question."

"It doesn't have an easy answer."

She frowned at him. "Fine."

Gabriel hissed through clenched teeth. "I thought I explained last night…"

"And I thought I said not to worry about me so much."

"I tried and failed. How's that?" he sighed, frustrated.

"So, you're stalking me," she said simply.

"No, I…" he started, then went silent. *That's better than revealing the alternative.*

"Don't worry about it, detective," she sighed, waving her hand in the air at him and standing from the bar. "Have a good evening."

She ended their conversation with that. She couldn't think of anything better to say.

Grayson wandered off into the crowd, feeling too agitated to go back to the booth and her friends. She made her way around the club until she found the ladies' room. It was humming with activity. Women in beautiful cocktail dresses milled around in pairs and groups of three, chatting in line and checking their makeup. She stepped in line behind an older woman in her early sixties and waited patiently. The woman was looking at herself in the full-length mirror as she waited and saw Grayson step in behind her. She turned right around.

"My dear," she drawled in a heavy southern accent. "I am sorry; I hope you don't think this too forward of me, but I saw what happened with that rascal at the bar. I was about to send my Frank up there to give that boy a talking-to and you up and put him in his place. I don't think I've seen anything better in all the years of my life, save for my children."

"Um, I...thanks," she managed to squeak out.

"If I had any sons near your age, I'd be introducing you to them. They married off long ago, of course. But I'd say you have quite a looker with his eyes on you already."

"Excuse me?" Grayson replied, startled.

"That young man you're with," she replied.

She has to mean Noah. We walked in together, we've been dancing...

"Actually, we're just good friends."

The woman adamantly shook her head. "Oh, no, dear. Not that young man at the bar with you just now. Friends don't look at each other like that. He's much more than a friend. Or at least he should be." She smiled, then stepped forward into a free stall.

Grayson blinked rapidly after her. Noah hadn't been at the bar. She doubted he even knew what had happened to her. Kyle had been there, of course, but the woman hadn't said bartender. The only person there had been Gabriel. The man had accused her of murder five days ago and was now intent on watching her every move.

He said it was all about the job. He's just interested in me because of the case…right?

She took her time, touching up her lipstick as best she knew how and smoothing back a few stray wisps of hair. She mentally steeled herself as she walked back out into the club, expecting to find Noah, Babs—or worse, Ryder—waiting outside the door. She was almost disappointed that there wasn't anyone waiting to pounce on her when she walked out the door.

Idiot.

Grayson headed back into the main room, which had become even more crowded in her absence. The bar was completely packed. Detective Ryder was gone. She scanned the dance floor, and she didn't see either of her friends.

They must be taking a break.

She maneuvered around the small tables and waitstaff toward their booth. Sure enough, Noah and Babs were sitting there, looking slightly worn out and laughing over glasses of champagne.

"Gray!" Babs squealed, jumping up and hugging her.

"Hi to you, too," she said stiffly.

Grayson couldn't hug her back; her arms were trapped against her body.

"Isn't this great? They sent over a bottle of champagne! Really good stuff, too," she said, taking a long drink from her champagne flute.

"You've read up on champagne recently?" she asked sarcastically.

"Nope. It just tastes so good!"

Grayson nodded and slid in next to Noah, leaning down toward him. "How much has she had to drink tonight?" she whispered.

"Enough that she's drinking a glass of water in between each glass of something with alcohol in it," he smirked in reply.

"Okay."

Grayson poured herself a glass of champagne and relaxed back against the cool leather.

"Where have you been?" Noah asked after refilling his own glass.

"At the bar. Where have you been?"

"Keeping my eyes on this one on the dance floor."

"Probably for the best. Oh, speaking of the bar, you have a job to do tonight, you know," she grinned.

It took Noah a second to catch on. When it clicked, he dropped his head into his hands and groaned.

"I wasn't serious when I made that promise."

"I was."

"Gray…" he warned.

"What? What's the problem?"

"Are you really making me do this?" he whined.

"My night, right?"

He nodded.

"Then yes. I'm making you do this. Give me one good reason why not."

Noah scowled at her over his fingertips. "I don't have one."

"I figured," she said, sliding out of the booth. "Get going."

He rolled his eyes at her and slid out, taking aim for the bar. "If this goes tits-up, we're leaving."

"Fine."

He took off for the bar. Grayson smirked after him. She was halfway back into the booth when she felt a hand rest on her shoulder.

Same shoulder, same hand, same reaction.

The same shiver ran down the length of her spine. She spun around. "What is it now, detective?" she sighed wearily.

He looked slightly unsure of himself. His foot was tapping against the floor.

Grayson's face softened. *He's nervous? This is something new.*

"I thought you might like to dance."

She stood rooted in place, chewing on her bottom lip. "I might," she replied boldly. "Are you asking?"

Where the hell did that come from? Oh yes, thank you, tequila. I sound like a raving lunatic.

Grayson saw a spark flash across his eyes, just briefly, and it cut off her inner monologue.

Gabriel's lips curled up into a warm smile. "I might be."

"Well, when you make a decision one way or another, let me know," she bluffed, turning back toward the booth.

He stopped her, gently grabbing her upper arm. "I would've grabbed your wrist, but I've seen what happens," he countered, setting his other hand lightly on her waist.

"That only happens when I don't want to be touched."

"And now?" he inched closer.

She looked him straight in the face. She could feel the heat radiating off of his body. "I might," she whispered.

The heady look in Ryder's eyes softened the smirk that rose up on his lips. He turned and led her out onto the dance floor without another word, his hand pressed firmly against her hip.

As the night had worn on, the light emanating down from the chandeliers had softened, bit by bit, replaced with the addition of dozens upon dozens of candles throughout the room. It was difficult to see more than fifteen feet across the thick crowd.

Ryder led her several couples deep onto the dance floor. He took her right hand in his left and pressed his other hand onto the bare skin of her back. Suddenly, and without warning, he was very, very close to her.

Grayson could smell his cologne, the same scent he'd worn at Lisa's funeral. The same he'd worn last night. It wrapped around her like smoke, blissfully suffocating. Even in heels, there was a significant height difference between them, but she didn't mind it. It was safer not to look in his eyes.

He started slowly, leading her around the floor in a simple pattern. It didn't take long for her to fall into his rhythm. Their pace ebbed and flowed with the music. Soon, her head was resting on his shoulder, his fingers gliding along the bare skin of her spine. When the first few bars of *La Vie en Rose* began, she smiled.

"I like this song," she said absently.

That earned her a slight pressure on her back and a nod from her dance partner. Gabriel spun her out, to one side then the other, then pulled her back into his chest. He muttered something into her hair that she didn't quite catch.

"What was that?"

"I said you look incredible in that dress," he replied softly, dipping her backward just enough that she arched into him.

Grayson blushed. "I feel naked."

"If that's what naked looks like, you should do it more often," he said absently.

Gabriel continued on for several beats, then abruptly lost his step when he realized exactly what he'd said. And out loud. He cursed under his breath.

Grayson giggled into his lapel. "Easy, detective," she chided gently.

He opened his mouth to say something, but she stopped him, stepping onto the tips of her toes to reach his ear.

"If this is what naked gets me, I'll have to do it more often."

Ryder stopped dead in the center of the dance floor, his right hand molding Grayson firmly into his body. His fingertips flexed against her skin. She could feel the tips of his fingernails bite into her skin. He closed his eyes for a moment, his breathing suddenly haggard and shallow. She looked up at him, concern in her eyes.

Oh no, what did I just say to him? Goddamn you, tequila. I'm acting like a complete...

Gabriel didn't give her the time to finish her thought. He stepped back, clasped her hand tightly in his, and headed directly for the stairs that led up to the club's entrance. It never crossed Grayson's mind to tell him to stop.

The host immediately jumped up to get their coats when he saw them round the corner. He looked like he was about ready to ask a question, but Ryder waved him off and he returned silently to his post.

Gabriel waited until Grayson had her coat firmly around her shoulders, then pulled her out the wooden doors and up to the street.

12

GABRIEL TOOK ONE look at her when they reached the street and dropped her hand, lurching away as if she'd burned him. Grayson waited patiently, stunned, her ivory wool coat pulled up around her ears to ward off the cold.

Ryder paced frantically up and down the sidewalk, running his hands through his hair.

Get the fuck ahold of yourself.

He willed his breathing to even out, and with it, his pacing slowed as well. Several long moments passed. When he finally felt in control of himself, he sought her out.

Grayson was standing in the middle of the empty sidewalk, framed by the light drifting down from one of the street lamps. Her hands were buried in the pockets of her coat. She was calmly watching him, as though his frantic pacing was the most natural thing in the world.

When he didn't make a move to close the distance between them, she did and got just as close to him as he had gotten to her downstairs.

"You want to tell me what that was about?" she asked gently, placing a hand on the collar of his coat.

Ryder stared off over her head, avoiding her. When he didn't say anything, Grayson decided an apology was in order. "I shouldn't have said that," she said quietly. "I'm sorry."

He reached down and gently grabbed her chin, tilting it up so she was looking at him. "I'd rather hear you say it again," he replied, just as quietly.

Grayson cocked her head to one side, studying his face.

She could see it, the tension threatening to burst through the slightest crack. He was holding back from her. But what? And why?

A cold burst of wind blasted down through the skyscrapers, and she shivered, snuggling into her coat as best as she could. Ryder stepped in front of her, shielding her from the icy blast. He quickly wrapped an arm around her waist and started off down the street.

"Where are we going?" she asked when she realized they were moving.

"Down the street."

"What for?"

"Just trust me on this."

Truthfully, Grayson would have rather gone back and kept dancing the night away until she couldn't move an inch, but it didn't look like there was any way she was going to change his mind.

They walked a block and a half east before Ryder led her up a set of modern gray stone steps, into what looked like an office lobby. There were floor-to-ceiling windows, gray walls, and an abandoned security desk.

"You're taking me to work?" she asked, amused.

"We'd have a much longer walk if I'd meant to take you to the department," he replied, leading her down a hallway on the right.

He ushered her through a dark, almost black wooden door adorned with a large, golden monogram, a solitary C.

Once her eyes adjusted to the dim light, Grayson found herself in a rather cozy room. Floor to ceiling mirrored windows looked out on the street. There were wingback and club chairs in groups of two and four clustered around low-lying coffee tables, each decorated with clusters of votive candles and bud vases. A small but ornate bar lined the back wall. There were already several groups of well-dressed couples chatting around the room.

Ryder slipped Grayson's coat off her shoulders and handed it off, along with his own. He nodded to the bartender as he steered her toward a set of velvet wingback chairs in the far corner. She gave him a curious look, but dutifully took the seat on the left. Grayson settled in and relaxed back against the plush fabric.

"So, where exactly are we and what are we doing here?" The words were out of her mouth before he had even sat down.

Gabriel sighed and shook his head. "Do you always have to have everything answered right away?"

"Usually." She nodded. "I wouldn't be good at my job if I didn't."

"I imagine you'd still be very good at your job," he replied tersely.

One of the staff appeared in between their two wingbacks with a silver tray, which he wordlessly placed on the low table in front of them. Ryder reached for a small white cup, then nodded toward the larger one.

"That's yours."

Grayson reached forward and took the warm, steaming cup off of its accompanying saucer. Whatever it was, it smelled heavenly and was topped with a small pillow of whipped cream. She took a tentative sip. *Oh, wow.*

Gabriel watched the smile spread onto her face and relaxed, silently sipping his own espresso. Without warning, Grayson set her cup back onto the silver tray and stood up. A feeling of panic set in low in his stomach.

Shit. She's leaving?

But almost as quickly as it set in, the panic was replaced by curiosity.

Grayson steadied herself on the back of the wingback chair and, one by one, took off her high heels. She tucked them away underneath the table, sat back down, and twisted her feet up underneath her left hip. The move caused her body to shift and angle toward him, a perk Ryder rather appreciated. She reached across to the table and picked up her cup again, taking a long sip and closing her eyes.

Gabriel sat back and studied her. All done up for her night out, not a hair out of place, a gorgeous dress…drinking hot chocolate with her feet tucked up and a smile on her face. He cleared his throat to fight off the tightness that suddenly loomed in his chest.

Grayson opened her eyes and paused, staring back at him with her lips just the slightest bit open. She looked at him with a mix of fascination and contentment that was completely unexpected.

It took the breath right out of his lungs. He immediately schooled his own features when he realized he was doing the same.

"They know you here," she said, not able to think of anything better to say.

"I've been here once or twice," he said evasively.

"You have a standing order for hot chocolate when you bring a girl here?" she asked, clearly half-joking and half-curious.

He shook his head. "I've never brought another person here. Of either sex."

"Then how did you know…"

"Some things in life remain a mystery, Dr. Carter," he replied.

"So, you, what, read in some secret file somewhere that cinnamon hot chocolate is my favorite? I don't remember putting that on my residency application."

Gabriel shrugged and sipped at his espresso. She stared into her cup for a minute, then looked back up at him. "Will you at least answer one of my questions tonight?"

"Yes. But just one. Pick it wisely," he replied, smirking.

She didn't hesitate. "Why are you so protective of me?"

It wasn't the question he'd expected her to ask, and it caught him off guard. Gabriel continued to sip at his espresso, desperately trying to think of a response. He'd settled on something vague but appropriate when Grayson started talking again.

"And I don't mean protective like from a possible mass murderer. I mean like tonight, from some drunk jerk in a bar. Or outside in the rain during Lisa's funeral."

"You would've preferred me to leave you on your own?" he balked. "Outside a funeral, cold and miserable?"

"Of course not," she countered. Grayson didn't hesitate. It surprised both of them.

"Then what's the problem?"

"There isn't a problem. I just...I want to understand why." She sighed, staring out the window.

When he didn't respond, she rolled her eyes and took a deep breath. "Look, let me make this simple. I understand there's an active murder case. Somehow, I'm connected to it. But what I don't get is why you spend any excess time dwelling on what happens to me. I mean, me personally. It would be so much easier to park a squad car outside of my house. In fact, that would make more sense."

She sighed deep in her chest. When he didn't stop her, she kept going.

"You won't tell me why you were at the Petal Club tonight, and quite honestly, I don't know how or why I was either, but despite all the drop-dead gorgeous women in that place you decided to spend time with the introverted, completely-out-of-place surgical resident. And now this place?"

She waved her hand wildly around the room.

"I just...I don't belong here, and you...you clearly do, and I don't understand it. So..." She sighed, slowing her breathing down, not looking up from her nearly empty cup, "I'll ask again. Why are you so protective of me?"

When she didn't hear him respond, let alone take a breath, Grayson closed her eyes and dropped her face to the floor.

Great. The one time I really open my mouth I'm a whining, blabbering idiot. Not happy with you again, tequila.

She opened her eyes, intending to stare out the window and cleverly blame her little outburst on the alcohol. Instead, she ended up looking straight into a pair of raging dark blue eyes.

Grayson jumped back in her chair, startled. He'd knelt down in front of her while she'd had her eyes closed. Ryder took the cup from her suddenly shaking hands and set it on the table, gently taking her right hand in his.

"You want the truth?" he asked.

She nodded warily.

"I have absolutely no idea."

Grayson wrinkled her forehead, clearly not believing him. He kept talking, his voice low and smooth.

"I have an unexplainable, psychotic, alpha-male drive to make sure you're taken care of. Whatever it costs me. I felt it at the seminary when you were upset. I felt it when Carrol attacked you in the lecture hall. I felt it yesterday on your front porch. I felt it tonight at the bar when that asshole was all over you. I feel it now when you're completely safe. And I haven't the slightest clue why."

Gabriel looked steadily at her. His eyes were shining in the low candlelight. Grayson's heart was beating out of her chest, but she didn't look away. He was so close, so very close to her.

"Does that answer your question, Dr. Carter?"

She paused briefly, then nodded, absolutely breathless. "I think you can start calling me Grayson again, detective," she said softly.

"I think I can manage that." He stood, sat back in his chair, and smiled at her.

13

THEY SAT AND talked for the better part of an hour. Grayson had never felt as at ease and on edge at the same time in her life. It was an oddly thrilling combination. Every time he said her name, she felt a blush rush up to her cheeks. Okay, so he had some strange need to make sure she didn't turn up dead on his watch. That didn't mean anything.

But damn it, she wanted it to.

It was well after midnight when Ryder stood up from his chair and motioned for their coats. Grayson noticed that there was no bill asked for or offered up. He returned to her side with his coat already on, hers draped in the crook of one arm. He held out his hand to her and she accepted it, uncurling herself from the chair and bending down to gather up her shoes.

Grayson swung her legs out to the side, sliding her feet into the shoes as gracefully as she could manage. The movement caused the layers of her dress to gather up, and as she stood up, hanging onto a combination of the back of the chair and Ryder's hand, she flashed the briefest glimpse of the edge of her stockings and the garter belt that held them up.

She felt Ryder's hand clench around her fingers. She inwardly grinned. Now that dress had a whole new set of possibilities to consider.

Enough, Gray.

Ryder bundled Grayson into her coat and ushered her out the door with a quick nod back to the bartender. He'd be back to settle his tab later in the week. He always did, and the management never questioned it.

They walked out into the frank cold of early Saturday morning. The damp chill in the air hinted at the possibility of snow. Ryder walked slowly, partly because Grayson had to navigate the uneven sidewalk in rather high heels and partly to delay their eventual return. When she stumbled for the third time, due to a combination of exhaustion and not paying a bit of attention to where she was going, Gabriel slipped his arm around her and took most of her weight off of the concrete.

"Thanks," she muttered, embarrassed by her clumsiness but ecstatic at the result.

Ryder just smiled down at her and kept walking. When the Petal Club came into view, she let out an audible sigh.

"What's wrong?" he asked softly.

"Does it have to be over?"

"It won't be the last time," he replied.

"When will I ever do something like this again?" she countered sarcastically.

"Maybe sooner than you think," he muttered.

Grayson stared out across the deserted street. "This is going to seem like a dream tomorrow."

Yeah, no kidding. He was about to say just that when she pointed up into the sky in front of them.

"Look! It's snowing!"

A few stray flakes floated down toward the street, followed by several thousand more. In less than a minute, the deserted street became hazy as a midnight flurry passed through the city. Grayson grinned from ear to ear, staring up at the sky, watching the flakes come down.

They were everywhere. On her coat. In her hair. On the tips of her eyelashes.

The heat of her body made them melt, one by one. She could feel him watching her, not more than two feet away. She turned to look at him, and she giggled. He cocked his head to one side. Grayson covered her mouth with a gloved hand in a futile attempt to stifle her laughter.

"What?" He smiled back, hands in his pockets.

"You're covered," she giggled, brushing off his shoulders and the front of his coat.

"So are you," he replied gently, steeling his nerves and reaching a hand out to brush a few flakes off of her cheek.

Grayson watched him like a deer in headlights. At his touch, her eyes closed, and she tipped her head into his hand. It was subtle, but to Gabriel, it was screaming loud and clear. And suddenly, the tightness in his chest had returned full force.

He gently wrapped his free arm around her waist and pulled her into him, never taking his hand off her face. Everything slowed down. She looked right at him, blue eyes sparkling and expectant, one hand on his arm and the other laid softly on his chest.

At that moment, Grayson knew exactly what she wanted, but from the look on his face, it was the one thing she couldn't have.

"Gabriel?" she asked softly, registering the hesitation in his eyes.

He leaned forward and gently rested his forehead on hers. His lips moved, not saying anything she could hear, except the last two words. She barely caught them over the snow.

My name.

He took in a deep, steadying breath. Then another. She could feel the wrinkles furrowing his brow. "Grayson," he began, the conflict heavy in his voice. "I can't." He shook his head softly, raining flakes of snow gently down into her hair.

"Why not?" she whispered.

He pulled away from her and bent down to catch her downcast eyes. "Because I won't be able to stop," he replied.

Gabriel ran the side of his thumb across her cheekbone to clear away the snow. He looked down at what little space they had between them, then dropped his hand from her face and grasped her right hand in his.

"This will have to do," he said absently, bringing her hand up to his lips and lightly kissing the back of her leather glove.

Grayson swallowed hard. Her breath hitched in her throat. Despite the snow and the whipping wind, she was incredibly too warm. She gathered her bottom lip in between her teeth.

From the look on his face when he looked up, the detective clearly regretted his decision to keep his hands to himself. Gabriel swore under his breath and leaned forward, pressing himself closer to her.

"Stop."

He pulled her lip free and ran his finger along the edge, weighing his options.

A sudden dash of movement in his peripheral vision brought them both out of the moment. When he raised his eyes to look beyond her, Grayson turned to follow his gaze.

A town car had pulled up outside of the club, and the scuffle from the door was clearly recognizable. Noah was using all of his powers to steer Babs into the car without both of them falling over on the slick cement.

"Come on." Ryder's voice was low and demanding in her left ear. "It's time to go home."

Grayson nodded and let him walk her to the car.

Thankfully, Babs had managed to get in without a scrape. Noah was waiting at the open backseat passenger door, her clutch in hand. She smiled gratefully as he handed it over but hesitated at the thought of getting into the car. She turned slightly, enough to find him in her peripheral vision.

Gabriel nodded toward the car, a silent command. She suppressed a small grin and got in without a word.

Grayson slid into the middle seat, next to a very sleepy Barbara Parker. Noah followed behind her. With the door still open, she was able to hear Gabriel speaking to the driver.

"I'll take good care of them, Mr. Ryder. Good to see you again, sir," he said in reply.

He knows the driver?

She glanced at Noah, who gave her a slight grin that said, "don't try asking, I'm not telling." The car started up, and warm air from the heater blew in from the air vents on all sides. It felt wonderful, but Grayson hardly noticed.

As they pulled away from the curb, she turned around and looked through the back window. He was standing in the same spot on the vacant sidewalk, and he stayed there until they rounded the corner and were out of sight.

14

THE NEXT MORNING, Grayson woke up peacefully, without the usual intrusion of her squealing alarm. She stretched from tip to toe, lazily, inching her way further under her comforter. She rolled onto her side and opened her eyes, blinking against the sun.

Wait, the sun? What time is it?

She reached out for her alarm clock and pulled it toward her. *Eleven o'clock? I haven't slept that late in…wow.*

She felt well rested for once, and there was an unfamiliar hum just below the surface of her skin. She sat up slightly in bed and looked toward her bathroom, where a very distinctive dress was hanging from a hanger hooked on the door.

Did I really wear that? Did any of that actually happen?

She smiled and wrapped her arms around her waist. She'd worry about figuring out what on earth had actually happened tomorrow. Today, she would sit around and remember the look in his eyes in the middle of the falling snow when he kissed the top of her hand.

A quiet knock sounded on her bedroom door, and Barbara walked in carrying two cups of coffee.

"Well, well, look who's finally up," she giggled, handing over a cup and sitting on the edge of the bed.

"Thanks." Grayson nodded her gratitude and took a sip.

"How do you feel?"

"Good."

"Did you have fun last night?"

She nodded.

"So, just where did you run off to?"

Grayson's eyes went wide. *Shit. I thought no one noticed.*

"What are you talking about?" she asked, trying for innocent.

"You know damned well," her roommate replied, scowling over her pink coffee cup. "One minute, you're cheek to cheek with that detective on the dance floor, and the next he's hauling you up the stairs. I didn't see you until we went home."

"Don't worry about it," Grayson replied warily, vacating her bed for the window seat.

"Oh, come on. What'd you do? Make out with him in the alley?" Babs teased.

"Not exactly," she said, rolling her eyes.

"Spill it."

"No."

"Gray, there's no way he was around you all night in that dress and didn't have his hands up your skirt."

"Is it so hard to believe that he didn't?" she grumbled.

"After seeing the way he looked at you? Yes!"

"Get off it, Babs. You find him creepy, remember?"

"There is no way he wasn't dying to see what was underneath."

"Barbara!" She blushed.

"I'm serious! You can't tell me he didn't try to pull something."

"He didn't!" she sighed exasperatedly. "Not that I didn't want him to. I mean… Oh, I don't know."

"Talk to me, sweetie," Babs said, getting up from the bed and sitting on the other side of the window seat.

Grayson grabbed a blanket and threw it over her legs. She quickly summed up the remainder of her evening after she'd left the Petal Club. She left out several particular details.

Those are mine.

"So, let me get this right. You got hauled out of an exclusive club by a semi-unhinged man who's accused you of murder and magically appeared out of nowhere…and he took you for hot chocolate?"

She nodded.

"I think that's one of the best things I've ever heard, Gray," she murmured, leaning back against the wall. "Especially after this."

Barbara waved a familiar piece of expensive card stock in the air over their heads. Grayson eyed her roommate warily over her coffee cup. That was definitely not the response she had been anticipating.

"What?"

"Oh, come on, I know you. Gustavo's was delicious. The Petal Club was incredible. But can you really tell me those were the best parts of the night? For you?"

She couldn't. *Shit. She knows me too well.*

Grayson dropped her head into her lap and shook her head.

Babs grinned. "That's what I thought. Besides, I give the man credit. I saw how he was looking at you. If he kept his hands to himself, he might be worth keeping around."

"It would be nice if he wanted to be around, Babs, but that's not the case."

Barbara sputtered over the latest sip of coffee, spilling several drops onto her shirt.

"Are you insane? What are you talking about?"

"He's got some weird thing about protecting me. That's it. It's not a…liking me thing. It's a police protection thing. If something happens to me, he doesn't get the glory of solving a case."

"Bullshit. Right up there with…never mind."

Grayson was instantly intrigued. "Never mind what?"

Barbara tried to get up from the window seat, but she was held down. She struggled to get out of the hold, but Grayson's grip was firm and demanding on her arm. Almost desperate.

"What are you talking about?" she pressed.

"Are you serious, hon? Because this conversation is really starting to hurt my head. The man is staking out our house and when he royally fucks up, he calls in favors at Gustavo's and the Petal Club. Just. For. You."

What?

Grayson's eyes went wide and her face went white. Her heart pounded inside her chest. The room started to tilt. "You're not serious."

"Of course I'm serious! How the hell else do you think we got in that place? Where do you think that dress came from?" She pointed across the room. "You were right. It cost a pretty penny. Elie Saab."

Her head was spinning. *She can't be serious. He couldn't. He didn't. Did he?*

Grayson dropped her head into her lap and let out a sob. She was suddenly and completely overwhelmed.

"Breathe, sweetie," Babs said, rubbing her shoulder in circles.

"He told you he was doing all this?"

Barbara chuckled. "No, but I don't have any other good explanations, do you? The dress showed up at the door by private courier. Out of nowhere."

"Why would he do that?"

She shrugged. "Most men buy flowers when they screw up. The one interested in you apparently goes a step or two beyond that."

"He's not. Interested, I mean."

"You don't buy Elie Saab for just anybody. Especially on a cop's salary."

Grayson's eyes shot up from her lap. *No.* "Oh my God, Babs! There's no way he can afford that."

"So? What's the problem?"

"Babs, the cost of dinner alone was too much. If he actually did all this..."

"Sweetie, just go with it." Barbara stood up and grabbed their cups. "For once, please remember you're awesome. And even though I'm not sold on him, you really looked happy last night. Try doing that more often."

Barbara smiled and disappeared downstairs.

Grayson leaned back against the wall and stared out her bedroom window.

Babs can't possibly be right about him. He said so himself. Protection. That's all it is. Right?

15

LOGAN STORMED DOWN the hallway toward a familiar white apartment door, a mixture of anger and worry etched on his face. He'd last spoken to his partner on Friday, in the elevator as they'd left the squad. Gabriel had been agitated, off his game all day. With how piss-poor their week had been, Harrison had been more than a little worried.

He'd talked Ryder into meeting him at the boxing gym on Saturday morning. He'd waited for forty-five minutes. When his ridiculously punctual friend was clearly not coming, he'd shoved himself into his car and driven to the ostentatious sky rise Ryder called home.

When Logan reached the last door on the right, he squared his shoulders and pounded relentlessly on the door with his fist.

"Ryder. Ryder, get your ass out here!"

He heard the shuffle of feet on the other side of the door and the hasty pull of the lock.

"Logan?" came the muffled voice on the other side of the door. "What the hell are you doing here?"

Logan barreled into the apartment without acknowledging the man on the other side of the door.

"What am I doing here?" Harrison shook his head and spun around angrily. "You have got to be…" He trailed off when he actually got a good look at him. "…kidding me…"

Ryder looked good, if a bit disheveled. He was dressed in a white T-shirt and loose black sweatpants, running his left hand through the back of his hair and looking sheepishly at the floor.

His eyes weren't bloodshot. He didn't look hung over. There was a cup of what suspiciously looked like unspiked coffee on the table in the living room and a book overturned next to it. And it was a novel, not a textbook.

"Ah, shit. The gym. Logan, I forgot."

"Clearly," he said.

"Sorry."

"Don't be. I'd rather see you like this than hung over and hitting a bag. You got coffee?"

He nodded.

Harrison sauntered into the kitchen, poured a cup for himself, and brought it back into the living room. Ryder grabbed his from the table.

"So, you look good," Logan said, taking a seat on the couch.

"Thanks, I guess."

"You got laid, didn't you?" he smirked.

"No, asshole, I didn't," Gabriel replied quickly, then immediately regretted it. He'd been too quick to answer. Harrison was going to have a field day with this.

"Wait, hang on, you're calm and collected on a Saturday morning and there isn't some barfly back in your bed?"

When Ryder didn't answer, he raised his eyebrows.

"Okay, now I'm really curious," he said, resting his coffee cup on his knee. "What did you do last night?"

"Why is that any of your business?"

"Because in less than twenty-four hours you've turned back into a human being. It's nice to see. And I want to know for future reference."

Ryder sat down in one of his club chairs, nervously tapping his foot against the floor.

"Any day now, buddy," Logan chuckled into his cup.

"I went out."

"Not intending to get some."

"Yes. Well, no."

Logan smirked. *I'm enjoying this too much.* "I'm not follow-ing. You did or you didn't?"

"If you're going to be a complete jackass…" he hissed.

"All right, sorry. Where did you go?"

"Petal."

Logan raised his eyebrows.

"Pretty ritzy."

"Sure."

"Don't you have to be on a list for that place?"

Ryder nodded.

"And you are?"

He nodded again.

"Figures." Harrison rolled his eyes.

"Logan…"

"Fine. So you went hunting."

Ryder grimaced into his coffee cup. Hunting was their term for finding something quick and easy on a Friday night. Something distracting enough to dull the pain of the job for a few hours. As a rule, nothing permanent. Nothing complicated. No names. Always disposable.

"No, I didn't."

"Really? Then what were you doing there?"

"Keeping an eye on something."

It took a moment, but realization dawned slowly and smugly on Logan's face. "You took her there?"

"Not exactly."

"Explain it to me."

"What for?"

"Because I told you to, rookie."

"Fine." He sighed, sipping his coffee. "After what Nolan said in interrogation, I cornered Mason at the hospital. I made him a deal. I'd arrange a night for them if I could keep an eye on her. Out of sight. He agreed. Gustavo's, the Petal Club, all of it. I was supposed to have a drink and stay out of their way."

"And you didn't because..."

"Some drunken asshole was all over her."

Logan chuckled into his coffee. "So, you charged in all knight in shining armor?"

Ryder grinned at the memory. "Actually, I tried. I wasn't fast enough."

"Huh?"

"She took him down herself," he smirked. "Locked his wrist and spun him to the floor in four-inch heels and a cocktail dress."

Logan whistled through his teeth in approval. "Fuck. My kinda woman."

"Your kind of nothing, Logan," Ryder spat across the coffee table.

"Hey, I was just kidding," he countered, holding his hands up in mock defeat. "So, you failed at being a Disney prince. Then what?"

"We danced. I took her to Calvario. She went home," Ryder shrugged, attempting to keep his pulse under control.

"She look good?"

"Oh, dear God, yes."

Again, way too quick to answer. Fuck.

Harrison nodded to himself. "You paid for it?"

He nodded.

"She know?"

Ryder scowled into his coffee cup. "Not that I know of, apart from Calvario. I'd rather she didn't."

"She's smart; she'll ask questions."

"She's already asking too many."

"Good for her. Did you answer any of them?"

"Of course not."

"What a fucking surprise."

"Did you come here for something?" Gabriel spat.

"To make sure you're okay, which clearly you aren't. Whatever the good doctor has stirred up, keep it going, because you're looking human for the first time in months."

Ryder didn't answer. He kept drinking his coffee.

"Kiss her yet?"

"How the hell is that any business of yours?" Gabriel raised his eyes at his former partner, the fire evident behind the dark blue irises.

"Aw, lay off. I've never seen you fawn over someone before."

"I'm not fawning. I'm keeping her safe."

"Call it what you want. You can't tell me you don't want to see her again." Logan went back to drinking his coffee.

Ryder knew he couldn't argue.

16

OFFICER SUTTON WAS running on fumes. Three days awake with a new baby girl coupled with night patrol in the Highlands had just about done him in. Thankfully, his partner had taken pity on him. When his thermos of extra-strong coffee had run out early in their shift, she'd pulled into an all-night Starbucks for a refill. He picked up his cell phone as it vibrated against his hip and answered it.

"Hey, babe."

"How's the shift?"

"I'm dragging. Martinez is a godsend."

"Why's that?"

"She found Starbucks."

Giggling echoed on the other end of the line. "Remind me to get her a nice gift this Christmas, Ted."

"I will. Why are you awake?"

"Why would I possibly be awake with a three-week-old baby?"

"Sorry. Dumb question. She's okay?"

"Of course. Just hungry. You've got to stop worrying so much."

"Yeah, right."

"Honey, if you're this worried now, what are you going to do when she's sixteen and brings a boyfriend home?"

"Eh, I have that handled. I'll just answer the door with a loaded shotgun."

"Ted…"

"I'm kidding. I've gotta go."

"Be safe."

"I'll see you in the morning." He shut his phone off as his partner opened the passenger door. Officer Sally Martinez slid into her seat, passing over a large cup of coffee and a very full thermos to her partner.

"Think that'll be enough to get you through?" she joked.

"At least until sunrise, sure."

"Good. And here, eat something," she said, passing him a small bag with a pastry in it.

"Hey, I'm trying to lose my baby weight here."

"Is that the excuse you're going with? I don't see you doing pushups in the parking lot. One doughnut isn't going to kill you."

"Vicki's on this whole low sugar thing…" He hesitated.

"Which means you have zero chance of getting away with this in the house. So eat it."

He grinned and turned the car on, sliding the pastry out of its package as he pulled back out onto the deserted street.

"Thanks for taking over the wheel, by the way," she added.

Ted smiled and started in on his doughnut.

He drove under the highway, then up, up, up the hill to 38th and back into the surrounding neighborhoods. As much as he didn't care for the cold change in the weather, it had forced people inside. Patrols had been quieter over the past few days.

His partner was in the middle of explaining her husband's most recent run-in with his power tools when Sutton slowed the car down to a crawl. Martinez immediately stopped talking.

"You see something?" she asked.

"I don't know. I thought I just saw somebody come out of the church," he said, pointing over toward the impressive edifice.

The sign out front read Our Lady of Mt. Carmel, Highlands.

"You live over here somewhere, Sal. Does the church usually leave the light on?"

They were far enough around the side of the building to see a weak light coming through the stained glass at the back of the building.

"No. Not this late at night," she said, putting her coffee cup in the center console.

"And I thought we were going to have a quiet night. C'mon," he replied, shifting the cruiser into park in the middle of the road and stepping out.

Sutton grabbed his gun from its holster. He looked up and down the street. Nothing. Not even a stray cat. His partner came around the front of the cruiser, her gun in her right hand.

"Maybe I was seeing things," he mused.

"Maybe, but we should check the church anyway."

He reached into the cruiser and spoke briefly into the radio. "Central, this is Sutton and Martinez in the Highlands. We're at Our Lady of Mt Carmel off of Navajo and 36th. Going to check the place. Might be somebody messing around with the church."

"10-4," came the static-heavy reply.

Sutton led the way up the front steps, his partner right behind him. He gently tried the main door. It didn't budge. She motioned to their left.

"Side door," she whispered.

He followed her around the corner to a small door hidden behind an overgrown hedge. Martinez tried the latch, and it gave. She raised her eyebrows, took a deep breath, and pushed her shoulder into it.

They made their way into the church slowly, checking each corner they crossed. It didn't take long for them to find their way into the main chapel. It was impressive. Two columns of long wooden pews were ensconced in stained-glass white-domed ceilings, and gold detailing...all of which was perfectly visible thanks to the candlelight coming from the altar.

Six ivory candles were clustered at the base and lit, small trails of hot wax pooling on the floor. From the looks of them, they hadn't been lit for very long. Sutton and Martinez looked rapidly around the church. Nothing moved.

"What in the hell?" Sutton muttered, stepping forward toward the altar. "Who the crap left the candles burning?"

He'd almost made it to the base of the stairs when Sally called his name. He turned to see her moving the opposite way down the aisle toward something. The low light and her moving body blocked whatever it was from view. He moved quickly to follow her as she knelt down.

"Oh shit," she muttered.

She rolled the bundle over, and Sutton instantly fought back the bile in his throat. A young woman, probably Indian descent, was staring up at them. Well, her eyes were open, anyway. They were glassed over and she wasn't blinking. Her skin looked almost too pink to be real, like she had bathed in cheap blush. There was something white crusted around her lips.

His partner was attempting to get a response out of the woman, and it wasn't working. From what he could tell, she wasn't even breathing. Sutton grabbed the radio hooked to his shoulder. Sally was about to tell her partner to just call for the coroner when the young woman's body jerked violently, then set into a mild but noticeable tremor. The woman groaned softly, and Martinez could actually see her breathing...just barely but breathing.

"She's alive! Sutton, call for a bus!"

Ted swore under his breath and turned away. "Central, this is Sutton. Get an ambulance up to Mt. Carmel now. We've got a young woman here who's in bad shape. Send backup, over."

"10-4, ambulance is on the way. Two units en route to your location. Any identification on the young woman, over."

Martinez dug into the woman's front jeans pocket and came up with nothing. She rolled up her sleeves and found a medical bracelet on her right wrist.

"Priya Malhotra, MD," she read off.

"You think she's one of them?" Sutton asked.

His partner nodded. Sutton cocked his head sideways toward the radio again.

"Central, better have that bus take our vic to St. Joe's."

"10-4. Ambulance informed of destination hospital."

Sutton looked back down at his partner who was still trying to get the young doctor to respond to her. She wasn't having any luck. "I guess that means we need to call Major Crimes, huh?" he said.

Martinez stood up from the floor, took out her cell phone and dialed. "Ted, stay with her," she pointed as the call connected. "This is Officer Sally Martinez, patrol in the Highlands. I need to speak to the captain of Major Crimes. It's an emergency. Yes, I'll hold."

17

THE SHRILL RING of her cell phone woke her out of a hazy, instantly forgotten dream. She jolted awake and reached out toward the sound on autopilot, disconnecting her phone from the charger. She briefly looked at the screen to see who was calling at two in the morning.

Noah?

"Carter." She answered with her last name, out of habit.

"Gray, get out of bed. Right now. Get your shit together. I'm coming to get you," Noah said frantically.

He was panicked. And Noah rarely panicked.

Grayson instantly sat upright in bed. "What's wrong? What happened? Are you okay?" she asked, now completely on edge.

"I'm fine. Look, I'll explain more on the way, but here's the short version. My juniors just called me. Priya Malhotra was found unresponsive in a church in the Highlands about fifteen minutes ago. They're bringing her to Joe's. I'm going in. I could use some help here."

Oh. Shit.

"I'll be downstairs in five minutes," she said, ending the call before he could reply and turning on her bedside light.

Grayson scrambled around her bedroom, throwing on the pair of scrubs she kept in her closet for emergencies. She rummaged through her bag and pulled out her pager, ID, and house keys. She clipped the pager and her cell phone onto the waistband of her pants as she shoved her feet into a well-worn pair of sneakers. Not her usual hospital footwear, but they were the closest available to her in the closet. She scribbled a quick note to Babs on a Post-it note and put it on her bedroom door before racing down the stairs. She grabbed a black North Face fleece from the coat closet and yanked open the front door.

Across the street, the flash of the automatic porch light immediately caught Ryder's attention. His hand instantly went for the gun at his right hip. He looked out the driver's side window, anticipating an intruder, or at the very least, a squirrel. Instead, he saw Grayson, dressed in scrubs, locking up her front door. He watched her shove her keys in her pocket and throw on a black jacket against the cold.

She's just going to work, he thought absently.

Then panic set in.

Wait, why the hell is she going to work at two a.m.? And why is she leaving through the front door? Her car's parked in the back alley.

He had his hand on the door handle when he saw her look down the street and sprint off the porch. A black car was speeding down the quiet street toward the house. Gabriel recognized it as Noah Mason's. She ran toward it, opened the passenger door, and threw her bag into the back seat. The car took off with her before she even had the door fully closed.

What the hell?

He put the key in the ignition and started the car just as his cell phone began to vibrate in his pocket. He looked at it.

Nolan.

"Ryder," he answered tersely, pulling the car out into the street after the black sedan.

"I'd ask if I woke you, but it doesn't sound like it. You okay?"

"She just left the house in a hurry. With Mason."

"You're still watching her house? Buddy, you have a problem...wait, she what?"

"Something's wrong. She's dressed in scrubs. They're headed to the hospital."

"Well, guess what? So am I. I suggest you follow her."

'What's going on?" he asked as he put the siren on and sped through a red light.

"Patrol in the Highlands just found a vic inside Lady of St. Carmel. Get this, she's still alive."

"Really?"

"Barely, but yeah. They're taking her to St. Joe's." Nolan paused for a moment. "Um, you...you want me to head up to the Highlands?"

"No. See if Logan can go start up there. I...I think we both need to be at the hospital if the victim is alive."

Ryder swerved, pitching the SUV out of the way of an oncoming car in the intersection.

"All right. See you in a minute," Nolan replied, ending the call and immediately dialing the other detective's cell.

It took three rings for him to answer.

"Logan," came the groggy greeting.

"Time to get up, buddy."

"I hate Sunday mornings for the first time in my life. It's all your fucking fault, Nolan."

"Complain later. We need you to go to a church in the Highlands."

"And you two ladies are going to sleep in and have brunch?" he asked sarcastically as he swung his legs over the side of his bed.

"No, we're going to the hospital."

"Dead bodies don't need immediate police attention."

"True, but live victims do."

It took a minute for Harrison to process the sarcastic remark through the early morning haze. His eyebrows raised up high as he sat up on the edge of the bed. "Shit, really?"

"Yeah, alive but barely. Ryder and I are headed in now. I guess he saw the doc and Mason speed off from her house. The word's out."

"I'll handle the scene. Don't worry. Check in when you know something."

"Will do. Thanks, Logan."

"Just bring me coffee when you two haul your asses up here, will you?"

Blake ended the call as he pulled into the ER parking lot. He didn't have to wait long. A black car raced into the same lot and pulled into an on-call physician spot. Noah and Grayson jumped out and sprinted toward the emergency room doors. They disappeared through them as a department SUV pulled into the spot next to him.

Nolan hurriedly got out and locked his car, clipping his badge onto the outside of his coat so it was in plain view. Gabriel walked around to the front of the SUV, badge clipped to the outside of his left pocket and gun strapped to his right side, just barely visible underneath his overcoat.

"They're inside already," Blake said.

Gabriel nodded, not saying a word.

The two detectives took off at a jog toward the entrance to the ER.

18

GRAYSON AND NOAH sprinted into the ER from the parking lot. They were halfway to the trauma bays where the ambulance elevators were located when Noah's pager went off. He ripped it from its holster and looked at the message.

"They're taking her straight up to the ICU. Come on. We'll meet them up there."

They changed course, running out into the hallway and up several flights of stairs to the back entrance of the intensive care unit. Grayson swiped her badge through the lock, and the door automatically opened. They looked wildly from left to right. A large group of people had gathered outside of one of the rooms, and they immediately went in that direction.

Noah and Grayson threw their coats over a random chair at the nurse's station. A nervous-looking kid in a white coat was making a beeline for them. He was white-eyed, flushed, and completely panicked.

"Dr. Mason, thank you so much for coming in," he said hurriedly. "I…I didn't know what else to do. I…"

"Don't worry about it, Oscar. Who's your attending tonight?"

"Keefer. But he's downstairs. Some OB patient is tanking out. Between that and a consult that we got earlier tonight in the cardiac wing that's a train wreck, he hasn't been able to get away to do anything else."

"So, we're on our own until his backup gets here?"

The young man nodded.

"Any idea on ETA?"

"No."

"Wonderful," he muttered under his breath.

Noah turned to face the whole group and raised the volume of his voice.

"Okay, people, here's the deal. You all are well aware of who's coming in. Priya Malhotra. We don't have any idea what in the hell happened to her. She was found down. Until we get an attending up here, I'm running the show. We're going to get her tubed, lined, and stabilized as quickly as possible. Draw all the usual labs, including tox. The works. If you are not actively doing something in this room, do not crowd around and gawk. Understand?"

The group nodded just as the EMTs came into view, jogging beside a stretcher. Noah moved to the head of the bed and started barking orders at the nurses.

"Everybody move. Get in position to move her. Respiratory, get ready with the vent. Greg, pull up etomidate and succinylcholine."

The EMTs moved the stretcher into position by the hospital bed. Grayson took up a position on the opposite side as one of them started talking. The rest of the staff worked quickly but silently to follow Noah's orders.

"Okay, we've got Priya Malhotra, found down in the Highlands by the cops. We found her nearly unconscious, unresponsive to sternal rub, intermittently jerking and shaking. Eyes are glazed over, pupils are real dilated. She was breathing on her own but barely. Narcan didn't do anything. We put her on ten liters which didn't do a damn thing to her sats, so we put a temporary airway in. IVs in both antecubs, 16s. She's had a total of 1700 of fluid. Vitals..."

The EMT's voice faded away into a background hum.

Grayson focused all of her energy on Priya and listening to Noah's instructions. They got her off the stretcher and onto the hospital bed. Two quick injections of medication and she was paralyzed, intubated, and hooked up to a ventilator. Nurses were throwing leads on her to get her heart rhythm up on the monitor.

Jesus, her skin looks really red. Like a full-body sunburn.

"Grayson."

She blinked rapidly and looked across the bed at Noah.

"Can you throw in a subclavian line for me, love?"

She nodded, ducking underneath IV lines and EKG leads to move to the head of the bed. Noah ordered everybody to put on a mask. On autopilot, Grayson threw on a gown and gloves, prepped the skin, and threaded a central line into the large vein underneath her right clavicle in under two minutes. She sutured the catheter in place and placed the dressing, immediately getting out of the way so the nurses could hook up fluids and draw some more blood for lab work.

She looked around the room and noticed the young girl hovering over Priya's left arm, her own right hand holding a large needle and violently shaking. Grayson pushed the poor respiratory therapist-in-training out of the way and placed the arterial line herself. When she was finished, she worked her way toward the back of the room where Noah was leaning up against the counter, reading through a few pieces of paper and intermittently glancing up at the monitors above the bed.

"Her medical file," he said, waving the papers around, not looking up to see who it was. "Her medical bracelet says she's a Type 1 diabetic. So does this. Great control. Her glucose was fine in the field. That's not what's causing this."

He looked up at the monitor again, then back to Grayson. "Shite, love, are you done with that central line already?"

She nodded. "And the art line."

"Right. I forgot I'm dealing with a surgeon, not one of my interns. Thank God for you." Noah's eyes fluttered back up to the monitor above the bed.

"Her rhythm doesn't look great. Not frankly dangerous, but her T-waves are worrisome. We need to get her electrolytes back."

"Hey, Dr. Mason, wanna come take a look at this?" Greg, one of the nurses, called from the head of the bed.

Noah walked over to a clear canister on the wall which was filled with a dark brown, nearly black, liquid.

"What the hell is that?" he cringed.

"Came out of her nasogastric tube. All that was sitting in her stomach," the nurse replied.

"Get some of that and put it in something to save it. We'll send it for testing. Get her started on stress steroids and IV PPIs."

"Got it."

Almost on cue, another nurse called to him.

"Yeah?"

"I just ran her ABG. It says her hemoglobin is five."

"Recheck it."

"That is the recheck, Dr. Mason."

Noah grimaced. "Shite. Call for blood. Have them send up four units and start thawing some more."

"On it," the same nurse replied, disappearing from the room.

"Order platelets and FFP with that!" Grayson called out the door after her.

While he went back to reviewing her chart, Grayson looked back at the bed. She tugged gently on his shirt sleeve.

"Noah…why the hell is she shaking like that?"

He looked up, confusion plain as day on his face. Grayson pointed. Sure enough, Priya's arms and legs were twitching, all out of rhythm.

"That's not the paralytic wearing off, is it?"

Oh please, let me be dumb and let it be the paralytic wearing off.

"No. What the fuck…"

The young intern who had initially met them at the door Oscar, squeezed between two nurses with several pieces of paper in his hands. He shoved them in Noah's face.

"Stat labs are back," he huffed.

Noah scanned them quickly.

"Jesus, it'd be easier to say what is within normal range than what isn't," he muttered to himself.

"What's wrong with her?"

"Everything's failing. Her creatinine is up, so her kidneys are shot. That helps explain all of her electrolytes being off, but not this acutely. Her liver's failing. I can't get her oxygenated. And that…" he said, pointing toward her twitching limbs, "…looks like a seizure. She's anemic without a source for bleeding, and wildly hypertensive and tachycardic. She's got benzodiazepines in her system. Shite, a lot of them."

He barked out a few medication orders and changes to her ventilator settings, then looked up at the charge nurse, who was standing by the doorway and waiting for any additional instructions. Noah motioned her over to the bedside.

"Can you give nephrology and neurology a call? They need to get in here. The attendings, not their damned residents. She's going to need emergent dialysis. And we need to figure out why the hell she's twitching like that."

The woman silently nodded and quickly left the room.

Grayson sighed and rubbed her eyes with the palms of her hands.

I am so out of my league here.

This was Noah's world, not the operating room. She imagined he would have the same feeling if she dressed him up in a gown and gloves and told him to go fix a hip fracture. She opened her eyes and gently touched his arm.

"Come on. Give this stuff a chance to work. Let's get you a cup of coffee so you can think straight."

Noah opened his mouth to argue with her, but Grayson narrowed her eyes at him, making her point. He nodded and followed her out of the room. They walked down the hallway toward a recessed counter where the nurses always kept a fresh pot of hot coffee and a small refrigerator with various kinds of creamer. The ICU nurses were all well aware of how a fresh cup of coffee could make or break a doctor in their unit.

Grayson poured two cups and added creamer, handing one to Noah. "What now?"

"We watch her. I'll have to put a temporary catheter in her neck so she can get emergent dialysis. That won't take too long. They're bringing the kit up now. My guess is we'll scan her, but it doesn't look like she was attacked. I don't see any bruises."

"You think she took something?"

"It's possible." He shrugged. "It might help explain the benzos, and why just about everything is abnormal, but it can take a long time to get tox panels back. Even the quick ones take over an hour. Most of the medications we have to treat that stuff are also extremely toxic. I can't just go loading her up with something until I know what it is I need to treat."

"Have you ever seen anything like this?"

He shook his head. "I wish I had. It would make this easier."

Grayson nodded. She knew the feeling.

From down the hallway, alarms began to sound and someone began shouting for respiratory. Grayson looked at Noah. Her stomach dropped to the floor when she saw the look on his *face*.

No. No, no, no, NO!

They took off running, their coffee forgotten, as a static voice came over the PA system.

"Code Blue. Intensive Care Unit. Medical Team One. Code Blue."

19

RYDER AND NOLAN used their badges to push their way into the hospital and up to the ICU without much resistance. It wasn't hard to figure out which room the young doctor had been taken to. They arrived just as the EMTs were wheeling out their empty stretcher.

Ryder started toward the door, but Blake grabbed the sleeve of his jacket and pulled him back behind a counter on the other side of the hallway. His partner glowered at him as he leaned against the faux countertop.

"Let them do their thing, man. We'll get our shot."

Ryder nodded and relaxed, which let Blake focus his attention on the flurry of activity in the room across from them. Mason was apparently running the show, barking out orders in an exhausted British accent. He noticed Grayson wind her way to the head of the bed and watched curiously as the young surgeon put on a blue gown, surgical cap, and gloves.

She's gonna operate on her in the room?

A minute later, she was shoving a very large needle underneath Malhotra's clavicle. Blake looked away, suddenly queasy.

"It's a central line," Ryder mumbled.

"A what?"

"It's an IV that empties right to the heart. Easy access for blood and efficient delivery of medication for an unstable patient."

"Of course you know that." He rolled his eyes. "You know how to put one in, too?"

"We can always find out while we're here," Ryder replied, smirking. "Are you volunteering?"

"No, thanks."

Nurses fluttered in and out of the room. Grayson and Mason stood together in the back of the room, looking over some paperwork a young kid in a white coat had shoved at them. After a minute, Noah dejectedly followed her out of the room, and they disappeared down the hall. The two detectives remained hidden across the hallway, unnoticed.

"What do you think her chances are?" Blake asked absently.

"You'd have to ask a doctor that, Nolan."

"Were you really outside her house again?"

Ryder didn't answer.

"Hey," Blake said, lightly hitting him on the shoulder. "I asked you a question."

"Does it matter?"

"Yes."

"Would you believe me if I told you no?"

"Hell no. You already told me you were there."

"And if I lied?"

"I've known you to be evasive as shit, but not a liar."

"Point taken."

"Being a bit paranoid?"

"Considering the circumstances," Ryder waved toward the scene in front of them, "I'd say no."

"We can always put a squad car on her, Gabe."

Ryder had opened his mouth to respond when alarms started sounding from the room in front of them. A male nurse at the head of the bed called for something Blake didn't quite catch, then hit a button on the wall above the bed. In the periphery, he saw several nurses poke their heads out of other patient rooms, then start hurrying over.

The sound of heavy running snapped his attention to the left. Noah and Grayson were sprinting down the hall. The PA system sounded. Blake glanced over at his partner who was staring into the room across from them and repeatedly opening and closing his left fist.

"What the hell is going on?"

"Her heart's stopping," Ryder replied. "She's dying."

20

"WHAT THE FUCK happened?" Mason shouted as he rushed into the room.

"I don't know, doc," Greg replied from the door, wheeling the crash cart into the room. "She was fine, then her rhythm just went haywire. I can't get a pressure on her."

"Shite! Put her bed down flat. Get the epi out and get the pads on her."

Grayson moved around to the side of the bed.

"Do we have a rhythm?" Noah asked, looking at the monitor himself.

"Not a good one," Greg replied.

"Push the epi. Start CPR," he said, looking at Grayson, pleading with his eyes.

She immediately put her palms down on Priya's chest and started compressions. After the first few pulses, she felt ribs break under her hands. The sickening crunch echoed off the walls. It was an expected complication, and a marker of compressions that were strong enough to reach down to the heart muscle, but it was still horrific to feel the ribs of someone you know breaking beneath your hands. Grayson fought off the bile rising in the back of her throat.

Noah continued shouting orders, every few minutes ordering another burst of medications and a pause in compressions. Grayson cycled through with some of the other residents and nurses, everyone taking turns on compressions until they were tapped out and a fresh set of hands moved in.

Ten minutes later, they were still working on her. Nothing had changed.

"Back off. Check her rhythm," Noah barked out.

Everyone paused, suspended in midair. Noah swore under his breath.

"She's in Vfib. Fuck. Charge the defibrillator. We've got to shock her."

Noah grabbed the paddles, and when the machine indicated it had a full charge, he brought them down onto Priya's chest. Her body rose off of the bed slightly at the current.

"Start compressions again. Load up the amiodarone. Charge again."

It continued in cycles. Compressions. Meds. Shock. Repeat. Nothing changed. When they hit a half hour in, Noah looked up at the rhythm on the monitor and shook his head. One of the nurses tried to hand him the paddles again. He didn't take them.

"Right. We're done here, gents."

"Noah, we can't just quit…" Grayson started to argue from her perch, midway through a cycle of compressions.

"She's gone, Gray. We're thirty minutes into this. I'm calling it."

"He's right," came a voice from the door.

Dr. Keefer stood in the doorway, his white hair askew and glasses falling out of his front pocket. "It's time."

She backed away from the bed.

"Time of death, 03:16," Noah said flatly.

Dr. Keefer patted Noah on the back as he walked out of the room, head down, to call the coroner. Grayson remained in the back of the room, watching as the nurses switched off the monitors and covered Priya up with a sheet. She took a few shaky breaths and stepped up to the bed.

"Goodbye, Priya," she whispered.

She went to find Noah.

She found him several nursing stations down, slumped over in a chair. She bent over his shoulder and wrapped him in a hug.

"You did your best."

"I know that. She's still dead."

"It looks like Keefer is taking care of the paperwork for you."

Noah blankly looked down the hallway at the elderly attending. He was bent over the chart, his pen flittering around erratically in his left hand.

"Oh joy. I just…give me a minute, okay?"

"Sure."

Grayson walked back toward the ICU room. She was almost to the door when she noticed them. She stopped in her tracks.

What the hell are they doing here?

What a stupid question. She changed course.

"Detective Nolan. Detective Ryder." She nodded by way of greeting.

"Dr. Carter." Blake smiled.

Ryder nodded at her. Grayson tried to keep herself in check. Her heart was already pounding inside her chest. She nervously tucked a loose piece of hair behind her ear. She could feel the blush creeping across her face. "What are you two doing here?"

"We were hoping to, well…" Blake replied, trailing off.

Grayson's face fell. "Oh. Interview her."

"Who was she?" Ryder asked.

"Priya Malhotra. She was one of our palliative care fellows."

"What was your relationship with her?"

"She was nice. I met her last year, on my orthopedic oncology rotation. She took great care of our patients. They loved her."

"You personally come to the rescue every time something happens to one of the residents in this place?" he asked gently.

She meekly smiled, exhaustion quickly blanketing her features.

"No. The ICU service was slammed tonight. One of the junior residents panicked when he found out who was coming in and called Noah. He needed help, so I came with him."

"Did anyone have any problems with her?"

"The only people that ever took issue with her were people who don't like, um, homeopathic and naturopathic medicine."

"In English, please, doc," Blake said.

"Alternative forms of medicine, basically." She shrugged, staring over toward the dimly lit room. "There are people who believe that all traditional medicine is poison. There are people who believe that homeopathy is all fairy dust and make-believe. And there are people in the middle somewhere. Priya was in the middle. Her treatment recommendations had a bit of both worlds. There are a few attendings that have a problem with that, mainly because they think it gives false hope, but that didn't stop her. And her patients appreciated the approach."

"Anyone in particular?"

"Nobody comes to mind offhand, but I can ask around."

"We'll take care of that," Blake said. "I need to go talk to Mason," he muttered, walking off toward the young doctor sitting in the corner with his head in his hands.

Grayson stared across the hallway at the white sheet draped over the hospital bed. Over Priya. She leaned her weight back against the counter and sighed.

"Are you all right?" Gabriel asked.

The genuine concern in his voice made her breath hitch.

"This has to be a bad dream," she muttered. "Who would want Priya dead?"

"That's for me to worry about."

"How did you know?" she asked, turning to face him.

"I, um…" The way his eyes darted to the floor was a dead giveaway.

"Did you see me leave the house this morning?" she asked, reading the look on his face.

"Yes."

"You were watching me again?" she huffed. "Didn't I tell you…" *God, I just want to hit something. Of all the stupid, idiotic things he could've been doing at two in the morning…*

"You told me only when it made sense. And Saturday night makes sense. Clearly," he said matter-of-factly, motioning toward the room behind them.

Grayson felt her blood boil at the tone in his voice. She set her jaw and glared at him. "I didn't think you would actually…"

"Stop trying to pick a fight," he said calmly, cutting her off. "Now answer me. Are you all right?"

Grayson started.

How did he know I was trying to pick a fight? Damn him.

"Of course not," she murmured. "I just spent the better part of forty minutes breaking a colleague's sternum, pumping her full of drugs, and shoving needles into her neck. Oh, and then I had to stand around and watch my best friend pronounce her dead. Noah's going to be a wreck." She dropped her head into her hands before the tears could start up.

"What can I do?" he asked.

"Figure out who's doing this, detective. Please. I don't know how much more of this I can take."

We're back to detective. "Such a small request," he teased.

Noah suddenly appeared beside them, looking worn out and ready to break.

"All right, Gray. Everything's tied up. I need to get you home," he mumbled.

"Noah, why don't you stay with me?"

"I'd rather just go home, love." He shook his head.

Ryder glowered at the pet name.

"Okay. Then just take yourself home, Noah. I'll grab a cab."

"No, I will..."

"...go straight home. Now go," she chided, cutting him off and handing him his coat.

He took it without saying a word and sulked down the hallway. Dr. Keefer fell into step beside him halfway down.

Grayson grinned. The old doctor always seemed to know how to pick a resident back up after a bad case.

I hope he's up to the challenge tonight. Noah's going to need it.

She grabbed her own coat and slipped it on. She moved to grab her cell phone off of her hip, intending to call a cab to the hospital ER entrance, but a warm hand encircled hers before she could get there.

"Don't be ridiculous. I'll drive you home," Ryder said. "Come on."

Grayson didn't argue. She let him steer her out of the ICU and down to the ER parking lot. They parted ways with Nolan, who headed up to the Highlands to help Logan at the scene.

The ride back to the house was quiet and thankfully short.

———

Ryder steered the SUV into a vacant spot across the street and turned off the engine. They sat together for a moment, Grayson staring straight ahead out the windshield.

"Answer something for me," she said softly, breaking the silence.

"Of course."

"Do you really think someone is going to come after me?"

Gabriel saw her start to nervously wring her fingers together in her lap. *She's scared. But I can't lie to her.*

"Yes."

"Why?"

"There's a sadistic agenda at work here. The longer this drags on, the more I'm convinced that you're the end game. Whatever this is, it started because of you. And it will end with you."

She couldn't argue with that. She couldn't hide the shiver that rocketed down her spine. The car was suddenly freezing cold.

"Let me worry about it."

"It's kind of hard to just let that go, detective."

"Try," he said softly. "I told you I'll take care of it. Just trust me."

Ryder walked into the crime scene a little after seven in the morning. Nolan was the first one to notice him.

"Where in the hell have you been? We left the hospital hours ago."

Gabriel didn't answer.

21

BRIGHT AND EARLY Monday morning, the trio of detectives made the trek down to Carla Pelton's office. She met them at the door, arms crossed over her chest, her foot tapping furiously on the floor.

"I swear, you are going to give me an ulcer, boys," she said the moment they walked off the elevator.

"Nothing personal, doc," Logan replied.

"Shove it, Harrison. I've heard that line from you before. As I recall, I got a whole squad from the Lobos cartel a week after you last told me that."

"Yeah. Sorry about that one."

"Ruined my whole weekend," she mumbled, turning and walking into her exam room.

"So, what did you want to see us for, Carla?" Blake asked as she reached for a file folder.

"I think you all need a major update on your victims. Considering we're up to six bodies and, as I hear, still suspect-less."

"That's cold, doc," Logan mumbled.

"I've been here since noon yesterday, detective. I'm allowed to be cold. Now," she snapped, opening the file, "let's review. Lisa Oakes overdosed on narcotics, specifically fentanyl. Dr. Nelson bled out. We never found his missing parts. Marcus Porter literally ate himself to death, since his food was laced with Botox."

She flipped to another page.

"Our next three were also unique. Pretty boy James was strangled. Fibers indented into his neck confirmed it was with his own tie. Dr. Carrol had his tongue cut out, but a little digging showed it was likely just before he died. Official cause of death was blunt force trauma. He had damage to his spleen, liver, kidneys, and lungs. Someone took a boot to him, judging from the bruises that popped up postmortem."

Pelton sighed wearily, shaking her head as she turned to the third page in the file.

"And lastly, our most recent unfortunate, Priya Malhotra. What a loss."

"You knew her?" Blake piped up.

"I did, yes. A good friend of mine has stage IV breast cancer. She went into the hospital with a little bit of back pain, came out with a get-your-affairs-in-order diagnosis. Priya was the palliative care fellow who saw her in the hospital."

"What did you think of her?" Ryder asked, his interest masked behind a blank expression.

"I liked her. She spent hours with Katie. Helped her through a lot. And got her hooked up with her naturopath."

"Her what?" Logan asked, eyebrow raised.

"Her naturopath," Pelton repeated. "I like to call it her Whole Foods doctor. Vitamins, diet, supplements, the whole nine yards."

"You believe in that shit?" Logan balked.

Carla just shrugged. "It doesn't matter what I believe. Katie says it helps. And quite honestly, if it makes her happy and she feels better, I couldn't give a crap. Anyway, she was going to stay on at St. Joe's if they offered her a job after her fellowship, and they were keen to keep her."

"Did you find anything else that we should know about?" Ryder interjected, clearly losing his patience with the side story.

Carla rolled her eyes at him. "Yes, detective, I did. Since

you're about to jump out of your own skin, I won't keep you waiting."

She pulled a series of photographs out from her file and laid them on the countertop.

"Just as you suspected. A single mark on the abdomen of each victim. Each in a slightly different location."

"That could just be random," Blake said.

"That's what I thought, but I took measurements and sent them up to the lab. They're all perfectly spaced, as long as you account for a difference in body size."

"That sounds like math." He grimaced.

"Yes, high school geometry is actually useful. Go figure." Carla rolled her eyes yet again. "I had the forensics guys run it. Each mark makes a predictable jump inward, in a spiral."

"Have you been able to figure out what made them?" Ryder asked, bending down to get a better look at the photographs.

Carla shook her head.

"I sent specimens to trace."

"Anything else?"

"Yes. I confirmed what they suspected in the hospital. Malhotra had an extremely high amount of benzodiazepines in her system. Even if she had been taking them chronically, which there's no evidence of, this would have been a dangerously high level. Enough to stop breathing. But what I found in her stomach was a bit more interesting."

She held up a small container of dark liquid with a bright orange lid.

"That came from her stomach?" Logan balked.

Blake held a hand over his mouth. Pelton nodded.

"It wasn't the color that surprised me most, but the smell…"

"I'd rather you didn't, doc," Blake said as she went to open the lid. "I get enough of that shit at crime scenes with Ryder."

"Suit yourself." She shrugged. "It was an odd combination of almonds and something I couldn't quite place."

"So, she ate an almond biscotti before she died? Who cares?" Logan quipped.

"Doubtful, detective. Everything in her stomach was liquid. And she didn't ingest any of it voluntarily. There was tearing along her esophagus and the back of her throat mucosa. Something was shoved into her throat and she was force-fed. After the benzodiazepines. There was trace around her mouth. I sent that off to the lab, too, just to be sure it's the same stuff."

"So, she was drugged, then poisoned?" Logan grimaced.

"It appears so."

"Seems like major overkill," Blake muttered from the corner.

Ryder's head popped up. "What?"

"Nothing."

"Say it again," he said forcefully.

"I said it seems like overkill. If she was going to stop breathing from the benzo-whatever anyway, like Lisa, why poison her?" He shrugged.

"To make a point," Ryder said softly. He turned on his heels and bolted out of the M.E.'s office without saying another word. Harrison looked over at Nolan, shrugged, and walked out after him. Blake sheepishly turned back to her.

"Uh, sorry, Carla…" he mumbled, rubbing his palm along the back of his neck.

"Oh, stop apologizing, Blake. I've stopped paying attention to him completely," she replied sternly, waving her hand around in the air in reply.

She scooped up the photographs that were strewn across the table and tucked them back into the file folder. "Here, take these."

"Thanks," he said, grabbing the file and hastily walking out of the office.

He caught up with them in the crime lab. He walked up next to Harrison, who elbowed him in the shoulder.

"Thanks for joining us, Nolan."

"Shut your trap, Logan." That earned him a sly grin.

"If you two ladies are finished," Ryder hissed, slapping his palm down on the table to draw their attention.

Olivia Forester leaned back on the lab counter and smiled. She'd come into work expecting a normal day in the crime lab. Instead, she'd found a pile from the M.E.'s office on her desk, all marked RUSH, and now a live version of *The Three Stooges* was playing out in front of her desk. She shook her head.

She knew Blake Nolan well. He'd come to the department about the same time she had, and he'd always been nice to her. Especially in the beginning, she'd been the butt of more than a few jokes. A girl with purple hair, tattoos, and a closet full of leather wasn't exactly typical around the department.

Nolan had stood up for her until her work had started speaking for itself, and they'd stayed friendly since. She'd done work for Logan Harrison before, too. He seemed to think too much with his below-the-belt anatomy, but he'd always been pleasant to her.

Nolan's partner was another story. Gabriel Ryder always got her guard up, usually because she was worried he would find something she had missed. He never missed anything. He was driven. Intense. Harsh. And he was just…a bit odd. She couldn't put her finger on what it was. He had a temper, sure, but there was something else.

"Um, yeah, so…" she mumbled, nervously eyeing Ryder, "…it didn't take long to run what Pelton sent up. The stomach contents were easy, and the trace matched. Three simple ingredients."

She handed a piece of paper over to Ryder, whose eyes widened as he read the list. He handed it back. "Really?"

She nodded her head. "Ensure, mercury, and cyanide."

"So, she got a geriatric suicide cocktail?" Logan asked.

"Basically, yes."

"No benzos?" Ryder asked.

"No. No pills or evidence of it in the recovered fluid. Those must have been given intravenously."

"Carla needs to look for the needle mark. Probably around the neck, like Lisa." Ryder scowled. "And the other samples?"

"Oh, yeah. From the skin, right? Also easy," she replied, handing over another sheet of paper.

"Ink?"

"Yeah. Plain old black ink. Like you find in any dollar-store ballpoint pen."

Harrison grabbed the paper to read for himself. "This guy's what, checking these people off?"

"Or marking them in some other way. Maybe he's trying to keep them in order," Olivia replied, shrugging her shoulders.

"There's only one mark per vic," Logan argued. "They still look random to me."

"It was just a suggestion, detective," she said, turning toward her glowing computer screen.

She tapped a few keys and brought up photographs of each victim, which spun around and were ultimately linked together by a red line spiraling between all of the points.

"It's Mensa-level stuff. I had to have the computer double-check, but it works out. Each mark makes a predictable jump forward if you account for the difference in body size. They all spiral inward toward one specific point."

Before he could think of something smart to say back, Logan's cell phone rang. He scowled and picked it up.

"Harrison. Hey, captain, we're...no...yeah...all right. Yeah, yeah, now. Got it."

He ended the call.

"As fun as this has been, we have to go. Dad's angry."

"Great..." Ryder groaned.

"See ya around, Olivia," Blake said, winking as they hastily left the lab.

22

CARRICK McCALLISTER WAS pacing in his office when the three detectives walked in. He was getting damned tired of Sunday morning phone calls and weekly meetings with the chief of detectives. With the body count now at six, he wanted answers. Today. And no excuses.

"Sit down. All of you," he barked, directing his second sentence toward Ryder who was positioning himself along the back wall. "If anybody's going to angrily pace up and down in here, it's gonna be me. Sit."

The detectives complied, each finding a seat, while their captain remained standing. He glared down at them over the bridge of his nose.

"I want to know where you three stand on this case. Now. And I don't want any of the typical placate-the-captain bullshit. Start with the new vic."

As usual, Blake took the lead. "The newest victim is Dr. Priya Malhotra. She is…was…a palliative care fellow at St. Joe's. From phone interviews and talking to staff at the hospital on Sunday, she was very well liked. Her department was hoping to keep her on after she finished training, at least that's the rumor per Pelton."

"So, there isn't one single thing wrong with her? Like the Oakes girl."

"Apparently, some of the staff took issue with her using alternative medicine on her patients. Natur… uh, homeo…what the heck was it?"

"Naturopathic and homeopathic," Gabriel corrected from behind his binder.

"Oh, yeah, my wife's into all that," the captain replied, leaning back against his desk. "I thought it was all hippy nonsense for a while, but she gave me something when I got the flu and I was fine two days later. So, who knows. That's it?"

"As far as we can tell." Blake nodded.

"Is there a cause of death?"

He sheepishly looked sideways. "Um, I'm gonna let these two take that one. I walked in halfway through that conversation."

Gabriel cleared his throat. "She had benzodiazepines in her system, captain, so she was drugged. Heavily. She probably would have stopped breathing just from that. But she was also force-fed a liquid that contained mercury cyanide," Ryder said coolly.

"Those come together?"

"Apparently. From what I saw at the hospital, she was exhibiting more signs of acute mercury poisoning than cyanide toxicity, but the few cases reported in the literature have shown either one can kill you. It just depends on which is more concentrated, the mercury or the cyanide. This woman had three strikes against her. She would have died no matter what was done for her."

"And you know that how?" Blake hissed. *He's such a fucking know-it-all.*

"I have access to the Internet and can read." Gabriel shrugged sarcastically.

"So why didn't we find her dead like the others?" the captain asked.

"Dumb luck," Logan piped up.

"Excuse me?" McCallister glared.

"Hey, don't look at me like that, cap," he replied, throwing his hands up. "I talked to the patrol officers that found her. I know one of 'em, Sutton. He's a good man. He said he and his partner stopped for coffee, which delayed their patrol in the Highlands by about ten or fifteen minutes. When they drove by the church, he thought he saw someone leaving through the side door. Of course, by the time he did a double take and parked the cruiser, whoever it was was long gone. But they found her in less than five minutes and called a bus. She had a medical bracelet on, so when they saw she was a doc and put two and two together, they told the bus to go to Joe's."

McCallister squeezed the bridge of his nose under his reading glasses. He could feel a headache coming on behind his eyes. "And the others?"

"We got the update today. Trust fund baby was strangled with his tie. The surgeon had his tongue cut out, but apparently, somebody kicked him so hard he bled out into his organs or something. And then Malhotra makes six."

"So, basically, there's no pattern. Goddamn it. Thoughts, Ryder?"

The detective shifted uncomfortably in his chair. *I'd give anything to be able to pace around the room right now.*

"Detective?" McCallister tried again, clearly impatient.

"They're all connected, captain. Our perp is tied to the hospital."

"And you know that how?"

Gabriel shifted uncomfortably, desperately trying to keep his urge to pace at bay.

"Because the only solid connection we have between all the vics also works there," Blake interjected, trying to give his clearly agitated partner a break.

The captain raised his eyebrows. "This is news. These people are being specifically targeted because of their association to someone? I was beginning to think it was random."

"So did we, until recently."

"Who's the link?"

An uncomfortable silence fell across the three detectives. McCallister lost what little patience he'd had left. He slammed his hand down on his desk, the vibration upturning a coffee cup full of pens. They scattered noisily across the floor.

"Detectives, I want an answer. Who is connected to all these people?"

"Dr. Carter," Blake said hesitantly, looking sideways at his partner.

Ryder had his head buried in his binder. McCallister didn't notice. He was too busy trying to place the name with a face.

"Carter…that young woman who was mentoring Lisa Oakes?"

They nodded. McCallister smirked.

"So, she's having these people killed."

"No!" Ryder shouted, jumping from his chair.

Blake immediately shot him a look to keep his mouth shut. Gabriel briefly nodded and started pacing frantically in the back of the room, his binder discarded on the floor. McCallister had his mouth open, ready to reprimand the young man when Harrison waved him off.

"We already went there, cap. Didn't go well. She's not pulling the strings here. We think whoever is behind all of this has some kind of sick fascination with her. Whether she's the prize at the end of the tunnel or the last name on this psycho's list, we don't know."

The captain leaned back in his chair, shutting his eyes and sighing heavily. "We have a serial killer with no discernible M.O. except for dumping bodies in churches on Sundays who's somehow connected to one of the physicians in training. Fantastic. Any more good news?" he asked sarcastically.

"No, cap," Logan replied.

"Thank goodness," he grumbled sarcastically. "So, what do we do here, guys? We can't just let the medical staff get picked off one by one. I'm open to ideas here."

The office went silent, except for the sound of Ryder pacing in the back of the room.

"We could go public," Blake muttered.

"Are you nuts?" Logan fired back. "Can you imagine the panic that would cause? That hospital would shut down."

"Not necessarily," Blake replied. "Look, we just have to make it clear that this involves the staff only. You said it yourself, captain, we could use some help here. We're six weeks in, and we've got nothing. So we go public. Hold a press conference. Release the names. Hell, it could be as easy as mentioning the churches. Some old blue hair might remember seeing someone out of place at mass, scoping the place out. Who knows?"

"That's true. We can't be everywhere at once. As it is, we spend half of each week interviewing people at the hospital," Harrison admitted.

"I can't say I'm opposed to the idea." The captain nodded. "Ryder?"

The two other detectives turned in their chairs. Gabriel stopped pacing and stared out the window.

"We don't have a choice. Just keep Gray's...Dr. Carter's name out of it. That could spook this guy off," he said quietly.

"Then it's decided. Get me names and pictures for the press. I'll handle the rest. You three just be ready to smile and curtsy for the news crews this afternoon."

"Ugh," Harrison moaned and rolled his eyes. "I'm gonna need more coffee."

He stood and walked out of the office. Ryder picked his binder up off of the floor and was quickly on his heels.

"Nolan..." The captain held him back. "Everything still okay?"

"Sure," he replied evasively.

"Harrison is working out well?"

"Oh yeah. No complaints there."

"And your partner?"

"He's fine, captain. I told you I'd let you know of any problems."

"All right. See you at three this afternoon."

"Wouldn't miss it," Blake replied, feigning excitement.

McCallister scowled and emphatically pointed him out the door.

23

GRAYSON TAPPED SOFTLY on the apartment door in front of her. She didn't want to wake Noah if he was sleeping, but she sincerely doubted he was.

Word had spread through the hospital quickly on Sunday about what had happened to Priya. A series of phone calls had started with Dr. Keefer and ended with Dr. Sanders, who had personally called to tell both her and Noah to take Monday off to regroup. She'd protested, insisting that only Noah needed the time away, but Sanders hadn't given her a choice. She'd take the day off. End of discussion.

The sound of shuffling behind the wall confirmed her suspicion that he hadn't been asleep. Thirty seconds later, the latch unlocked. He opened the door and let her in, shutting it quickly behind her and moving back to his spot on the couch without a word. Grayson stayed standing by the door.

Noah looked terrible. He'd clearly spent the majority of Sunday, and all of last night, on the couch. The bottle of vodka on the side table wasn't a good sign. She briefly wondered how full it had been when he'd started. There wasn't much left in it now.

"I'd have cleaned up if you'd told me you were coming," he said, his voice pitifully hoarse.

"Which is why I didn't tell you," she replied.

She pushed the balled-up blanket to the other side of the couch and sat down next to him. "What's going on with you?"

"Oh hell, love, I don't know," he said, putting his head in his hands.

From the looks of his hair, he'd spent a lot of time in that same position recently.

"I know I did the best I could. I even went over the files with Dr. Keefer again. He agreed. He said he wouldn't have done anything differently. That means a lot, coming from him."

"So..."

"So, why do I feel so awful? Why do I keep going over it and over it in my head? Could I have given the epi quicker? Should I have shocked her sooner? What if I hadn't gotten coffee? If I'd stayed in the room..."

Grayson felt a pang of guilt stab into her heart. She'd been having the same thought, but now was not the time to admit it.

"...you would've done the exact same things in the exact same order. Noah, you were gone for maybe two minutes. Literally five doors down. And you had some of the best nurses in the ICU watching her. They caught her rhythm. There's nothing else you could've done. You followed protocol, what works."

"And I keep telling myself that, and then I start thinking..."

She waved her hand in front of his face. "Don't. For once, shut your mind off. Stop thinking about it. You're taking this hard because you had an extra reason for saving her. You knew her. It always makes it that much worse when things go wrong. You think I was high-fiving people when you pronounced her? It took everything I had not to throw something at the wall. I haven't felt that helpless in the hospital in a really long time."

He looked up and managed a small grin. "Things had to be really bad for you to feel helpless, hon."

"Yeah, no kidding." She grinned back, shoving herself into his side softly. "You feel like eating real food?"

"Not really. What time is it?"

"After two."

"Good God. I had no idea it was that late already."

"Yeah, vodka and blackout blinds will do that to you."

"Oh, ha ha," he mumbled sarcastically.

"Look, I'm hungry and I drove all the way up here, so the least you can do is come with me and watch me eat," she said, standing up. She grabbed his arms and hauled him to his feet. "Go shower and change into something with fewer coffee stains on it."

"I, um, I should probably..." He motioned toward the mess strewn across his small living room.

"I'll do it. Just go," she insisted, pushing him down the hall toward his bedroom.

Grayson lurked outside the bathroom door until she heard the shower turn on, then walked back into the main room and started straightening up. Dirty glasses and one dirty dish went into the dishwasher. The vodka went back into the cabinet. Blankets and pillows were piled into the small storage closet by the door. By the time Noah reappeared, looking much more like himself, his apartment was back to normal, and Grayson was waiting by the door.

"Thanks, love. You didn't have to..."

"Yeah, I did," she said, waving him off. "Now, let's go eat. I'm starving."

"You and your one-track mind," he replied, smiling.

"Hey, you know I get dangerous and cranky when I'm hungry."

"Yes, yes I do. Speaking of which..." He held out his hand for the keys. "That probably means I should drive."

"Why?"

"You can't parallel park when you're in a good mood. I don't want to see you try on an empty stomach."

"Oh, ha ha," she parroted, rolling her eyes at him and handing over her keys as they left the apartment.

It was well past the usual lunch rush when they walked into the D&C. There were only a few people scattered here and there across the tables. Kyle was behind the bar and waved them in with a smile, which meant they could sit wherever they wanted. They chose their usual booth in the back. He strode up a few minutes later with menus.

"Sorry, guys, one of the waitresses called in sick today, so we're a bit short. You'll have to put up with me waiting on you."

"We'll live," Grayson replied.

"What'll it be?"

She ordered a burger and fries, and surprisingly Noah asked for the fish and chips. Secretly, he'd been hungrier than he'd made it out he was back at the apartment. As Kyle walked back to the bar, she leaned over the table.

"So..." she said with a smirk on her face.

"So, what?" he said evasively.

"Did you go through with your half of the deal from Friday?"

"Gray..."

"Out with it."

He rolled his eyes. "Fine. Yes. I held up my end."

"And..."

"And...I hate saying this...I should have listened to you sooner, damn it."

Grayson grinned from ear to ear and had to keep herself from jumping up and hugging him. "Noah!"

"Keep it down," he said, breaking into a grin himself.

"So, you spent time with him?"

"Saturday," he replied, nodding. "It was nice."

"And you're seeing him again?"

"This week."

"Well, I finally get to say I told you so, Dr. Mason."

"Yeah, yeah, you earned this one."

Grayson sat back in the booth and sighed. Noah was smiling and acting more like himself. She'd been worried in the apartment. Fresh air and getting the hell out of there had done him some good. When Kyle brought their food, she didn't miss the look that passed between him and Noah. They ate in comfortable silence, each just happy to be out in the normal world for once.

She was about two-thirds of the way through with her meal when she felt Noah nudge her leg under the table. She didn't respond, thinking it must have been an accident. He did it again not a moment later.

Grayson looked up, ready to say something smart about him playing footsie with the wrong person when she saw his expression. He jerked his head above hers, and she twisted around to look at the television that was suspended above their table.

There was a distinguished looking man on the screen, dressed in a formal police uniform and standing behind a conference lectern. A hoard of press was standing in front of him, and he was attempting to calm them all down. The banner on the screen read: "Live: Police Release Statement on Saint Joseph Hospital Deaths."

Behind him, Grayson recognized the faces of city's mayor and the chief of detectives on the left side of the screen. What had caught Noah's attention, however, were the three men on the right.

"Hey, Kyle," she called across the room, "can we turn that up?"

He nodded and aimed a remote control at the television. Grayson slid out from her side of the booth and moved in to sit beside Noah.

24

"PEOPLE, PEOPLE, PLEASE calm down. We'll get to your questions in a few minutes."

I fucking hate this.

Captain McCallister absolutely despised press conferences. As far as he was concerned, the press were vultures sent to suck the life out of his department at every opportunity. But he couldn't disagree with his detectives on this one. They needed the public to be on board with what was happening at St. Joseph's. He'd have to fight off his headache long enough to get through the viper's nest in front of him.

When the reporters finally had enough good grace to get settled into their seats, he took a deep breath and started talking.

"Thank you all for coming on such short notice. We're going to give a quick statement here, then we'll open up the floor for questions. Please understand that this is an ongoing investigation, and please respect the victims and their families.

"As you all are aware, there has been a series of murders in the Denver area in recent weeks. We can now confirm that all of the victims are connected to one of our local hospitals. We have reason to believe that the medical staff at St. Joseph's Hospital is being targeted. In addition, it's true that all of the victims have been discovered in local area Catholic churches. With one exception, none of the victims were known to have attended the churches in which they were found.

"We are asking for several things here today. The first is not to panic. There is no evidence that the general public is being targeted. Neither are the patients that attend St. Joseph's Hospital. I have been assured by the hospital administration that business will continue as usual, and we are encouraging people to continue utilizing the resources that St. Joseph's provides to the community.

"We are also asking that the hospital staff be vigilant in the coming weeks as our investigation continues. Take precautions. Utilize the security available at the hospital whenever possible. Report any suspicious activity to the appropriate personnel or to our offices here downtown.

"Lastly, we are asking for the public's help, particularly those of you who are members of the Catholic community here in Denver. The person responsible for these crimes has a clear predilection for leaving his victims within your churches. If anything comes to mind, or if anyone sees anything suspicious, please alert your pastors or call the police.

"Now, we'll take a few questions..."

The room erupted into chaos as every reporter jumped to their feet, hands raised and jostling for attention. McCallister chose his reporters carefully. After years of navigating the viper pit, he knew who asked fair questions and who went for the jugular just for the fun of it. He pointed toward a young woman in a blue blazer seated in the second row.

"Captain, is there any evidence that the person responsible for these crimes works at the hospital?"

"Not as of yet, Michelle," he said, his expression deadpan. "We are keeping our suspect pool very broad at this point."

Not a blatant lie.

He pointed to a young man almost directly behind her.

"Captain, have any other patterns emerged beside the connection with St. Joseph's Hospital and the Catholic churches?"

"No, Brian, but we are continually reexamining the evidence from each crime scene in the attempt to find one. We hope members of the public will be able to help point us in the right direction."

Okay, now I'm lying.

The questioning went on for almost twenty minutes before the mayor rose from his seat and took his turn at the podium. McCallister walked back and took his seat next to his detectives, exhausted.

"Nice job, cap," Harrison said, leaning over slightly.

"I hope something comes of it," he replied in a low voice, "because next time, I'm personally feeding the three of you to those vultures."

Logan just nodded and smiled.

25

IT WAS GOING on five-thirty when Harrison looked up from the paperwork on his desk. The press conference had gone well, and they'd been flooded with calls with potential leads. Thankfully, a call bank staffed with eager volunteers had been set up in anticipation of the deluge, so they'd personally been spared the initial onslaught. Now it was their job to sort through each of the reports and figure out which ones were credible enough to go after.

So far, none of them, but hey, at least people are trying to get this psychopath busted.

Nolan and Ryder were back in the interrogation room, doing God knows what. He was happy to stay out in the open squad room. It got a bit claustrophobic in there with the three of them.

He glanced over at the captain's office. Through the open blinds, he could see him sitting at his desk, his phone up to his ear and his fingers pinching the bridge of his nose. He wasn't having any better of an afternoon, clearly. Logan wondered if that was the chief of detectives on the phone or his wife. He shrugged and turned away when his own desk phone started ringing.

"Harrison," he said into the receiver.

"Hey, Logan, it's Fred at the front desk."

"Hey, buddy. What's up?"

"I've got somebody down here that wants to talk to you about that St. Joe's case."

Logan groaned. "Tell them to give the phone bank a call."

"I tried that. She's pretty insistent. Asked for you by name."

"Really?"

She? That has possibilities. That piqued his curiosity.

"Okay, I'll be right down."

"I figured as much."

He grabbed his badge off the desk and clipped it onto his belt, then headed straight for the elevator. He strode out into the lobby and looked around. He didn't recognize anybody. Fred was waving him over toward the main information desk.

Logan shook the man's hand when he was within reach. "Hey, Fred. How's it hangin'?"

The older man shrugged. "Nothing to complain about."

Fred Williams was one of the oldest cops on the force. A gunshot to the leg had wounded him late in his career and taken him off active duty. He'd been in and out of the hospital for almost a year. At one point, the doctors were talking amputation just to give him a better quality of life. But he'd toughed it out and now walked with the help of a cane and a bit of a limp. The department had offered him his full pension and retirement early, not to mention a medal for getting shot in the first place. He'd politely told the brass to shove it and was working the front desk until he hit his actual retirement date.

"So, whatcha got for me, Fred?"

The older man pointed toward one of the couches in the front lobby. "That pretty one there on the right. She's all yours." He winked.

Logan followed the older man's line of sight. *Well, well...*

"Thanks, buddy, but that one's already spoken for," he replied, grinning, then left the desk without another word.

He walked around the back of the couch and into the young brunette's field of view.

"Dr. Carter," he said, holding his hand out to her.

"Detective Harrison," she replied, standing and shaking his hand.

"I'm surprised to see you down at headquarters on a weekday. What can I do for you?"

"Um, nothing really," she said, fidgeting slightly with the hem of her sweater.

Logan took a second to look at her while she had her eyes on the floor. Jeans, white sweater, leather jacket and boots, hair a little windblown, cheeks a little flushed. He was almost jealous of Ryder. Almost.

"Well, you've got me confused then, doc. Most people don't voluntarily hang out in a police station."

"It's more of what I can do for you, I guess," she replied, shrugging her shoulders.

He just looked at her, face calm and completely blank, waiting for her to continue. She huffed and pursed her lips. "I saw the press conference this afternoon. Your captain didn't mention me, but...I...I know you think I'm involved. I'm really starting to believe it myself. I just thought I'd see if there's any way I can be helpful."

Logan cracked a smile at her. He was really starting to like this girl. She wasn't one to go hide in a corner and wait for someone else to solve her problems. In another life, she would've made one hell of a cop.

"All right," he said. "Can't hurt. Let's get you a visitor's pass so you're legal."

He guided her up toward the front desk.

"Fred, meet Dr. Carter."

"Hello again, missy," the older man smiled.

Grayson managed a small one in return.

"She needs a visitor's pass for today. And put her on your list, will ya? She's helping with the St. Joe's thing. She can come up whenever she wants to."

"You've got it," he replied, handing over a visitor's badge on a lanyard.

Grayson cautiously navigated the badge over her head and around her neck.

"Okay, let's go," Logan motioned toward the elevator.

He guided the young woman into the gray box ahead of him and pressed the button for Major Crimes. Grayson nervously tapped her right foot on the linoleum floor.

As they neared their floor and the elevator car slowed, Logan took another glance at her and smiled to himself. *This is going to be interesting.*

He guided her off the elevator and into the squad room. He wasn't more than a foot out of the door when he heard his name.

"Logan, where in the hell have you been, you lazy asshole?" Nolan called from across the room. "I'm not running through all these goddamned leads by myself."

Blake's face turned beet-red when he saw Grayson step off the elevator behind Logan. He nearly spilled his coffee. "Oh shit, I mean, I..."

"Don't even try to get out of that, bud." Harrison grinned. "It's too much fun to watch you turn colors."

"Shut up," he mumbled. "Um, hi, Dr. Carter," he added hastily.

"Hi, detective." She smiled, trying not to laugh.

"What are you doing here?" he asked, still trying to recover himself.

"The good doctor is here to help us with our investigation," Harrison said, winking over her shoulder. "I thought I'd take her to the cave."

"The what?" she asked, confused. *Where the hell did he say he's taking me? The cave?*

"Don't worry about it. You'll love it." Logan winked.

"That sounds like a great idea," Nolan nodded. "I've gotta talk to the captain. I'll be back there in a few minutes."

Grayson cemented her boots as best she could against the floorboards. "Okay, wait, what exactly is the cave and why am I going there?" *Am I missing something here?*

"Just come on," Logan said, guiding her down a side hallway, his palm pressed firmly into the small of her back.

There was light coming from under the last door on the left, and he was guiding her straight toward it.

26

RYDER LEANED HEAVILY over the rickety metal table, his head in his hands, absorbed in the photographs Pelton had sent back up with Nolan. He was exhausted, not that he'd admit that to anyone. He was convinced, now more than ever, that the markings on the victims were important. It was more than keeping score. The spiral meant something. It had to. Their killer was too calculating to do something that complicated by chance.

I just can't fucking see it.

And unfortunately, his usual method of staring at the evidence until an answer came to him wasn't working.

The press conference was generating a lot of buzz, none of which seemed very credible. It was just going to mean chasing down leads that were a waste of time, which was just going to add to his oh-so-chipper mood. He was considering getting another cup of squad room grade coffee when there was a knock on the door. He looked up as Logan pushed it open.

"So, Wonder Boy, anything new?"

"What do you think, Logan?" he sighed, dropping back down into his chair.

"I guess not. You look like hell."

"Brilliant, detective," he replied sarcastically.

"You want some help?"

"From you?" he asked, surprised. Gabriel knew that Logan hated being stuck in a confined space with him when he was working a case. He always had, ever since their days in narcotics. Ryder chuckled to himself.

"Are you feeling okay, Logan? You hate it back here."

"I feel fine, ass. And for the record, I didn't mean me."

"Blake's suffered in here enough today. Give the guy a break."

"Yeah, saw him in the hall. He's voluntarily spending time with the captain. That says it all."

"Did you want something?" Ryder asked, sighing into his hands.

"I asked if you wanted some help."

"Not if this is your idea of helping, Logan."

"Nah, this is," he replied, sidestepping away from the doorway.

The older detective watched his former partner's face as the young brunette stepped into the room. The look of shock was priceless. Harrison shook his head, chuckled, and walked back down the hallway toward the squad room, waving his hand behind his head. "Enjoy," he hollered back at them.

Grayson rolled her eyes and leaned against the doorframe. Gabriel didn't move. He sat perfectly rigid, staring at her. They passed several minutes in complete, uncomfortable silence.

"Well, do you want some help or not?" she asked, crossing her arms over her chest.

When he didn't answer her, Grayson pushed herself off of the doorframe, shut the door, and began wandering slowly around the room. She spent more than a few extra minutes looking at the photographs from Lisa's scene. There was something peaceful about it, strangely enough. Compared to the others, it looked like someone had actually taken time to make her comfortable.

Weird.

Ryder watched her closely as she made her way around the room. *What in the hell is she doing here? Is Logan insane? She can't be in here.*

She'd take one look at all this, at him…how he functioned… and she'd run screaming. He nervously tapped his pen against his thigh, waiting for her to bolt. Waiting for the look of disgust and fear to wash across her face. It wouldn't be new. He'd seen it from enough colleagues and former week-long partners.

But she didn't run. She didn't scream. She just kept working her way through the photographs. She made it to photographs from the fourth scene before she said anything.

"What is this?" she asked, pointing to a particular shot from the M.E.'s office.

Gabriel blinked rapidly and shook himself out of his head. "It's…it's ink," he replied, once he'd remembered how to speak.

"Ink," she repeated. "Like from a pen?"

He nodded.

"Why is this guy injecting ink into people?"

"Injecting?"

"Yeah," she replied. "If it was just a pen mark, it would wash off, right? That looks like a tattoo, which means the ink is below the skin. Somebody used a needle to do that. Do they all have one?"

He nodded again, then motioned toward the photographs in front of him. Grayson grabbed the photograph off the wall, then leaned over his right shoulder to get a better look at the ones on the table. Gabriel's heart rate kicked up when her hair fell against his shoulder. She didn't notice.

"These are in order?"

"Uh…" He took a quick inventory, hastily placing the James photo in its place. "Yes."

"Huh. That's weird."

"What is?"

"They're heading toward McBurney's."

Ryder looked over his shoulder and gave her a questioning look. She stared back. It took Grayson a second to realize he had no idea what she was talking about.

"Oh, sorry!" She shook her head several times, clearly admonishing herself. "McBurney's point. Find your anterior superior iliac spine—your ASIS—on the right and draw a line to your belly button. Divide that line into thirds. The point that's closest to your ASIS is McBurney's."

"And it means what to you, exactly?" he asked.

"It's the textbook place to look for pain when somebody has appendicitis. Technically, it's not diagnostic and pain there can come from things other than the appendix, but it's what every medical student memorizes for their exams. And look," she said, hitting each mark with her right index finger in succession, "The marks are getting closer to that point. Like a spiral."

Ryder looked back and forth between Grayson and the photographs several times. She was right.

"Maybe whoever you're looking for has some medical training," she suggested quietly.

He faced the table and shut his eyes, rubbing his forehead with his hands. His headache was getting worse. The incessant throbbing was moving backward around his temples to the base of his skull. The knives were multiplying behind his eyes.

Grayson noticed him tense up, and she figured she'd said something either very wrong or very stupid. Or both. Really, what did she know about this stuff? She stood up straight and bit her lip. Without thinking, she put her right hand on his shoulder.

"I'm sorry. It was just a stupid idea. I didn't mean to say something wrong…"

Ryder's left hand shot up and covered hers. He pressed it further into him until he could feel the pads of her fingers through his shirt. "It wasn't a stupid idea," he said softly. "I've been staring at these marks for weeks, and in just five minutes, you..." He sighed and shook his head.

"So, I found some pattern in a bunch of dots. So what? Does it actually mean anything?" she asked, trying to lighten his mood.

Gabriel folded further into himself, his mood darkening. Grayson wrinkled her forehead. *Good God, is he always this hard on himself?*

"It might. If there's an end to this, the body with a mark directly on that point will be the last one on the list. And judging by the trajectory..." he paused, doing the math in his head. "We're looking at three, maybe four more in all."

"Nine, maybe ten victims total? That's kind of a random number, isn't it?"

"Not necessarily. It depends on the motivation behind it. This guy is a calculating son of a bitch. If it's nine or if it's ten, he has a damned good reason for it."

"That doesn't particularly make me feel any better, you know," she joked.

Gabriel's grip on her hand tightened considerably, almost painfully. "He's not getting anywhere near you," he hissed.

"You may not get much of a say in the matter, from the looks of it. It doesn't seem like anybody ever sees him coming. Do any of them have defensive wounds?"

He shook his head. "No, they don't."

"Well, there you go then. Whether I'm number nine or number ten, unless you pick him up before he gets to me, it looks like I won't have much of a fighting chance," she said shakily. Grayson attempted to laugh to lighten the mood. The sound was eerily high-pitched and completely hollow.

Ryder lifted her hand off of his shoulder and gently pushed her into the seat beside him. Her eyes were fixed on the floor and glassy.

"Grayson, look at me." He waited patiently for her to look up, and when she didn't, he gently grabbed her chin and forced her. Her blue eyes were full of fear.

"Listen to me," he said softly but firmly. "No one is going to get close enough to touch you, let alone hurt you. We don't even know for sure that you're on this guy's list. But it doesn't matter. He's going to have to go through me to get to you, and that's not an option. Understand?"

His words hung in the air between them, his hand still on her face. She took in a shaky breath, then nodded. He managed a small smile and wiped a tear away from her right cheek with his thumb. A knock at the door broke the silence.

"Hey, Ryder?" Nolan's voice came through the door as they shoved away from each other.

"Yeah?"

"Captain wants to see you," his partner said, poking his head in.

"All right." He nodded, standing and holding his hand out to her. "Come on. You've spent enough time in this hellhole. And I think it's time I introduced you to the captain."

He steered her out the door and shut the door behind him. If he could help it, she'd never set foot in there again.

27

THE REST OF the week was business as usual for the two young physicians. Noah returned to his ICU team and Grayson went back to the trauma service. Adams had held down the fort well, and it helped that the service had been relatively quiet in her absence. Now that it was getting colder out, fewer and fewer people were outside doing stupid things. As the ski season picked up, that would change. It did every year. But for now, things were relatively quiet and steady.

The rumor mill was running full force within the hospital walls. Everyone had their opinions about what was going on and who the next victim was going to be. All kinds of wild theories were floating around the locker rooms, but in reality, nobody had the slightest clue what was going on. That made things worse. Everyone was scared and on edge.

On Friday morning, Grand Rounds convened in the conference room. Residents scurried around the hospital, scrambling to finish patient rounds and get to their seats on time. It was the same battle every week.

Grayson and her team arrived a few minutes into the start of the conference. It had been a hard decision: get to conference on time or get coffee. Coffee had won out, especially with the topic that was being presented. She hated to admit it because she had been the one on stage two weeks ago, but she had absolutely no interest in learning about recent advances in the treatment of sexually-transmitted diseases in the developing world.

There were only two seats left in the orthopedic section. Several rotating medical students had taken up the usual extra seats. Grayson ushered her two juniors down the stairs, then found a seat for herself in the back row.

Out of respect, and a little bit of guilt, she spent a few moments listening to the poor OBGYN resident stammer through the first few slides of her presentation. When it was clear she wasn't going to miss anything important, Grayson pulled out her patient list and started working through her day's to-do list, splitting up the work equally amongst her team.

She saw someone sit down in the seat next to hers in her peripheral vision but didn't pay much attention until a low voice whispered in her ear.

"You should be paying attention, Dr. Carter."

She whipped her eyes up. Dr. Cain had a condescending look on his face, and his green eyes were focused directly on her. She shifted, moving as far away from him as she could without moving seats.

She managed a small, wary smile and shrugged. "It's not exactly my field, Dr. Cain."

"Nonsense. Everyone gets into a little trouble now and again, so to speak."

"Um, I guess," she replied, turning back toward the front of the lecture hall and feigning interest. *What the heck does that mean?*

Suddenly, a talk on STDs in third-world countries was absolutely riveting.

Thirty minutes later, the first presentation was over and a short break was called before the start of tumor board. Grayson started to stand up, hoping to make her way out of the back row and down toward the other residents.

Dr. Cain motioned for her to keep her seat. "A moment, if you would, Dr. Carter. I have a few questions about my patients."

"Oh, um…all right," she said, sitting precariously on the backs of the chairs of the row in front of them.

Her junior residents shot her a do-you-want-us-to-save-you look as they passed on the stairs. She waved them off. "I didn't think we had any of your patients on our service."

"454 A. Mr. Carlton," he replied sharply.

Grayson wrinkled her nose as she checked her list. "Um, we signed off."

"You aren't seeing him anymore?" Cain balked.

"No. He's only in the hospital for medical reasons. We fixed his hip a week ago."

"Fine," he replied, clearly unimpressed. "623."

"Final washout was yesterday. He's following up in clinic in two weeks. The wound VAC stays on until we see him. Home care is going to come out to the halfway house to change it. He looked fine this morning. We signed off."

"638."

"Non-operative ankle fracture. He can go home in a walking boot."

"ICU 116."

"Everything's done. We fixed the last of her fractures over a week ago. Her problem is getting off the ventilator."

Dr. Cain's face progressively darkened. "Do you always fail to treat your patients appropriately?"

Grayson blinked in surprise. "Excuse me?"

"My understanding, *doctor*, is that you are supposed to care for your patients while they are in the hospital. Failing to round on them is a gross violation of that duty," he hissed.

"With all due respect, Dr. Cain," she said, standing, "My

service takes very good care of our patients. We are consultants, which means we are able to sign off on our patients when we have nothing additional to add to their care. If you have an issue with that practice, you can speak to my department chairman."

"Hmmm, such spirit," he cooed softly as she attempted to walk past him. "You'll be a challenge."

Her spine shivered. She spun on her heels when she reached the safety of the stairs. "A challenge for what, exactly, Dr. Cain?" she shot back.

He glanced at her. "You need to learn your proper place, Dr. Carter."

"Trust me, I know my place, and it has nothing to do with you."

"You'll reconsider," he chuckled, standing.

"Doubtful."

"Trust me," he said, grabbing her right arm as she passed him. "You'll see things my way."

Grayson twisted her arm and wrenched it out of his grasp. It came away easily.

He smiled brightly at her as she backed away from him and headed down the stairs.

Noah met her about halfway. "Hey, Gray, are you...whoa! Hang on!" he hollered as she barreled past him. "Stop, stop! What's going on?" he said, grabbing her by the shoulders and spinning her around to look at him as she reached the stage.

"Ugh, I can't stand him," she said, shaking her head.

"Who?"

"Cain. He's such an ass. And he gives me the creeps."

"Join the club, love. The administration adores him. The rest of us cringe when we have to work with him."

"He just..."

"He gets his weird moods and obsesses for a bit and then moves on. He's the St. Joe's bogeyman. Don't worry about him. Just come sit with us."

"Fine. Thanks."

She followed Noah over to the medical side of the lecture hall and took a seat beside him. She hoped for Cain's sake that he backed off. Whatever she might think of the man, she didn't want him dead.

And lately, anyone who'd gotten close to her had ended up in the county morgue.

28

"OKAY, ADAMS, YOU know what to do. Go for it." Grayson nodded.

She watched from the door as her junior started working on their most recent ER consult, a known drug addict with a massive forearm abscess. The guy was only nineteen, but he was in the emergency room at least once a month. He had to have at least ten or twelve scars from her personal scalpel alone. How he wasn't one big scar ball from the elbows down was anyone's guess, but he was somehow still able to find a vein, shoot meth, and get infected.

These consults were never pleasant. He'd cuss and swear and threaten whoever walked in the door, then cry like a baby the second they started talking about numbing up the skin before they opened it up. It never made sense to her.

How can you shoot up multiple times a day but cry at the sight of a 25-gauge needle? Your body is covered in tattoos, for God's sake.

"You okay in here for a bit?" she asked.

"Yup, I'm okay," Adams replied, ignoring the epithets being slung at him from the hospital gurney.

"Okay, I'm gonna go take a look at the next one. Be back in a bit."

She pulled the curtain behind her as she left and walked several bays down. She picked up the chart from the door, made sure she was at the right place and walked in the room.

"Mr. McIntyre?"

"Yeah?" a sixty-something-year-old man replied from the gurney. A woman about the same age with graying hair sat next to him, rubbing his hand.

"I'm Dr. Carter from orthopedics. One of the chief residents. The ER asked me to come down and take a look at your shoulder. What happened?" she asked, walking to the other side of the bed.

"Oh, just me being stupid. I went out this afternoon to start putting up our Christmas lights and wasn't watching what I was doing, and down I went. Landed on my shoulder," he said, motioning toward his right side.

"It says here you fell off of a step stool?"

The man's eyes shot to his lap, clearly embarrassed that he'd fallen at all.

"No, the roof," the woman beside him scolded.

"Doc, this is my wife, Martha," he chuckled, rolling his eyes. "She does most of the talking."

"I told him we should just hire somebody this year, but no, he doesn't listen." The older woman glared at her husband.

"Do they ever?" Grayson smiled.

"No. So don't ever go thinking you're gonna change any of them that way." She shook her head and her face softened. "He's always been a stubborn idiot."

"Hey, I'm the one with the broken bone here. No ganging up on me," Mr. McIntyre said jokingly, grimacing when he felt pain shoot through his shoulder.

"Okay. Let me take a good look at you from head to toe. Mrs. McIntyre, if you wouldn't mind moving down here," Grayson pointed toward a chair away from the gurney.

"Oh, sure, hon." She was mid-rise when a horrified look washed over her face. "Oh, I'm so sorry. I'm sure you hate being called that."

"I've gotten used to it," Grayson said honestly. "You don't mean it as an insult, so why should I take it as one?" She smiled and started her exam.

Midway through, Mr. McIntyre jumped when she touched his right ankle.

"That hurts?" Grayson asked.

"Oh yeah," he nodded. His skin was black and blue, and the joint was clearly swollen. Less than a minute later, she hit another sore spot on his right wrist.

"Hey, quit that," he joked through his grimacing.

Grayson's forehead scrunched. "Did they take x-rays of your ankle or your wrist?"

He shook his head.

"Did anybody even examine you?" she asked, not bothering to hide her disgust.

"Not like that," his wife said. "They asked him where he hurt, he said his shoulder, and that was it."

Grayson scowled. "Lovely. Okay, I'm going to get some more x-rays, folks. Hang tight."

"What about his shoulder?" the wife asked.

"Well, it's broken," she said, "but what we do about it partially depends on what's going on with your wrist and your ankle. Let's wait on those new x-rays, okay?"

"Sure, honey."

Grayson stepped out of the room and grabbed the chart from the wall again. *Who in the hell saw this guy?* The name on the chart was illegible, so she went to the nurse.

"Hey, Jim?"

The bald middle-aged EMT smiled as she approached his station. "Hey, kiddo. How're the bones?"

"Mine are fine. His..." She motioned toward Mr. McIntyre's room. "Not so much. Any idea who saw him, resident-wise?"

"Yeah, Harlan," he replied, nodding. "Why?"

Carter wrinkled her nose in disgust. "He never touched the guy. He's probably got a broken wrist and a broken ankle on top of his broken shoulder. Oh, and he fell off a roof, not a stool like they told us."

"Shit, really?"

"Yeah. Where's Harlan at?"

"He's working under Dr. Meyer tonight. Section Three."

"Thanks."

Grayson found a computer, put in orders for more x-rays, then went in search of Dr. Harlan. Instead, she found his attending, Dr. Meyer. He was on the phone with someone in the doc box of section three. She waited patiently until he was finished.

"Dr. Meyer?"

He swiveled in his chair to face her. He was all of 5'3", but he was a firecracker. He didn't put up with bullshit from anybody, but deep down, he was a lovable Santa Claus-type. Once a year, he'd have a bit too much to drink and talk about his secret missions with the Marines in Vietnam.

"Dr. Carter, haven't seen you down here in a while. Did they demote you?" he teased.

"No, sir. Just helping my junior while he's in with that forearm abscess so we don't get behind. Are you taking care of Mr. McIntyre in bed 43?"

He looked at his patient list. "Yeah. Harlan saw him, I think, but I haven't looked at him myself yet. Why?"

"Well, I hate to blow the whistle on people, but according to the McIntyres, Harlan never did an exam. He's clearly got a broken ankle and a broken wrist on top of that broken shoulder. My junior was told he'd fallen off a step stool. He actually fell off of his two-story roof hanging Christmas lights. Did Harlan even really go in the room?"

"I assumed so," Meyer said, scowling, "but honestly, I trust you more than I trust him. Can you stay for a minute?"

"Sure. I have to wait on these new x-rays anyway." She shrugged and took a seat.

They made small talk until Greg Harlan turned the corner. At 6'2", muscled and tan, he was a formidable-looking guy. He had a reputation for having a quick fuse, and rumor had it he knocked his wife around when he didn't get his way. Nothing was ever proven, so he'd never done jail time, but the guy had a huge ego and a temper to match.

"Harlan! Get over here," Meyer called across the room.

Harlan's face dropped immediately. He stalked over toward his attending, eyeing up Grayson in the process.

"Yeah, what?"

"Yeah, nothing. Tell me about Mr. McIntyre in 43."

"I told you about him already."

"So, tell me again," Meyer snapped coldly.

"He fell. His shoulder's broken. I called them," he said, pointing at Grayson. "What more do you want?"

"Well, since he's probably got a broken ankle and a broken wrist, I'd say start with a goddamned basic exam," Meyer replied.

"She doesn't know what she's talking about," Harlan spat.

"Really? The chief of orthopedics doesn't know how to spot an ankle fracture? Tell me another one," he shot back sarcastically.

Dr. Meyer stood up and shoved a finger in Harlan's face, which of course caught everyone's attention in the whole section. "What the hell were you thinking? Did you even examine this guy?"

"Doc, I…"

"Shut. Up. It's cocky, lazy pieces of shit like you that give our department a bad name. Now, you haul your ass back in there and do a FULL. FUCKING. EXAM. Then you apologize to Mr. McIntyre and his wife. And then you come back here and apologize to Dr. Carter. You should know better."

Meyer turned around to walk away, then whipped back around.

"And for the record, a simple shoulder fracture like that doesn't even need orthopedics. You're capable of putting someone in a sling. Now get the hell out of here."

Harlan glared at Grayson and opened his mouth to say something to her.

Meyer caught him. "Keep your damned mouth shut. You'll have enough explaining to do in front of your program director on Monday."

Harlan turned on his heels and stalked off down the hallway.

"He'll cool off. Thanks for the heads-up, Carter. Feel free to call his ass out anytime."

"See ya, Dr. Meyer," she said, heading back down the hallway to check on Adams' progress.

29

SEVERAL HOURS LATER, Grayson was walking down the back hallway of the ER, her eyelids heavy, completely lost inside her own head.

Thank God. We're finally caught up.

Saturday night had turned out to be busier than she'd anticipated. Too many people had attempted to fight the ice and try to put up Christmas decorations after dark. The ice had most definitely won out. Adams was finishing up the last splint and was going to meet her back in the consult room in a few minutes to run the list.

Dot the t's and cross the i's. Shit. Either way, I'm tired.

Grayson yawned and put her hand up to her mouth to stifle it. She swiped her hospital badge through the card reader on the wall, and the door to the consult room clicked open. The room was pitch-black. The computer screens were all turned off, and the lights were out. She was halfway into the room before she realized that wasn't right.

Something was wrong.

Wait. Why is the room dark?

Without warning, two hands landed on her throat, squeezing and lifting her off of the floor. She tried to scream, but the fingers tightened. Someone swung the door to the consult room closed. Grayson kicked her legs wildly and only made contact with air. Her lungs were on fire. She couldn't see in the dark, but she could feel herself start to go fuzzy.

Suddenly, the hands let go, and she dropped to the floor, gasping and coughing for air. The moment she felt she had enough power in her lungs, she tried to yell for help, but something cold and hard struck her in the chest. She whimpered and doubled over in pain. The crack that echoed around the room was unmistakable.

Broken ribs.

Pain rocketed through her side with her next breath and she clutched at her chest.

"Feels good, doesn't it?" she heard someone hiss into her ear.

She tried lifting her head to see who it was, but a hard strike to her cheek put her back on the floor. It was too dark to see anything, anyway.

"You need to learn your place."

Grayson struggled to keep conscious, edging back from her attacker as best she could in the dark. Her side was on fire. It was getting harder and harder to breathe. Even in the dark, she knew the edges of her vision were starting to blur as she hyperventilated. Strong fingers wrapped around her throat again.

"Feel me, sweetheart. You'll never forget me."

Her vision went black.

———

Adams walked down the hallway toward the consult room. He wasn't happy with his splint, but it would be good enough to last Mr. Stewart until morning. He was so tired. All he needed was a twenty-minute nap, and he'd make it through the rest of the night. He reached up to swipe his badge through the card reader, but the door to the consult room was already cracked open.

Strange.

They usually locked automatically. He pushed the door open.

Why the hell are the lights off?

He flipped the switch on the side wall and immediately ran into the room.

"Carter? Carter! Grayson? Holy...holy shit, hang on!" he called out, bolting from the room.

A minute later, Dr. Meyer burst into the room with two nurses and a gurney, with Adams hot on his heels.

"Goddamn it, call a code! We're taking over trauma bay one. Get her on the gurney now! Move!"

30

HE'D BEEN EXPECTING a call out.

Hell, he hadn't even bothered to try to go to bed after he'd dropped his girls off at their mother's house after dinner. He'd gone home, cleaned up their room as best he knew how, and put their toys away. The house was always too dark and too quiet without two rambunctious little girls running all over the place. He'd cracked a beer, settled in on the couch, and waited.

His phone went off just after one o'clock, jolting him awake from a dead sleep. Blake looked around wildly, momentarily disoriented, but quickly got his bearings. He'd fallen asleep on the couch, his feet still on the coffee table. He flailed around for his phone, finally remembering that it was in his front pocket, and answered without looking at the screen. "Yeah?"

"Sleeping beauty, I presume?" came the soft chuckle across the line.

"Gabriel?" he croaked. "Fuck, man, what the hell time is it?"

"It's a little after one in the morning."

"So technically it's Sunday."

"Yes."

"We have work to do?"

"How did you possibly guess?" Sarcasm practically oozed out of the phone.

"All right, all right, I'm getting up, I…wait, they called you first?"

"Is that a problem?"

"They never call you first, Gabe."

"I asked to be first call. I didn't know how late you had your girls."

"Oh." Nolan stared blankly across the room. That hadn't been the response he'd been expecting. "Thanks."

"Get your stuff together."

"Yeah, yeah. I'll be at your place in…"

"Don't bother. I'm outside in the SUV. Logan's meeting us there."

Blake peeked out his living room window, and sure enough, there was the SUV parked in his driveway.

"Well, hell, just let me get my coat then," he pouted, throwing on the closest coat on the coat rack and stuffing his keys into his pocket.

"Don't forget your badge."

Nolan scowled. "Shut up, it's…ah, hell…"

He hung up the phone as he trudged up the stairs to his girls' room. The game of the month was "Officer Princess," and quite often his badge, his sunglasses, and his ID went missing when he had his kids. He pawed through their room like a rabid raccoon, disrupting all of his previous attempts at cleaning.

Not in their room. Damn it.

He took a quick look through the bathroom before it dawned on him. He stalked into the laundry room. Sure enough, there was his ID, along with his partially warped badge, in the dryer with their princess costumes from Halloween.

"Perfect," he muttered.

He stuffed both into his coat and headed out the front door. He slid into the passenger seat without a word and sized up his partner. Jeans, gray sweater, and what looked like hiking boots.

At least it's not a fucking suit.

"Something wrong?" his partner quipped.

"No, nothing."

Gabriel smirked. "You find your badge, Officer Princess?"

"Shut up, Ryder."

Gabriel pulled out of the driveway and maneuvered out onto the main roads. Nolan tried his best to enjoy the ride. It was strange to be in the passenger seat. He took note of the two travel mugs in the center console.

"You brought coffee?"

"Huh? Oh, yeah, sorry."

"You had time to make coffee and drive out here after the call out? That must mean our guy's getting antsy and dropping off bodies on Saturday now, huh?" he joked, reaching for his mug and taking a long sip.

Hell yeah. That's the stuff.

He had his complaints about his partner every now and again, but the man could make a good cup of coffee.

"No, the drop was made after midnight."

"And you know this how?"

"The people who reported it witnessed the drop."

"Oh, okay."

Nolan took another sip of coffee before nearly spitting it out on the dashboard. "Wait, what?"

"It'll make sense when we get there, Blake. And I didn't have that far to drive."

"It takes you a good twenty minutes at least to get to my house."

"I wasn't at home."

"Oh, okay," he shrugged, then smiled. "Ooohhhhh…"

Ryder shot him a glare from across the car.

"You were keeping watch on the good doctor again."

"On the *house*, Blake."

"On *her* in the house," he corrected. "You ever going to let me just put a squad on it?"

Ryder didn't respond, but his grip on the steering wheel tightened. Blake dropped it.

They pulled up outside of St. John's Cathedral minutes later, parking just behind Harrison. The church was an impressive sight to behold. It was a towering mass of gray stone guarded by two towers and laced with stained glass. A swarm of blue and white cruisers, lights blazing, were already scattered across the street. The entire front lawn was draped off in yellow tape. Uniformed officers were walking around the perimeter in pairs with scent dogs. Several others were interviewing neighbors dressed in winter coats thrown over pajamas. The lights inside the church were on full blast and, combined with the lights coming from the cruisers, strange and distorted shapes were crawling along the magnificent outer walls.

Blake opened the passenger door and stepped out onto the lawn. His partner did the same. Harrison got out of his own car and walked up to meet them. He looked like he'd just rolled out of bed...or around in one.

"Thanks for this." He grinned at Ryder. "I clearly didn't have anything else to do tonight."

"Knowing you, there'll be another one waiting when you get back," Ryder stated coolly. "You were just planning to sit back and make this a spectator sport?"

"No, asshole, I figured since you're our department's resident bloodhound, I'd wait until you got here. I'm not into sniffing bodies on the front lawn."

"The body's inside the church, Logan. Have a bit of respect here," Nolan scolded.

"Uh, not this time, buddy."

Blake wrinkled his forehead in confusion. "You've lost me."

"Just follow the bloodhound," Logan sighed, motioning forward.

Ryder was already five steps ahead of them. The two other detectives followed behind at a leisurely pace.

Sprawled across the front steps of the church, fresh blood still trickling down the stone, was the body of a man. Or what Nolan assumed had once been a man. The hair was cut short and the build was right, but beyond that, it was hard to tell. The face had been beaten to a pulp. The skin was purple and shredded. Here and there, white specks poked out beneath the exposed muscle.

What are those?

His partner apparently had the same question as he snapped on a latex glove onto his right hand and reached out to touch the body. He went over several places, quickly and carefully.

"It's bone," Ryder said calmly.

Nolan felt his stomach churn. *Okay, so somebody hit this guy so hard his bones are poking out of his face. Great.*

Nolan looked over the rest of the body. The left leg was twisted around in a way that couldn't be natural, the right arm was at an odd angle... There wasn't an inch of skin that wasn't bruised, beaten, or just completely missing.

"Jesus, somebody beat the shit out of this guy," Harrison mumbled.

"And dumped him on the front steps," Ryder nodded, standing up and peeling the glove off his hand. "Didn't even bother to take him inside."

"Didn't want to stain the carpets?" Harrison asked smugly.

"It's out of character, certainly," he replied, starting to pace when he was far enough away from the body not to track blood away from the scene. "Even Nelson and Carrol were found inside of a church, and their scenes were particularly brutal. There are no candles. There's no staging."

"Are we sure this isn't a copycat?" Nolan spoke up. "Or just some local psycho?"

Ryder stopped his pacing for a moment to consider it. "It's a good thought, considering the press conference and the inconsistencies, but I don't think so. Something tells me it's related."

"We know if this guy works at St. Joe's?" Nolan asked.

Harrison nodded. "He had his badge on him. Oh, and we're like a minute from the hospital. So, yeah, there's that."

"There's never been rage quite like this," Ryder continued, almost to himself, as he resumed his pacing. "This isn't just escalation. Something triggered a reaction like this. Something unplanned and unexpected. This was sloppy."

He turned to look at Logan. "There was an eyewitness?"

Logan pointed to a middle-aged man in a blue bathrobe and snow boots a hundred yards away. "He was out walking his dog after coming home from a late shift. He was across the street when the dog started going nuts. He spent most of his time trying to shut the dog up so it wouldn't wake the neighbors but got worried when the dog wouldn't behave. I guess it's a pedigree-something-something-specially-trained whatever, so it should have stopped barking.

"Anyway, he saw a man about six feet tall throw something onto the church steps. He assumed it was some teenager trying to be funny, but the dog insisted on going across the street. They nearly got run over by the car that peeled out of the parking lot. Dark sedan, no make, no look at the plates. The guy wanted to know what had been dumped before he called the priest, so he went in for a closer look. He and Fluffy found this."

"Shit," Nolan muttered as his cell phone started ringing in his pocket. He frowned at the caller ID and walked off several feet to answer it.

"Well," Harrison started, edging closer to Ryder, "Our witness swears that it was right at midnight when he heard a car door open by the church. Think our guy was waiting for Sunday?"

Ryder nodded. "But I can't explain why. The stroke of midnight hasn't seemed to matter before. At least, not that we've known about. Why now?"

"That's your department, buddy, not mine. I'm just here to look good."

"So you keep telling us," Ryder replied and turned sideways, looking for Nolan. One look at his partner's face as he walked back toward them was enough to get Ryder immediately on edge.

"Uh, Gabe..."

"What?"

"You said you think this guy snapped. Like, he lost his shit? And it probably wasn't planned?"

"Sure."

"What would cause someone to snap like that?" Nolan asked hesitantly.

"Any number of things," he replied, shrugging nonchalantly. "But it's usually an attack on a person or an object with particular significance. Why?"

"The attack on Dr. Carrol. That was similar?"

"I assumed so, though this one is much worse. That's why I accused..." he faded off. "Blake, what's wrong?"

Nolan shook his head and turned toward the SUV. Ryder looked at Logan, alarmed, but his former partner just shrugged.

Gabriel sprinted forward and grabbed his partner by the shoulder, forcing him to stop.

"Nolan, what the hell is going on? Who was that on the phone?"

Blake didn't answer. He just held out his hand for the car keys.

"I'm not…"

"Just give me the damned keys, Gabriel," he said forcefully, grabbing them from inside his partner's coat pocket. "Logan, stay here and finish up. We're going to St. Joseph's. Come find us when you're done."

Logan nodded silently and walked back up the lawn toward the church.

"Blake, what the fuck is going on?" Ryder asked, the irritation plainly evident in his voice.

"Just get in the car, Gabriel," he spat, the tension heavy in his voice. "I'll explain on the way." *I really, really don't want to, but I guess I don't have a choice. Fuck. I hope we don't wreck.*

31

NOAH HATED THIS. Absolutely hated it.

He'd gotten into medicine to be the person in the room with the clipboard and the white coat, the person with the answers and the plan. He didn't sign up to be a patient, or worse, a patient's family member.

He fidgeted in his chair with his head down until he couldn't stand it any longer, then craned his neck upward. He stared at the monitor above the bed. He knew what every number meant. He knew which colored squiggly line matched which number. He knew when to pay attention to the alarm that intermittently went off and when he could easily ignore it. Hell, he knew how to silence the damned thing.

Speaking of which…

Noah stood up from the exceedingly uncomfortable plastic chair and hit a yellow button on the side of the screen, shutting off the monotone beeping. He focused on the monitor, checking over each number once, twice, three times. He read out her heart rhythm strip again, just to be sure they hadn't missed something.

The monitor seemed to think everything was fine. Her heart rate was on the high side, but stable. She was breathing fine. Her blood pressure was perfect. She was getting enough oxygen.

Now, he mused sarcastically.

The gray box said she was fine. He shot a quick glance at the form on the gurney beside him and instantly cringed.

No, not fine.

Grayson was anything but fine.

He'd been seeing another patient with one of his junior residents down in the ER when he'd heard the commotion. He'd peeked out of the door, morbid curiosity getting the best of him. He'd instantly recognized Dr. Meyer's voice among the crowd, and it took a lot to get that man agitated. Noah had followed the crowd of ER staff and nurses down the hallway toward the trauma bays. They were bringing someone in from the back hallway, not from the elevators.

How do they have a trauma patient that didn't come in by ambulance or helicopter?

He'd casually hung by the wall until he'd recognized Adams, Grayson's junior, sprinting to catch up to the gurney with a green hue to his face. The hairs on the back of his neck had stood up immediately.

Noah had taken off in a run, arriving at the trauma bay doors just as Meyer and a few of the nurses placed a limp body on the trauma bed in the middle of the room. He'd pulled on gloves and stepped up to the bed, about ready to open his mouth to ask how he could help, when he'd noticed the black fleece pullover and surgical scrubs. Grayson always got cold on call. She wore it even in the dead of summer.

The room had started spinning. Meyer shouted instructions but he didn't register them. A nurse had wheeled in a crash cart. One of the general surgery residents had pushed in toward the right side of the bed and started examining her neck.

Wait, what the hell is wrong with her neck?

Bruises. Slowly coming to the surface. All around her neck. Not just bruises. Whole fucking handprints.

Oh, my God, someone attacked her.

He'd instantly and violently snapped out of his head. By now, Dr. Meyer had been leaning over her at the head of the bed with an endotracheal tube in his hand, having already given medications to paralyze her.

"Hey, Mason," the general surgery resident had said, nudging him in the side.

"Yeah?"

"Think you can throw a central line in her? I've got to go get radiology off their asses so I can get a chest X-ray. She might have pneumo."

He'd nodded and immediately stalked to the corner of the room, grabbing the sterile trays from the locked cabinet. Noah had worked on autopilot, all the while repeating 'It's Grayson. It's Grayson. Be careful. It's Grayson' in his head. By the time he was done with the line, she was hooked up to a ventilator and her oxygen saturation was trending toward normal.

The surgery resident had looked her over from head to toe, and when he'd seen the bruises developing on her stomach, he'd immediately called for a CT scan. The second Noah had had the line sewn in, they'd wheeled her away. He'd hung back, trying to stop his hands from shaking. That's when he'd noticed Adams glued to the back wall.

"Adams, right?"

The young man had almost jumped out of his skin. "Yeah? I mean, yes, sir," he'd stammered.

"It's okay. Calm down. Here, better yet, sit down," he'd said, motioning toward two plastic chairs in the hallway. "What the hell happened?"

The young man had taken one shaky breath, and then he'd started talking a mile a minute. "I...I don't know. She was on with me tonight. We'd finally caught up. I was supposed to meet her in the back consult room. Just…just to go over all of our patients since it had been so crazy, you know? Didn't want to miss anything. Anyway, I got back there and the computers were off and the room was dark. I turned the lights on, and th…th…there she was. She, she wasn't moving. I couldn't get her to wake up. Aw, hell, I don't even know if she was breathing. I…I just ran and found Dr. Meyer. I didn't know what else to do," he finished, hanging his head in his hands.

"Hey, you did just fine. You got help. Nobody can ask more than that."

"I…I spent more time talking to the last patient's family than I should have. I caught up with one of my ER buddies. What if she was there the whole time? I could've been there sooner. I could've helped her, maybe," he'd said, his voice cracking.

Holy shit, he's going to cry.

He knew the juniors liked Grayson, even if she didn't, but he didn't know they liked her this much.

"It doesn't matter. The point is you found her. Period."

"I guess," he'd replied, trying to maintain some air of professionalism. The tears threatening behind his eyes told another story.

"Did you see anybody around?"

He'd shaken his head dejectedly.

"Okay. Look, get on the phone with whoever you need to so you have some backup tonight, okay? Get your service straight. I'll keep an eye on her. Come back and check on her when you can."

"Okay," he'd nodded, walking off toward the main ER.

Noah sighed and rubbed at his eyes. That had been about two and a half hours ago. He'd followed his own advice, calling in a favor to one of the senior medicine residents. Allison had agreed to come in at the drop of a hat when he'd explained what had happened.

They'd taken Grayson straight from the CT scanner to MRI and then back to a room in the ER. Noah hadn't left her side. She was intubated, paralyzed, sedated, and so far very, very lucky. The scans and x-rays had shown a few broken ribs and some internal bleeding in her abdomen, all of it minor. She had a pneumothorax, but it was small. Nothing that would need a chest tube and nothing that would require surgery, but she would be sore for a while and need another chest x-ray in a few hours. For the amount of force she'd taken, she'd come out relatively unscathed.

Because of her unknown down time, they'd done an MRI and an arteriogram of her brain, which all looked good. No bleeding. No signs of swelling or herniation. They were going to move her up to a room in the ICU shortly. Once she was stable for a few hours, they were going to try to wake her up and get the tube out of her throat.

Noah stared down at the bruises on her neck, which were becoming harder and harder for him to look at without his stomach turning over.

Who in the hell could have done this to her?

Then it clicked, and he broke out in a cold sweat. He fumbled in his pocket for his phone and dialed. With any luck, he could sweet-talk his way into what he wanted.

32

IT WAS A little after 2:30 in the morning when Noah raised his head from in between his hands. There were voices in the hallway, just outside the door, talking animatedly. He assumed it was a few of the medics until a soft knock came at the door.

Blake Nolan peeked around the corner and instantly sought out Mason. The doc looked like hell—that was for sure. His eyes were bloodshot. His white coat was tossed in the corner. He looked like he'd been up for a week.

Blake took a chance and glanced over at the body lying still on the gurney. He felt his stomach heave at the sight of her.

Oh no...

"Hey, man," he said, by way of greeting. Formality just didn't seem appropriate at the moment.

"Detective Nolan." Noah nodded by way of greeting.

"Can I...can we, uh..."

"Sure. She's stable." He nodded, standing to shake the detective's hand. "Thanks for coming."

Blake just nodded, then stepped to the side. Ryder walked in behind him. He didn't suspect a thing. Nolan hadn't said a word to him on the car ride over, afraid his partner would go ballistic if he told him who the phone call had been from and what it had been about.

Gabriel walked into the small ER room, utterly annoyed that he'd been dragged away from the one crime scene that might actually lead to a break in their case. It was sloppy. There was a credible witness. If their killer was ever going to leave behind something for them to find, this was it. And instead of letting him work the scene, his partner had shoved him in the SUV and insisted he come with him to the hospital on some wild goose chase. His anger had been boiling the entire ride.

What on earth could be so motherfucking important?

The moment he registered the bedraggled young man standing beside the gurney, Ryder felt his stomach drop. He rapidly cataloged the room: ventilator, blood and fluids hanging from an IV pole, Noah Mason hovering at the bedside. He could only come to one conclusion.

No. It can't be. She was at home when I got the call. She was safe at home...

Gabriel remained rooted to the floor by the doorway. He couldn't get his feet to cooperate. He was paralyzed.

Blake broke the silence. "How is she?"

Noah shrugged. "As far as we know, she's very lucky."

"What happened?"

"We don't really know. Her junior resident found her in the consult room, on the floor and not breathing. He called for help. She's been undergoing testing for the last few hours. She looks to be okay."

"She has a fucking tube down her throat," Ryder growled from the doorway. "How is that possibly okay?"

"Gabe, enough," Nolan instantly shot back, spinning his attention back to Mason. "Was she supposed to be working tonight?"

Noah shook his head. "She switched shifts with one of the other seniors. His kid was sick."

"Why is she, um, not breathing right?" Blake asked hesitantly.

Noah looked at the detective for a second, confused, before realizing what he was talking about. "She's paralyzed and sedated right now, so the machine is breathing for her. Once they get her upstairs, they're going to try to wake her up and take the tube out."

"Can I, um, look…look at the, um…you, you said there were…"

"Sure," Noah nodded, pulling the blankets down a bit.

"Holy shit…" Blake gasped when he saw the handprints on her neck. He could almost hear his partner's fists clenching behind him.

"And these," Noah said, pulling the hospital gown aside just enough so they could see the bruising on her chest and abdomen. "She has broken ribs, a pneumothorax, and internal bleeding. Nothing that needs surgery, or so I'm told. They scanned her brain. Everything looks okay. We just have to see if she wakes up."

"If?" Blake asked.

"Yeah. If," Noah repeated. "She got hit hard. More than once."

The sound of breaking glass made both men jump. Blake whipped around and looked over his shoulder. His partner's fist was clean through the glass door, his blood trickling down the lower panel to the floor.

"Aw, shit, Ryder, what the hell?" he groaned.

Gabriel looked across the room at his partner, calmly, like nothing out of the ordinary had happened. He withdrew his hand from the hole in the glass, not paying attention to the shards embedded in the skin or the blood running down his arm. Several nurses and two security guards were on their way over to the room, but Noah stood up and waved them off.

"Don't worry about it. They're detectives. It was an accident," he called out.

Noah stepped forward and grabbed the detective's hand. "You should get this looked at."

"I'm fine," Gabriel snarled, wrenching his hand away.

"Grayson would say otherwise," he retorted, moving over toward the cabinets and grabbing some gauze. "Sit down."

"I said…" he began, growling.

"I heard you," Noah snapped. "While I personally think you should just bloody figure it out yourself, she would kill me. So sit down, shut up, and let me take care of this. Detective Nolan, the man you want to speak to is Dr. Meyer. He's in section three," he said.

"All right, I'll be back. Behave, Gabe," Nolan commanded as he left the room.

Ryder sat down in one of the plastic chairs while Noah pulled on a pair of gloves and opened up a laceration tray he found in the bottom drawer. In short order, he had the glass shards out, the wounds cleaned, and the larger gashes stitched together. He huffed in satisfaction as he finished applying a dressing and tossed his sharps in the back container.

"I'll write you a script for some antibiotics. Fill them and take them. I'll scrounge up some for you to take here tonight."

"Thanks," Ryder nodded. "You're good at that," he added, nodding toward the dressing on his hand.

"Comes from having an orthopod as a best friend. She'd rag on me every time a bad dressing or bad stitch job would come into her clinic. I learned quick. She's the reason I could…" he trailed off.

"What?"

Noah glanced briefly at the IV in Grayson's neck. Ryder immediately understood.

"She made sure I could do everything she could for a trauma. I might not splint an ankle often, but I can put in lines and chest tubes against any surgeon. The surgery attendings take me seriously, for a medicine guy, and that's saying something. She'll never admit to being the reason why." He smiled sadly.

Ryder glanced hesitantly at the still figure in the bed. "What are her chances? Really?" he asked quietly.

Noah almost smirked at him. His eyebrows narrowed skeptically. Then it hit him. The detective actually had no idea how serious her condition was. For all his intelligence and charm, he was just like any other scared family member. It was a sharp slap in the face.

"She's going to be okay," Noah said, putting his hand on the detective's shoulder. "As long as she wakes up and starts breathing on her own, she's going to be fine."

Gabriel hung his head. "I...I didn't know..." he muttered.

"What?"

"I thought she was at home. I wasn't here..." he said softly.

"And you think you should have been? What for? You don't owe her that," Noah said.

"I should have been here," he said, looking longingly at the bed.

Noah took one look at him and stood up.

"I'm going to go get those antibiotics," he said and walked out of the door, closing it behind him.

Ryder grabbed the bottom of his chair and scooted over to the side of the gurney. He didn't register the pain shooting through his hand.

She was so pale. The bruises were darkening before his eyes, and all he could focus on was the rise and fall of her chest in time with the soft beeping of the ventilator. It took a few minutes to build up the courage, but eventually he reached out and stroked her hair. He secretly hoped her face would turn into his hand, just like it had weeks ago in the middle of the snowstorm on a deserted downtown street corner. She didn't move. He dropped down so that his lips were beside her ear.

"Wake up," he whispered. "Do what you want to me. Yell, scream, take a shot at me. I don't care. I promised I'd protect you. I failed. I'll never forgive myself. Wake up, Grayson. Please, wake up."

He kept whispering to her until Noah walked back into the room, and even then, he didn't stop.

And she never moved.

33

THE FOG WAS excruciatingly thick. She'd tried to break through it a few times, but it didn't let her go. Gray fingers kept hold of her, pulling her down and down and down into the haze. She'd heard Noah's voice, telling her to keep fighting, only once, and it had faded away quickly. The fog didn't like to let the voices in. It got thicker.

Now, she heard a different voice. It was low and soft and strong and always present. It fought off the fog. She couldn't quite place it, but she could hear it saying her name over and over and over again. It was definitely familiar. Every time she got close to the edge of the fog, the pain in her side crashed over her like a wave and sent her tumbling back down.

Why does my side hurt? And my stomach…and my neck… And why does it feel like something's down my throat? My throat… My throat!

Grayson's eyes shot open, wide and full of fear. She couldn't see anything. All her eyes saw was white. Her gag reflex kicked in full force. She coughed against the wretched thing in her throat, moving her hand to her face in a desperate effort to pull it out. Something stopped her before she got close. Strong, warm fingers gently interlaced with hers.

"Shhh, calm down," she heard the voice say into her ear.

Calm down? How can I calm down? There's something down my throat! I'm going to choke. I can't breathe!

She tried to shake the hand off of hers, but it held her firmly.

"Grayson, it's all right. Breathe."

Goddamn it, I can't breathe with something jammed down my throat!

She tried speaking, but the effort just made her gag harder against the tube. She took a deep breath and coughed violently. She couldn't see anything. The light above her was blindingly bright. Everything was white. She clamped her eyes shut against it.

She heard more voices. They started far away, then came closer and closer. The first voice stayed close, whispering to her.

Then someone called her name. Loudly.

Noah. It's Noah!

He was telling her to squeeze her left hand. She did. He told her to do it again. She did, harder this time. She felt something shrink inside of her throat, and then the obstruction was gone. She sucked in a ragged breath and coughed again, which sent pain rocketing down her chest wall. She moaned and curled onto her side, desperate to make the pain go away. The other voices said something she didn't understand, then faded away into the background. Noah faded away. She felt warm fingers run through her hair and a soft hand on her cheek.

"Good job," the voice cooed over her. "Close your eyes. Go back to sleep."

She didn't argue. She wanted to, but her chest hurt so badly. It was agony just to breathe. She curled even tighter into a ball and closed her eyes shut, fading back into the fog without resistance.

34

HOURS LATER, THE ICU room was quiet. The soft hum of the blood pressure cuff came and went every ten minutes, but he didn't pay attention to it. They'd taken the tube out of her throat, thank God. He'd coaxed her back to sleep without much of a fight. Since then, she'd been breathing on her own and sleeping fitfully. Every time her nightmares brought her close to consciousness, she would toss and turn, flail her arms and kick her legs, scream, call out in pain, beg for someone to stop hurting her. She'd needed wave after wave of sedation from the nurses to keep her from hurting herself, and the medication never lasted long.

This time, he heard her first low whimper echo in the darkness. Gabriel turned away from his vigil at the window and eased himself toward her bedside. Her face was twisted, contorted in pain. Beads of sweat were forming on her forehead. He reached out, stroking her hair. Grayson turned toward him in her morphine-fueled haze, and he let her nuzzle her face into his palm. Her face softened. Her shaking subsided. She sighed and gently dropped back into a deeper sleep.

Once she'd quieted back down, Gabriel tried to move back to his chair beside the window. He was restless enough as it was. He didn't need to disturb her because of his uncontrolled agitation.

Grayson started whimpering as he pulled his hand away. He sat back down on the edge of the bed and stroked her hair. *Relax. I'm not going anywhere. You're safe.*

"You're going to have to stay there all night, you know," a kind voice said from the doorway.

Gabriel looked up to see the night nurse smiling warmly at him. He thought her name was Linda, but he honestly hadn't paid much attention to anyone but Grayson since they'd brought her upstairs. His first instinct was to immediately back away from the bed, detach himself from her, but he forced himself to remain still.

The nurse checked on something around Grayson's IV, then grabbed some supplies from the cabinet. The hair on the back of Gabriel's neck bristled protectively.

Just what the hell do you think you're doing to her?

Ryder was about to demand an explanation when he saw the blood running down Grayson's neck, soaking the white sheets. He swallowed hard.

"Don't worry," Linda said as she stepped back up to the other side of the bed, seeing the concern on his face. "When patients toss and turn, they pull on the stitches a little. This just needs a new dressing. Hopefully, we'll be able to get it out sooner rather than later."

The young man just nodded.

Linda smiled as she gently changed the dressing around Grayson's central line. She'd volunteered to change patients when she'd heard who was coming up to the unit, and this young man had been right with her when they'd wheeled her up from the ER. Dr. Mason had made it quite clear that if he wasn't personally at the bedside, this young man or his partner should be.

It didn't take long to figure out the two new faces were cops. It made sense that someone needed to stay with her, considering what had happened. But the way this young man was with her, the way he looked at her...

Linda shrugged as she finished with the dressing. She'd never heard Dr. Carter talk about having someone special in her life, but the way this handsome detective was looking at her, she'd strongly consider looking into it.

"Just push that call button if you need anything. I'll be in with the patient next door," she said, quietly shutting the door behind her as she left.

———

Ryder hardly acknowledged her exit. He just kept his place on the bed and watched Grayson breathe. He counted her breaths. He felt her pulse at her wrist. He wrapped her fingers into his. The doctors seemed happy with how things were looking, but of course, breathing on your own and being able to remember how to fix a femur were two completely different levels of functioning. She was young and healthy, but there was always a chance she'd never be the same.

Gabriel shook his head. He'd been sitting outside her house, thinking she was safe inside, while she was suffocating at the hands of a psychopath. If there was any permanent damage, he'd never forgive himself.

Who the hell am I kidding? I'll never forgive myself anyway. I promised her.

The door opened again, snapping Gabriel out of his head.

He watched his former partner walk into the room. Even after all of his years on the police force, it never sat well with

Logan to see a young woman hurt. The purple handprints on Grayson's neck were easily visible from across the room. Gabriel watched his mentor's fists clench at his sides.

"Holy shit, Ryder," he mumbled, stopping halfway to the bed.

Gabriel just nodded in agreement.

"Nolan's downstairs finishing up. He told me what happened. She's lucky to be alive."

"Yeah, she is."

"I thought he said she wasn't breathing."

Gabriel heaved a heavy sigh. "When they found her, she wasn't. They took the tube out a while ago. She's been fine."

Well, her breathing has been fine. The rest…

"That's good, man," he said, pulling one of the plastic chairs up to the foot of the bed. "Is she waking up?"

"Trying to. I think the pain is too much," he said, stroking her hair again when she started whimpering and moving around on the bed. She calmed down almost immediately.

"Looks like you've got the touch."

Ryder just shrugged, keeping his eyes trained on her face.

"Look," Harrison started, "there was nothing you could have done to prevent this. You were where you should have been, where she was supposed to be. Even if you'd known she'd switched nights, what would you have done? Follow her around the hospital like a lost puppy?"

Ryder didn't respond. He pushed a stray lock of hair out of her eyes and wrapped it gently behind her ear. Logan kept talking.

"I know that fucking look in your eyes, Ryder. Snap out of it. You did not do this. So stop acting like you did. Those handprints on her neck aren't yours. She's going to be angry and scared as hell when she clears that pain medicine. Somebody's going to have to be the voice of reason. Oh, and right now, about everybody in this hospital wants to form a lynch mob to go after the bastard."

"I don't necessarily disagree with that approach," Ryder replied.

"I don't either, but it doesn't mean I can publicly endorse it." Logan grinned, sprawling back into the chair with his arm draped over the back. "Look, Gabe, you've latched onto this girl. I'm not looking for particulars here. But if you're going to take responsibility, real responsibility for her, then you're going to have to find the bastard and keep her safe while you're doing it. So, drop this lone wolf shit; let me and Blake help you. And when the time comes, you'll take the shot."

Ryder curled his free hand around his mouth and sighed, nodding.

"All right."

"Although, you know, she might just want to take the damned shot herself," Harrison replied, chuckling under his breath. "You might have to get in line."

"I wouldn't argue," he replied, smirking.

The door opened again, and Nolan stuck his head in, peering around toward the bed like a little boy. "Okay to come in?"

"Yeah, buddy, c'mon in," Harrison nodded, reaching over to pull another plastic chair up to the bedside.

"She's okay?" he asked, sitting down.

"Won't know for sure until she wakes up," Logan summarized, quickly changing topics at the sight of Ryder's clenched fists. "What did you find out downstairs?"

"It's hard to pin anybody down. It's chaos down there. Best I can figure, she was attacked around ten. I honestly don't think she was down for very long before that Adams kid found her. But here's the interesting part. The doc that treated her, Meyer, said she blew the whistle on one of his residents. The guy nearly smacked her in front of him in the middle of the ER. The nurses said he's a hothead, and Mason told me there are rumors he beats his wife. So I checked. He's got multiple trips out to his house for domestic disputes. Never arrested. He apparently shows up to all the hospital functions and gets trashed, then calls her to come pick him up when he's done and usually is scream- ing at her before they ever pull out of the parking lot."

"Nice, so this guy is a violent asshole who likes to beat women. I'd say getting called out by a woman would set this guy off. You get a name?"

Blake pulled out his notebook and flipped through a few pages. "Yeah, um...Harlan. Greg Harlan."

He looked up from the pages and registered Logan's blank stare. He rapidly blinked back and forth between the two men sitting before him. "What? Did I miss something?"

Harrison shook his head and turned toward Ryder.

"Well, buddy, remember when I said you'd get the first shot at the son of a bitch? Turns out, I lied. Somebody got to him first."

"You've lost me, Logan," Nolan said from his chair.

"After you two left St. John's, we rolled the vic. Hospital badge was in his pocket. Dr. Greg Harlan."

"Oh, you've got to be fucking kidding me," Blake moaned, dropping his head into his hands. "So he's not the mastermind? We have to treat the asshole who probably beat her up like a victim? This Sunday keeps getting better and better."

"It fits," Ryder mumbled. "It's all about obsession. Whoever killed Greg Harlan was eliminating a threat to Grayson."

"But he was dumped, not posed. And outside of the church, not in it," Logan argued.

"Sloppy." Ryder nodded. "We'll need DNA to prove it, but my guess is, Harlan lost it. If he's the one who attacked Grayson, he took the place of our would-be victim number seven when he laid a hand on her. Our killer had to scramble to compensate, for Harlan's spontaneity as well as his own response to it."

"So we are looking for somebody at the hospital then? Someone who works here, and not only knew about the attack on Grayson but knew who did it."

"Yes. It narrows our field substantially."

"Okay, but what about the others? How was Oakes or Malhotra or even James a threat? This Harlan guy is an outlier. A big one. We're back to the same unanswered questions, Gabe."

"I don't know. Somehow that's how they were chosen. I just can't..."

He was starting to fidget, his agitation getting the better of him. The movement was causing Grayson to wake up. Gabriel stopped his train of thought midstream when he heard her whimper and felt her move closer to him on the bed. He dropped his right hand from her hair down to her right arm and gently rubbed up and down her soft skin, careful to avoid any pressure that would transmit over to her broken ribs. He took hold of the top edge of the flimsy hospital blanket with his other hand, pulling it up around her shoulders as she nestled into his side. He leaned his full weight onto the back railing of the bed and let her head fall into his lap.

Harrison knew it was time to quit for the night.

"All right, buddy, we're going home for a few hours of sleep and a change of clothes. Be back in the morning with coffee. You want me to bring you anything from the apartment?"

There was no question. He was staying the night with her. Ryder shook his head and nodded at the small bag in the corner that Nolan had brought up with him.

"I have all I'll need in there."

"All right. Behave for a few hours," he murmured with a wink as he ushered Nolan out the door and down the hallway.

Ryder rolled his eyes and went back to concentrating on the small bundle curled into his right side. He focused on the steady rhythm of her breathing and stroked her hair almost in time with it.

Logan was right. He was in deep trouble. And he was going to need some help.

35

FOR WHAT SEEMED like the thousandth time, she swam up from underneath the fog, desperate to break through the surface. She could hear voices talking, and they were close. She couldn't place any of them, but they made her feel safe. And warm. She was warm. Something was wrapped around her back and it wasn't a blanket. It was warm.

She fought against the pain in her right side and took a few deep breaths. It wasn't as bad as it had been before, but she still winced at the shock rocketing across her chest. The fog started lifting. The voices got stronger. The light in the room started getting brighter. She attempted to sit up, but the thing at her back wrapped around her shoulder and gently held her down.

She could make out one voice now. It was that same voice again. It was close and soft and telling her to stay still. To open her eyes. It was calling her name.

She took another deep breath and nuzzled her face one last time into the warm pillow she was laying on. Then, slowly, Grayson opened her eyes. Her vision was blurry, but it cleared quickly as she rapidly blinked her eyelids.

She was instantly on edge. There were several things very, very wrong with this picture.

Fearfully, Grayson processed her surroundings. The green walls, the monitors, the supply closet full of syringes, the crash cart. She was in the intensive care unit. She was lying in a hospital bed and wearing a hospital gown.

A very perky-looking Detective Harrison was sitting at the bottom of the bed. He was staring at her with a goofy grin on his face.

Why is he here? And why am I in a hospital bed?

She stretched gently and felt the tug of the dressing on her neck.

What the...? Oh God, my neck!

The memory of the attack came flooding back. She slammed her eyes shut. The room was dark again. She could feel the pressure building around her neck, squeezing, cutting off her air supply. Her heart rate skyrocketed. She reflexively reached up, trying to grab at her neck, desperate to claw the invisible hands away.

A warm hand came up and stopped her, pulling her arm back down to her side. She twisted to her left, trying not to turn too much through her torso, (*why does that hurt so much?*) and locked her eyes onto a gray sweater and the top edge of a pair of jeans. She startled.

That is so definitely not a pillow.

Confused, she wrinkled her forehead and followed the sweater fabric up to a shirt collar and then the top of the collar up toward a face. She nearly had a stroke when she saw Gabriel staring down at her, a completely unguarded look of relief washing across his face.

Grayson looked back and forth along that same route several times, jeans-sweater-face-repeat, desperately trying to find a good explanation why she had woken up with her head in his lap and why he was in bed with her. The morphine slowed her thoughts. She wrinkled her forehead. Nothing was clear. Frustrated, she went back to blatantly staring up at him, her bottom lip sucked nervously in between her teeth.

"You have an admirer," Harrison chuckled from the bottom of the bed.

"I see that," Gabriel said softly, running his left hand across her cheek. "Hi there."

"Hi," she whispered hoarsely, attempting a small smile.

Ryder reached behind himself and grabbed a small foam cup off of the side table.

"Here, have some of this," he said, handing over the cup.

She winced reaching for it but was able to get a few sips in. *God, water is amazing.*

"If you keep that down, sweetheart, I'll take you out for tequila shots later," came the voice from the bottom of the bed again.

She shifted just a bit to put Logan into her field of view. "You're buying," she managed to squeak out.

Logan hooted in amusement. "Well, it's official. She's up for tequila, and she remembers me. She's fine," he announced, slapping his hand down on his thigh as he stood up. "I'll go get the troops," he said, walking out the door.

Grayson went back to staring at Ryder. There were so many questions floating around in her head, but she was struggling to keep hold of any of them. She started with the shortest and easiest.

"What happened?" she croaked.

"You were attacked," he replied gently.

Her hand instantly shot toward her neck. The darkness threatened from the periphery of her vision. The hands were waiting to clamp down on her throat...

"None of that," he said gently, grabbing her hand again and lacing his fingers into hers. "Don't want to mess up your IV."

"My wh...oh," she said. *I have a line in?*

She moved on to the next easiest question. "What are you doing here?"

Gabriel thought for a moment before answering that one. He wanted to keep her calm, and she was obviously still clearing her pain medication. Anything complicated would just make her anxious.

"Noah called my partner. I came to watch over you."

"Noah called?" she asked hazily.

He nodded.

"Oh. Noah called," she repeated.

Grayson could already feel the exhaustion creeping in, and she slid back down on the bed. When she rested her head in Ryder's lap instead of on the anticipated pillow, she startled and forced herself back up. She hissed against the pain in her side as she pushed up through her arms. She stared at Gabriel for a moment, fighting desperately to get the fog to clear again. Her nose wrinkled and her eyes narrowed.

Ryder stared back at her, his arms supporting her, patiently waiting.

"I used you," she said, the narcotic slur heavy in her voice.

"Pardon?" he asked, startled and stifling a laugh.

"I used you," she repeated, looking down at his sweater and picking at the fabric. "As a pillow," she added, after a minute.

"Yes, you did. It's okay."

She yawned.

"Why don't you lie back down? Come on," he said, gently guiding her back down onto the mattress.

"You're not a pillow," she said lazily, resting her head on his lap again.

"No, I'm not," he chuckled. "Would you prefer one?" he asked softly.

Grayson shook her head violently, spreading her hair out across his lap and the sheets beneath. "I prefer you," she whispered before closing her eyes and drifting back to sleep.

Oh, I am in so much trouble here.

36

SEVERAL HOURS LATER, Grayson was sitting up in bed and staring with more than mild disgust at the breakfast tray in front of her. Noah was standing at the end of the bed with Dr. Keefer, his fingers pinching the bridge of his nose.

"Gray…"

"Come on, Noah. You know I can't eat this. Look at it. I don't even know what it is. The Jell-O doesn't even jiggle."

"You've got to give me an inch here, love," he countered, smiling to hide the exhaustion in his voice. "You manipulated Linda into taking out your central line before any of us had a chance to look at you…"

She scowled, changing targets. "She owed me one. Dr. Keefer, back me up here. I can talk. I don't have dysphagia. I can drink liquids just fine…"

"…and manipulated Detective Nolan into getting you coffee…" Mason grumbled loud enough so everyone could hear.

"…I can handle more than nectar-thickened liquids for breakfast."

The elder attending chuckled, shaking his head. He slapped a hand on Noah's back. "It's your decision, Dr. Mason."

Noah pinched the bridge of his nose again. "Eat what you have there for breakfast. Maybe we'll compromise for lunch," he said firmly.

Grayson folded her arms across her chest and pouted. "Well, then maybe you should get used to the idea of a nectar-thickened Thanksgiving, Noah," she replied.

The young doctor's eyes jumped up immediately. "You wouldn't dare..."

"If I don't get a real breakfast, I can't be held accountable for my actions," she griped.

"You fight dirty, Gray. I'll go change the order," he mumbled, walking out the door.

Dr. Keefer winked at her and followed.

Grayson smiled to herself and pushed the tray away.

"That was quite a show, sweetheart," Harrison chuckled, standing up from his chair in the corner and removing the offending tray.

"Hospital food is bad enough. That doesn't even count as food." She grimaced.

"And Thanksgiving is a threat?" Blake asked.

"In our house, it is." She nodded.

"Are you feeling all right?" Nolan asked.

"I'm feeling better," she agreed. "My right side is killing me."

"That would be your fractured ribs and bruised liver, love," Noah said, walking back into the room.

"We'll go try to track down a decent breakfast in this place. Come on, Blake," Harrison said, dragging the other detective with him.

Noah took a good look at his friend and smiled.

Grayson warily eyed him from her bed. "What?"

"You gave me a big scare, Gray," he said.

"I'll try not to next time," she said quietly.

"Do you remember anything?"

She shook her head and tentatively rubbed the bruises on her neck. She winced as her fingers glided across the darkened skin. She hadn't seen the bruises yet, but the fact that they were so tender meant they were probably pretty bad.

"I remember walking into the consult room. It was dark. Then someone grabbed me by my neck and lifted me off the ground. I tried fighting back. He dropped me and I tried to scream. I...I think he kicked me. I didn't stay conscious long."

"Did you see who it was?"

"No. But something was familiar..." she drifted off and nervously eyed the small door to the bathroom. "Um, Noah?"

"Yeah?"

"Did he stay...you know...all night?"

Mason's face softened. "Yes, love, he stayed all night."

"Why did you call him?"

"I didn't. I called his partner."

Oh, right. Somebody told me that. Did he tell me that? I can't remember. Damn morphine.

"Blake? Why?"

"Because I knew he would keep it together long enough to get his partner here."

"Oh. Wait, what?"

"Sweetheart," he said, sitting on the bottom edge of her bed, "you should have seen his face when he showed up in the emergency room. He didn't leave your side the whole night. Oh, and he slammed his fist clean through one of the ER doors at the sight of you hooked up to a ventilator."

"What?" *He punched through a door?*

Noah waved her off. "I took care of it. Thank God you taught me how to stitch properly."

Grayson sighed and shook her head. "I don't get it."

"Don't get what?"

"Why stay? I had a tube down my throat and paralytics on board. Even if I'd been conscious, I wasn't going anywhere."

"Are you kidding me? Gray, do you really not see it?"

"See what?"

The bathroom door opened, interrupting them, and Gabriel walked out. He had showered and changed, mostly at Grayson's insistence. When she'd woken up a second time with her head in his lap, she'd been more than a little embarrassed. Technically, the showers were for patient use only, but she'd insisted, stuttering her way through an apology about the drool on his pants. It had given her a bit of distance and time to think, both of which she'd desperately needed.

Grayson chanced a look at him out of the corner of her eye. He looked good, that was for sure. Dark jeans, black cashmere sweater, wet hair hanging off his face. She felt a strong urge to wrap herself up in his arms and run her fingers through his hair. A long shiver rippled down her spine before she could get a hold of herself.

Wait, whoa, that has to be the morphine.

Noah gently tapped her lower leg with his finger, twice, and winked as he walked out the door. Grayson watched him go, scowling. When she turned her attention back to Ryder, he was standing directly beside the bed, staring at her. She startled.

Shit! I didn't hear him move!

"Hey," he said softly, sitting down on the edge of the mattress.

"Hey, yourself," she replied, smiling slightly. "Feel better?"

"I do," he said, running his hand through his hair. "And you?"

"I could use a shower probably, and a change of clothes," she said, eyeballing her tacky, oversized hospital gown.

"Then, come on," he said, holding out his hand to her. "It's your turn."

"Oh, um, I…I can…" she stuttered, hastily swinging her legs over the side.

"…accept a bit of help. Now, here," Gabriel scolded, putting both her hands in his and pulling her to stand.

Grayson swayed on her feet and stumbled forward into his chest. She winced against the pain that reared its head on impact.

Okay, so, the morphine's still clearly working…and making me look like a complete moron.

"Careful," he admonished softly.

They stood together for several minutes. Gabriel watched her face intently, waiting for the slightest hint that she was going to pass out. There was none. Satisfied that she could stand on her own two feet, he guided her toward the bathroom.

"I can take it from here, detective," she murmured softly as she reached the door.

"Mason brought you a change of clothes. On the counter." He pointed, then brusquely turned away.

Grayson shut the door and peeled herself out of her hospital gown. She forced herself not to look in the mirror and instead stepped directly into the shower. The hot water felt incredible pelting against her sweat-sticky skin. She let it run through her hair and trickle down her legs. She watched the dark rust-tinged water swirl at her feet, disappearing through the metal drain… *that's blood…*then set about washing her hair and scrubbing her body clean.

Noah was a godsend. He'd brought all of her usual toiletries from home. Grayson took her time cleaning up and emerged from the shower feeling marginally like herself again. She brushed out her hair and gritted her teeth against the pain long enough to rub lotion onto her skin. She caught a glimpse of the bruises around her right ribcage, which automatically reminded her of her neck.

Grayson hesitantly glanced up into the mirror and, for the first time, saw the full extent of the damage. The pair of purple handprints wrapping around her neck was sickening, contrasted against her fair skin. She brushed her fingers over one side of her neck and cringed. Pain shot through her neck and down into her chest.

God, it looks awful. I look awful.

She took a full inventory of herself. She had a bruise on her right cheek and several around her waist. There was a massive one on her back spanning both her shoulder blades.

From when he dropped me onto the floor.

The bandage over her removed central line certainly completed the look. She shook her head at her reflection, then tore the wretched dressing off of her skin. She awkwardly pulled on the yoga pants and blue cashmere sweater that Noah had packed for her.

At least I have comfortable clothes to look like hell in.

Grayson stepped out of the bathroom as quietly as she could. Ryder looked up from the book he was reading at her bedside and stood.

"Feel better?" he asked as she walked toward the bed.

"I feel human again," she said. "Even if I don't look it."

"What?" Gabriel's eyes narrowed at her comment.

"You have seen this, right?" she said, pulling down the collar of her sweater to put her neck on full display. She hissed as the material pressed against the skin.

"Of course," he said. "It doesn't make you less human."

"It looks awful," she mumbled pathetically.

"Bruises fade, Grayson," he said softly, caressing her cheek. "Don't worry about them."

She sat down in one of the plastic chairs, shy and shaking against the flimsy plastic, and looked up at him. "What are you still doing here?"

"What?"

She didn't respond. She just kept looking up at him, a genuinely curious expression on her face. He closed his eyes and sighed, frustrated, then sank down to a crouch on the floor in front of her. A vision flashed in front of Grayson's eyes, of Gabriel in a tailored suit crouched down in front of her at Calvario.

Déjà vu.

"Do you have to ask a question about everything?" he inquired.

"Usually."

"It would be easier if you asked me questions that I actually have answers to."

"I'll keep that in mind next time."

He raised a hand to her face and placed his palm on her cheek. Grayson startled, only for a moment, then turned and nuzzled her face gently into the roughened skin.

"Don't scare me like that again. Please," he murmured.

"I'll try not to," she said, smiling. "Don't let me get strangled half to death again."

Ryder pulled his hand away as if she'd burned him. Grayson startled backward in her chair, confused. She watched the anger and the guilt build behind his eyes, darkening their blue color into something unrecognizable. She understood.

"Oh, I...I didn't mean..."

"I made a promise to you I didn't keep," he said. "You have every right to be angry at me."

"Wait, what? Angry with you? For what?"

"For not keeping you safe," he murmured.

Grayson nearly fell out of her chair. *Is he for real?*

"You were supposed to keep me safe at work?"

"Yes."

"Twenty-four/seven?"

"Yes."

"You realize that's impossible." She rolled her eyes at him.

"It's not impossible…"

"Yes, it is. Look at me," she coaxed, boldly placing a hand on his cheek and turning him to face her. "You are too hard on yourself. I know you'll find who did this. I trust you. I've seen the cave, remember?"

"And you didn't run away."

Was I supposed to?

He smiled slightly at her. "You got lucky, Grayson."

"Yeah, I did," she replied. "So don't waste it."

"I don't intend to," he said forcefully.

Before she could react, he'd halfway stood from his crouch on the floor and leaned forward, kissing the top of her hair. He backed away almost immediately and reached down, grabbing their bags in one hand and holding out his other to her.

"Breakfast is waiting downstairs," he said, smiling.

Grayson took his hand without a word and followed him out the door, stunned. She had no idea where that had come from, but she would have given anything for him to do it again.

37

FOR THE REST of the week, Ryder kept himself safely sequestered in the interview room.

The body outside St. John's was Greg Harlan's. DNA proved it. A visit to his widow late Monday afternoon had confirmed the stories floating around the hospital. He was a wife-beater and a steroid abuser, and he had been for years.

The surprise had been that earlier in his life, Greg had been a cutter, relying on self-mutilation to get a buzz. When he'd discovered in high school that the scars were associated with people he considered weak, namely suicidal emo teenagers in tight jeans, he'd stopped drawing his own blood and started fighting. It had quickly escalated from barroom brawls to living room matches with his wife while his one-year-old son slept in the nursery. Truthfully, his wife had seemed relieved that he wouldn't be coming home.

Ryder leaned back in his chair and glanced over at the photographs pinned up to the wall. He was so close, he could feel it. As horrific as Grayson's attack had been, it had narrowed their suspect pool. Substantially. They had a list of all active and on-call staff that had been in the hospital the night she'd been attacked. They'd already cleared the general surgery, ER, and intensivist staff. Now he just had to figure out the pattern. He closed his eyes and relaxed, letting his mind wander back.

He'd taken Grayson out to breakfast on Monday with Harrison and Nolan. He'd noticed her trying to shrink into her sweater—to hide the bruises around her neck—before they'd even left the hospital. Every time she'd reached up to cover the hideous purple handprints, she'd whimpered in pain. Gabriel had nearly drawn blood, he'd fisted his fingernails so vehemently into his own palms at the sight of her cowering behind blue cashmere.

At a red light somewhere in the middle of Cherry Creek, he'd decided he couldn't take it anymore. He'd reached into the back seat of the SUV, grabbed his black cashmere scarf, and gently wrapped it around her neck. She'd startled at the gesture, and he'd nearly missed the light, but it had been worth it. She'd spent the rest of the ride and most of breakfast running her fingers back and forth over the material. He hadn't missed the questioning looks she'd given him during the meal. Or the ones from his partners. He'd just chosen to ignore them.

Barbara had been waiting on the front porch, full of questions and glaring daggers at Ryder, when they'd pulled up outside the bungalow. Harrison and Nolan had thankfully steered her away into the living room while Gabriel had helped Grayson up the stairs to her room, by carrying her. She had been too exhausted to even attempt to make it up the front porch steps.

Gabriel sighed as he remembered pulling down her comforter and guiding her underneath it. She'd refused to take anything for pain at breakfast, but it was clear by the time they'd gotten her home just how much pain she was really in. When he'd offered her two pain pills after tucking her in, she'd taken them without argument. Her eyes had quickly drifted shut as they'd taken effect.

Gabriel had intended to quietly leave her be, but in the opiate-induced haze, she'd reached out for him. He'd sat down on the edge of her bed, just like he had in the hospital, and stroked her hair as she'd drifted off. Once he'd been sure she was asleep, he'd brought the blanket higher around her shoulders. A soft chuckling from the doorway had interrupted him.

"You've got it bad, Gabe."

Harrison had been leaning against the doorframe, watching them with a knowing grin on his face. Gabriel hadn't responded. He'd just finished tucking her in and walked out the door without a word.

"Good memory?" Blake asked from the interview room doorway, interrupting his stream of consciousness.

Ryder opened his eyes, shrugged, and leaned forward to set his elbows on the table.

"Something like that. What do you want?"

"Making progress?"

"Yes."

"You got a name and address for this psycho yet?" Harrison interjected, coming in through the door and pulling up a chair.

"Of course not."

"Okay, so lay it on us. You've got ideas. I know that look."

"Sloppy was an understatement this time," he said. "The lab found another set of hair and skin cells underneath Harlan's fingernails besides Grayson's. Nothing's in the system, but if we get a suspect it'll be an easy DNA match. Pelton sent up the autopsy report a few hours ago. There isn't an organ system that didn't get hit. Even if he had survived, he would've been a vegetable for life. And there are handprints on his neck."

"Like the ones on hers?" Logan asked.

Ryder nodded.

"So, it was a revenge kill."

He nodded again.

"Apparently, he was choked post-mortem."

"Wait, wait, wait," Blake interrupted. "Why would he get choked after he was dead? He was already dead, right? This whole double-kill thing is starting to drive me nuts. This guy needs to pick one idea and run with it."

"You die the way you live, huh?" Harrison joked, leaning back in his chair.

Across the table, Ryder stopped fidgeting. "What did you say?" he asked, looking up at Logan.

"Nothing, I…"

"No, what did you say?" he hissed emphatically.

"I said 'you die the way you live,'" he repeated. "So?"

Ryder stood up and started pacing, thinking out loud. Nolan hastily moved his chair to get out of his partner's way.

"So…so what if that's it? We have seven bodies, all left in or around Catholic churches, all with some kind of association with Gr…Dr. Carter. What if they're being selected and killed off because of how they live their lives? What if our killer, whoever he is, thinks their faults define them as dangerous to her, so one by one, he kills them. And they suffer in death the way they lived in life."

"Aw, shit, Ryder," Harrison groaned in his chair, rolling his eyes back into his head, "please don't tell me we have some whack job seven-deadly-sins asshole running around."

"Well, look at the people we have. The number of victims. It makes sense."

"So, Harlan got his ass kicked and got strangled after he died because he attacked her. Nelson was a dirty old man, so he lost a few choice body parts. Carrol yelled at her and tried to get physical, so he got beaten up and his tongue cut out. Pretty boy tried to get in her pants a few times by showing off like a peacock and he got strangled in his Saturday-night best with his own tie. Porter was an obese slob, and he ate the poison that killed him."

"Correct." Ryder nodded enthusiastically.

"Those I can get my head around, Gabe." Harrison continued. "That's five down. But here's who I can't explain: Priya Malhotra. Everybody loved her."

"Not everybody," he said, shaking his head and pushing up from his chair. "Some of the staff didn't agree with her methods, especially her holistic approach with the homeopathy. She was killed with a combination of mercury and cyanide. There have only been a few reports in the medical literature. Most of it is decades old. But mercury is an additive found in some holistic medicines, and it causes a great deal of harm. There isn't a national check on traditional medicines, so it's easy to get something that has been tampered with."

"So she was poisoned because someone thought she was poisoning her patients."

"Exactly. And Gray...Dr. Carter liked her. The association was dangerous."

"Fine. That's six. Explain Lisa Oakes."

Ryder sat back down in his chair and studied his binder. When he didn't speak after a few minutes, Logan continued.

"Okay, so let's try it this way. Lust, check. Nelson. Gluttony covers Porter. Greed, check plus. James. Wrath, double check. Carrol and Harlan. Pride, maybe Carrol goes in that category instead. But that leaves Envy and Sloth."

"How the hell did you rattle those off?" Blake asked, his eyebrows rising. "I didn't even bring them up that quick on Google."

"I was a good Catholic boy in a past life," Logan sneered sarcastically, then looked across the table at Ryder. "So, yeah, I get it, Malhotra was killed with the mercury whatever. But that doesn't fit with Envy or Sloth. And other people envied Lisa Oakes, not the other way around. She wasn't lazy, either; she worked her butt off. We have seven bodies and only five that fit the deadly sins."

The interview room went silent. Blake was still trying to pull up the internet on his phone. Harrison was staring at his former partner across the table. Ryder was onto something, but the seven deadly sins wasn't right. Whatever the pattern was, it had to include Lisa Oakes. There had to be a good reason why her death started the whole mess.

"So, back to the drawing board, Wonder Boy," Logan said nonchalantly.

"No, this should fit," came the reply.

"It doesn't fit, Gabe, and you know it. If it was as easy as the seven goddamned sins, you would've figured it out a long time ago. It wouldn't have taken seven bodies. I agree, something's fucked up here, but the seven deadly sins isn't it. You've got to keep looking."

He stood up from his chair and hauled Nolan to his feet by his collar. He pushed the younger detective out the door first, then paused at the doorway.

"You know you have to make Lisa fit, Gabe. When she fits, you'll have it. Just remember what happened the last time you went blindly barking up the wrong tree."

Ryder didn't look up from the table as his former partner quietly shut the door behind him.

Goddamn it, I hate it when he's right.

38

THURSDAY NIGHT AT the Carter-Parker household was turning into a chaotic mess that Grayson was all too happy to stay out of. Barbara was flying around the house, curlers in her hair, evening gown half on, trying desperately to find her missing shoe. The night of her benefit gala had finally arrived, and with her work's hired limousine due to arrive any minute, she was a complete disaster.

Grayson sat curled up on the couch, sipping on a glass of wine, and took in the scene before her with a small grin on her face. Barbara hardly ever got flustered, especially when it came to getting ready for a night out.

Babs can be just as scattered as me…who knew?

Of course, the moment the thought entered her head, Grayson felt guilty about it. Barbara had been wonderful to her over the past few days. She'd taken time off of work, waited on her constantly, and cooked all of her favorite foods as best she knew how. And when she'd set the fire alarm off in the kitchen after an ill-fated attempt at stir-fry, she'd gone out for her favorite takeout as a backup.

All of it had been completely unnecessary, but Grayson had secretly been grateful for the company. The thought of being alone frightened her, especially alone and in the dark. She kept the lamps turned on in her room, even while she slept. For the first time since she was eight years old, Grayson Carter was afraid of the dark.

Her department director had told her to stay off work through the end of the Thanksgiving holiday. She'd protested, not wanting to be away from her service for that long, especially after her already extensive list of recent absences. He had been insistent that she take time to recover, and Dr. Sanders had seconded that sentiment. She'd had no choice but to agree.

Grayson unconsciously brought a hand to her neck and rubbed at the bruises. They were starting to disappear, but she was still wearing a scarf or a turtleneck around the house to keep them hidden. It was too painful to look at them in the mirror. Every time she saw them, she had a flashback. She could always feel the hands clamping down on her airway, the lack of oxygen starving her brain and forcing her heart to race to keep up. It was terrible. Barbara had broken down crying the first time she'd really seen them in the light.

A sharp knock at the door pulled Grayson out of her head. She set her wine down and walked over, peering through the peephole, her heart beating out of her chest. She breathed a sigh of relief and opened the door.

"Miss Parker?" a man in a chauffeur's uniform asked politely.

She shook her head "Um, no. Sorry. You're looking for my roommate. She's not quite ready."

"Not a problem, miss. She's my first stop, and I'm early. I'll just idle outside. She can come out when she's ready."

"Okay, thanks," she replied, shutting the door as the man walked down the porch steps.

"Who was that?" her roommate called from the second floor.

"Your limousine is here, Babs. He's going to wait for you," she called back, settling down on the couch.

Three minutes later, Barbara came down the stairs, dressed up and looking fabulous, as usual.

"Well?" she asked, twirling around in a circle in the middle of the living room.

"You look very nice."

"Good enough to snag me a millionaire?" she replied, preening in the hallway mirror.

"That would be a good place to start," Grayson inquired, grinning.

"Are you sure you're going to be okay here by yourself?" Babs asked, walking back into the main room while putting an earring in her right ear. "I don't have any problem telling my boss I can't come."

"I'll be fine." Grayson waved off her roommate's concern. "I have a bottle of good wine and a ridiculous amount of food in the refrigerator. What else could I need? Besides, tonight is going to be great for your career. You have to go."

"I don't like leaving you alone."

Grayson made a face. "You don't have a choice. Stop mothering me and go have some fun. Shoo!" she said, motioning her roommate out the door.

"Okay. But I'll have my phone on just in case."

"Stop worrying."

"All right…" she sighed, throwing a coat over her shoulders and opening the door. "I'll see you later."

"Bye, Babs."

The door clicked shut, and Grayson slid the deadbolt into place. She picked up the remote control and flipped through the channels, ultimately landing on an old episode of *Scrubs*. She'd just curled underneath a blanket and wrapped her fingers around her wine glass when there was a knock at her door.

"Ugh, she must have forgotten something," she mumbled to herself, pushing up from the couch.

She held on tightly to her right side in an effort to stabilize her broken ribs. It didn't help much. She hissed against the pain.

Her ribs hurt almost constantly, but she absolutely refused to take any of the painkillers shoved in the junk drawer in the kitchen. They made her sleepy, hazy...

Too slow to react to a threat.

"What did you forget?" she asked as she blindly opened the door.

Grayson looked out onto the porch, expecting to see her flustered roommate shivering against the cold. Instead, Gabriel was looking down at her, a small smirk across his face.

"Oh! I...I'm sorry," she stammered.

He really looked good. Dark suit, black shirt undone at the collar, camel overcoat, and a sparkle in his eye that glinted off the slowly falling snow.

Damn it, Gray, get yourself together, she hissed into her own ear.

"What are you...um...doing here?" she asked, swallowing hard.

What in the hell is wrong with me? Stop stuttering, Gray.

"I need to talk to you," he said calmly, taking his time to examine her.

Sweatpants, slippers, a turtleneck, loose wavy hair and a blush spreading across cheeks. She looked good.

Healthy. Finally.

Her skin had lost the sickening gray hue from Sunday afternoon. Her lips had color to them again. But she was shaking, and it wasn't from the cold.

"Oh, um, well...come on in," she said, stepping aside to let him in.

Gabriel slipped his coat off and hung it up on the coat rack by the door, followed by his jacket. Grayson watched him as he casually walked around the living room, taking in the books in the built-ins and the pictures above the fireplace. He picked one up to look at it more closely.

"This is you?" he asked, pointing to a young child in the photograph.

"Yeah, that's me," she replied, walking up to his side in front of the fire. "That was taken at the San Diego Zoo. I was probably six in that picture. We'd been at the park all day, and all I wanted was a picture with the kangaroos. Of course, I ran around for six hours straight and fell asleep about ten minutes before we got to the kangaroo exhibit. So my parents thought it would be funny to put me in the pouch of the guy dressed in the kangaroo outfit. That was our Christmas card picture that year," she smiled.

"Were you upset you missed it?"

"For a minute. And then I got my stuffed kangaroo Charlie as a present at dinner, and I was fine," she said, taking the picture and setting it back on the mantel. "Can I get you something?"

He hesitated for a minute, then looked behind her to the coffee table at the glass of wine. "You're drinking?" he asked, eyebrow raised.

"A glass of wine never hurt anyone, detective," she said defensively.

"I didn't say it did," he replied, chuckling. "What are you drinking?"

She handed him the bottle from the table.

"This is a good bottle," he said smoothly. "What's the occasion?"

"Babs has her gala tonight. I'm home alone." She shrugged. "Why not?"

"Good answer," he said, handing it back to her. "May I join you?"

She nodded, set the bottle down, and went into the kitchen. He heard tinkling as she pulled a glass out of the cabinet, followed by hissing and a mumbled epithet.

Her ribs.

She returned and sat down on the couch, grabbing the bottle and pouring him a glass. Gabriel accepted it, then immediately set it aside on the table. He sat down beside her and, without a word or warning, reached out to grab the edge of her turtleneck. Gently, he pulled it down to expose the bruises on her neck. Grayson tried to pull away, but he steadied her with his other hand.

"Stop," he commanded softly, taking the time to examine her entire neck.

The bruises were fading, but they were still painful to look at. He brushed his fingers against them. She didn't wince.

"They look better."

"They don't feel much better," she said, pushing his hand away and tugging her turtleneck back into place, which of course made her side hurt.

Ryder noticed the pain in her face as she turned away from him. He grimaced in turn. "They'll fade."

"Not the memory of them."

She grabbed her glass of wine and leaned back against the arm of the couch. It was as far away from him as she could get without retreating to the edge of the room.

"You said you had to talk to me. So talk, detective." It came out harsher than Grayson had meant for it to, but if she kept him at arm's length, she figured she would be able to think straight.

He turned to face her on the couch, drawing his left leg up onto the cushions. He knew he had to broach the subject gently. "Tell me about Greg Harlan."

She tensed. Her fingertips immediately started ghosting over the rim of her glass.

"What about him?"

"I need to know what kind of relationship you have with him."

"I don't have one," she said immediately. "Harlan is a pompous ass. He thinks he can get away with anything. He thinks he's so good he can diagnose from the doorway. He beats his wife."

Okay. I clearly hit a nerve. He pressed further. "Have you had any problems with him?"

"Once or twice. Most recently Saturday. Why?" Grayson tried to keep her palms wrapped securely around her trembling glass. She failed.

"What happened?"

"I called him out to one of the ER attendings when he didn't examine a patient. Missed a couple of obvious fractures. I've had to do it before."

"Have you seen him since?"

"No, I haven't been back to work since...since all this happened. Why are you asking about Greg?"

There was no pause. No hesitation.

"Grayson, he attacked you," Ryder said bluntly. "He's responsible for what happened. He tried to kill you Saturday night."

Her eyes went wide, and her breath caught in her throat. She unconsciously rubbed the edge of her turtleneck. Her fingertips trembled against the material. Gabriel could see her fear written across her face.

She can feel his hands on her neck again. She can't breathe...

She swallowed, hard. "How...how do you...are you sure?" she asked, her voice shaking.

"You got in a few good shots. There were scratches on his forearms. We found his skin cells underneath your fingernails."

Her face darkened. Ryder saw her fingers tighten around her wine glass.

"That son of a bitch," she hissed.

"Grayson..." he started, trying to calm her.

"No! I can't believe this! That asshole tried to kill me. Are you kidding me?"

She stood up and hurled her wine glass into the fireplace, screaming. The alcohol sparked the flames, and they licked upward against the bare brick. The glass shattered against the back of the hearth, the shards glimmering in the heat.

Ryder started to open his mouth, intent on calming her down and soothing her anger. Instead, he fell silent when he caught sight of the tears falling down her cheeks. Her arms were wrapped protectively around her waist, and she was shaking uncontrollably. He grabbed her hand and gently tugged her toward him. She didn't fight him. He leaned back against the edge of the couch and brought her with him, letting her curl into his side. He shushed her and rubbed circles along her back. Slowly, very slowly, her sobbing quieted and she calmed down.

"Sorry," she mumbled. "I shouldn't act like that."

"Don't be," he replied, wrapping an arm around her back. "I'm sorry I had to tell you, but I thought you should know."

Grayson nodded into his damp shirt.

"Miss Parker is gone all evening?"

She nodded.

"Is someone coming to stay with you?"

She shook her head against his chest.

"You shouldn't be by yourself, Grayson."

"I don't need a babysitter." She scowled, pushing back.

"No, you need someone to take care of you."

"That's the same thing."

"I beg to differ," he countered, turning her on the couch and propping her up on some of the pillows.

He pulled a blanket up around her shoulders, then pulled his cell phone out of his pocket and stepped into the kitchen.

———

Grayson could hear him on the phone with someone, but she couldn't make out what he was saying. She desperately tried to clear her head and get the pain in her side under control. Now that the adrenaline was out of her system, she was paying dearly for throwing that glass of wine. The burning in her side was excruciating, crawling from one side of her ribcage to the other. She wiped her eyes and tried to get ahold of herself. The shaking just wouldn't stop. She pulled the blanket higher.

Ryder walked back into the living room with a clean glass, grabbed the bottle of wine, and poured her another glass as he sat back down on the couch.

"So, you have nothing better to do with yourself on a Thursday night?" she asked, trying for a joking tone of voice.

"I can't imagine where else I should be," he said, grabbing his own glass and leaning back against the couch.

He stared right at her, his bright blue eyes never wavering from hers.

Goddamn it, blink or something!

"A bar with beer, NFL football, and scantily-clad college girls comes to mind," she said, taking a blissful sip.

"Not all men spend their time in bars."

"Most single men do," she countered.

"I'm single now?"

Grayson choked on her wine. "Oh my God, I didn't…"

Gabriel smirked into his. "You're right. I am." He chuckled. "I still don't spend much time in bars."

"Then where do you spend your time, detective?"

"Usually in an empty squad room with a case file and bad coffee."

"Oh. That doesn't sound like fun." She wrinkled her nose.

"It isn't."

"So, why do it?"

"Why do you take call at the hospital?" he countered.

"Because it's part of my job. And honestly, sometimes it's fun."

"Same answer," he said, running a free hand through his hair.

They sat in silence for a few minutes. Grayson could see the cogs turning in his head, trying to come up with the proper answer. She sat patiently and waited, for a moment. When he didn't answer her, she got bored.

"Well, I guess that explains why my director doesn't want me back at work until after the holiday. They have to figure out what to do about Greg."

Gabriel growled under his breath.

"I think that has more to do with your injuries, my dear."

"I might not be able to wield a hammer quite yet, but I can round and see consults. I should be at work," she grumbled.

"You should be at home," he chastised gently.

"Why? It's all over, isn't it?"

He gave her a questioning look.

"You said so yourself, detective. Whatever was going on was going to end with me. So, Harlan snapped, and I was his final target. You guys put him in jail, he's out of the hospital, and I go back to work. No more danger. Case closed."

Grayson smiled and relaxed back into the couch. It hit him like a ton of bricks.

No one told her. She doesn't know Greg's dead. No wonder she talked about him in the present tense.

"Not exactly," he mumbled, pouring more wine for both of them.

"Not exactly what? I think that's a pretty good story right there," she said, shifting on the couch in a half-hearted attempt to get comfortable.

"Grayson..." he hesitated.

"What?"

"Greg Harlan is dead. He was found early Sunday morning outside of St. John's Church. Beaten to death." Ryder saw the utter confusion on her face.

"Wait...what? Greg's dead?"

"Yes."

"Are you sure?"

He nodded.

"But he's the one who attacked me."

"Yes."

"But then someone killed him."

"Correct."

"Who?"

Ryder took a deep breath.

"Whoever is responsible for the other six bodies on my list," he said calmly. "That's where I was when Mason called my partner. We were less than two minutes from the hospital."

He watched her take a few shaky breaths, in and out. She unconsciously set her glass down on the table before she spilled wine all over the place. Her shaking was getting worse, nearly uncontrollable.

"You think he was killed," she swallowed hard, "be...because of what happened to me?"

Gabriel nodded gently. "Yes. He was found almost next door to the hospital. The scene looked like a dump job. Someone got to him and disposed of the body quickly. He had handprints on his neck, just like yours."

Grayson unconsciously wrapped her own fingers around her neck. "But...but who...who would have known?"

"My guess is someone in the hospital that night. Someone either saw him attack you or saw your confrontation in the emergency room and put two and two together."

She swallowed hard and nodded. "How bad was it?"

"You don't need to..."

"How. Bad. Was. It?" she asked again, sharply.

"We officially identified him with DNA. We couldn't use his dental records or his fingerprints." There wasn't anything left to use.

"So, whoever has been doing all of this...they're...they're still out there?"

Ryder nodded.

"And whoever it is works at the hospital. My hospital."

He nodded again.

"Jesus Christ," she said, shaking her head and dropping it into her hands. She sat still for several minutes, eyes closed, her breathing erratic and forced. Abruptly, she lifted her head to look at her companion across the couch.

"Well, detective," she remarked sadly, "you really know how to ruin a girl's Thursday night."

"I didn't mean to…"

"Oh, stop. I'm not trying to be cruel," she said, waving her hand in the air and picking up her glass. "I guess they do have a decent reason for keeping me off of work then," she mused to no one in particular.

The sound of the doorbell made her jump. Gabriel got up from the couch to answer it.

Grayson's eyes went wide. "I…I'm not expecting anyone," she panicked.

"Don't worry. I am," he said, smiling back at her.

She looked at him quizzically as he accepted a large white paper bag from a well-dressed man at the door, signing something the man held out in front of him. When he set the bag down on the coffee table, she immediately read the scrawling print on the front.

"Gustavo's?" she asked. "I didn't think a place like that did takeout, much less delivery."

"They make exceptions." He shrugged.

"And you're one of the exceptions?"

He just smiled. "Where do you keep your plates?"

"In the kitchen."

"Yes, I figured that. Where in the kitchen?"

"I'll get them."

Gabriel tried to tell her to stay on the couch, but she was already up and through the threshold. He followed her. She opened a set of high cabinets and started to reach up to grab them, grimacing when pain shot through her side.

Gabriel reached up around her to grab two dinner plates. She rolled her eyes at him and reached into a drawer, grabbing knives and forks instead.

"I can handle two plates," she said, annoyed.

"So can I. And I don't have broken ribs. Is it so hard to let someone do something nice for you?"

Grayson turned around and leaned back on the counter. He was exceedingly close to her, his hands gripping onto the counter on either side of her hips. "It is when I don't understand the motivation behind it."

"You question my motives, doctor?" he asked, chuckling and taking the silverware from her.

"If the roles were reversed, wouldn't you?"

"That's entirely different." He scowled, pushing back from the counter and stalking back into the living room.

"No, it's not," she replied, pulling two napkins from another drawer and chasing after him.

He was already sitting on the couch, portioning out their dinner like it was any other Thursday night in. For a quick second, Grayson was struck by how normal it seemed to see him there. Then she shook her head and got hold of herself.

"You really wouldn't think twice if some hot girl just showed up at your house unannounced with special-order takeout?"

He chuckled and continued dishing out the food without saying a word. She let it go. The food smelled incredible. Filet mignon, ravioli in some kind of rosé cream sauce, and Caprese salad.

Yum.

Grayson took the plate he offered her and balanced it on her lap. The food was incredible, just like it had been weeks ago at the restaurant itself. That triggered more questions in her mind, but she stuffed them down for the time being. The ravioli was causing sensory overload as it was.

They finished the meal in comfortable silence. Gabriel cleared the plates and put away the leftovers before Grayson ever had a chance to tell him not to.

Sighing, she walked over to the front window and wrapped a blanket around her shoulders. The snow was getting heavier. They'd have a few inches on the ground before morning, at least.

She heard Ryder come back into the room. Grayson turned around to find him leaning casually on the threshold between the kitchen and the living room. He was watching her, studying her. It was unnerving to stand under his fixated gaze.

"Please tell me you're not planning on spending the night out in that," she said, motioning out toward the snow.

"If I have to." He shrugged. "It wouldn't be my first time on a surveillance job in a snowstorm."

"Gabriel…" she sighed, shaking her head and pinching the bridge of her nose. "You know that sounds completely…"

"What else should I be doing?"

"I'll mention again the bar and college girls suggestion from earlier."

"Don't be ridiculous," he said, walking toward the front door and reaching out for his suit coat. "I'd prefer surveillance in the snow to that nonsense any day."

"And if I tell you you can't?"

"Can't what?"

"Sit outside my house and freeze to death in a department-issued SUV tonight."

"Why not? It has heat, by the way." He chuckled.

"Of course it has heat, you ass! The point is it's Thursday, not Saturday, and I don't want you to!"

Grayson crossed her arms over her chest and stared at him, silently daring him to put his overcoat on. She saw the amusement flash across his face, which made her scowl at him even more.

"We've been over this. Now more than ever, you shouldn't be by yourself," he said gently.

"I'm not arguing with that."

"Then…"

"I don't want you freezing to death thirty feet from my front door in the middle of a blizzard," she declared.

Before he could fire back something sarcastic, she held up her hand and cut him off.

"Look, this is exhausting. I just had a completely unexpected, fantastic dinner, half a bottle of pretty good wine, and all I want to do is spend the rest of the night on the couch watching a movie. You have two options: stay in this house or go back to your own. If you leave and go out in that," she said, gesturing toward the window again, "you are driving home. Immediately. If I see you sitting in that black behemoth, I swear to God I will have it towed with you in it. I'm apparently responsible for seven bodies in as many weeks. I'd rather not make it eight."

With that, she stalked off into the kitchen to make herself a cup of tea. By the time she'd dropped the bag into the hot water, she'd calmed herself down.

Holy crap, I just threw a tantrum in my own living room. Real smooth, Gray.

She played around with the teabag, pulling it in and out of the water and watching the liquid darken. She grabbed the cup and walked back into the living room, surprised to find Gabriel standing at the bookcase where Barbara kept the DVDs.

She sat down quietly on the couch and watched him. He'd seen her out of the corner of his eye but waited until she was curled up with her tea before saying anything.

"You're not going to make me watch something with subtitles, are you?"

She raised her eyebrows in surprise. "I would've thought subtitles would be right up your alley, detective." She smiled softly.

"Not when I have something more important to pay attention to," he mumbled. "Which of these do you want to watch?"

"Oh, I don't care. Pick something."

Really? She's letting me pick?

"I just had a very nice dinner. The least I can do is let you watch something you'd enjoy."

He continued to peruse the shelves, which clearly held a mix of two unique collections. He was curious as to which half of the collection was Grayson's and hoped he'd guessed correctly when he made his selection. He crouched down in front of the television and put the disc in the DVD player, pushing a few choice buttons to make the picture appear on the screen. He heard her mumble into her teacup behind him.

"What was that?" he asked, smiling at her as he sat back down on the couch and hit Play on the remote control.

"I said, 'boys and their toys.' How is it that you all know exactly how to work an entertainment system, no matter how many remotes there are?"

"Call it a gift."

"Or something," she muttered. "What are we watching?"

"A movie," he said, attempting to skip ahead to the main menu. "You don't ask questions through the whole movie, too, do you?"

"Not if I understand what's going on," she smirked, then looked at him with a questioning look on her face. "You really don't like it when I ask questions, do you?"

"It's not the questions you ask, Grayson," he said quietly.

"So what is it?"

"It's the self-deprecation behind them," he said simply, then pressed another button and the main menu flashed onto the screen. "It pisses me off when you try to make less of yourself than you actually are, and the last thing I want is to direct any of that anger at you. Understand?"

She nodded, barely, stunned.

Gabriel watched the conflict play out across her eyes. She didn't side with anyone but him. He knew by the shy smile she raised a moment later.

"Good. Now, come here," he said, holding his hand out for her.

She took it, and he gently pulled her across the couch to sit beside him.

"Bring your blanket."

She grabbed it and draped it around her legs, bringing part of it over on top of his.

"Keep that for yourself," he said, attempting to drape it back over her.

"Just take it," she said, batting his hand away.

She looked up at the TV screen as he switched off the side table lamp.

"Indiana Jones? The first one?"

"Mmm-hmm." He nodded. "Do you approve?"

She nodded. "It's one of my favorites."

"Good," he said, starting the film. Oddly enough, it was one of his, too. A selfish choice, but it had paid off.

Ten minutes into the movie, she was sinking down into the couch cushions and trying to find a comfortable position that didn't hurt her ribcage. Ryder let her toss around for a few minutes, and when it was clear she wasn't going to find a good spot sitting straight up, he draped one arm over the back of the couch and gently guided her head onto his shoulder. He pulled the blanket up around her.

"Better?"

She nodded. A few more minutes passed. "Thank you for dinner," she whispered.

"You're most welcome," he replied, running his left hand down her arm. He felt her close her eyes.

"And thank you for staying with me."

"It's a pleasure. Especially when warm."

"You weren't really going to sit out there all night, were you?"

"Of course, I was. At least until Miss Parker came home."

"It's not Saturday night."

"I know."

"We agreed."

"Your nearly being choked to death changed that agreement."

"Why?"

"Shhh," he hushed, running a hand through her hair. "Watch your movie."

She turned into his side a bit more and sunk down underneath her blanket. She was warm and comfortable and completely safe. It was nice.

Ryder sat as still as he could, intermittently running a hand down her arm or fingers through her hair. He was having a very hard time fighting the urge to cup her cheek in the palm of his hand, turn her head up to face his, and kiss her. He'd stopped paying attention to the film a long time ago. It was too distracting having her pulled up to his side and breathing softly onto his neck.

Oh, this is really not a good train of thought.

When the credits came on, he turned to look at her. She was curled up against him, wide awake.

"You ready for another one?" he whispered into her ear.

She turned her face up toward his and nodded. He helped her slowly sit up before he stood and walked over to the bookcase. As he pulled out another DVD case, she stood and walked into the kitchen.

Another cup of tea, he said to himself, listening to the sounds coming from the dimly lit room.

He sat back down on the couch once he had the disc in and started to bring up the main menu. By the time he had it up and running, she was standing in the doorway, looking at him.

"What?" he asked, noticing her staring at him.

"I was thinking," she started, leaning against the wall, "that since you've been behind one, maybe two, nice dinners recently, I should return the favor somehow."

"You don't need to do anything like that," he said, refocusing on the TV remote. This was not supposed to be some quid-pro-quo arrangement. At least, it wasn't to him.

"No, no," she said hurriedly, seeing his reaction. "I don't mean it as a repayment thing. I'd like to."

She sat down next to him on the couch again, her teacup refilled and cupped safely between her palms.

"What are you doing for Thanksgiving?"

"Thanksgiving?" He startled.

"Yeah, Thanksgiving. That holiday where everybody gets together and watches football and eats too much? End of November-ish every year? There's a parade in New York City on TV with obnoxious floats?" She smiled sweetly at him.

"I'm familiar with it, yes."

"Barbara and I cook every year. Well, I cook. She taste-tests mostly. Noah always eats too much. I'd like to invite you. And Detective Harrison and Detective Nolan. We always have too much food."

Gabriel was momentarily speechless. She was inviting him—and for all intents and purposes, his family—to her family's house for the holidays? His face must have betrayed his shock because she started rambling.

"You probably already have other plans, and they probably do, too. And…and that's fine. But if you don't, it would be nice to have you all. Kind of a way to say thank you, I guess. I…I don't know…I…"

She dropped her eyes to the floor, obviously having second thoughts.

Ryder regained his mental footing first and cleared his throat. "I can't speak for Harrison or Nolan, but I would be honored."

Honored? That's a bit much. "It's just Thanksgiving," she replied, immediately blushing.

"Your Thanksgiving," he corrected. He motioned for her to lie back down against him, which she did, and he started the next film.

"Oh, good, you put in *The Last Crusade.* I hate the second one."

"The bugs?" he asked, smiling and glancing down at her.

"No, the whiny blonde actress," she said, then dropped her voice, "…and maybe the bugs."

He chuckled and turned up the volume slightly. "You're certain Barbara and Noah won't take issue with my invasion of your holiday?"

"They'll be fine."

"I get the feeling she doesn't like me."

"Has that stopped you before?"

"No."

"Then don't start the habit now." She yawned and snuggled underneath the blanket. "Just bring wine."

"I can handle that."

By the time Harrison Ford was making his way into the Temple of the Crescent Moon, Grayson's head was resting in Gabriel's lap. He pulled the blanket around her and then placed his left arm protectively on top of hers, occasionally running his hand up and down across her skin.

When the first of the credits came rolling onto the screen accompanied by the well-known upbeat score, Gabriel glanced back down. Grayson was fast asleep, breathing softly and occasionally mumbling into his shirt. He glanced at the clock on the wall. It was going on midnight. Barbara Parker would be home soon. He assumed that, as much as he personally liked his current position, she wouldn't take too kindly to it.

Ryder eased himself out from underneath her and stood beside the couch. Grayson grimaced and pulled the blanket higher around her shoulders in her sleep. He shut off the television, then bent down and lifted Grayson into his arms. Waking slightly, she turned into his chest and wrapped her arms around his neck.

"Time for bed," he whispered softly into her hair, climbing the stairs and easing open her bedroom door.

He pulled out her comforter and gently laid her down into bed, tucking the sheets and heavy comforter back up around her shoulders. She instinctively turned onto her side to try to find him, and he put a hand out to touch the skin on her cheek. She sighed, completely content and completely asleep. He leaned down and kissed her forehead.

"Goodnight, Grayson," he whispered before leaving her bedroom and shutting the door.

He made his way down the stairs, collected his belongings, and threw on his overcoat. He left through the front door, jiggling the handle slightly to be sure it had locked behind him. He walked once around the house, just to be sure it was secure, then headed to the car.

The snow was still coming down heavily as he slid into the driver's side of the SUV. It took a while for the heat to kick on and the inside of the car to warm up. He'd shut off the engine and turned off the headlights only a minute before he saw the limousine turn down the street. Barbara Parker was escorted up to her front door by the same chauffeur he had seen pick her up hours ago. She shut and locked the door behind her and turned off the few lights he had left on downstairs.

Satisfied that Grayson was safe and wasn't alone in the house, he turned the key in the ignition and pulled the car out into the street. He smiled to himself as he drove through the snowstorm. He had the feeling that extending Grayson's invitation to his partners the next morning was going to be interesting.

39

SOMETIMES GRAYSON WASN'T exactly sure how she and Barbara Parker had ever become friends. If they'd met now, today, each in their respective careers and each with their respective quirks, she doubted they would've given each other a second thought.

Thankfully, they'd met each other young, before elementary school. They'd never attended the same schools and had moved across the country from each other for college. Somehow, they had both decided to migrate home to Denver when all was said and done.

Grayson had bought the bungalow to be close to work without really being able to afford it. Barbara had needed a place to live and somewhere to keep her shoe collection when she'd moved back to the city. The arrangement had worked out perfectly at the time.

Right now, the tenacious blonde was following her roommate around the kitchen with an open eyeshadow palette and a brush aimed at her right eyelid. Grayson was silently cursing her decision to ever let Barbara live with her.

"Babs, seriously. Quit. I need to check on this," she scolded, pushing her roommate aside so she could resist the temptation to shove her back into the oven with the turkey.

"Hey, one or two extra minutes won't kill anything."

"So says your extraordinary cooking skills?" Grayson smirked.

"So says the guy I get most of my takeout from. Now, stop moving and let me do this. You're not even dressed yet."

"I spend Thanksgiving in the kitchen. What do I need to wear besides an apron?"

"Well, since we'll be having company and I don't swing that way, a pair of pants and a shirt would be nice."

That comment earned Barbara Parker a dinner roll thrown at her head from across the kitchen countertop.

"Hey! I wasn't the one who invited lover boy over for lunch, dinner, whatever we're calling this," she retorted, picking up the roll and ripping it in two. "You want a piece?"

"You're the taste-tester. No thanks."

"Suit yourself." Babs shrugged, popping the warm bread into her mouth. "Mmmmmm," she sighed, closing her eyes, "homemade carbs."

"Yes, evil carbs." Grayson rolled her eyes. "God forbid you should ever have one." She pushed the turkey back into the oven and increased the time on the clock.

"Okay, now that you're done with the turkey, can I please finish what I started an hour ago? They'll be here soon."

Grayson rounded the counter and sat down on the kitchen stool without a word.

"Much better. Eyes closed," Barbara scolded before putting her brush to work.

A soft knock at the kitchen door a few minutes later offered Grayson a reprieve from the constant assault on her eyelids. Noah pushed through, smiling, with several paper grocery bags in his hands.

"Hello, lovies," he greeted them, smiling.

"Busy," Babs replied without looking from Grayson's face.

"Hi, Noah," Grayson replied, her eyes scrunched down against the feel of the brush.

"She's got you trapped, eh?" he remarked, his casual tone laced with humor.

"Well, she wasn't planning on even wearing mascara, for heaven's sake. I mean really, Gray."

"Oh, that's right." He nodded, setting the bags down on the countertop. "Tall, dark, and overprotective is coming to dinner. At least tell me we've picked an outfit."

Grayson motioned to the yoga pants and flour-stained T-shirt she had on underneath her apron. Noah visibly grimaced in disgust.

Babs rolled her eyes. "See what I have to work with here, Noah?" she said, the annoyance heavy in her voice.

"Honey, you have to put in a bit of effort. A little blonde birdy tells me you like this one."

"I thought dinner was the effort. Whatever happened to the old saying 'the way to a man's heart is through his stomach'?"

"Honestly?" He shrugged. "The way to a man's heart is a little further south than that."

Grayson slapped him on the shoulder.

"Ow! No hitting. C'mon, get up. Babs, hold down the fort here for ten minutes. I'm going to help our little helpless princess find something respectable to wear."

"You get five minutes," Grayson scowled, scooting off of the stool and following Noah as he made a beeline for the stairs.

In no time, he had several outfits flung out onto her bed. She went with something she could spend the rest of the day in, both in and out of the kitchen. Dark jeans, ballet flats, and a V-neck sweater in a light rose. She hazarded a looked at herself in the mirror. Not half bad, considering her hair was going to end up in a messy bun within ten minutes anyway.

"You clean up nice, love," Noah said from his perch on her bed.

"So you keep telling me. I wish you'd stop."

"Fine. Then tell me something."

"Sure."

"Where do you and this Ryder guy stand?"

She turned from her dresser and gave him a confused look. *What the…?*

"Where do we stand on what?"

"On the two of you. Together."

"I wasn't aware there was a 'together,'" she scoffed.

"You're certainly not apart. Babs said he was here the night of her big shindig downtown. She found leftovers from Gustavo's in the fridge. Hon, they don't do takeout. For anybody."

"They do for him." She shrugged. "Hand-delivered to the door."

"So, just how the bloody hell did that happen?"

She sighed and leaned back against her dresser. "Does it matter?"

"Have you asked him about the night we went there for dinner? Or about the Petal Club?"

"No."

"Have you asked him about that dress?" he asked, pointing to the garment bag hanging conspicuously in her closet.

"No. Noah, where are you going with this? Are you saying he really did all of that?"

Noah wrinkled his forehead at her.

Grayson wrinkled hers back at him.

Why is he looking at me like I should already know the answer to my own question? Did I miss something here?

He shrugged as he shook himself out of his own head. "Suppose he did. You know what a cop makes, Gray. Even a detective. On his own, he can't afford any of that. But maybe he does, and then some. What is his deal?"

"Again, I ask, does it matter?"

Noah sighed and pushed himself up from the bed. He walked to her and set his hands on her shoulders, crouching down so he was eye level with her. "Not if you're happy with whatever is going on here. Look, I'm with Babs on this. He's a charmer. But there's a side to this bloke that doesn't show. Let's not forget he was here just weeks ago accusing you of murder."

"I...I..." Grayson didn't quite know how to start. She closed her eyes and took a few deep breaths, then opened them and started again.

"You're right, Noah. There are big parts of who he is that I don't get. But why should I? We're not in a committed anything. Jesus, we're not even in a non-committed anything." She threw her hands up in the air and leaned harder on her dresser, catching her breath. Noah sat still, patiently waiting for her to continue.

"There was a point when he was here last week when Barbara was gone. He was dishing out dinner on the couch. It was like he was supposed to be there. But then, I know absolutely zero about him. And right now, there's so much other stuff going on, I...I just don't care. Does that make sense?"

"Of course it does. Sweetheart, you should have seen my face when I walked into your ICU room. I found him in bed with you, and you with your face snuggled down in his lap."

Grayson cringed. A rip-roaring blush flew into her cheeks. "Yeah, that was a bit embarrassing. I can't believe he let me do that."

Noah shook his head. "No, Gray, I mean the way he was looking at you. I'd give anything for a man to look at me like that. I can't even really describe it. Like gentle and incredibly possessive at the same time. Every time you had a nightmare, all he had to do was touch you. You calmed down every time. Instantly. Hell, the drugs didn't even do that. It was just like you said. Like he was supposed to be there."

She stood in front of her dresser, dumbfounded.

"Oh." *WHAT?* The room started to spin.

"Whatever 'it' is, it's there for both of you. All I'm saying is, be careful."

"Okay."

"Gray!" A loud call came from downstairs. "Is the turkey supposed to be boiling?"

"What on earth?" Noah asked, eyebrows raised.

"Who knows? I've gotta go," she answered, taking the stairs two at a time and then dashing into the kitchen.

40

ABOUT AN HOUR later, the three friends were sitting around the kitchen counter, having already cracked into a bottle of wine, when there was a knock at the front door.

Babs shot out of her chair. "I'll get it!" she chimed, scampering toward the front door.

"You ready to play hostess, love?" Noah asked, smirking.

"Ready as I guess I'll ever be. I can't get arrested for making bad food, can I?"

"Doubtful. And your food is delicious."

"Hey, lazy butts, we could use some help out here!" Babs called.

Noah shot Grayson a confused look, which she returned, as they made their way out into the living room.

Logan and Blake were trying to take their shoes off in the entryway while balancing two paper grocery bags and a six-pack each. Babs was attempting to carry in something rather heavy, also in a paper shopping bag.

"Hi, detectives," Grayson said warmly, stepping forward to grab one of the bags from Nolan.

"Eh, it's just Logan and Blake today, doc. Happy Thanksgiving, by the way," Harrison replied.

"I think I've got this," Blake said, finally getting his second shoe off. "Probably could use some help outside, though."

"Oh, all right," she replied, quickly slipping on a pair of boots that were sitting by the door. "What is all that?"

"Football essentials," Blake grinned.

Grayson stepped out onto the porch. It was definitely a winter afternoon, but the bite in the air wasn't too bad with the sun shining. She wrapped her arms around her chest and walked down the steps toward a black car parked in front of the house. She didn't recognize it, but the trunk was open and the bottom half of a familiar camel overcoat was jutting out the back of the open hatch.

"You know, I was kidding about the car," she chuckled, stepping up to the trunk and mentally reading off the SL65 AMG stamped over the rear taillight.

"No, you weren't," Gabriel replied, pulling himself upright. "But you happened to make a very good guess."

"One of these days we're going to have to talk about how you can afford all this on a cop's salary," she said, shaking her head.

"We can do that now," he shrugged, his voice suddenly cold.

Grayson bit the inside of her cheek.

What did I say? Shit. Great way to start things off, Gray. "I'll pass. It's too cold out here for that, and I have a house full of guests. What can I help carry?"

"You can take these," he answered.

Gabriel slid past her to the open passenger door and pulled a large bouquet of flowers from the seat.

"Wow."

It was all she could think of to say. White lilac, deep pink and red ranunculus, Queen Anne's lace, and a whole host of other flowers she didn't recognize. The arrangement itself was so big that it took two hands to carry it properly. She let it rest gently in the crook of her right arm. They were gorgeous.

"What's this for?"

"For you, of course," he said, pulling a large box out of the trunk.

He motioned for her to start back toward the house. They walked in the front door one after the other. Blake took the box Gabriel was holding and hauled it off into the kitchen. Noah, who was in the process of helping Logan dish out snacks on the coffee table, raised two eyebrows at her from the couch when he saw the flowers.

Barbara was less subtle when she made it to the kitchen with them. "Holy shit! Look at those!" she squealed.

Grayson blushed as red as the blooms.

"Where did these come from?" Babs asked, angling closer for a better look.

Grayson smiled shyly, handed them over, and started rummaging around in a high cabinet for a vase.

"They're from him, aren't they?" she asked, sniffing the flowers. She got a nod in return.

"Gray, these were not cheap. I think the only thing in season is the Queen Anne's lace."

"You're an expert on flowers now?"

"I spent a summer in my aunt's flower shop, remember?"

"You were fifteen, Babs."

"Still…I remember what I put into bouquets and what I didn't. Sweetie, these are freaking gorgeous."

"Yeah, they are…" Grayson said, smiling and cutting off the protective plastic wrapped around them. She gently pulled away the tissue paper and cut the elastic band that was holding the stems together, then one by one pulled out the stems and took a bit off the bottom of each one.

Babs pulled out the bottle of wine they'd already opened and watched from the kitchen table. It didn't take long for a particular shadow to fall across the kitchen floor. She stood and slipped past him into the living room, leaving them alone.

Grayson was almost finished arranging the flowers when she felt him step up behind her.

"You like them?" he purred into her ear.

She shivered slightly, only enough for him to notice, and nodded. "They're...they're too much."

"No, they're not," he replied, resting a hand on her arm and leaning in to kiss her temple. "Happy Thanksgiving."

Grayson had to resist a very strong urge to turn around, grab him by his hair, and kiss him until she ran out of oxygen. Her ability to keep her head on straight around him was basically becoming nonexistent. *Holy shit.*

"Come on. Everyone's in the living room," he said quietly, putting a hand on her right hip to steer her around the counter.

Grayson kept enough of her wits about her to put the vase on the kitchen table and grab her wine glass. She walked silently into her living room and found it in complete chaos.

Logan and Blake were on the couch, arguing over which football game to put on, the Bears versus the Lions or the Eagles versus the Cowboys. Noah had answered the door and was motioning Kyle in out of the cold. Barbara was trying to put in her vote for no football at all, which was just making things worse. The coffee table was full of food, and it all looked fried, fattening, and fantastic.

Grayson paused in the doorway, not exactly sure what or who to try to tackle first. Gabriel slid past her and grabbed the remote from his partner, hitting him on the head with it.

"Ow!" Blake yelped, rubbing the side of his head.

"All right, enough. The games are staggered, idiots. We're starting with the Bears, whether you like it or not. Go crack a beer before you both kill each other."

"Yes, mother." Harrison grinned, shoving up from the couch and heading to the kitchen.

On instinct, Grayson discarded her wine glass and followed him. Logan opened the back door and grabbed two bottles from the cardboard carriers on the back porch.

"You want one, doc?" he asked when he saw her looking at him.

"Sure," she nodded. "And it's Grayson, by the way."

He nodded at her and pushed the back door open wider. "You want the IPA, the amber, the porter…" he drifted off, reaching down toward the amber.

"The porter," she said.

His eyebrows shot up and he grinned, changing trajectory and bringing up another dark bottle.

"You drink that?" he asked, setting the bottle on the counter and reaching for the opener. "It's kinda strong."

"Girls aren't allowed to drink dark beer?" she asked with a smirk.

"Can't say I've ever met one that prefers it," he responded, handing her the open bottle.

She took a drink. "Well, now you have," she said, tipping her bottle toward him and grabbing the open one meant for Nolan. "I'm glad you all could come, by the way."

"This is already the best Thanksgiving I've had in a good decade." He smiled at her over his shoulder, grabbing another two bottles from the porch. "I usually spend it at home on my own."

"Beer, underwear, and football?"

"Pretty much, yeah."

"Well, hopefully, this is a bit of an upgrade."

"Big upgrade. Nolan would have been doing the same thing. Kids are with the ex."

Her face fell. "Oh."

"Yeah. Maybe don't mention that."

"Oh, I won't. Don't worry."

"Are you two done gossiping?" came Noah's voice from the living room. "The game's starting."

Grayson grabbed her beer, Nolan's, and one for Babs. She walked out into the living room and sat down in one of the armchairs, handing a beer over to her roommate and then another across the coffee table to Blake.

"Thanks," he said, angling to look at the television behind her.

Babs just nodded and kept chattering away with Kyle. Logan walked into the room carrying the rest of the bottles. When he handed over Ryder's, he leaned down close to whisper in his ear.

"The girl went for the porter, Gabe. Voluntarily. If you don't jump on that, I swear to God, I'll steal her."

Gabriel took the offered bottle and glared at him. "Back off," he hissed.

Logan pulled back and smirked. "Call it incentive for you to keep it together," he murmured with a grin, then took a seat and angled toward the TV.

The next few hours passed with ease. Between the seven of them, they blew through the snacks and a good portion of the beer. Logan and Blake spent a good part of the time arguing over football statistics, which Kyle was all too happy to join in on. Babs and Grayson kept intermittently running in between the living room and the kitchen, checking on dinner.

Grayson was surprised to see Noah latch onto Gabriel. When they weren't watching the game, they were talking amongst themselves side by side in the set of armchairs beside the couch. She was struck by how normal it seemed to have all of them in her living room, arguing over football and which local brewery was going to have the best Christmas Ale this year.

She was in the kitchen finishing up with the scalloped potatoes when Nolan came lumbering in, looking for another beer. "On the back steps." She motioned with the paring knife.

"Thanks. You want one?"

"No, I'm good. Thanks."

He popped the cap and took a drink. "Thanks for this. Hosting all of us, I mean."

"Oh, you're welcome. I'm glad you could make it."

"The kids are with their mom. This is much better than my planned alternative," he said, taking a drink from the bottle.

"Well, hopefully, it's a relaxing day off. I'm sure you lost another weekend at a crime scene."

"Nope. Not this weekend," he replied.

"Really?" Her eyes widened.

"Yeah, go figure. Sunday was quiet. Looks like we're at the end of it."

"That would be great, wouldn't it?"

"Keep your fingers crossed, doc," he replied, winking as he walked back into the living room.

Grayson stayed in the kitchen a few extra minutes, thinking. If it was all over, she could get back to her normal life. Her lack of a life. Work. The hospital. That was all she had to go back to. She couldn't decide if that was necessarily a good thing.

41

DINNER WAS A rousing success, even though the seven of them just barely managed to squeeze around the kitchen table. They served up turkey, stuffing, scalloped potatoes, green beans, homemade dinner rolls, the works.

Grayson smiled to herself as she watched Nolan and Harrison eat. Two plates in and going strong, it was clear that they both were starved for a good home-cooked meal.

Kyle and Barbara were at one end of the table, chatting about the pros and cons of the different ski resorts nearby. Noah was finishing his latest glass of wine, and Gabriel was opening another bottle beside her. That had made up, in part, the contents of the box he'd brought into the house. He'd apparently taken her seriously when she'd suggested bringing wine. And good bottles, too. What else was left in there, she hadn't any idea, but it was far from empty. Gabriel set a glass of wine from the new bottle down in front of her.

"Try this," he said quietly into her ear.

"What is it?"

"Always with the questions, doctor." He chuckled as he poured a glass for Noah.

"Always so hesitant to answer, detective," she replied, taking a sip of the wine. *Oh, wow. This is really good.*

The wine was bold, heavy, with just enough sweetness to stave off any harsh aftertaste. Right up her alley. Grayson decided she really shouldn't argue with him when it came to food and wine. He had yet to go wrong in either department.

She looked up to try to grab the bottle and take a look at the label, but it had already been passed down the table. *Damn.*

"I put a bottle in the pantry," he added quietly.

"Confident, were you?"

He shrugged and went back to talking to Noah. She watched them contentedly and sipped at her wine.

Another forty-five minutes later, everyone was thoroughly stuffed and, as Nolan reminded them, there was another football game on. Chairs noisily scooted back against the wood floor as everyone made their way into the living room. Barbara led the way. Grayson hazarded a quick glance at the table and turned down the kitchen lights. Really nothing was left, except for a few pieces of turkey and half of the cranberry sauce. She shrugged. At least they wouldn't be stuffing themselves with leftovers for weeks on end.

Now the only one left in the kitchen, she stacked up the dinner plates, grabbed the silverware, and hauled it all to the sink. A quick rinse and it was all loaded in the dishwasher. She was midway through her second pass over the table, carrying serving trays back to the sink when she heard a throat clear in the doorway. No surprise. There he was, his scowling face trained directly on her.

There's that shiver down my spine again. Can I ever be around him without feeling that pull?

"What are you doing?"

"Um…clearing the table?" she replied, turning on the faucet in the sink.

"Leave it. You've worked all day. Just come out with everyone."

"You go ahead," she said, starting to scrub one of the trays. "This will drive me nuts. Besides, I don't want to spend my last day off of work doing dishes."

An eerie pause settled over the kitchen. "What was that?"

"Really, go have fun. I'll be there in a few..."

"No," he interrupted forcefully, barreling around the counter. "What did you just say?"

"I said this will drive me nuts. So?"

"The second part. About going back to work."

"I go back Saturday," she shrugged, continuing to wipe off the platter in front of her. "Considering I've spent most of today in or around the kitchen, I'd rather spend tomorrow on the couch."

Grayson went back to washing the dishes, completely unaware of the storm building behind her. She didn't see his jaw clench. She didn't hear his teeth grind together. She didn't see his fingernails dig into his fisted palms, his shaking fingers rhythmically opening and closing at his sides. He forced air into his lungs in a last-ditch attempt to calm down. She didn't heed those, either.

"You're not going back." It was said simply. Coolly. And all it did was send fire through the backs of her eyes.

"Excuse me?"

Grayson stopped scrubbing but kept her back to him. She felt him come up behind her, his body heat penetrating into her personal space. She could see his reflection in the window above the sink. His eyes were completely black and glistening with rage. He was furious.

"You. Are not. Going back. To work," he said sharply, caging her in on both sides, his fingers digging into the countertop.

"Yes, I am. Saturday," she countered.

Her voice sounded more confident than she felt.

"No," he hissed in her ear, "you're not."

She could see the tension in the muscles beneath his

shirtsleeves. Hear the strain in his voice. He was so close to losing control. She didn't care.

"You have no say in this, Gabriel," she replied, her voice low.

"I have every..."

"No, you don't," she hissed, whipping around to face him.

She could see the anger on his face. If the lights had been fully up, she would have seen the fear that the anger was masking. But the lights were down low. She wasn't looking for it. She missed it.

"My time's up. My department says I'm due back, so I go back. If I don't, I don't graduate; I lose my fellowship. Everything I've worked for, for close to thirteen years. Done. I can't lose all that. I have to go back."

"And if you end up a corpse?" he seethed, trying to rein in his temper.

"Who says I will? Blake told me there wasn't another victim on Sunday. What does your conspiracy theory say about that?" she spat, momentarily throwing him off balance.

When he didn't immediately answer her, she continued. "And where has your little theory gotten you, huh? I still see a pretty long list of bodies without a single suspect, detective. Oh, except for me, of course, but we scrapped that one.

"So, Harlan got himself killed after he kicked the shit out of me. He had enemies, inside and outside of the hospital. He had patients send him death threats. Have you looked into them?" She slammed the kitchen towel she had been holding in her hand onto the counter. "I refuse to lose my career over the half-cocked conspiracy theory of a Major Crimes rookie detective!"

"Grayson, please," he pleaded, his eyes closed. "Don't do this."

"It's not up for discussion." She tried to turn back to the dishes, but his hands shot up from the counter to hold her in place. He gripped her by the shoulders and stepped even closer to her.

"I can't...I won't..." he stammered, pleading with her through his eyes.

She stared straight back at him, her blue eyes cold and piercing. "Careful, detective. I bruise easily."

Gabriel immediately released her, and he dropped his hands to his sides. His eyes shot to her neck, where Barbara's careful application of concealer had hidden the final few purple streaks. His right hand reached up to brush her hair out of the way so he could see them better.

Grayson steeled herself against him, ready to jerk out of his reach. She was furious, a cat ready to claw at whatever came near her. The second his fingers hit her neck, she closed her eyes and let him brush her hair away. The anger faded.

Goddamn it.

"I can't stand around and watch you get yourself killed," he whispered.

"No one is asking you to," she replied.

"Stubborn girl," he said against her forehead, gently resting his hands on her hips.

"Overprotective caveman," she whispered back.

He chuckled and pulled her to him, wrapping his arms around her back and resting his chin on her head. Grayson hooked her fingers through the rear belt loops of his jeans and rested her head on his chest. "You're going to be the death of me. You know that?" he said into her hair.

She nodded slightly, and he laughed again. "Don't make me send in an armed escort after you."

"You wouldn't."

"Try me. I have beat cops that owe me a few favors."

"I'll send in my interns to run interference."

He tightened his hold on her. "I mean it, Grayson. I don't like this."

She sighed in protest but didn't move.

He continued, "Call it overprotective. Obsessive. Whatever. I have a very bad feeling about this. The minute something doesn't feel right, you need to get out of there."

"I'm supposed to, what, drop my scalpel and run?"

"No. Take the scalpel with you. Then run."

"Gabriel..."

"I'm not playing around, Grayson. Please," he begged, forcing her eyes up to his. "I know I haven't figured this thing out. I know I don't have any idea of who's behind this. You're right. I can't explain why we didn't have a body this week. You don't have to remind me that I've dropped the ball here."

She started to say something, but he put his fingers over her mouth and continued on without breaking pace.

"But it doesn't negate the fact that the psychopath responsible is still lurking in the halls of your hospital. His kills are violent. They're getting more and more personal. He's getting close to what he wants. And what he wants is you. I just had to see you in the ICU. I'd rather not repeat the experience."

She sighed into his chest and mumbled something he couldn't hear.

"What?"

"We really have to work on you and Thursdays, Gabriel."

He chuckled and kissed the top of her head. "I'll put it on my to-do list for next year."

Another low chuckle from the doorway startled both of them. On instinct, Gabriel put himself in between the door and

Grayson. She just managed to unhook her fingers from his jeans before he whipped her behind him. Logan was standing in the doorway, his arms crossed over his chest.

"Hey, I'm unarmed," he said playfully, throwing his hands up. "I come in peace. I've been sent in for pie and...something else...Hey! What else was I getting besides pie?" he called into the living room.

"Scotch. Top shelf!" came Noah's voice over the NFL commentators.

"And scotch. Apparently, it's on the top shelf." He smiled.

Putting a reassuring hand on his back, Grayson moved out from behind Gabriel's protective stance. She grabbed two pies out of the oven. Once she'd set them on the counter, she grabbed dessert plates from another cabinet, silverware from the second drawer over, and napkins.

Logan was practically drooling standing up. "Oh, please tell me you have..." He cut himself off when she pulled ice cream out of the freezer and homemade whipped cream out of the refrigerator. "It's official. I've died and gone to heaven. Oh, Gabe, if you don't keep her, I swear to fucking God..."

Gabriel ushered him out of the kitchen with one of the pies and the whipped cream before he got any further with that thought, then ducked into the box that was still sitting by the kitchen table.

Grayson was sure she was blushing crimson from head to toe. *Thank goodness I dimmed the lights.*

Logan came back in for the second pie but instead had a bottle shoved into his abdomen.

"Ooof!"

"Take that in."

"What is it?"

"Scotch. Top shelf."

"Oh, okay."

He turned around without saying another word, raising the bottle to eye the label.

Logan was less of an ass when he'd had a few, but he definitely had a loose tongue. It was a fine line Ryder had learned to walk during their time in narcotics together.

When Grayson slid past him with the second pie and the ice cream, he didn't stop her. He grabbed the plates and silverware and followed. Everyone was still sitting around the TV, clearly focusing in on the dessert instead of the game.

"Gray, these look awesome. What did you make?" Noah asked as Harrison handed over the bottle of scotch.

"My usual. Pumpkin and apple."

"Just so everybody knows, her 'usual' should be put into a museum somewhere," he said, rolling his eyes before looking at the bottle of scotch in his hands. "Hey, this isn't my…"

"See if you like it," Gabriel interrupted, putting the plates down.

"You'll like it," Logan piped up, already mid-pie. "Trust me."

The group ate their dessert in the midst of a happy cacophony. Logan and Blake kept fighting with each other about the game. Kyle tried to correct them when they got their statistics wrong, but before long he cut his losses and gave up entirely.

Eventually, Noah and Kyle got into a debate about scotch, whiskey, and bourbon, which Gabriel seemed happy to join. One glass turned into two, then three.

The game ended. The pies were gone. Since no one was eager or sober enough to go home, they pushed some of the chairs back out of the way and decided to put in a movie. When Noah pushed play and the beginning titles came onto the screen, Grayson rolled her eyes.

"*Ghostbusters*? Really?"

"What?" he replied. "It's funny. It's got Bill Murray. And we can all sing along when the song comes on. Like we're sober enough to watch anything serious, lovie."

"Here, here!" Blake hollered from the couch, waving his scotch in the air.

"Okay, okay, I didn't mean to start a war," she agreed, her hands thrown up in defeat.

Grayson scooted backward on the floor to let Noah get to the couch, knocking into the lower part of one of the armchairs in the process. Once he was past her, she tried to move forward again. A hand dropped down on her right shoulder, gently but emphatically keeping her in place. She settled back down against the front of the chair, a jean-clad leg on each side of her.

Gabriel shifted in an attempt to stand and give her the chair. She shot her right hand out and clamped down on the fabric of his jeans to keep him where he was.

She reached over and grabbed a blanket, throwing it over her legs, lap, and conveniently, her right hand. She felt him try to move again, and this time she reached her fingers out, finding the top edge of his dress sock. She pulled it down so she had unobstructed access to the skin covering his lower leg.

Grayson smiled when she felt him tense up, his fingers flexing against her collarbone. Emboldened, she lazily ran the pad of her index finger along the joint. That earned her a moaned four-letter word from the man sitting behind her, just loud enough for her to hear.

"Are you planning on keeping that up all night?" he

murmured quietly into her ear, his fingers ever-so-slightly increasing their own pressure.

She didn't dare look back at him, but she nodded.

"Good."

Grayson shut her eyes. It made the shiver running down her spine all the stronger.

Holy shit.

42

IT WAS A RELIEF to finally have a day off. A real day off, where there was literally nothing he had to do and he had nowhere to be.

Nolan walked leisurely in between the rows of treadmills. The gym was packed, of course. Everyone was trying to burn off the Thanksgiving damage. It was almost time to suit up for the holiday party season, after all. Soccer moms in oversized cotton shirts, cougars in two-piece matching spandex, corporate weekend warriors in too much Under Armor, muscle heads who needed to put their shirts on…everyone was sweating and out of breath.

He grabbed one of the last remaining treadmills on the line, set his water bottle down, and pulled his phone out of his pocket. He turned up Pandora and settled into his usual eight-minute-mile pace. His mind drifted back to the holiday.

When Gabriel had extended Dr. Carter's invitation earlier in the week, both he and Logan had burst out laughing. They'd teased him mercilessly for an hour until they'd finally figured out that, not only was the invitation for real, but Gabriel had already himself accepted it. They both had rapidly agreed to go, on the premise of keeping Ryder in line. Truthfully, Blake had just been excited at the prospect of getting out of his own house.

The whole day had been great, as far as he was concerned. He and Logan had stopped off to get some food for the game, not really knowing what time actual "Thanksgiving" was going to be served. That pit stop put them at the young doctor's front door right when Gabriel had pulled in driving that car.

Blake shook his head to himself, sweat already running down his face. One of these days, his partner was going to let him take that damned car of his out for a test drive on the highway. At two a.m. At 190 mph.

Everyone had gotten along well, with the help of a little alcohol. The food had been incredible, and they hadn't left a scrap. Even the pie didn't last. And when everyone had been too blitzed on wine and scotch to even think about driving, the doc and her roommate had just shoved chairs aside, made room, and put on *Ghostbusters* like it was no big deal.

The fact that they had all fallen asleep in her living room and were a snoring, hungover mess the next morning hadn't been great. Well, all but two of them. At some point, Dr. Carter had gone upstairs to her own room.

Or someone took her up there, he thought to himself.

Either way, when the hungover mass of arms and legs and bedheads had actually woken up the next morning around ten, it had been to the smell of bacon, eggs, coffee, and something wonderfully sweet. They'd all groggily shuffled into the kitchen to find Grayson nearly finished preparing breakfast and Gabriel popping the cork on the first of several bottles of chilled champagne.

Even in his hungover haze, Blake had seen the smile on his partner's face and the way he'd always kept one eye on the young brunette as she'd moved around the kitchen.

Of course, Logan had noticed it, too. He'd smacked Gabe on the back and given him the most obvious "you-need-to-hit-that-and-soon" look that Nolan had ever seen. Thankfully, for Ryder's sake, nobody else noticed. They'd all been paying attention to the bacon.

The group had squeezed themselves around the kitchen table again and proceeded to stuff their faces with bacon, sausage, scrambled eggs, mimosas, and made-from-scratch cinnamon rolls. Just thinking about all that food made Blake kick up the speed on the treadmill.

Afterward, they'd all tried to help clean up, but Grayson had shooed them out of the kitchen. They'd said their good-byes in the early afternoon, and he'd reluctantly piled himself into Harrison's car for the drive home. Gabriel and Grayson had sequestered themselves on the front porch and had been in the middle of a heated discussion when Logan had pulled his truck away from the curb.

He'd spent the rest of Friday on the couch feeling like a bloated whale carcass but utterly happy. He'd talked to his girls on the phone and watched a bit of football, then called it a night. He'd hauled himself out of bed and out to the gym first thing Saturday morning. Or at least, he'd tried to. The flat front tire that had greeted him in the driveway had interfered with that plan a bit, so now here he was, with the midday rush, sweating his ass off with the rest of his neighborhood.

Nolan hit his target thirty minutes on the treadmill, searing pain shooting through his left ribs. He immediately hit the button to decrease the track speed and grabbed onto the bars, breathing hard.

I've gotta get my ass to the gym more. It didn't used to be this fucking hard to breathe.

He started his cool down and was just taking an inventory of which weight bench might open up first when the music abruptly dropped off. The handset vibrated against the treadmill console. An incoming call. He grabbed it and brought the screen close to his face.

Logan.

He pulled his earbuds out of their jack and held the phone up to his ear. "It's Nolan."

"Hey, buddy. It's Logan."

"So says the caller ID. What's up?"

"Uh, I've got a favor to ask."

"Okay."

"Are you okay? You sound out of breath. You having a heart attack or something?"

"Maybe. I'll have to ask the treadmill that just kicked my ass."

"Slaving away at the gym with the rest of the supermodels?"

"You can't tell me you weren't at least five pounds heavier on the scale on Friday."

"Yeah, but my girlish figure just bounces right back," came the sarcastic reply.

"Ugh. Screw you. So, about that favor?"

"How soon do you think you can make it down to the squad room?"

"Showered or not?"

"Dear Lord, shower. Please. For all of us."

"Thirty minutes, to be safe."

"Okay. Just meet me in the deck. We'll go up together."

"What's going on?" Nolan asked as he jumped off the treadmill and immediately started toward the locker room.

One of the staff tried to yell at him for not wiping down his machine. He flipped up a choice finger and kept walking.

"I'm going to need some help is all. Just get here."

"Okay."

Nolan shut off his phone, grabbed his bag out of his locker, and half-sprinted into the showers. Four minutes flat and he was out. Another two, and he was dressed and out the front door. In just under a half hour, he pulled into the parking deck next to Logan's truck.

The older detective was leaning against his trunk, waiting. He pushed himself up to standing when Blake hit the pavement. He didn't say anything, just started toward the elevators.

"Wanna tell me what the hell I'm doing here on my day off, Harrison?" Nolan asked coolly.

"Helping me with Wonder Boy," he said flatly, punching the up button.

"Well, I figured that much. What's he done now?"

"Nothing yet."

"So, I'm confused. What are we doing here?" he asked as the elevator dinged in arrival. "And how did you even know he was here? He's not supposed to be in today either."

"He didn't answer his phone this morning. I got nosy and went by the apartment. Nothing," Harrison replied, stepped in and pushing the button for Major Crimes. "Gym gear wasn't touched. Usually, he's either at the bar down the street or here. I tried here first since it's still a bit early to get fashionably hammered. Well, in public, apparently..." he trailed off, rolling his eyes.

"I don't like the sound of that."

"Yeah. And just take a guess as to where the hell he is."

The elevator dinged, announcing their arrival on the squad floor. Nolan walked out first, shaking his head and turning toward the interview rooms.

"Goddamn it, Gabe," he mumbled before pushing the door open.

Logan was right behind him.

There was Ryder, sitting in his usual seat, staring into his binder, tapping away with his right foot. He was dressed like he always was at work. That wasn't the problem.

The problem was the two-thirds empty bottle of scotch sitting by his right arm. The files on the desk weren't neatly arranged. There was no order to whatever he was doing here. And by the look of the hand he had fisted into his hair, things were not going well.

"See why I called?" Harrison mumbled.

"Um, yeah. I get it."

Blake walked a few steps into the room. "Gabe? Whatcha up to, partner?" he asked, trying to sound nonchalant.

He got a pair of bloodshot eyes to momentarily scowl at him, which was a plus, but that was all the response his partner gave him. It was enough to see how horrible he looked. In fact, Ryder looked sick.

His skin was pale; his eyes were red and rimmed with very dark circles. He was almost as pale as his white shirt. His forehead was wrinkled with intense concentration. This was not the partner he'd seen twenty-four hours ago.

Nolan grabbed a chair and turned it around so he could lean over the backrest. Logan hugged the wall and discreetly closed the door. There were only a few other people in the squad room today, but if voices got raised, nobody needed to know what was being said or by whom.

"Hey. You wanna fill me in here?" Nolan tried again. "What the hell is all this?" he asked, motioning to mess on the desk.

"I'm running out of time," he said hoarsely, not looking up from his binder.

"Running out of time for what?"

"Nine hours. I only have nine hours," he mumbled.

Nolan glanced at the clock. That would take them to about midnight.

"Nine hours to what?" he pressed. "Gabe, you know you've gotta help me out here. What happens at midnight?"

"It's Sunday."

"Yeah, I know that. Buddy, remember, we're probably done with this weekly shit. Nothing happened last week." He put a hand on top of Gabriel's notepad in the binder to break his focus and get him to look at him.

It didn't work. Gabriel just shoved the hand out of the way. "It's not done," he hissed.

"Gabe. Look at me. It's done."

"It's not done!" Ryder spat loudly across the table. "He's not done. He's coming back. He's not done. He doesn't have what he wants. He's coming back," he mumbled in circles, over and over.

This must be what it's like inside of his head, Blake thought to himself. *Jesus. Every single case. No wonder he drinks. Speaking of which...*

He reached over and grabbed the bottle of scotch from the table. There was no cap. *Probably already in the trash.*

"Put that back," his partner growled.

"You've had enough of this for now. By the way, you're not allowed to drink in the squad room. You know that." He handed the bottle over to Logan, who placed it down by his leg, effectively hiding it from Ryder's view.

"Go to hell."

"Already kinda there, buddy. I'm stuck at work on a Saturday afternoon because you're drunk. Now, get up. You're going home."

"Fuck you. I'm staying."

"No, you're not."

"I'm not leaving."

"Oh, for the love of Christ, Gabe, enough!" Blake shouted, throwing his hands up. "Arguing with you when you're sober is a pain in the ass. Right now, you're just impossible."

Ryder ignored his partner. He kept staring at the notes in his binder, his lips subtly moving back and forth. He was reading to himself.

"Okay, fine. Fine. You give me one reason. One really fucking good reason why I should let you stay in the department, shit-faced out of your mind at three in the afternoon and raving like a lunatic. You convince me there's a need for this, and… and…I'll go buy you another hundred dollar bottle of fucking scotch."

When his partner didn't look up, Nolan slammed his hand down on the metal table, sending several files onto the floor. "I don't have all fucking day, Ryder. Answer me."

For once in their four years together, Blake Nolan had finally had it with his partner.

Ryder's lips moved, but no words came out.

"Speak up so the back of the room can hear you," Logan said cheekily from the corner.

"She…she went back. He's there," he said softly, the hoarseness making him barely intelligible.

"What?"

"She's there. With him. Alone."

Blake shot Logan a questioning look, and all he got was a shrug in return. "Gabe, who's with who?"

He took a shaky breath. "Grayson. She went back. To work."

Tick. Tick. Tick. Three. Two. One.

"Aw, shit!" Blake exploded, grabbing a stack of paper from the table and flinging it across the room. "What the fuck is she thinking?"

Ryder didn't answer. He just kept talking to himself. "I told her not to. She went anyway. He's there. He wants her. I know he does. He's not done. He can't have her yet. But maybe tonight. Maybe after tonight…then he won't have to wait anymore."

"So figure it out!" Nolan hollered from across the table.

"I can't!" Gabriel yelled back, snapping his head up to look at his partner.

The look on his face was one full of fear, helplessness, and a whole boatload of scotch. "What am I supposed to do?" he asked, his voice back to its normal decibel level.

"Well, I can tell you one thing, buddy," Logan said, pushing off from the wall, "getting soused before five when you've got a midnight deadline would not have been high on my priority list."

Gabriel dropped his head into his hands. "I've been here since yesterday. Caffeine and endorphins haven't helped. Alcohol seemed like a good next step."

"You've been here since yesterday?"

Nolan paused, momentarily confused, and then it hit him. "You came here after we left her house, didn't you?" he asked.

Gabriel nodded.

"Did you drive?"

He shook his head. "I walked."

"Well, at least you had that much fucking sense. Get up. Now. You're going home."

Ryder's face instantly darkened. "I told you, I'm not leaving," he said, his voice menacingly deep.

"Yeah, well, newsflash. You are. If you're so fucking convinced we're not done with this bullshit, then I guess we're not done with it. But you being drunk off your ass isn't going to help anybody. And for the record, I'd like to have a partner at the end of all this. You dead from choking on your own vomit in the interview room isn't really what I wanna see Monday morning."

Nolan hauled Ryder to his feet and shoved his binder at him. "You have two fucking minutes. Grab whatever of this shit you need and then we're leaving. Logan, give me the bottle."

The older detective held the scotch out at arm's length. Ryder made a swatting grab for it, which went wide. Blake shook his head and headed for the bathroom to dump it.

Ryder stood still for a moment, trying to get the room to stop spinning, then grabbed what folders he thought he would need from the table. "You ratted me out, you asshole," he spat at his former partner, who was leaning against the wall and grinning.

"Yup. You needed it."

"Fuck you."

"Eh, I don't swing that way, buddy. We've had this talk before when you've been hammered. Several times."

"I don't need a goddamned babysitter."

"No, you need a shower, a change of clothes, and a strong cup of coffee. And you need your partner."

Blake took that moment to show up in the doorway. "Let's go, asshole. Car's waiting downstairs," he said, motioning out the door.

Gabriel growled in his throat as he staggered out of the interview room toward the elevators.

Logan came up behind Nolan and slapped him on the back. "You may just have what it takes to keep that boy in line after all, Blake."

"Dear God, man, I hope so. I don't know how much more of this case I can take."

43

COMING BACK TO work had been a horrible idea.

She was fourteen hours in, and for the first time in a very long time, all Grayson wanted to do was go back home, curl up in her bed, and forget she was a doctor.

She'd snuck into the building easily enough, but the second one of the ICU nurses had recognized her, all hell had broken loose. Everyone wanted to know how she was, who had attacked her, and if it had anything to do with Greg Harlan's murder. His name had finally been released to the press the day after Thanksgiving, and the hospital had been awash with gossip ever since. Only this time, there was someone alive that the gossiping masses could get answers from.

She was lost in the swarm of multicolored scrubs and shrill voices until Linda grabbed her out and told her bloodthirsty coworkers to shove it.

She's a saint.

Adams had clearly not been sleeping. The poor kid had jumped to his feet and started stumbling over some kind of awkward apology when she'd walked through the door for rounds. She'd hugged him fiercely, thanked him for finding her, and put an end to the rest of it.

Breathe, breathe, breathe. Calm down. Just keep your head down and get through the day.

By 6 p.m., she was starving. Despite having three fractured hips waiting in the ER, she called time and went with Adams to the cafeteria. She got something simple, a small soup and salad. After all the food at Thanksgiving, she needed a break from anything heavy or loaded with cheese. They ate at a quick pace, but even so, the familiar whirring of the trauma helicopter started before they were even halfway finished. Adams' pager went off not a minute later.

"Ugh! You have got to be kidding me," he groaned, grabbing it from its holster and reading off the screen. "Trauma, level one. Twenty-year-old MVC. GCS 5. Intubated. Polyextremity. Wide mediastinum. Oh, that's good. Nice way to start the evening."

"All right, let's go," she said, standing up from her chair, her dinner barely touched.

"Oh, please. Sit down, Carter. They're not gonna even let me do anything for a good ten minutes if he's that bad," Adams said, grabbing his cheeseburger with one hand. "Besides, I can eat this on the run. Soup and salad? Not so much. I'll see you when you're done and I'll page if it really looks like a disaster."

"Okay. If you're sure…"

"Yeah, I'm sure. Don't worry about it. See ya in a few," he said.

Or at least, the last sentence was what she thought he said. He had a cheeseburger stuffed into his mouth and she couldn't quite tell.

It was a minute or so later when she looked over toward his vacated seat and noticed he'd left his pager sitting on the table. She grabbed it and was about to put it into her coat pocket when someone stepped up beside her. She assumed Adams had come back for it. She looked up with a smirk on her face, attempting to hide the pager under the table.

Dr. Cain was hovering over her, his green eyes focused directly on her, not saying anything. She jumped in her chair.

"Oh! Dr. Cain! I'm sorry, I thought you were Adams. He forgot his pager," she said lamely, bringing the little black box up from her lap and holding it out for him to see.

"Dr. Carter. Good evening," he said, slightly bowing to her. "May I join you?"

"Oh, um, sure? Help yourself."

He gracefully folded his six-foot frame into the seat that Adams had vacated, the one right next to her, and regarded her coolly.

Seriously? There are seven other chairs at this table, Cain.

"You are back at work already?" he asked, taking the lid off his dinner. Salmon. Mashed potatoes. Asparagus.

Wait, does our cafeteria even serve that stuff?

"Yes, they finally gave in and let me come back after the holiday."

"Quite soon after your ordeal. You should be resting."

"Um, I feel fine. A little sore in the ribs, but that will go away. I can manage a service by now. But thank you for the concern."

He started cutting up his dinner into fine, independent little cubes, all the exact same size. He set his plastic cutlery down when he was finished and looked at her over tented fingers.

"There are no other ill effects remaining after your attack?"

"Um, no."

"The bruises. They have faded?"

Grayson instantly sent a hand up to encircle her neck. "Mostly."

"That was a terrible thing that happened to you, my dear. No one so pretty should ever have to have some sadist's hands wrapped around her throat."

Grayson didn't know how to respond to that. Was "thank you" appropriate? She stayed quiet.

"It would have been even worse, would it not, to have to come back to work every day and see him, knowing what he did to you?"

Grayson cleared her throat. "I can imagine that being unpleasant."

"Still. Now it is assured."

"What's that?" she asked, inching away from him as best she could while still staying in her chair. *Dear God, Adams, page me so I can get the heck out of here.*

"Your protection, my dear. A sadist can't hurt anyone when he's dead." He said it coldly. Smoothly. Like it was something he was proud of.

"I would have preferred a disciplinary hearing. Or a police record."

"It doesn't matter now. What was done has resulted in your safety."

"What was done is considered murder, Dr. Cain."

"From a certain point of view."

She wrinkled her forehead at him. The hair on the back of her neck was at full attention. Grayson decided it was time to leave. "If you'll excuse me," she said, standing, "I have a trauma patient to see and a pager to return. Enjoy your dinner, Dr. Cain."

"Good evening, Beatrice," he said, looking right at her and not giving a damn about his fish.

She cocked her head to one side and was alternating between correcting him and just leaving the damned room when he kept talking.

"Aparet autem mea beautido," he said softly, still looking at her.

She backed out of the room and jogged out of the cafeteria.

What is his deal? First, he's the smartest guy in the hospital and now he can't keep my name straight or speak English? I have no idea what he just said.

She shook her head.

Cain's weird.

44

TWO HOURS LATER, Grayson had extracted herself from the emergency room and made her way up to the ICU to see a consult for Noah's team. By some blessing, he was also on call tonight. Knowing she could call him if she truly lost it had been a nice safety blanket.

There wasn't much to do for his patient, unfortunately. He'd been an active guy once, according to his chart, but years of drug abuse, followed by a bullet to the spine courtesy of his unpaid dealer, had aged him quickly. His liver was failing. His lungs refused to work properly after all of his infections. And his legs were covered in ulcers. How he'd managed to even live with the smell was beyond her.

Grayson had done what she could for him with dressings and wraps to the wounds, but ultimately, he was going to need to lose his legs…if he ever got healthy enough to tolerate the surgery. And things weren't particularly looking good at the moment.

She was finishing the last few lines of her note when she felt someone walk up behind her. "Any questions about our plan with him, Mike?" she asked, assuming it was the night nurse.

"You would have to ask Mike that question, my dear. But I have a few," came the cool reply.

Grayson's spine instantly stiffened. "Dr. Cain." She nodded in greeting as he circled around to her left side. "This is your patient?"

"Yes, he is. But I'm not interested in your opinion of him just now. I can read the consult form later."

"Then how can I help you?" she asked, trying to keep her voice steady.

He leaned closer to her, resting against the wall. "Tell me, how did it feel to have the boy look after you when you were here?"

"The boy?" She narrowed her eyes.

"Yes, young Dr. Mason. He was flustered when they brought you up to us."

"I don't think he would be pleased with being called 'the boy,' Dr. Cain. He isn't one. And I can understand why he was upset. If someone tried to choke the life out of him and he came up here with a line in his neck and a tube down his throat, I'd be climbing the walls. What does that have to do with…?"

"And poor Dr. Keefer. So far beyond his prime."

"I wouldn't say…wait, what?"

"Of course not. Because you are young and kind and care for others. But not to worry. I made sure you were taken care of."

"You did?" she asked incredulously.

"Of course. No one else could've done it properly."

"I was on Dr. Keefer's service, Dr. Cain. There was no reason, and you had no right, to interfere with my care."

"Not interfere, my dear. Just watch. And double check." He shrugged. "And improve."

What the hell? "Dr. Cain, I…"

"I would not entrust your care to an inferior, my dear. You are too precious," he said, his green eyes sparkling intently at her.

"You talk like I'm some kind of valuable commodity," she said, trying to lighten the exceedingly creepy mood that had descended over the ICU.

He smiled at her. "Valuable, yes. In a way. Commodity? Absolutely not."

"Dr. Cain, I should be getting back to my patients," she said, folding the chart closed, her note unfinished, and turning away from him.

"Of course." He nodded. "Ever the calling of the injured. Just be careful. Your safety is not guaranteed."

"What?" she asked, turning to face him head-on.

He leisurely pushed off the counter and strolled past her, leaning toward her as he passed by her ear. "Not yet."

By the time Grayson had regained her ability to breathe, he was gone.

45

NOLAN GRABBED HIS beer bottle off the coffee table and drained it. They were getting nowhere, and even he was beginning to become annoyed.

They'd left the squad room with a very drunk Gabriel Ryder hours ago. They'd taken the shortest route back to his apartment, thrown him into the shower, and gotten some decent food in him.

Granted, decent to him and Logan meant a cheeseburger and fries, but hey, whatever would help soak up the alcohol. Gabriel had fought them and complained the whole time, but neither he nor Harrison had been in the mood for any more of his bullshit.

Blake stood up and walked into the kitchen, grabbing another two bottles out of the fridge. He popped the caps off and took a long drink from one. As he walked back into the living room, he handed the other bottle over to Logan, who nodded his thanks and took a long drink himself.

"Well, it's almost midnight," he said, flopping down into his chair.

"Yup."

"Think he's gonna be right?"

"Oh, probably. He usually is."

"He's a pain in the ass."

"Yup." Harrison smiled as he took another long swig from the bottle.

"Think we're being a bit hypocritical here?" Nolan asked, holding up the beer bottle.

"Nah. This is a proper way to spend a Saturday night. He's the one that went face-first into a bottle of scotch."

"Still."

"Don't worry about it."

Nolan grabbed one of the files from the table and scanned his partner's notes that were paper clipped on top of it. "This has to be driving him nuts."

"Worse than that, buddy. This is starting to kill him. He's not eating. He's drinking, worse than I've ever seen. He's not sleeping. We both know he can't do this forever."

"Well, what am I supposed to do about it?"

"This is it."

Harrison pointed over to the couch where Ryder was asleep, his back to the room. "There gets to be a point where nothing you say or do is going to solve the case and it's all up to him. That's usually when it gets like this. You've got to be the one to put your foot down and call him on his bullshit. It was the same way when he was my partner in narcotics. Sometimes, you just have to get him to shut off for a few hours. Most of the time, it's by force."

"Great. I have a career of this ahead of me." Nolan rolled his eyes.

"Give him some room, Blake. Coping skills were not learned well in the Ryder household."

"They weren't learned in the Nolan household, either."

"Heh," Logan grinned.

He was about to take another swig from his beer when he jumped slightly in his chair. Blake registered the low hum of a vibrating cell phone. Logan pulled it out of his pocket and wrinkled his forehead.

"Who is it?"

Logan didn't answer but stood and walked over toward the windows. Blake could at least still hear his muffled side of the conversation.

"Yeah, Logan…well, isn't this a surprise…no…doesn't ring a bell…no…no…wait, you did *what*…Goddamn it…yeah, yeah, okay. I'll be there. Give me fifteen minutes." He shut off his phone and shoved it back into his pocket.

"What was that?"

Harrison shook his head. "Nothing. Look, I've gotta run out for a few minutes. Think you can keep an eye on Sleeping Beauty for me?"

"Yeah, sure, but…"

"Just keep him here, okay? And make sure when he wakes up, he doesn't put his head right back into that bottle."

"All right."

Logan grabbed his coat from the coat rack and threw it on, collecting his car keys from the counter. "Just. Stay. Here," he said as he walked out of the apartment.

Blake watched him leave and took another swig from his almost-drained bottle. *What the hell was that about?*

He turned back in his chair, preparing to take a little catnap himself, and ended up looking right into a pair of very angry blue eyes.

Aw, fuck…

46

NOAH SLID HIS badge into the door lock and quickly threw himself into the pitch-black hallway.

This was ludicrous. This was nuts. She'd come back to work too soon. They were going to get caught, lose their jobs, and end up doing physicals at some free clinic somewhere. If they were lucky.

But here he was, in the middle of his call shift with a few precious minutes to put his head down on a shitty call room pillow, breaking into the department because his best friend had asked him to. He was an idiot. A bona fide idiot.

The light was minimal, with only small streaks of starlight coming in through the slits in the blinds. But it was enough to see her waiting for him.

Noah quickly loped down to her. He opened his mouth to try to tell her he was having major second thoughts when she grabbed his badge, swiped it through the door lock, and pushed him through the door. She gently shut it behind them as he flipped on his phone to provide some light.

"Gray," he hissed as loudly as he dared to. "What the hell?"

"Thanks," she said, handing his badge back to him and beelined toward a file cabinet in the back of the room.

"We really shouldn't be in here. We'll lose our jobs."

"Just tell them I had a psychotic break and forced you into it," she said, dropping down on her heels so she was face-to-face with the third drawer.

"Right, like anybody's going to buy that," he said, rolling his eyes. He crouched down beside her. "What are we looking for?"

"Employee records. The sealed ones. They're in here." She gently tested the drawer by pulling on the handle. It was locked.

"They do lock cabinets around here, love."

"Where are the keys?"

Noah reached into his pocket and pulled out a pair of small silver keys, dangling them in front of her.

"Thanks," she said, grabbing them from him and opening up the lock. She didn't have time to ask where they came from or how he'd gotten them.

It was actually simple. Dr. Sanders' secretary kept them in a small dish on her desk. No one knew what they were for, so she didn't feel the need to lock them up when she left for the day. And every medicine resident had access to Dr. Sanders' office after hours because of his extensive library…so they all had access to her desk.

His well-known open-door policy. Noah grinned to himself. Shelly was not the smartest secretary.

Grayson quickly located the file she was looking for, opening it on the floor.

"What are you…whose is that?" Noah whispered. He looked at the photo in the front jacket of the file. "Seriously?"

She nodded and started flipping through pages.

"What's got you all riled all of a sudden?"

"I don't know. A feeling."

"You're risking your job on a feeling, Gray?"

She shrugged.

"What are you going to do with this now that you have it?"

She looked up wildly around the room. "I need…I need to copy it."

"What? Why?"

"I can't take the real one out of here, Noah," she hissed, walking over toward the copier that was sitting by the far wall.

"Shite," Noah swore under his breath as he followed her. He grabbed the file from her and straightened the two metal prongs at the top, pulling the large stack of papers out all at once.

"We're doing this quickly," he said, shoving the stack into the copier and punching the green copy button.

The machine whirred to life and started sucking the pieces one by one into itself.

"Shit, Noah, they're double sided!" She pointed at the papers.

"Geez, five years in this place and you haven't figured out how to make the copier do two-sided pages?" he chided.

He repeated the same with the other side of the file, and in five minutes they had the original safely back in the locked file cabinet. She went with him to put the keys back in Dr. Sanders' office, then followed him back to the main hospital, the paperwork hidden underneath her white coat.

Noah guided her up to the medicine call rooms and shoved her into his without hesitating. "All right, now what the hell is going on?" he asked once his door was shut and locked behind them.

Grayson sat down on the pathetic excuse for a bed and wrapped her arms around her knees. "I think the cops should look at Cain."

"Cain. Seriously? Why? He's harmless." Noah raised his eyebrows and sat next to her on the bed. "Honey, we all know that one has too many bats flying around in his belfry. He's strange, but he's a bookworm."

"I don't know. He said some pretty weird stuff tonight."

"Weirder than usual?"

She nodded.

"Maybe he's sleep deprived."

She started to protest but yeah, on the one hand, that did make sense. On the other… "That shouldn't be for me to decide."

"Can't they come talk to him without all this?" He grabbed the paperwork she'd placed between them and waved it in front of her face.

"I...I don't know."

"Gray..." he cooed softly, throwing an arm over her shoulder and running a reassuring hand up and down her right arm. "You came back too soon. Everything's still fresh. It's okay. Stay up here tonight. Let Adams do his thing. He can handle it. And get out of here early tomorrow. Tell them you need more time."

"I don't need more time."

"Love..."

"Don't 'love' me right now, Mason," she spat, standing up and walking to the tiny window. "There's something wrong with Cain. I can't put my finger on it. But he got to me tonight. A lot more than he usually does. And he called me Beatrice."

"Beatrice?"

"Yeah."

"Old girlfriend?" he smirked.

"I don't know."

"That's off. He knows every intern's name and face and GPA and Step One score before they start in July. He knows your name."

"Right."

Noah didn't understand why one little slip-up suddenly had Grayson so riled up. She clearly wasn't in the mood to explain to him any more than she needed to. Not right now.

"So, you've risked your career for this small tree here," he said, handing her the file. "Now what?"

"I need to make a phone call."

47

LOGAN PULLED THE collar of his overcoat up around his neck and swore against the biting storm.

Goddamn it, it's freezing out here.

The wind kicked up, relentlessly slamming snow into his face. He blew into his hands and rubbed them together briskly to get them warm. "Why couldn't we meet at a bar like normal people?" he muttered to himself.

Two minutes. He was giving her another two minutes and then he was getting the hell out of here. Or at least telling her their meeting venue had changed. He had his cell phone halfway out of his pocket when he saw a small figure in a black coat cross Colfax and walk toward the northeast corner of the capitol building lawn. When it passed under the streetlight, Logan knew it was her. Scrub pants and long, brown hair. It couldn't be anybody but her.

He met her halfway between the street and the capitol building wall where he'd been leaning. "Well, doc," he drawled, "You couldn't have picked a nicer night for a meeting outside."

"Hi, Logan. You're blaming me for the weather now?"

"Nah. But maybe next time, let's meet inside, okay?"

"I didn't want to give you this in the middle of Applebee's," she said, opening her coat and pulling out a manila envelope.

Logan stepped up close enough so she could pass it to him without anyone noticing, including the security cameras on the Capitol building. He tucked it safely away underneath his coat. "What did you do?"

Grayson avoided looking at him and instead glanced around the park to keep her eyes occupied. "I think you should be looking at one of the attendings. Douglas Cain."

"I told you on the phone. He wasn't on the list of names we got. We cleared all the intensivists that were in-house the night you were attacked. Name doesn't ring a bell."

"Well, it needs to."

"What happened?"

"Nothing dramatic," she said, shaking her head. "He's always creeped me out a little bit, but since I've been back to work, it's gone up. Several notches."

"I can't get an arrest warrant on somebody because they're creepy, doc."

Grayson scowled at him through the snow. "Look, he just started talking about Harlan. Like he was happy he was dead. He said it ensured I was protected."

"Really?" That piqued Logan's interest.

"And he said he watched over me when I was in the hospital. I wasn't on his service, Logan. There was no reason for him to even know I was admitted. He wasn't on call that weekend. He shouldn't have been in the hospital. He started talking about how my safety wasn't guaranteed yet. Even the way he looked at me…it really freaked me out."

"So what is this I'm hiding under my coat?"

"His personnel file. Well, a copy of it."

"And you got this how, exactly?"

"It just…I…I found it," she said evasively.

Logan nodded. "You could lose your job for this."

"I know."

"Why risk it? What's in here?"

Grayson rubbed her hands violently up and down her arms, scattering snowflakes wide. It was really getting cold. "Cain has a sealed personnel file. He has for a couple of years. It means there was some kind of complaint filed against him."

"So, he got sued?"

Grayson fidgeted from one foot to the next, constantly moving against the cold creeping through her scrubs. "No. Lawsuits are part of the public record. Personal complaint. Harassment. Something like that. He's the golden boy of the hospital, so whatever it was got shoved under the rug. But all of the records are there, including a psych eval."

"You read through this already?"

"No. Not really. I recognized one of the forms. It's a standard part of a generic psych battery. All those forms are pink."

"We can't use this as evidence."

"I know that. But if it somehow puts the pieces together…"

They stood in silence for a few minutes, the snow whipping around them in circles. Logan eyed her, his curiosity finally getting the best of him. "All right. So here's my next question. Why call me?"

"Who should I have called?" she asked, staring at the snow-covered concrete.

"I can think of one other detective who probably should be higher on your call list than me."

"He wouldn't approve."

"And I do?"

"Don't you?"

Logan smiled. "Touché, doc."

"Look, just tell him…I don't know. Something. Anything."

"I'll come up with something."

"Thanks."

Logan grinned, but concern quickly washed over his face. "Hey, you okay? You're shaking."

"Oh, yeah. I just…something just popped into my head. Something Cain said to me tonight. It just gave me the chills."

"What's that?"

"He called me precious."

Logan's eyebrows rose. He opened his mouth, ready to say something smart.

A deep, hoarse, threatening voice bellowed menacingly from the shadows of the capitol building. "He called you *what*?"

Harrison recognized the tone and shut his eyes. *Shit.*

Grayson's eyes widened in horror when she looked over Logan's right shoulder. "Gabriel…" she whispered.

He stalked out of the shadows, his eyes blazing at the both of them. Logan knew that look. He was stone-cold sober and furious. Logan had only seen it twice before, and both times things had not ended well. For Ryder or their perp.

He registered Nolan sheepishly standing over by a lamppost.

Damn it. He wasn't asleep when I left. Fucker played us.

Ryder had probably been awake in the apartment the whole time, just listening to them gab like biddies at a beauty parlor. He'd strong-armed Nolan into following him.

Shit.

———

Ryder barreled past Logan, grabbed Grayson by both shoulders, and violently spun her around toward the park.

"Hey, Gabe, easy," Logan started in, trying to put himself between the two of them.

"Back off, Logan," he spat.

Logan shot a look of apology toward Grayson and got one from her in return.

Ryder didn't notice. He was focused on the frightened woman in front of him, completely oblivious to the fact that he was the thing she was so afraid of. "What the hell did you do?" he asked, the venom dripping from his voice.

"Wh...what are you doing here?" she stammered. Grayson had never seen anyone this angry.

Why is he here? I called Logan, not him. Why is he here?

"Answer me, goddamn it!"

"I...I...I..." She couldn't remember how to speak. All she could do was focus on the fire behind those blue eyes. All that rage. All that venom. It was directed at her. Focused on her. Her breathing hitched. She couldn't get enough air. It was paralyzing.

Ryder turned his head toward his former partner. "Give me the file."

"No."

"I'm not asking."

"Don't care. Same answer."

Ryder's fingers dug into Grayson's arms. She winced but refused to cry out.

Nolan and Logan both took steps toward them. "All right, all right. Take your hands off her and I'll hand it over. Although I'd rather not in front of the cameras," he said, motioning up to the corners of the capitol building.

Ryder kept glaring at him, incrementally tightening his hold. From out of nowhere, Nolan ran forward and threw his body weight into his partner. Ryder stumbled sideways, breaking his grip on her arms. He looked back at his partner, foaming at the mouth and ready to fight back.

"Fuck you, asshole, you're hurting her!" Blake hollered.

Something clicked. Ryder shook his head, resetting. The fire in his eyes vanished. The aggression in his shoulders died. In an instant, he changed into a different person entirely.

Grayson had her arms wrapped protectively around her waist. She was desperately trying to bury herself inside her coat. Her breathing was shallow and fast. She was shaking, and not from the cold. As hard as she tried, she couldn't keep the fear off of her face. At that moment, she was completely and utterly scared to death of him.

Ryder took a step toward her and she skittered backward toward Logan. He tried again, the begging evident in his gaze. He was trying to apologize to her with one long, pleading stare.

She took another step back. *I can't…*

Logan shook his head and put his hand up. "Stay put, Ryder."

Grayson kept shaking. "I…I need to get back to the hospital," she whispered.

"I'll walk you back to your car," Harrison said, stepping up behind her and putting a hand on her shoulder. "Nolan, take his ass home and this time, keep it there."

Blake nodded in agreement.

Logan started to walk forward, wrapping his arm protectively around the young doctor's shoulder. She didn't move. He tried again, firmer pressure this time, and she didn't budge. He turned his gaze sideways to look at her, smirking.

"Hey, doc, we can go now if you…" The smirk dropped off his face.

She was white. Pale-as-snow white. Her arms had dropped loosely to her sides and she was breathing even faster. Her eyes were focused straight out in front of her. Not at Gabriel, but beyond him.

Logan hesitantly followed her line of sight.

A hunched-over figure was lurching through the park, head down and breathing hard, from the look of the steam coming from its mouth. At first, Logan thought it was one of the drunken bums that were known to hang around the capitol building, but the guy wasn't dressed like one. He was in work clothes. Stained work clothes. And he wasn't veering around like a drunk. He was limping.

"Guys..." Nolan's hand drifted to the side of his hip where his sidearm was holstered.

The man heard Nolan's voice. He looked up and, seeing people, started heading straight toward them.

Logan stepped protectively in front of Grayson. Both Ryder and Blake stepped in on either side of her. Gabriel fought back a curse when Grayson backed away from him. He couldn't tell if she was more scared of the thing advancing toward them or of him.

The man was close now, stuttering in an attempt to say something. When he passed under the halo of light from the streetlight, Blake swore under his breath.

The man was clutching his side where a bright red stain was starting to make its way down toward his leg. He was pale and his eyes were glassed over.

"Hhh...help..." he managed to squeak out over the wailing of the storm.

That single, simple word snapped Grayson out of her catatonia.

She shook her head rapidly to clear the haze. The moment she registered the man in front of them as an injured patient instead of a threat, her instinct kicked in.

She shoved her way past Harrison. She grabbed the man underneath his right arm, and he collapsed part of his weight onto her.

Grayson quickly but awkwardly worked her way out of her coat, threw it on the ground, and then lowered the man on top of it. She ripped the shirt apart and was instantly met with a gush of blood and air. Droplets splattered over her neck and chest, running down her shirt.

Grayson slammed both of her hands back onto the spot, blood-soaked pieces of fabric pressed in between her skin and his. She looked up at Logan. "Goddamn it, don't just stand there. Call for a bus! He's been stabbed in the chest!"

Logan yanked his cell phone out of his pocket, motioning for Ryder to keep his spot on the pavement.

Blake ran over and knelt down beside her. "What…what do you want me to do?"

"Just keep holding pressure here," she said, exchanging her hands with his. "Don't let go, or he's going to bleed out."

She ran her hands through the snow to get some of the blood off and dried them on her scrub pants. She shifted her attention up toward the man's face. He was conscious, but barely.

Harrison was in the background, gruffly telling whoever he was talking to hurry the hell up already. Grayson opened her mouth, intending to ask the man who he was and what happened, but his hand shot out and grabbed hers before she could react. She looked at his face, momentarily shocked in place. He was using all of his strength to stay conscious and make a point, so she shut her mouth and leaned closer.

"Hhh……hhelp……" he said softly, a faint gurgling audible at the end of each gasping breath.

He's drowning in his own blood. Fuck!

The man took a few more ragged breaths, then tried again. "Hhhelpp……ch……churchhhh……"

Grayson narrowed her eyes. She'd barely heard him over the whipping wind around them. The man released his hold on her arm and closed his eyes, overwhelmed by the pain and the blood pooling in his lungs. She could feel the seconds pass…*one, two, three…click, click, click…*

Grayson felt her body freeze, and it had nothing to do with the subfreezing temperature or her lack of a coat. Her eyes shot up across the street. Sure enough, there were two identical white spires visible among the buildings just to the east, intermittently obscured by the swirling snow.

No…

Realization came crashing down, hard. Her heart rate sped up. She could feel it hammering mercilessly against her chest.

Grayson looked at her watch. It read 12:17 a.m.

"No," she whispered, staring down at the clock face.

Blake quirked his eyes at her, thinking she was talking to him. "Doc?"

She started shaking her head rhythmically, over and over.

"You okay?"

Faint ambulance sirens could be heard in the distance, growing louder, headed their way. Harrison was still on the phone, calling in for squad cars and the crime scene techs.

Grayson hardly registered his voice. All she could hear was the blood rushing to her head and the thumping of her heartbeat. She stood up, shakily, as Logan shut off his phone.

"Okay, bus is on the way and……doc?"

She was staring off across the street, but there wasn't anybody there.

"Hey, doc?" Logan tried again, stepping forward.

Nothing.

"Grayson?" Gabriel stepped forward, his voice guarded.

She turned to look at him.

One part of her wanted to attack him. Scream at him. Demand to know what in the hell his problem was. Another part of her was too scared of the consequences of doing just that. The third part, the part that won, knew she had other things to deal with right now.

Gabriel opened his mouth to call to her again, but faster than anyone would ever have given her credit for, Grayson spun around and took off across the lawn, aiming for the main road.

"What the hell...?" Blake started.

"Grayson!" Gabriel shouted after her into the snow.

She heard him. She didn't stop.

Behind her, the trio tried to track where she was headed. When Gabriel saw the spires in the air, he took off after her, calling out her name, begging her to stop.

"Oh, fuck!" Harrison swore, making the connection. "Nolan, stay with him. Call when you have a hospital," he said as the ambulance came into view.

"Wait, what? Where the hell are you going?" Blake called, covered in blood and crouched helplessly in the snow.

"After them!" Harrison called back.

"Why?"

"He was right!" came the echoing reply.

48

GRAYSON CHARGED HEADFIRST through the snow. Her lungs were burning in protest. She wasn't a runner in any sense, but right now it didn't matter. The adrenaline coursing through her system was more than making up for any cardiovascular shortcomings.

The church. He said the church. Get to the church!

She kept repeating it over and over in her head.

She pushed her way past the few partygoers on Colfax brave enough to be out in this weather, their high heels slipping and sliding on patches of ice. Her scrub pants were soaking wet with a mixture of blood and melting snow. Her socks were fully drenched. It was cold enough with the wind that they were starting to freeze solid. She was losing the feeling in the tips of her toes.

Someone was screaming her name, telling her to stop and wait. She ignored it. She ran harder.

There were lights on inside the church. Soft colors from the stained-glass windows were floating down with the snow onto the waiting ground.

Grayson took the front steps two at a time. She slipped and lost her balance halfway up, slamming down on the stone steps. She swore and pushed herself back up, biting her lips against the gravel digging into her palms.

She slammed her side into one of the great doors and it gave way, groaning under the strain of the hit. Her still-healing ribs screamed in protest.

She looked around the entryway wildly and saw a trail of blood smeared on the floor, heading from the chapel to the front door. She followed it with her eyes down the front steps.

That man. He was stabbed here...

Grayson bolted into the chapel. There were candles lit at the altar, four on each side.

Lying sprawled out on top of the altar itself was a man, blood dripping from his hands and his face.

She ran forward. The slapping of her wet sneakers echoed off the stone walls.

She got within twenty feet of the altar before she recognized him. She stopped dead in her tracks.

"Nathan?" she called out.

The young neurosurgery resident didn't move. Didn't groan. Didn't take a breath. There was just the sound of the slow *drip, drip, drip* of blood from his fingertips onto the marble floor.

"Nathan!" she called out louder, starting toward him again.

Grayson got within five feet of the body before strong arms grabbed her around the waist and violently hoisted her backward off of the floor.

She shrieked and struggled against the hold, flailing wildly and hitting air.

No! No! Not again!

"Put me down! Let me go!" she screamed, her voice echoing off the stone walls.

Her arms were trapped at her sides. She was losing strength, fast. She could feel it. If she didn't get out soon...

He found me. I have to get out! I have to get away...

"Grayson, stop!" A familiar voice hissed in her ear. Her eyes snapped open at the feeling of his hot breath on her neck, but she didn't stop struggling against him.

"Put me down!" she protested, her strength weakening. "It's Nathan! Put me down! Let me go!"

She repeated it over and over. With each breath, it became more of a plea than a command.

Grayson didn't take her eyes off of the altar, and Gabriel didn't let her down. She was barely mumbling by the time Logan jogged past them and up to the altar, checking for a pulse on the victim's neck.

"Please, Gabriel…" she whimpered. "Please, let me go…"

Grayson's head lolled to one side. Exhaustion was taking over, the rush of adrenaline rapidly crashing out of her system.

Carefully, Ryder turned her in his arms. He grabbed her chin with one hand, tipping her face up to his. He kept his other arm firmly wrapped around her waist, holding her off the floor.

Her eyes were glazed over. She was whimpering, soaked to the bone, and shivering. Her hair was damp and plastered to her forehead, melting snow mixed with cold sweat.

He raised the hand that had been under her chin to brush the hair away from her eyes.

Grayson let out a strangled cry and threw her arms around his neck, burying her face in his coat. She started sobbing, hard.

Gabriel wrapped both his arms around her and just let her cry, whispering words of comfort in her ear. Nothing helped. She had completely lost control.

When she didn't calm down, Gabriel moved them both into one of the pews. He sat down and pulled her into his lap. She kept her arms around his neck as he shushed her and rocked her back and forth.

Sirens could be heard coming down Colfax.

Logan came over to them and spoke briefly to Gabriel.

Grayson didn't register anything he said. She was only aware of the low, soothing tone of Gabriel's voice. She felt something heavy and warm drape across her shoulders. She quickly buried herself underneath it.

Harrison gave his former partner a sympathetic look and then went toward the front door to greet the squad cars, with just a T-shirt to guard against the cold.

49

GABRIEL SAT WITH Grayson wrapped in his arms as the squad cars arrived and the crime techs descended on the cathedral. She kept herself folded safely inside of Logan's coat.

She had calmed herself down enough by the time the first officers walked into the chapel to look respectable, but Gabriel could still feel her shaking in his arms. She no longer wailed against his shoulder. Her tears had turned silent.

"Shhh, Grayson," he kept whispering in her ear.

Each time, he was met with a small whimper and her nose nuzzling into his neck.

"Hey, hey, come on. Look at me," he said after a time, pulling her face up so he could look at her. He tried putting a smile on his face, but it fell when he saw how pale and drawn she looked. He sighed, running his fingers over her face. "We need to get you home."

He made a move to stand, gathering her in his arms, and she instantly tightened her hold around her neck. She mumbled something that he couldn't hear.

He dipped his face closer to hers. "What?"

"I have to go to the hospital."

His stomach dropped. "What? Are you hurt?" Gabriel panicked, lifting the coat up to try to get a better look at her. His eyes darkened as he examined her for the slightest scratch.

"No," she croaked, "I have to go back to work."

"Absolutely not."

"But…"

"No," he whispered. Under normal circumstances, he would have raised his voice. Fought with her. Argued with her. Right now, all he could think to do was be gentle with her. "We've notified the hospital. They know."

That was a lie. He didn't care. They'd take care of it later.

Logan appeared by the side of the pew. "Just got off the phone with Nolan," he said quietly. "That guy in the park was one of the custodians of the church. He was here doing some maintenance work. Probably going to plow out around the building with the snow, according to his wife. Liked working at night. He took a knife to the lung. Did a lot of damage. They don't know if he's going to last the night. He's still in surgery."

"Okay."

He felt Grayson start to shake again and looked down worriedly at the top of her head nestled against his chest. "I need to get her home. She's in shock."

Logan fished in his pocket and grabbed his car keys. "My truck's around the corner. I'll get it. Bring her out the side entrance and I'll meet you. Take her home in that."

"But..."

"I'll have a uniform drop me off at your apartment when we're done here." He waved away the concern. "Won't be the first time."

Gabriel nodded. While Harrison brought his truck around, he carried Grayson down one of the side hallways. He kept her hidden in the shadows of the side entrance until Logan pulled up next to the sidewalk. He gently laid her in the passenger seat and pulled her seatbelt across her chest. He shucked out of his own winter coat and replaced Logan's with it.

"Here, you'll need this," he said, handing it back to its rightful owner.

"You could've let her keep it for now," he replied, throwing it over his shoulders.

"She should've had mine in the first place," he mumbled under his breath, pulling open the driver's side door.

"I think you'll be forgiven."

"For that, or for the rest of my bullshit?"

"Just get her home, Ryder. Worry about the other shit later."

Gabriel nodded and slid into the driver's seat.

Logan hit the top of the car twice to indicate he was good to go, and he watched him drive off into the snowstorm. Once he couldn't see the taillights anymore, he headed back inside to deal with their latest bloodbath.

50

GABRIEL PULLED UP in front of the bungalow shortly after two a.m. The lights were out. The snow was still falling heavily, but at least the wind had eased up. It was actually quite peaceful watching it fall in the soft light of the street lamps.

Unfortunately, Gabriel was too worried about the young woman riding in the passenger seat to take any comfort in it. He pulled into a spot a few car lengths down the street from her front door and shut off the engine. She was staring out the window, just like she had for the entire ride home, with a blank look on her face that had him on edge.

"Grayson?" he whispered, reaching out to run his fingers through her hair.

She didn't respond. She didn't move. She didn't turn toward him. He wasn't surprised. He got out of the car and walked around to her door, opening it and unclipping her seatbelt. She nearly fell into his arms.

"Come on. You're home."

Slowly, Gabriel tried to guide Grayson down the sidewalk. She could barely support her own weight. It took all of three stumbling steps for him to growl in frustration and scoop her up into his arms.

He carried her the rest of the way to the porch. He kicked his shoes clean on the front step and tried the front door. It was locked. He ducked his mouth down toward her ear.

"Where are your keys?"

She mewled softly and tried to move in his arms. He put her feet down on the deck so she could stand, and shakily she withdrew her keychain from her back pocket.

He took it from her before she dropped it completely and unlocked the door. He kicked it open as he hoisted her back into his arms.

Ryder strode into the entryway, closed and locked the door with his free hand, and took stock of the dark living room as his eyes adjusted. Everything was still and quiet.

"Where's Barbara?"

"Ski weekend," she murmured.

"Oh." *Good.*

He turned on his heel and took her upstairs, shoving open the door to her room. She turned her head into his shoulder, hiding her eyes when he turned on the overhead light.

Too bright.

Gabriel immediately turned it off, instead turning on a lamp in the bedroom. He took her directly into the bathroom, letting the softer light filter in from the open doorway. He set her down on the closed toilet seat.

After he was sure she was steady on her own, he turned on the hot water in her claw-foot bathtub. He methodically adjusted the knobs until the water coming out of the faucet was the perfect temperature and then opened up the cupboard below her sink.

"What are you doing?" she asked. Her voice was hoarse. Flat. Hollow. Inhuman.

That's not her voice.

"Bubble bath."

"What?"

"Do you have any?"

She nodded. "In the back. But…"

He pulled the bottle out of its hiding place in the back corner and quickly looked over the label. Lavender and black orchid. Subtle and calming. Something that would help her sleep.

Perfect.

He poured some into the hot water, directly under the faucet, then turned his attention back to Grayson. She hadn't moved. Her shoulders were slumped. Her arms were wrapped around her waist.

She's still shaking.

"Come on. You need to get out of those clothes. We need to get you warm."

She didn't move.

Gabriel sighed and started with her scrub top, removing it to reveal a soaked undershirt beneath. He took off her shoes and then her socks, tossing them aside. He took her pager and her cell phone clips off of her waistband, turning both machines on silent before he set them down on the edge of the sink.

What to do next presented much more of a challenge. The most rapid plan involved taking the rest of her clothes off himself and lowering her into the bathtub, but he wasn't about to violate her privacy. That would only open up a whole new can of worms he wasn't ready to face. She was going to have to help herself a bit.

Gabriel knelt in front of her and tapped the bottom of her chin so she would raise her eyes to look at him. She did. Her eyes were completely glazed over. There was no life in them.

"You need to get in the bath. Can you manage to step in on your own?"

It took her a moment, but she nodded.

"Okay. Where are your pajamas?"

"Top right drawer," she croaked.

"Okay. I'll get you something to wear." He kissed the top of her head gently as he stood. "Get in the bath, sweetheart."

Ryder waited by the door until he saw her grasp the ties of her scrub pants, then pulled it partially closed behind him—closed enough to give her privacy but open enough to leave light for her to see by.

He opened the top drawer and took a quick look through her things. He made his choice and walked back to the bathroom door. He didn't hear much on the other side. The faucet had been shut off. Everything was quiet.

He knocked softly. "Grayson? Can I…are you…" He was suddenly tongue-tied. *How should I ask this?*

He heard a small splash of water and a soft sigh, but nothing more. Gabriel pushed the door open, slowly, ready to retreat if there was even the slightest hint of indecency. There was none.

Grayson was submerged in her tub, bubbles billowing over the sides. She'd already dunked her head in the water. Her hair was straight and wet and glued to the back of her neck. Her eyes were closed and she was breathing steadily. When the door squeaked on its hinges, she turned to look at him.

She didn't react to him, didn't startle. She simply looked at him, then rested her head back on the edge. Gabriel set her clothes on the edge of the sink and sat down on the floor, facing her across the length of the tub.

"How do you feel?" he asked softly.

"Horrible," came the shaky response. "What just happened? What did I just…this, this isn't going to stop, is it?"

He didn't know exactly how to answer her. So, he didn't speak. He just let her talk.

"I froze. I'm a doctor. I know what to do. Why didn't I move? And Nathan…oh my God, Nathan…"

Gabriel could hear the grief and the guilt in her voice. The tears she was trying so very hard to control were still falling, causing little ripples to form beneath the bubbles.

"I saw his face. His eyes…someone cut out his eyes. He wasn't moving. What if I'd gotten there sooner? I could have helped him…I could have…could have…done…something…"

The last two words were lost in the middle of a gut-wrenching wail. Her hands flew up to her face.

Gabriel gave her a moment, then reached out and took one of her hands away from her eyes. He put it inside his own, resting them both on the edge of the tub.

"Nothing that happened tonight was your fault. Do you understand? The only reason the custodian had any chance is because of what you did. And what Blake did. There was nothing you could have done at the church. Look at me, Grayson," he said, tugging on her hand gently. "You have to let this go."

Her blue eyes were big and glassy and completely focused on him. "I don't know if I can do this anymore," she said, shaking.

"It will be all right." He managed a small smile for her. She didn't return it. "Are you warm now?"

She nodded.

"Good. Do you want me to leave you alone for a while?"

"No."

"Okay."

He sat beside her, holding her hand and gently running his thumb along the soft skin on the tops of her fingers. Eventually, she started shivering. He gently dropped their hands below the water's surface. It had cooled to the point of being uncomfortable.

"Time to get out," he said, standing and reaching for two large fluffy white towels from the rack on the wall.

He set them down on the toilet seat and stepped out of the bathroom, leaving her alone.

Gabriel waited for Grayson in her bedroom, and when she emerged a few minutes later, she found him perched on the edge of her bed. She was dressed in the clothes he'd left for her, navy silk pajama pants and an ivory lace camisole. Her hair was towel-dried and hanging well below her shoulders.

She stood in the doorway, waiting like she needed an invitation into her own room.

"Bedtime," he said simply, standing and pulling her comforter aside.

Grayson hesitantly walked by him and slid underneath the covers. Gabriel pulled the comforter as high as he could without fully covering her head, then leaned down and kissed her forehead.

"Go to sleep," he whispered, then turned to head toward the door.

"You're leaving."

It was a statement, not a question, and he wasn't even sure he'd really heard it. But when he turned back around, Ryder found Grayson sitting straight up in bed and shaking.

"You...you want me to stay?" After his behavior earlier, he'd been surprised she'd even let him take her home.

She nodded. "Please," she begged.

Gabriel shut her bedroom door, took off his shoes, socks, belt, and now-wet button down. Under different circumstances, he imagined his first time undressing in her room would have been received differently. His mind envisioned flushed skin, trembling limbs, and her bright blue eyes locked on every inch of him.

Instead, he turned to find her sitting with her arms wrapped around her waist and her gaze firmly rooted in her own lap.

He put his cell phone on the nightstand and stood by the edge of her bed. "Where do you want me?"

She pulled up the covers and slid over to one side of her bed.

"You're sure about this?" he hesitated.

"Please," she begged again.

He nodded and slid in beside her, resting his back against the headboard. Just as she had in the hospital, Grayson gravitated toward him and molded herself into his right side, her head on his lap, his arm wrapped around her back.

He laced his fingers into hers. He whispered to her in the darkness, and the low, smooth sound of his voice lulled her to sleep within minutes.

"Don't leave me," he heard her whisper.

He kissed her forehead and then the top of her hair. "I won't."

I am in so much trouble here.

51

"WELL, THIS IS a treasure trove of information, isn't it?"

Logan grinned over the rim of his cup of coffee. He and Nolan were at opposite ends of Gabriel's kitchen counter, the contents of the manila envelope spread out between them. They'd been looking it over for the last half hour.

"Yeah, it is. Too bad we can't use it."

"Can't use it officially, is what you mean."

Harrison pulled a few pieces of paper closer to him. "We can do whatever we want with it now as long as we destroy it."

"Yeah, I think that's on page sixteen of the official Denver PD handbook." Blake scowled.

"I'm getting sick of just chasing our tails with this shit. This helps."

"Sure. As long as we don't get caught with it."

The sound of a key turning in the front door lock had both men look up just in time to see Ryder walk into the apartment, his coat slung over his shoulder and looking more than worse for the wear.

"Well, look what the cat dragged in this mornin," Blake said, grinning. "Want some coffee?"

Nolan got a silent nod as an answer. He got up off his barstool and lumbered into the kitchen.

Ryder slid into the vacant barstool as Blake poured him a large cup. "So, how is she?" He looked up hesitantly at his partner.

"Asleep," he replied, taking a long drink.

"You just left her at home? Alone?" Logan balked.

"You think I'm that much of an idiot?"

"After yesterday…"

Blake expected a sarcastic comeback. All he got was an understanding nod.

"No, I didn't leave her alone. Her roommate came home from her ski weekend and kicked me out of the house. Grayson is asleep, and she has someone with her."

"Did she say anything, after you took her home?" Harrison asked gently.

"No. She was in shock. I barely got her cleaned up and in bed before she collapsed."

"Shit. That bad?"

He nodded. "Are you surprised after what she saw?"

"Sorry, man."

"Yeah, me, too."

Ryder took another long drink of coffee, then turned his focus to the piles of paper on his countertop. There was no point in telling them that he'd been up most of the night trying to keep her nightmares at bay, or that they were getting much, much worse.

"What did you find in the file?"

Harrison grinned at him from his barstool. "All kinds of fun things. Here are the highlights," he said, pushing a small pile over to him.

"In a nutshell, the good doctor might just be onto something here. Dr. Douglas Cain, thirty-four, originally from Connecticut. Away-from-home fancy prep schools followed by Yale under-grad, majors in biochemistry and Italian of all things, and medical school at the same institution. Residency training in Boston. I'll give you one guess which hoity-toity program he went to, then fellowship out on the west coast in California. Actively recruited to come to St. Joe's since he was such a rock star in Cali. And when he got here, he started getting himself into trouble."

Nolan pushed several more pieces of paper toward his partner, who started reading through each one while Harrison kept talking.

"There are complaints of yelling at nurses, being inappropriate, stalking at the hospital, you name it. There were at least five or six complaints filed early on by residents, all female, about personal conduct issues. But here's what's interesting. About two weeks before some big hearing, a lot of these complaints got dropped. The girls changed their stories and things changed in the file. Cain never actually went before a review committee, and it looks like he's been a good boy since then. Not a blemish. At least officially."

"How does this help anything?"

"If you read the original statements, the ones that we think are the real versions, it sounds like Cain had these short bursts of intense obsession over these girls. He would pick one and just hone in on her. Follow her. Learn her habits and routines. The longest one we have here is six weeks. Then he would just drop them at the drop of a hat. One minute, stalker; the next minute, he couldn't care if the girl was the dirt underneath his feet. He wouldn't just ignore them. He would go out of his way to have no contact with them whatsoever like they were contaminated. The one girl said it was like he was looking for the perfect woman, someone without any vices. A year ago, it all stopped. That's when the new set of statements went in the file, and people went about their merry business."

"Interesting. High IQ, obsessive tendencies, history of stalking." Gabriel stood and started pacing with some of the papers in his hand. "He certainly fits the profile."

"But we can't use this to get him into an interrogation room," Blake said, sulking on the edge of the bar.

"And if we confront him now, chances are he'll go to ground and hide," Logan added.

"He's close to being done. He won't run. But he will hide." Gabriel nodded.

"So, here's my question then," Blake said, moving to the arm of the couch. "Is he our guy?"

"She brought us the file on him. She risked her career to get it. I heard it in her voice last night when she called me. She's scared of him," Logan said.

Ryder nodded. "It's more than enough for me."

"So we have to keep her out of the hospital. No question. I'll put in a call to her department chair first thing in the morning," Blake nodded emphatically.

"All right. My turn."

Harrison poured himself another cup of coffee and sat down in one of the club chairs in the living room.

"So, this Cain guy is obsessed with Grayson. Fine. People obsess all the time. I had a crush on Michelle Pfeiffer once. But I didn't go around killing people and putting them on display inside Catholic churches to get her attention."

"It isn't about attention," Ryder muttered, shaking his head.

"Okay, so what is it about then? Impress me."

"He called her precious."

Ryder walked over to the window and looked out across the snow-blanketed city. Snowflakes were still falling softly in between the skyscrapers. When he didn't continue, Harrison prodded him.

"And that means what?"

"It means he and I are after the same thing."

Blake shook his head violently. "I'm sorry. Maybe I heard wrong. Did you just say you have something in common with this nutjob?"

"He wants her for himself. He'll do whatever he has to do to have her. Eliminate any threats to her or to him having her. Anything that might damage her. She's precious to him. He wants to keep her safe. Protect her."

"And that makes you like him how?"

"Don't tell me you can't see it," Gabriel chuckled sarcastically, his blue eyes dark and threatening. "I want the same thing."

"Yeah, you've said that, but you aren't slaughtering innocent people to do it," Harrison argued. "So, each of these people posed some kind of threat to her?"

"Apparently."

"We've been down this road before, Gabe. We hit a dead end. Carrol, sure. Definitely Harlan. Maybe even Nelson and James. But we're back at the same roadblock here that we had with the deadly sins angle. We have people that don't fit. I can't see how some of these people were threats."

"It doesn't matter what we see," Ryder said, shaking his head. "It matters what he sees. He has a system for identifying them and killing them. Something that we see as acceptable, or at the very least a normal variant, he finds abhorrent and dangerous. Hence the history of fleeting obsessions and treating women like they're biohazards."

"Something stupid or insignificant made them worse than dirt?"

"Exactly."

"This guy's a real Prince Charming, isn't he?" Logan said, rolling his eyes.

"So, now what?" Blake asked.

"Now," Harrison said, "Wonder Boy needs to get his ass in the shower and change. Then we're going out for breakfast. I'm starving."

Ryder didn't argue. He just set his coffee down on the side table and headed back toward his bedroom, peeling his shirt off in the process.

"Shit. That can't be good," Blake said once he was out of earshot.

"What?"

"Comparing himself to a serial killer."

"Yeah, it's not ideal. But nothing that a good greasy spoon breakfast can't fix."

"I hope so."

Nolan bit the inside of his lip. He wasn't so sure.

52

GRAYSON'S EYES FLUTTERED open, her sleep disturbed by the sound of clattering and clanging from the kitchen downstairs. She squinted against the sunlight that was trickling into her bedroom through pulled blinds. She yawned and stretched out, savoring the feeling of being warm in her own bed. Then her mind cleared, and the reality of the night before came crashing back down on her.

Her heart rate skyrocketed, the muscle fibers hammering mercilessly inside her chest. Her breathing grew shallow. She turned in bed and felt the mattress beside her. It was cold and empty. He was gone. For a moment, she pretended she'd dreamed him, but there it was, his scent on her pillow and in the sheets.

She turned over and closed her eyes, desperate to go back to sleep. Desperate to make it a dream.

He'd promised he'd stay. He didn't.

Stupid girl, she told herself. *What did you expect when you're a blubbering, incoherent mess? He probably couldn't wait to get out of here, the way you were acting. Stupid, stupid idiot.*

She was nearly back asleep, a few tears trickling down her cheeks, when there was a soft knock at her door.

"Gray?" Babs' muffled voice filtered in beneath the doorjamb.

"You awake yet?"

She hurriedly wiped her eyes and sniffled. "Yeah, I'm awake."

"Can I come in?"

"Sure."

The door slowly opened, and in walked Barbara, two cups of hot tea and a plate with two croissants balanced on top of them in her hands. The moment she took a look at her roommate, she hurried toward the bed and sat down.

"Oh, sweetie, what's wrong?" she asked, putting the cups and plate by the bed and throwing her arms around her roommate's neck. "You've been crying. What did that psycho do to you?"

"What did who do to me?" Grayson asked, startled by the response.

"That creepy fucker I found in your bed this morning!"

"What are you...?"

"I came home early from skiing. Long story, some of my coworkers were fighting and I didn't want to hear any more of their shit. There were footprints on our front porch, and I heard somebody in your room. There he was, half-naked, in bed with you, mumbling with you passed out next to him. I asked him what the hell he was doing here and what the hell you were doing home. He gave me some song and dance about a rough night, which I didn't buy. I asked him again what the fuck he was doing in bed with you and when he didn't answer me I kicked him out of the house. So you tell me right now. Do I need to go hire people to have him killed in a dirty alley somewhere?"

Grayson pulled away from Barbara and looked at her with a blank expression. "You...you made him leave?" she asked softly.

"Of course!"

"Babs, I asked him to stay last night! He brought me home, he...you have no idea...what happened..." She broke off into a sob and ducked her head into her hands.

Instantly, Barbara knew something was wrong. "Oh, hon, I'm so sorry. I...I didn't know. Here, drink some of this." She handed over a cup of tea, which Grayson took into her shaky hands. "What happened?"

"It's...it's a long story."

"I've got all day, you know."

"Maybe later."

"Okay. Are you hungry? I brought you a chocolate cream puff from that bakery in Vail you like."

She shook her head.

"Okay. Maybe later, too."

Barbara looked around the room, from one corner to the next. Grayson knew the tactic. She was stalling, looking around for a safe topic of conversation. She finally seemed to find one.

"Did you sleep with wet hair last night?" she asked. "You never do that."

"I...um...got dirty. He gave me a bath."

Her friend's eyebrows shot up. "The uptight, creepy, super-hot detective...gave you a bath?"

"He sat with me. Probably to be sure I didn't try to drown myself." She shrugged.

Babs didn't seem to know which part of that to process first: the fact that Grayson had taken a bath while Ryder had watched or that she had actually thought about drowning herself. It didn't matter.

"Umm, I'm not really sure what to say to that."

"It wasn't like that, Babs," Grayson scowled, knowing where her roommate's mind was headed.

"He was taking care of you?"

She nodded.

"Wow. Can't say I've ever had that before."

"You probably haven't walked in on a murder scene after having one of your attendings stalk you through the hospital… or after stealing said attending's personnel file."

"Okay, wait, what? Grayson, back up. What the hell's happened in the thirty-six hours I've been gone?"

Grayson sat up in bed and put her back up against the headboard, clutching her teacup. "On call. Last night. That attending I've told you about before, Dr. Cain? He cornered me, in the cafeteria and then outside of a patient's room. He just… he said some things that weren't right. He was talking about how Harlan getting killed was justified…"

"I agree with him there."

"…to protect me, Babs. And then he called me precious and said I wasn't safe yet but that I would be. And then he called me Beatrice."

"Beatrice? Where the hell did he get that?"

"I don't know. But he's not someone to screw up something like that. It was just odd."

"I'll say. You think this Cain guy is involved with everything that's been going on? Like with Lisa?"

"I don't know. But he makes me incredibly nervous. There's just something about him. I stole a copy of his personnel file. I figured there had to be something in there worth seeing if it was sealed by the department."

"Good God, are you part of a spy agency now or something?"

Grayson ignored the comment. "I took the file to Logan last night and, long story short, I ended up at the murder scene of Nathan Alexander."

"Oh, no…"

"Yeah, one of our neurosurgery residents had his fingertips chopped off, his teeth knocked out, and his eyeballs gouged out. He was trussed up like a turkey inside a church downtown. The old man that takes care of the church got himself stabbed in the chest for being around at the same time Nathan was killed. He came staggering into the park. Oh, I left my coat there...." she finished absently, staring off into her bedroom wall.

"Gray..." Babs didn't know what to say. She just wrapped her in another bear hug. "Sweetie, I'm so sorry. And he brought you home after all that?"

She nodded.

"He stayed to make sure you were safe, didn't he?"

She nodded again.

"Are you going to go back to work today?"

"No. I don't...I don't know if I can go back."

"Good. I wasn't going to let you if you'd said yes. Where's your car?"

"Parked downtown near the capitol."

"We need to go get it or they'll tow it."

"Okay. When can you go?"

"Anytime, honey. I'm not doing anything. Look, why don't you get yourself cleaned up and get a nice warm sweater on. It's still snowing outside."

Grayson nodded and got up from the bed, slowly making her way to her closet to pick out something to wear.

"Since when do you sleep in silk, Gray?" Babs asked from her perch on the mattress.

She looked down at her pants, fingering the material. She hadn't realized she'd had them on. She smiled sheepishly. "I usually don't. He picked them." She grabbed a pair of jeans, a lace camisole, and a sweatshirt before making her way into the bathroom.

Babs watched her go, then cleared the dishes and headed out of the room, straight for her cell phone.

53

IT WAS LATE afternoon when Barbara herded Grayson into her car and took off toward downtown.

The snowfall had picked up over the past few hours, and they'd both changed into warmer clothes. Babs had opted for her trusty bright pink turtleneck. Grayson had stared into her closet until Babs had grabbed her ivory cable knit sweater from the hanger and practically shoved it over her head.

Her usual winter coat was bloodstained and covered under a snowbank by now, but Grayson had found a suitable replacement in the back of her closet.

Her poor friend was absolutely shattered. Barbara could see it in her eyes, her face, her body language, the way she couldn't quite keep her eyes open or hold her head up properly. She was seriously contemplating driving home directly behind her, just to be sure she didn't fall asleep at the wheel and wreck.

She'd spent a few hours on the couch, force-feeding her croissants and tea and fresh fruit. The more Barbara had heard about last night, the more shocked she was that Grayson was even out of bed.

They found the 4Runner on Sherman Street. It was buried under what was probably a pass or two from the snowplow, on top of the continued snowfall. They made quick work of brushing it all off since there wasn't any ice to deal with, and the engine easily turned over in the cold.

Barbara shut the driver's door, then knocked on the window so Grayson would roll it down. "Hey, I'm freezing. Why don't we get some hot chocolate? My treat."

"Oh, Babs, I don't think so…"

"Please," she pleaded, giving her friend her best puppy-dog eyes. "The best place for hot chocolate is just a couple of streets over. They even have a parking lot. I doubt they'll be busy. Please?"

"All right." Grayson forced a small smile. The poor girl looked like she just wanted to be back in bed. "I'll follow you. You'd better not be lying about the parking lot."

Barbara hopped back into her car and headed out, winding around several back roads before she pulled into a small parking lot off of 12th Avenue. The Art Museum towered in the distance. Grayson pulled in just behind her and took the last parking spot.

Barbara waited patiently while her friend bundled herself up in her oversized coat and walked over to the sidewalk. She looped her arm into hers, and they made their way through the snow to the corner where the scent of warm melted chocolate wafted deliciously through the air.

"What is this place?" Grayson asked.

"Mokaya. They do amazing things with all things chocolate."

"How did you find it?"

"Um, a friend told me about it. All right, in you go."

Barbara pushed her through the entryway. The lighting on the inside of the small cafe was dim, and it took a few moments for their eyes to adjust. Grayson kept her coat wrapped tightly around her shoulders as she surveyed her surroundings.

The décor was incredibly rich: mahogany wood, red velvet booths, art deco sconces on the walls, and two crystal chandeliers hanging from the ceiling. The place looked positively sumptuous.

Barbara shuttled her up to the counter and pointed to the menu elegantly sketched in gold on the overhanging chalkboards. "What do you want?"

"Um, I…I don't…" Grayson stared blankly ahead.

A thin young man with a goatee and a neck tattoo walked up from behind the counter.

"Good afternoon, ladies," he said, smiling warmly. "Glad you made it in with the snow. What can I get you?"

"This is her first time here," Babs said. "What do you recommend?"

"Well, we do it all here. Are you in the mood for hot chocolate, a soufflé, a warm cookie hot out of the oven?"

"Hot chocolate, please," Grayson said quietly.

"Alrighty then. We have different kinds listed up top, plus I can basically make whatever isn't up there."

"Do you have anything with cinnamon in it?"

The man smiled warmly. "Sure do. Milk, dark, or white?" When Grayson didn't answer, he elaborated. "Chocolate preference, I mean."

"Oh, um…can you mix milk and dark?"

"Of course. I'll put one of our homemade churros with it. Really tops it off."

"Thanks." She forced another smile.

"We bring everything out to the table, so please grab a seat and I'll have it out to you when it's ready."

"Go on, sweetie. This is my treat. I'll be right there," Babs said, taking her wallet out of her purse.

Grayson eased herself out of her coat and into one of the booths away from the door.

She rubbed her temples to try to keep her headache at bay, focusing on the polished copper tabletop in front of her. The crystal from the chandelier sent rays of colored light down onto its surface, and they bounced and moved in the breeze from the heating vents.

After a few moments, a shadow fell over the booth, obscuring the dancing light. Grayson assumed it was either Babs or the young man with her hot chocolate, so she lifted her eyes up and prepared to fake another smile.

Gabriel was staring down at her, his face drawn and heavy with concern.

Grayson registered Barbara standing at the door far behind him. She winked and pointed to a to-go cup in her left hand, then hurried out the door with a smile on her face.

Grayson scowled at her flamboyant exit, then turned her attention back to the man hovering over her. He was standing stock-still, staring at her and visibly uncomfortable, not saying a word.

"What are you doing here, Gabriel?"

He opened his mouth to answer but was immediately interrupted by the arrival of the young man from behind the counter. He set a small silver tray down onto the table with a stark white cup and saucer, a small teapot, and two warm churros drizzled with warm chocolate. He nodded silently before backing away from the table and heading back behind the counter. Grayson kept still.

Ryder smiled slightly. She asked again. "What are you doing here?"

"Buying you hot chocolate, of course."

"How did you know I was here?"

"Barbara called."

Grayson was too tired to play into his game. She turned her attention to the cup in front of her. She tried to pick it up, but she was shaking uncontrollably, partly from exhaustion and partly from the shock of seeing him towering over her.

The cup clattered against the saucer and she slammed it back down onto the tray, frustrated. It was all too much. The hint of tears started to well up at the corners of her eyes.

Gabriel hastily unbuttoned his overcoat and hung it on the side of the booth. He slid into the seat opposite her and gracefully poured a cup of the steaming liquid chocolate from the teapot. He handed the cup across the table to her.

She took it with both hands and took a cautious sip. Hot, but oh so rich and lovely. Just the right amount of cinnamon.

Grayson held her cup tighter and eyed him up from across the table for a few moments. He didn't look away from her, but she could tell he was uncomfortable under her scrutiny.

"Barbara called?" she finally parroted, almost annoyed.

"Yes, she did. This morning, after you woke up. She called to apologize."

"For kicking you out of the house."

"And other things. But yes."

"Why didn't you tell her what happened?"

"When? This morning?"

She nodded.

"I can't jeopardize an ongoing investigation," he said steadily, before lowering his voice. "Besides, you were in shock when I brought you home. I doubted you'd want me in the house anyway. Once you'd woken up."

"Why wouldn't I?"

"After how I treated you in the park?" he scoffed and dropped his head into his hands. "Can you honestly say you wanted to wake up to me? Jesus Christ, Grayson...the way I spoke to you. I hurt you. You have bruises on your arms where I grabbed you. You were afraid of me."

He emphasized the last sentence, the pain evident on his face. Silence hung in the air between them.

Grayson ran her fingers over the bruises she knew lurked underneath her sweater.

Gabriel kept his head in his hands and ran his fingers through his hair, agitated, unable to hold her gaze a moment longer.

"Yes."

It was so soft he almost didn't hear it. His head bolted up and he looked directly into a pair of watery blue eyes.

"What?"

"Yes. I wanted you there," she said softly, a tear running down her cheek. "You promised." Grayson hated the weakness she heard in her own voice.

Gabriel slid out from his seat across from her and into the booth beside her. He wrapped his arms around her and tucked her body into his, calmly whispering into her ear.

"I'm sorry. I'm sorry. I'm so, so sorry." Over and over and over.

"You left me."

"I know."

"You were supposed to be there when I woke up."

"I know."

"You took care of me. And…and then you left me."

"I'm sorry."

Grayson let him hold her for a few minutes, reveling in the scent of musk mixed with chocolate. Eventually, she pulled away from him and craned her neck back so she could look at him.

"What is this to you?"

"Excuse me?"

"You heard me," she replied, not believing the conviction she heard in her own voice. "This whole you-protecting-me thing. Is this just your tried-and-true way of getting into a girl's pants?"

"What? No!"

Her face immediately flamed red. *How did those words even come out of my mouth? Change topics. Now.*

"Why aren't you out arresting Cain? You've read what's in the file by now."

"What? I can't just go out and put handcuffs on someone because of what's written in a sealed work file. A file that was stolen, by the way. You know that," he replied gently. He stared down at her for a moment. She'd suddenly clammed up on herself, hands wringing nervously in her lap.

"You asked me a question, Grayson. What is this to me? You mean, what are you to me?"

She nodded.

"Do you still want to know the answer?"

She nodded, her eyes fixated on the table and away from him, steeling herself for an answer she didn't want to hear.

"You are…" he looked up at the ceiling briefly, praying that he could say something to keep her without saying what she was in no condition to hear.

"You are…unique. Complicated. Beautiful. Someone to cherish and protect and take care of. And you drive me absolutely fucking crazy. I can't think clearly when I'm around you and I can't stop thinking about you when I'm not. And then you run off and put yourself in danger and I fucking lose my mind every goddamned time."

He looked down at her and smiled. "Does that answer your question?"

"As long as you don't do that again," she murmured into his chest.

"Do what?"

"Leave me. Like that."

"Okay," he chuckled, kissing the top of her head. "Your hot chocolate is getting cold."

"I think this place has better hot chocolate than the last place."

"I'll keep that in mind," he said softly, motioning to the young man behind the counter, who immediately scuttled over with an espresso and a fresh batch of hot chocolate.

54

AN HOUR LATER, Gabriel paid the tab and stood up from the booth. He quickly pulled on his coat before grabbing Grayson's and holding it open. He smiled when he recognized the label at the back collar. No wonder it had looked too big for her when she'd walked in.

He pulled the collar up around her neck and laid a gentle pressure on her back as he guided her out of the cafe. They stepped back out into the cold, blowing snow, and she looped her arm underneath his. "It's a good thing you kept my coat," he said, leaning down.

"I've been meaning to give it back."

"I'd rather you didn't."

"Okay." She didn't offer up any fight.

She's beyond exhausted. She needs to get home.

Gabriel looked up and down the street. "Where did you park your car?"

"In the lot down the street."

"I'll walk with you. The sidewalks are getting icy."

"All right."

They started down the sidewalk in silence, Grayson gently leaning on his arm for support. A thought suddenly struck her and she shivered. "I'm sorry."

Gabriel looked down at her, surprised. "You're sorry? For what?"

"For the way I've been acting lately. Whining. Crying. Not being able to pick out my own pajamas. I haven't been the best company."

"Why in the hell would you apologize for that?" he balked.

"You have enough to deal with. You don't need me blubbering on and on and making an overly-clingy idiot of myself."

"Grayson," he scolded.

"I'm serious, Gabriel," she insisted.

"So am I. There's nothing wrong with being upset, especially under recent circumstances. It's nice to know you feel safe and taken care of when I'm around. That's the whole point. And for the record, I wouldn't call anything you've done whining or blubbering. Don't speak about yourself like that again."

"I've stained at least a few of your shirts."

"That's what the dry cleaner is for. Or I'll buy new ones. It doesn't matter."

"I never did say thank you, did I? For yesterday. When you brought me home."

"You don't have to thank me for that."

"Of course I do. It isn't every guy that would make up a bubble bath for a girl after a murder and then sit quietly on the floor of the bathroom while she has a mental breakdown. And, um, not take advantage of…um…the lack of clothing."

"You think I would have…"

"No!"

Grayson slipped on the icy cobblestones, and Gabriel tensed his arm to support her. She struggled to regain her balance.

"But it was nice to not have one more thing to worry about."

"Anytime, sweetheart," he said, pulling her closer and kissing the top of her head.

———

Grayson momentarily closed her eyes and wished that wasn't the only place he'd kissed her. He felt so warm. She could feel the heat radiating off of him in waves. She was so unbelievably tired. She could've fallen asleep standing up in his arms.

"On that note," he whispered while he still had her close, "you should sleep in silk more often."

"What? Why?"

"Because I like the feel of it on you."

If he hadn't been walking next to her, Grayson would have stopped dead in her tracks and fainted headfirst into the snow. When did it suddenly get too warm outside for her coat?

Gabriel saw her cheeks flush. He chuckled to himself and kissed the top of her head again.

Her car was covered in a good inch and a half of snow, which Gabriel insisted on cleaning off while she sat in the driver's seat with the heat turned up on high. That gave her time to look around for his car, which she didn't see. The windows fogged up as the temperature inside the car increased, and she hit the defogger to clear them.

Ryder came around the front of the car when he'd finished and tossed her scraper onto the floor in the back seat, shutting the door quickly to keep the warm air in. He cracked the driver's door enough to poke his head in.

"All right, you're ready. Be careful. People are going to be driving like idiots today."

He shut the door and started walking around the front of the car. Grayson hit the button to roll down her window.

"Wait, Gabriel!" she called after him.

He turned around and splayed his forearms on the window ledge of the driver's door. "Yes?"

"Where are you going?"

"Home."

"You're walking?"

He nodded.

"How far is it?"

He shrugged, remaining silent.

"Why don't you let me drive you? The weather's terrible."

"Absolutely not. You need to get home."

"So do you."

He shook his head. "Just drive home, Grayson. And call when you get there."

She wrinkled her nose at him. "How am I supposed to do that, exactly? Call 9-1-1?"

"What?"

"Gabriel, I don't have your phone number," she said, rolling her eyes.

He smirked at her. "You have my ex-partner's phone number, but you don't have mine?"

Her face blushed. He extended his hand. "Give me your phone."

She handed it over, punching in the security code for him. He spent a moment typing, then handed it back to her.

"Now get going," he said softly, turning away before she had a second to protest.

She rolled up her window and pulled out to the corner of the lot. The street was deserted. Since she had to turn the opposite way down the road, she waited until he disappeared into the swirling white snow, then headed for home.

The drive wasn't horrible, but it certainly wasn't a walk in the park. It took her more than fifteen extra minutes to navigate the snowy streets. As she walked into the kitchen through the back door, she saw Barbara huddled on the couch reading a magazine with the fireplace on.

She waved quickly as she shut the door, then immediately pulled out her cell phone. She scrolled down until she found his name listed in her contacts. He had entered everything: his home and work address, cell and work numbers with direct extensions, email, his captain's direct line, everything. She checked quickly and saw that the same had been done for Nolan and Harrison. She grinned.

Just in case he's indisposed, she thought to herself. She highlighted his cell number and hit 'call.' He answered on the second ring.

"Ryder." He sounded tense, his voice harsh and strained. So dramatically different from less than an hour ago. For a moment, she hesitated.

"Um, hi. It's…it's me."

"Hi there." His voice instantly softened.

"I made it home."

"In one piece."

"Yes, of course. Are you…I mean, did you make it…"

"Home? Yes. I did. Why, were you worried about me?"

His voice was low and warm. Grayson felt herself lulling off a bit on the phone, putting more weight than was necessary on the poor kitchen counter.

"Yes."

"You shouldn't worry about me."

"I could say the same to you, detective."

"I have reason to worry about you."

"Same answer."

Chuckling filtered over the line. "Grayson?"

"Hmm?"

"Did you enjoy your hot chocolate?"

"Yes."

"I'd like to take you there again. Under happier circumstances."

"I'd like that. Soon?"

"Of course."

She smiled. Several muffled voices filtered through in the background on the other end of the line.

"I have to go," he said, with the slightest hint of disappointment in his voice. "Stay inside tonight."

"I will."

The line clicked dead before she could say anything else. She looked up from the black screen of her smartphone to see Babs grinning at her from her perch on the couch.

Grayson sheepishly walked into the living room and hung up his coat on the coat rack, then sat down on the couch next to her roommate.

"So?"

"So, what?" the blonde responded with a Cheshire cat grin on her face.

"Was the plan always to abandon me downtown at a chocolate shop?"

Babs erupted into a fit of giggles, which took several minutes to calm down. In the meantime, she grabbed two bottles of Pellegrino from the refrigerator and brought them into the living room, along with two large fleece blankets from the downstairs closet.

"Well, yes and no," she said, twisting her bottle open. "After I realized what a freaking moron I had been to kick him out of here this morning, I called Noah. He confirmed my idiocy and gave me Logan's number. Thankfully, the big lug was sitting across the breakfast table from Hot and Dangerous. I apologized and said I wanted to make nice—which I think he marginally appreciated—and told him we still had to come pick up your car. He said he wanted to see you and apologize for something. I didn't ask what. I just went with it, and he gave me the name of the place and a time. When I tried paying for our order, the little geeky guy behind the counter said it was already taken care of, and by the time I'd turned around, there was Hot and Dangerous staring at you like a man in a desert who'd just found water. I figured you didn't need me." She winked.

Grayson just nodded.

"Did everything go okay?"

More nodding.

"Are you okay?"

More nodding.

"You're still going in to work tomorrow, aren't you?"

Hesitation, followed by less enthusiastic nodding.

"Gray..." she sighed, frustrated.

"I don't have a choice, Babs. I'm not happy about it and I'd rather not, but I don't have a choice. We're shorthanded in December as it is. Unless I'm on a gurney, I have to go."

"The fact that one of your attendings might be a serial killer with a crush on you doesn't muddy that hard line a bit?"

"Not in orthopedics." She smirked.

"Well, shit," Babs said, throwing up her arms and falling back on the couch.

"Can we just focus on something else, please?"

"Sure."

They spent the next few hours watching B-list reality TV and trying to decide when to pick out their Christmas tree. By 9:30, Grayson could barely keep her eyes open.

She trudged up the stairs to bed, leaving Babs in the living room. She cleaned up for the night and picked out a pair of pajamas, making a mental note to invest in a set or two of new silk ones.

She was climbing into bed when her phone vibrated. She picked it up, read the text message that was waiting for her, and smiled into her pillow. She read it twice, just to be sure she'd read it correctly. She had.

Sweet dreams, beautiful girl.

55

GRAYSON QUIETLY MADE her way through the halls of the intensive care unit. What little morning light should have been filtering in through the windows was completely obscured by the heavy snow.

The drive in had been absolutely horrendous. All she wanted to do was get through rounding and get to the operating room without acknowledging any of the gossip-heavy stares that were following her like starving wolves. She could even hear them.

"That's her…Did you hear?…Should we ask her?"

Grayson shook her head and tried desperately to block them out.

She flipped open Mr. Robinson's chart and tried to find the critical care notes from the day before. He was an elderly man who had fractured his hip and gone to surgery yesterday. Anesthesia hadn't been able to get him off the ventilator, so he'd been transferred to the unit postoperatively. From the looks of it, he hadn't made any progress overnight.

Sighing, she took off her white coat and laid it over the nurse's chair, then walked into the cool hospital room. She turned on the softest bedside light she could manage and pulled on a pair of exam gloves. She pulled the bedsheet aside by his right hip and looked at his surgical dressing; not a drop of blood.

"Perfect," she griped. "The only one I won't have to change this morning."

She felt for the pulses in his feet, which were bounding, and then pulled the gloves off. While she was washing her hands, she took inventory of the equipment in the room. Two IV poles, four total pumps, a myriad of drips, the ventilator…too much equipment to be good news.

She walked over to the IVs and started turning and twisting the bags around, trying to get an idea of exactly what medications and infusions he was getting and how much. Antibiotics, fluids, vasopressors…

"All that's a little out of your purview, isn't it, Dr. Carter?"

The hair on the back of her neck shot up. She turned around slightly, just to be sure it was him, then went back to mentally cataloging the bags. She forced herself to keep her back to him. She was in no mood for him this morning.

In fact, the longer she stood staring at the IV bags, the more she felt something dark stir in the pit of her stomach. She had trouble putting her finger on what it was for a few moments, then it clicked. She was angry.

More than that. She was itching for a fight.

"Mr. Robinson is my patient, Dr. Cain, and with all due respect, I went to medical school just like you did. I may not use these drugs anymore in my own practice, but I'm well aware of what they're for and what they do. If they're being used on one of my patients, they're well within my purview."

Her voice had a bite to it that she hadn't intended, but it felt incredible. If this self-involved jackass had it out for her, she wasn't about to be meek or deferential to him anymore.

Screw this. And screw him.

"Very well."

He nodded and continued watching her from the doorway, his arms folded across his chest. Grayson continued taking inventory of Mr. Robinson's various machines and medications until she was satisfied, then moved to the door. She stood stock-still in front of Cain, her own arms crossed in front of her chest and eyes blazing.

He moved out of the doorway and allowed her to grab Mr. Robinson's chart. She scribbled out a progress note as quickly as she was able. "Are you going to wean him off of the ventilator today?"

"Are you in some kind of rush?" he mused.

"You should be. Every day he stays hooked up to that thing his risk of ventilator-associated pneumonia goes up."

"You are fired up this morning, Dr. Carter," he chuckled, inching closer. "It's invigorating."

"Please just wean him when you can, Dr. Cain. The last thing he needs is pneumonia followed by an infected hip."

"As you wish, my dear." He continued lurking in her peripheral vision as she finished writing in the chart.

"Do you need this?" she asked, nodding toward the blue binder.

"No. I rarely need charts to take care of my patients. But I do need to talk to you."

"I'm in the middle of rounds."

"That's not relevant," he shrugged, still staring at her. "Have you been privy to the news about young Dr. Alexander?"

"From neurosurgery? No," she lied sweetly. "Is something wrong?"

"He had a rather unfortunate Saturday night." There was a smirk on his face. He was trying to hide it, but Grayson could see it simmering underneath his skin.

She pressed her nails into her palms, distracting herself with the pain. "What exactly does that mean, Dr. Cain?"

"I'm afraid Dr. Alexander will not be practicing medicine

within these walls anymore. The neurosurgery department will have an extra residency spot to fill next year."

"He got himself into some kind of trouble on Saturday?"

"Yes, my dear. The young doctor is dead. Unfortunate, but he did have his faults."

"And just which ones killed him?" Grayson was about to be physically ill, but she forced the bile down her throat to keep Cain talking. He'd been the one to bring up Nathan. Maybe if she kept him going, he would slip up somehow, give her something to take to Gabriel.

"He was a fraudulent, manipulative young man. Dangerous."

"Excuse me?"

Cain stepped forward, invading her personal space.

Is he wearing cologne?

For the first time since she'd known him, Mr. Fussypants I-have-to-keep-my-senses-clear was wearing cologne.

"His rather long list of credentials was sorely lacking. All rather brilliant, but forgeries nonetheless."

"And that's a reason to kill him?"

"Fraudulent egotists are rarely singular offenders."

"That's not an answer. How do you know Nathan's dead?"

"Word travels fast within these walls." He shrugged.

"Well, for the record, it isn't news. At least not to me."

"You knew?" he asked. His eyebrow rose only a millimeter, but she caught it. Clear as day. He was surprised.

"I more than knew," she hissed, lowering her voice for effect. "I. Found. Him."

It was satisfying to see the son of a bitch shift uncomfortably, the surprise now clearly evident on his face. Cain tried to hide it, but no amount of shifting and dropping his eyes could hide the shock.

Gotcha.

"In a church downtown," she continued silkily. "Blood dripping from his fingers, his eyes spooned out of their sockets and teeth ripped from his skull."

She watched as he slowly shook his head in disappointment. "No one so pure and precious should ever lay their eyes on something like that," he mumbled under his breath.

"What was that?" she challenged.

"Nothing. I'm sorry you had to see that, Beatrice. I hope it did not cause you any undue distress. Try to put it out of your mind."

She narrowed her eyes at him. "That's not my name, Dr. Cain."

His eyes sparkled at her and a small smile ghosted across his mouth. Without a word, he turned from her and walked down the hallway.

Grayson shivered despite her polar fleece pullover.

Well, that was exceptionally creepy.

She marked Mr. Robinson's name off of her rounding list and counted. Six more patients to go. She made a note to herself to start another list when she got home from work today.

If Nathan died because Cain thought he was a fraud and Harlan died because he'd assaulted her, there had to be a reason for the others. Maybe she could figure it out.

It was worth a shot.

56

"ALL RIGHT, I'M getting really fucking tired of saying this, but here's another one." Blake sighed, tossing a piece of paper onto a pile in between his desk and Ryder's.

"Another one?" Logan called from his desk across the squad room.

"Yeah. A recommendation letter from some guy at Yale. A guy who not only never taught at Yale but, according to their records, has never even been a student or a guest lecturer."

"That brings us up to, what, six?"

"Seven," Ryder said, fingers pressed to his temples as he tried to fight off a headache. "The prep school he listed on the east coast finally called back. They don't have any record of him either."

"How'd you get those pretentious bastards to call you back at all?" Logan asked.

"I called in a favor."

"You have people who do you favors in Connecticut?"

"A few."

"All at fancy prep schools?"

"No, asshole."

"Fuck the attitude, Ryder."

They were all a bit on edge. They'd spent two days digging into Nathan Alexander's past, and the more they tried to find out about the young neurosurgeon, the more roadblocks they'd hit.

They'd stumbled across a small discrepancy in his personnel file, usually nothing to think twice about. Ryder had been suspicious, so they'd gone digging. Sure enough, that one little flaw had led them to letters of recommendation, past employers, and now prep school records that had been faked.

Dr. Alexander wasn't a privileged Ivy-League gunner. He was a kid from small-town rural Pennsylvania who'd moved in with his aunt and uncle in New York City at sixteen, after the death of his single mother, and started running around with kids whose parents made more money in a week than his mom had made in a year.

Ryder had felt guilty leaving Blake and Logan to do the heavy lifting over the past weeks, so he'd forgone his usual place back in the interview room and stayed out in the squad room with them. The fluorescent lights combined with the usual din of the squad had forced a roaring headache in between his eyes.

Thankfully, they were now the only ones left in the squad room, except for the captain. He was on the phone in his office, behind closed doors and drawn blinds.

"I can't do much more of this, Ryder," Blake moaned, leaning back in his chair.

"Then go home. I can finish this."

"Don't be ridiculous. I just need a break. Can we get dinner soon?"

"It's not dinnertime."

"It's after seven."

Gabriel glanced up at the clock on the wall and swore. *How the hell did it get so late?* "Shit, I'm sorry. Get whatever you want. I'll pay for it."

"Don't worry, buddy," Logan said, slapping him on the shoulder, "we did that about twenty minutes ago. Food's on its way."

A few minutes later, Logan's desk phone rang. When he put the handset back in the receiver, he stood up and slapped his palm down on his desk. "All right, time out. We're eating. Put that shit away," he announced, backing away from his desk and heading toward the break room.

Nolan sighed with relief and started stacking the papers on his desk into a somewhat neat pile.

Ryder kept his head down, furiously writing notes in his binder, Alexander's files open in front of him. The others could stop for dinner. He still had too much to do. The sooner he finished, the sooner he could get home and drown his headache in a full glass of scotch.

The elevator dinged, and he heard the telltale clicking of a woman's shoes on the tile floor and the rustling of to-go bags.

What delivery girl wears heels?

The sharp sound was doing a number on his headache. Gabriel scowled against the shooting pain behind his eyes. The click-clacking stopped just shy of his desk.

"Anybody hungry?"

Gabriel's eyes snapped up from his binder. He twisted his body toward the source of a very familiar voice. He opened his mouth to reply, but his partner beat him to it.

"Oh, dear God in Heaven, yes!" Blake lunged from his chair, arms stretched out for the bags.

Grayson smiled widely as he grabbed them from her arms, careful of the cardboard drink carrier she was carrying in one hand. Once he'd squirreled away to the break room with the food, Grayson stepped up closer to the side of Ryder's desk.

What the hell is she doing here?

She was wearing a deep green sweater, black dress pants, pointed patent leather heels, and her ivory overcoat. Her hair was windblown and her cheeks were flushed from the cold. Her blue eyes were sparkling. The sight of her, standing innocently at the edge of his desk, had thrown him completely off guard.

"Hi," she said softly.

"Hi."

"I thought you might need this," she said, pulling one of the cups out of the drink carrier and setting it on his desk.

"Coffee?"

"Double espresso." She grinned, then plucked out a second cup and set it beside the first. "And coffee."

"Oh God, I could kiss you," he sighed, opening the first cup and breathing in the wonderful aroma.

The words were out of his mouth before he even registered thinking them, let alone saying them. His mouth gaped open when he realized what he'd said. He looked up with a sheepish grin on his face.

Grayson was perched on his desk, blushing beneath her long eyelashes. "Why don't you just come and eat some dinner?" she asked quietly.

"You brought me dinner?"

"I brought everyone dinner," she replied.

"Why?"

"Why not? You all have to eat. It's not Gustavo's, but I hope it'll be okay."

He stood up from his desk and wrapped one arm smoothly around her waist, underneath her overcoat. Grayson's hands flew up to his chest to steady herself. "You didn't need to do this, Grayson," he said in a low, smooth voice.

"I know. I did it anyway." She smiled back at him.

He saw something briefly flash over her face, like she was weighing options in her head. In one swift move, she pushed herself up on her toes and kissed his cheek.

"Come on," she whispered. "Your food is getting cold."

Grayson extracted herself from his grip and walked back toward the break room, taking her coat off along the way. He waited for a beat before following her, just long enough for the electricity to fade from the skin on his cheek where her lips had been.

Blake and Logan were dishing out the contents of foam containers onto paper plates when he walked in. Grayson was dividing up the remaining three large cups of coffee.

"Holy shit," Blake gasped into one of the containers. "Did you get us dessert, too?"

She blushed and nodded mid-pour. "Of course I did."

"Doc, this must have cost you a small fortune," Logan said. "Let us pay you back for dinner."

"You let her pay for this?" Ryder hissed from the doorway.

"Go easy on them," she said softly, walking over and laying a reassuring hand on his forearm. "I didn't give them much choice. Sit down."

Ryder glared at the two men over her head. Blake gave him a sheepish grin and shrugged. Logan just chuckled.

"Do what the doctor orders, Gabe," he said between bites.

They sat down to dinner, their plates full of chicken parmesan, garlic bread, linguine with clam sauce, and Caesar salad. Blake and Logan wolfed down two plates apiece before arguing over who would get the last piece of the chicken parmesan.

"This is really good, doc. Where's it from again?" Logan asked.

"Chew your food, you animal," Blake mumbled.

Grayson giggled at the two of them. "Mariello's. It's a little hole-in-the-wall Italian place close to me. I took care of one of the owner's sons when I was a second-year resident. We saved his leg, and when his son left the hospital, Mr. Mariello invited all of the residents who had taken care of him to the restaurant for dinner. I was a poor second-year, so of course, I said yes. The food was great, and I've been going there ever since."

"Well, thanks for bringing it. You showing up kept us from killing each other."

"What were you working on, if you don't mind me asking?"

"Trying to pin down Nathan Alexander. We found some discrepancies in his file," Logan answered, shoveling another forkful of food into his mouth.

"Oh…really? Like what?"

Grayson's right leg began to tap rapidly beneath the table. Her left hand balled up into a fist.

"Letters of recommendation, his time at a prep school he never attended in Connecticut, past jobs…they're all fake."

Grayson's eyes shot down to her dinner plate. She suddenly found something fascinating about what was left of her chicken parmesan. She began idly twirling linguine noodles around her fork while chewing her bottom lip.

"Doc?" Logan called over his plate of noodles.

"So, he was a fraud," she mumbled to herself.

"What was that?"

Her head shot up and she stared at Logan momentarily like a deer in headlights. She quickly remembered herself. "Oh, uh, nothing."

Shit, shit, shit!

The older detective smirked and speared a piece of chicken.

"You're in a room with three detectives, hon. No getting out of this one."

Her gaze darted quickly from Logan to Nolan, then finally settled on Gabriel, who was giving her a look of warm curiosity. She took a deep breath and closed her eyes.

"I had a run-in with Douglas Cain on Monday."

She waited for a beat, her eyes tightly shut. When a verbal outburst didn't assault her ears, she took a chance and opened them. The warm look he'd had a moment before was gone, replaced with firmly set lips and blue eyes darkened by fury. She couldn't handle looking at him, so she turned her gaze to Logan. Safer target.

"You ran into Douglas Cain on Monday," Logan parroted back.

She nodded. He waited for an explanation. Feeling a pair of steel-blue eyes boring a hole into the side of her face, she shakily continued. "I was in the middle of rounding. He cornered me in a patient's room."

"And said what, exactly?"

"Well, after he tried to tell me I was too stupid to look at an IV pole," she started, rolling her eyes, "he told me about Nathan. Like it was supposed to be a big surprise. He called him fraudulent and manipulative. Dangerous."

"Did he say how *he* knew about the death?"

She shook her head. "He was vague about it. I asked. Then I told him I already knew about Nathan because I'd found him dead in the church off Colfax."

Logan's eyes shot up. "Really? What did he say to that?"

"I don't think he believed me until I described it. In detail. Then he got nervous."

"What else did he say?"

Grayson fidgeted in her seat, remembering the sound of Cain's voice in her head. "He…he called me something."

"What, precious again?"

"No. Well, yes. He said I was 'too pure and precious' to see something like that. The crime scene, I mean. He said he hoped it didn't cause me stress."

"But that's not what you meant when you said he called you something. So, what did he call you?" Logan pressed.

"He called me…Beatrice."

The room was silent for a moment. Logan's eyes narrowed in confusion. "He called you what? Beatrice?"

She nodded.

"What the hell does that mean?" Blake asked. "Your name isn't Beatrice. Wait, is it? Is Grayson your middle name or something?"

"No, it's not. It's Ava. No one's ever called me Beatrice before."

"So, maybe it was a slipup." He shrugged.

"Cain doesn't make mistakes like that," she said, "And he definitely doesn't make them twice in less than a week."

"What do you mean twice?" Logan asked.

"Last week. When I called you to ask you to meet me in the park? He cornered me two times that night, once in the cafeteria and once in the ICU. The first time, he called me Beatrice."

"Doesn't make any sense to me. Gabe? Does this Beatrice thing make any sense to you? Gabe? Gabe? Hey, Earth to Ryder."

When Grayson registered Logan calling his name more than once, she took a chance and looked to her left. Gabriel's face was drawn, tight and tense. He was glaring at her. All the fire glinting behind those beautiful blue irises was aimed directly at her.

"What in the hell were you doing at the hospital on Monday?" he spat through gritted teeth.

She shrank into her chair. "Wh…what do you mean? I was at work." Grayson looked back at him, wide-eyed and instantly terrified.

"You weren't supposed to go back there."

"I…what the hell did you want me to do? I can't just not show up!"

"Yes, you can,"

"No, I can't!"

"What the fucking hell happened?" Ryder hissed, this time aiming his venom at his partner.

Grayson jumped back from the table. The rage rolling off of Gabriel was petrifying. She shrank back against the protection of the countertop.

"Didn't your department call you off?" Blake asked hesitantly over his shoulder.

"No." She shook her head. "Why, should they have?"

"Aw, hell," Logan muttered underneath his breath. "They didn't fucking pull her off duty."

"Wh…what's going on?" she asked, instantly hating the shakiness in her voice.

"We called your department on Monday and told them what happened. They said they'd consider taking you off of service," Blake explained. "You were supposed to be at home this week. Safe."

Nolan shot a quick glance at his partner, which Grayson caught.

She instantly understood. "Gabriel…"

His eyes were trained in her direction, but he wasn't looking at her. He was far gone, staring right through her. "You were supposed to be safe. You were with him," he hissed. "You were alone…with him." Ryder shoved himself back from the table and threw open the break room door. He stormed out, slamming it behind him.

Grayson looked after him, completely stunned. Blake swore under his breath. Harrison shook his head. He saw the anger brewing behind her eyes.

"Go get him, honey."

She took a deep breath, shoved herself off of the back counter, and walked out after him.

57

GRAYSON FOLLOWED GABRIEL out into the now-deserted squad room. He veered sharply into one of the open interview rooms and leaned up against the window, staring vacantly out over the twinkling lights of downtown. She leaned up against the doorjamb, patiently waiting for him to notice she'd followed.

He rhythmically clenched and unclenched his fists at his side. He was angry.

Really, really angry.

She waited silently for him to cool off, taking the time to selfishly ogle a bit. He really was rather gorgeous, even when steaming mad. Tall, muscular, dark hair that was just the right kind of too long…and all that muscle was balled up tight, tense, and on display underneath his white button-down shirt. She had a few choice words floating around in her head for the view below his belt loops, too.

Grayson sucked her lower lip in between her teeth. She wouldn't complain if she ever got her hands into his back pockets…

Goddamn it, focus!

After a long while, he leaned forward, resting his head against the cold glass. That was her cue. She walked up behind him and gently laid a hand in between his shoulder blades. Grayson felt the muscles shake and tense underneath her fingertips, the muscle fibers rippling in defiance. She moved her hand in small circles, trying to get some of the tension eased out of them.

Gabriel took a few shaky breaths and sagged forward, putting even more faith in the glass panes supporting his weight. "What am I going to do with you?" he murmured, shaking his head.

"For starters, you could explain why you're so upset with me."

"You can't guess?" he hissed.

"I'd like to know why something out of my control is my fault," she coaxed gently. "Or Nolan's or Harrison's. They tried to get me called off of work. They both tried, Gabriel. It just didn't happen."

He didn't turn around to look at her. When he didn't respond, she kept talking.

"Gabriel, I can walk. I can talk. I can use a saw and a hammer. In my department, that means I come to work. To be honest, I'm surprised they gave me the time off that they did after I was attacked. We're short this month. It's the holidays. We have junior residents away at conference. We can't spare anybody. You tried. Your partners tried. That's all anybody could do. Besides," she kept her hand on his back but moved toward his left side to try to get a look at his face, "Nothing happened. I'm fine."

"You're not fine."

"I'm standing here, aren't I?"

"That animal has been stalking you through the hospital all week. You think the incident in that patient's room two days ago, or the two times on Saturday, were the only times he was following you?"

Grayson thought about that for a moment. It made her skin crawl. "No. Of course not. But it's one of the only times he did anything about it. Does that matter?"

"I don't trust him."

"That makes two of us."

"You can't go back there."

"I have work tomorrow. I don't have a choice."

"Grayson." He folded his arms.

"Gabriel." She folded hers.

"Goddamn it, this isn't up for discussion!" he seethed, finally turning to face her. "For the past three days, I've actually been able to work and sleep knowing that you were nowhere near that son of a bitch. And now I hear that not only have you been in the same building, but you've been isolated and stalked by the man who has likely orchestrated eight murders in your name. He seems stable now, but if he gets spooked or thinks his position with you is failing, there's no telling what he might do. You. Cannot. Go back there."

"What are you talking about? Nothing's going to happen to me."

"I thought you were safe," he hissed. "You were supposed to be safe."

"I am safe," she said, stepping forward. "You're here with me."

"I'm not there. That's the point."

He turned back toward the window, gripping either side of the window pane until his knuckles were white. Grayson sucked in a breath, afraid his blanched fingers would rip through the wood.

"Stop it." Grayson ducked under his left arm and, before she could even think twice to stop herself, she placed a hand on his cheek.

Gabriel's breath hitched in his chest. He closed his eyes and turned his face into her hand. She wrapped the strands of his hair in between her fingers. His ragged breathing eased, and he dipped his forehead down to rest on hers. "I'm sorry," he whispered.

She didn't hesitate. "You're forgiven. Now go apologize to them."

"I'd never forgive myself if something happened to you." He slipped his left arm down from the window and around her shoulder.

"I'm just a case to you, Gabriel. Once you nail Cain, you'll forget all about me. It's okay. I get it." Grayson tried to keep her voice light. It shook more than she meant it to.

"I doubt that."

"You will," she insisted.

He pulled her closer to him and kissed the top of her head. "There's no forgetting you."

She laid her head sideways on his shoulder, her hand still rhythmically running back and forth over his shoulders. She felt the pressure of his palm against her hip. The heat was almost unbearable.

"Are you feeling better?"

"Mm-hmm."

"Are you ready to go back for dessert?"

"How are you still hungry?" he chuckled.

"I'm not. That doesn't mean there's no room for dessert." She smiled. "Come on. I have something to show you anyway."

She tugged slightly where her fingers were twisted into his shirt. He turned around and dutifully followed her back into the squad room.

She knew they weren't finished talking about her return to work, but his anger had faded to a low hum. She could barely feel the tension still simmering beneath his button-down.

She'd touched him, just once, and his brain had apparently short-circuited.

Gabriel followed her back into the break room and nodded brusquely at his partners. They nodded in return. All was forgiven.

"Did you two make nice?" Logan asked devilishly.

"Yes, we did. For now," she replied. "Who wants dessert?"

She dished out tiramisu and cannolis, along with the rest of the coffee. They were settled in and halfway through their plates when Grayson pulled two yellow lined pieces of paper out of her back pocket. She shakily placed them on the table underneath her coffee, using the foam cup as a paperweight.

Logan waited for a beat, then put his fork down. "What's that, doc?" he asked, motioning toward the papers with his eyebrows.

"Um, well..." she fingered the edge of the paper, "it's something I put together yesterday. I...I thought maybe it could help."

"Really?"

She nodded and unfurled the papers, then shoved them across the table at Gabriel. He took them with a slight smile, then started scanning the pages. His smile faded considerably.

"Gabe?" Nolan asked. "What is it?"

When he didn't answer, Grayson started talking.

"I, um...I made a list. Of everyone who died. I started thinking on Monday after...after things happened with Cain. He said something that stuck with me. He called Nathan a fraud. Not that he lied or cheated, but that he was a *fraud*. Like that particular word was the reason he had to die."

She was tapping her fingers on the table relentlessly in a predictable, rhythmic pattern. *12345, 54321. 2345. 2345.*

12345, 54321. With every passing minute, she was speeding up. "So, so what if there was a fault with each of them? This is what I came up with."

"You got something for everybody on that list?"

She nodded. "I think so."

"Whaddaya think, Gabe?" Nolan asked, looking over the table at his partner. "She on to something?"

He blinked quickly, then raised his eyes to look at hers. "Yes. She is."

He handed the pages across the table to his partners and then stood, walking out of the break room. When he came back with his binder, he laid a hand on the back of Grayson's neck and leaned down.

"Good job, sweetheart," he murmured in her ear.

She blushed crimson and focused her eyes on the half-eaten tiramisu in front of her.

"Finish your dessert. I like watching you eat."

Grayson jerked her eyes up and followed him as he walked back to his chair with a wicked grin on his face. She whipped her head to look at Logan and Blake. They hadn't heard him.

Oh good God, stop! Why is it so hot in here?

"This is good," Logan said. "How'd you come up with this?"

"It just came to me." She shrugged. "Why?"

"We've been trying to figure this out for weeks."

"Well, I wouldn't have done any of it if Cain hadn't been so creepy on Monday. He slipped up." She shot a guilty look at Blake. "Is that the term? Slipped up? Or is that out of date...like cowabunga?"

"Cowabunga?" Logan smirked.

"Hey, before I wanted to be a doctor I wanted to be a ninja turtle in a tutu. Shut up."

"Since I don't have a piece of paper in front of me, could somebody please explain?" Blake asked, spooning himself another helping of tiramisu.

"All right," Grayson nodded. "Working backward is easier. Nathan was a fraud. Apparently lying to me was enough to get him killed. Harlan attacked me, so I called him violent. Priya was tricky, but Cain thought she was a witchdoctor. There's more than one lecture where he calls naturopathic medicine modern heresy, so that's what I called her. A heretic. Dr. Carrol was easy. We all joked about not wanting to endure his wrath at Grand Rounds. Elliot was blowing through a trust fund and an expense account; couldn't get enough or spend it fast enough. Avarice. Marcus Porter was a fat pig. He ate and drank his way through everything. Gluttony. Dr. Nelson had certain, um…appetites, so I went with lust."

"What about Lisa Oakes?"

"I don't know. I'm too close to her. I couldn't find anything wrong with her."

"Damn."

"What?"

"That's our problem. Well, one of them. We can't make her fit."

"Sorry. I didn't get there." Grayson grabbed the sheets of paper and crumpled them up. "I guess this is useless."

"Not at all," Gabriel interjected, taking the sheets from her before she destroyed them.

"And I still don't know what the Beatrice thing is all about. I've been wracking my brain; I just don't have anything."

"Don't worry. Gabe will come up with something." Logan winked. "Wontcha, Wonder Boy?"

They sat around the table and chatted for an hour, trying to come up with a reasonable overarching theory. They came up empty-handed and switched to happier topics.

An hour after that, Grayson threw a hand over her mouth to stifle a yawn.

"You should get to bed, doc," Logan said.

"I'm fine." She yawned again.

"Come on," Gabriel said, standing and holding out his hand. "You can sleep in the crib."

Grayson's eyes weren't the only ones that rose at the comment. "The roads are a mess in this storm," he said by way of explanation.

"Um, okay…is that legal?"

Logan chuckled to himself.

Gabriel dropped his lips to her ear. "Yes, love, it's legal," he whispered in her ear.

"Noah calls me that," she whispered back.

"Then he'll just have to stop," came the response.

It made her shiver. She stood up without thinking and took his offered hand.

"Goodnight, doc," Logan chuckled as she walked out after his former partner.

Gabriel swiftly guided Grayson through the maze of desks in the squad room and down a short hallway. He pushed open a nondescript door and led her into a room. There were six bunk beds stacked one on top of the other in pairs and a single lamp on a lonely-looking side table.

"The crib?" she giggled.

"Yes. What's funny?"

"Nothing. Why do I need to stay here?"

"Because I don't want you to drive in this storm. And because I don't want you out of my sight."

The sentiment was endearing until she thought it through. *He wouldn't dare...* "You're not thinking of barricading me in here, are you?"

"Grayson..."

"Gabriel, please..." She grabbed the bridge of her nose and shut her eyes. "I can't have this argument with you again. I'll lose my job."

"You're not going back to that hospital," he said, pulling pillows off of an adjacent bed and turning down the covers on a lower bunk.

She rolled her eyes at him and crossed her arms in front of her chest. "Goddamn it, you can't keep me here!"

"Yes, I can."

"Gabriel, stop it! Some girls might find this little chase cute, but it's exhausting."

He sat down on the edge of the lower bunk bed and rested his elbows on his knees. "You think I chase after girls?"

"Don't you? Most men do."

"I'm not most men."

"For so...so many reasons," she scoffed sarcastically, shaking her head.

"Come here," he smiled, holding his hand out to her again.

She took it, trying to hold in a smirk. He pulled her into the bed and wrapped her in his arms. He swung his legs up and leaned against the headrest.

She snuggled into his side, unconsciously wrapping one leg around his. "What is it with you?" she asked. "You drive me up the wall one minute and the next I want to...to..."

Gabriel reached up and rested a hand on her cheek, brushing his thumb along the soft skin underneath her eye. They stared at each other for quite a long time, not saying a word.

"Don't go to work tomorrow," he whispered.

"Don't ask me to promise you that," she whispered back.

"I can't stand the thought of him watching you, let alone being close to you or touching you. You're mine and only mine. Do you understand me?"

Grayson sighed into his chest by way of response. She was already asleep.

He pulled the blanket around her shoulders and started rhythmically running his hands through her hair. "Sweet dreams, sweetheart," he whispered in between kisses to her forehead and the top of her head.

He was asleep a few minutes later.

58

GRAYSON WOKE UP just before midnight, feeling too warm and too stiff. She was momentarily disoriented at the sight of the dreary bunk beds, but it didn't take long to remember where she was. Or why she was warmer than usual. She propped herself up on one elbow and looked at him.

Gabriel was sound asleep on his back, his left arm curled around her and his right arm hooked underneath the back of his head. His chest rose and fell steadily with each breath. He looked so much more relaxed, and a lot younger. He barely looked thirty.

She put her head back down and ran a hand along his chest and stomach, on top of his undershirt. He stirred and reflexively brought the hand from behind his head to grab the one running over his abdomen.

Grayson stifled a giggle and stopped moving. She didn't want to wake him.

Good God, Gray, get ahold of yourself.

Before too long, her mind drifted to Lisa. And to Douglas Cain. It was the one connection she couldn't figure out. As far as she knew, he'd never had a problem with Lisa and Lisa had never had a problem with him. He hadn't been one of the attendings who'd given her a hard time. In fact, he'd been pleasant to her, like he'd enjoyed her company. Everyone had thought it a bit odd since it was well known that Douglas Cain didn't like anybody. She sighed softly.

Okay, fine, if I can't figure out Lisa, maybe I can figure out the Beatrice thing.

Grayson gingerly eased her hand out of Gabriel's and slid off the mattress. He groaned in his sleep at the loss of her warmth and turned in toward the wall. She stood stock-still until she was sure he was fast asleep.

Her eyes adjusted to the dark, and she noticed the two bunk beds opposite them each had an occupant. She rolled her eyes at the rhythmic snoring coming from each of them, one rising and the other falling in time with each another.

She quietly left the crib.

It took a minute looking around the squad room to find where they'd stuffed her messenger bag. It was underneath Gabriel's desk. She managed to get her laptop out and fired up quickly. She grabbed a lukewarm cup of coffee from the break room and sat down at his desk with her internet browser open and blinking.

"Well, here goes nothing. Needle in a haystack," she whispered.

Typing *Beatrice* into the search engine seemed like a rather stupid idea, but it was the easiest place to start. The screen lit up with results, most of them useless. Apparently, Mrs. Beatrice Evans, a Cherry Creek socialite, was throwing her annual charity auction to benefit the Children's Hospital autism unit. And Beatrice—aka Bea Mortero—had just been arrested on drug charges. Grayson began chewing on her bottom lip. The list went on and on.

Okay, so…not helpful. Let's try this.

She added "famous" to her search and tried again. After spending twenty minutes skimming links on everyone from Beatrice Arthur from *The Golden Girls* and Beatrice from Shakespeare's *Much Ado About Nothing*, she went for another cup of coffee.

As she waited for a fresh pot to brew, she tapped her foot on the linoleum floor and stared at the ceiling. It had to all be connected. Cain was too much of an anal-retentive bastard to call her Beatrice randomly. She rolled her eyes.

Egotistical bastard. Like he doesn't have a whole host of sins himself. He and the Devil would be great dance partners.

She stopped mid-pour and looked up at the wall, slack-jawed.

Holy shit, that's it.

Grayson immediately forgot about the coffee and jogged back to her computer, typing "Beatrice seven deadly sins" into her search engine.

Bingo.

She clicked on the first entry, a Wikipedia article on Beatrice Portinari, and started softly reading aloud to the abandoned squad room. Midway through the article, she clicked on a link to an article on the first of the three books in the *Divine Comedy, Inferno*. Halfway through that article, she found a list of the levels of hell.

She bit down on her bottom lip, hard, and read through them. Then again. And again. The hair on the back of her neck stood at full attention.

Grayson lunged for a piece of paper from Nolan's desk and wrote out Roman numerals one through nine, then the names of each level from the book.

I.   Limbo.
II.   Lust.
III. Gluttony.
IV.   Avarice.
V.   Wrath.
VI.   Heresy.

VII.   Violence.

VIII.   Fraud.

IX.   Treachery.

Shaking, she wrote out the names of each of the victims next to the levels, in order. They all matched, even Lisa. All except for number nine, which was still blank.

"There's still one more," she whispered, putting her hands over her mouth in surprise.

She tore her eyes away from the blank spot next to "treachery" and focused instead on the first entry. Lisa was matched with Limbo. She scrolled back up in the Wikipedia article and read over the entry again.

"*...In Limbo reside the unbaptized and virtuous pagans who, although not sinful, did not accept Christ...Dante implies that all virtuous non-Christians reside here...Beyond the first circle, all of those condemned for active, deliberately willed sin are judged...*"

Grayson wrinkled her nose, talking to herself under her breath.

"This doesn't make any sense. Lisa believed in God. She was a Christian. It's not like I've ever seen Cain go to church. The only thing he's ever worshipped is the damned hospital."

She shook her head and leaned forward, resting her face in her hands and rubbing her temples. Forward circles, backward circles. Forward circles, backward circles. Forward circles, backw...

It clicked.

We're not talking about real religion here. We're talking about Cain's religion. Medicine.

"She was a DO. Not an MD," she whispered. "Goddamn it, she died because I was friends with her and she had the wrong degree. Everything else was perfect, except for the two letters after her name."

She shook her head in disbelief. *You've got to be kidding me, Cain.*

Grayson kept her head in her hands, elbows on the desk, and shut her eyes. *Deep breath, Gray. You've still gotta figure out what he wants with you.*

It didn't take long to find the answer, also courtesy of Wikipedia. Not only was the tale's protagonist Dante obsessed with a woman named Beatrice, but so was the author, the real-life Dante Alighieri.

And in the story, Dante had to travel through all of the levels of hell to see her.

And he only has one more to go to get to me.

Grayson scowled at the brightly lit screen.

This is going to stop.

Now.

Quickly, she grabbed her notes and placed them in a pile in the middle of Gabriel's desk. She grabbed another piece of paper from the stack on Nolan's desk and scribbled a quick note, which she placed on top of the pile.

She threw on her coat and gloves, tucked her hair into her hat, and slung her messenger bag over her shoulder. She shot a quick look back toward the crib.

For a split second, she thought about waking one of them. Maybe Logan. Just to tell someone where she was going. Then she thought better of it. If she didn't go now, they wouldn't let her.

She fingered her car keys nervously in her right pocket. As quickly and quietly as she could manage, she took the stairs down to the ground floor and had the night guard let her out the front door.

She brushed the snow off of her front windshield and turned on her car, half-expecting someone to come bursting out the front door looking for her. No one did. She turned on her headlights and turned down the street toward St. Joe's.

Please, let this be the right thing to do.

59

IT WAS WELL after 3 a.m. when Gabriel stirred underneath the cheap flimsy blanket.

Goddamn it, why is the crib always so fucking cold?

He rubbed the back of his neck, trying to work out the kinks and the sore muscles. His eyes snapped wide open when the fog cleared.

I shouldn't be cold.

There was a damned good reason for that.

He reached out toward the other side of the small mattress. His hand found cold sheets and a cold pillow. Grayson wasn't there and hadn't been for a while.

His heart accelerated inside his chest as he sat up, swinging his legs over the side of the bed and onto the ice-cold floor. He could hear two different snoring patterns from the set of bunk beds on the opposite wall. Logan and Blake were passed out, oblivious to the world.

He walked out into the squad room. There were only a few desk lights on, casting an eerie glow on the furniture. He didn't see her. The light was on in the break room. He headed in that direction, expecting to find her curled up at the table with a foam cup of coffee in between her hands.

There was coffee, all right. In fact, a half-poured cold cup was resting on the countertop. A new pot was still warming underneath the machine. But no Grayson.

Fuck.

Now he was beginning to worry. And his blood was beginning to boil.

She better not have fucking gone home.

He stormed back out into the squad room and turned to go back into the crib, intending to wake up Nolan and Logan.

He was halfway to the door when he noticed his desk. There was no bag underneath it. No ivory coat on the back of Nolan's chair. And there was a new stack of paper on top of his blotter that hadn't been there when he'd gone to bed.

He walked over to his desk and lifted the first page up in the dim light. He read over the hastily scribbled note. He felt his gut suddenly sink into the floor.

No, no, no. No, goddamn it, fucking hell no!

He scanned the remaining pages, then bolted to the crib. He shoved the door open and flipped the switch on the side wall to turn on the overhead fluorescents.

Nolan groaned and rolled over on the top bunk, trying to cover his eyes. Harrison threw one hand over his face and squinted against the light.

"Gabe, what the shit? It's three in the morning," Blake muttered.

"She's gone!"

"Who's gone?"

Nolan was midway through rubbing his eyes when the stupidity of that question hit him. "Oh shit."

"What do you mean she's gone?" Harrison asked, swinging his legs over the side of the bottom bunk and rubbing his neck to work out the kinks.

"When did you two come to bed?"

"Uh, maybe an hour after you two snuggle-bugs came in here."

"Now's not the fucking time, Logan. She was here?"

"Yeah, of course." He nodded. "You two were sound asleep."

"You didn't hear her get up?"

He shook his head.

"You're sure she's not just in the break room or the bathroom or something?" Nolan yawned.

"Yeah, I'm sure."

He handed the pages from his desk over to Logan. Gabriel shoved his hands through his hair and started pacing in between the beds. It took Harrison a few passes to fully absorb what she had written down. He passed the pages up one level to Blake, then stared down his agitated former partner.

"Must've hit her during the night."

"Yeah, no shit." Blake whistled.

"So, Cain thinks she's a character in a book?"

"Not quite," Gabriel shook his head. "Dante Alighieri and Beatrice Portinari were real people. They both feature in the books as well, Beatrice less so until the second and third volumes."

"Don't tell me you're all read up on these, too," Logan griped.

"I took classics in college."

"Of course you fucking did."

"Hey," Blake piped up, "this Dante guy is Italian. Didn't Cain major in Italian?"

"Probably why he's so well-versed in murdering according to the book," Logan grumbled.

"So, Cain gets through this last level and then what?" Blake asked, climbing down from the bunk bed.

"He gets her," Gabriel sighed, leaning his head up against the concrete wall.

"Huh?"

Gabriel winced against the cold concrete. "Beatrice asked Virgil to guide Dante through the levels of Hell because she couldn't go with him to do it herself. Once he made it through to Purgatory, she came back and guided him to Heaven. Virgil hangs around for a while, but the point is: Dante makes it through Hell, and he gets Beatrice."

"You're sure?" Blake asked.

"Yeah, I'm sure."

"So, where the hell did she go?" Logan groaned.

Gabriel handed him a sheet of crumpled paper, the top page from the pile he'd found on his desk.

Gabriel-

I figured it out. Cain thinks I'm Beatrice Portinari. He's killing in order, the nine levels of Hell from Inferno. He has one more level to go. I can't let him kill anybody else because of me.

I'll be fine.

-Grayson

Harrison eyed his former partner. The rage and the tension were flowing off of him in waves.

So was the fear.

Logan couldn't understand what in the hell she had been thinking, going back by herself, but he had to give it to her. She had guts walking back into that hospital knowing what she knew.

He also couldn't shake the bad feeling that had settled in his stomach, but he wasn't about to say anything. It would just make things worse.

"She's already gone, Gabe. There's nothing we can do to stop her. You knew she was going to go into work in the morning anyway." That earned him a glare and a carefully chosen epithet.

He chuckled. "Oh, come on, Ryder. Like you were going to strap her down to the bed and keep her here. Don't be an ass."

Logan stood up and walked to the door. "Well, we're up now. Let's get the hell out of here, shower, and change. At least there's nobody on the roads. We'll drop in on her tomorrow after work, okay? Just let it go for now."

Harrison walked out of the crib, toward his desk. Blake hesitated for a minute, then slapped his hand on his partner's shoulder and forced him to turn away from the wall.

"C'mon, buddy. Let's go home for a few hours. She's okay."

"You don't know that."

"Gabe, the girl's a surgeon, for Christ's sake. She breaks bones for a living. She can handle herself."

Blake maneuvered his partner out of the crib and out to his desk. For good measure, they made sure Gabriel got into his car and drove out of the deck before getting in their own cars... just in case he decided to go back into the squad or worse, turn his car toward the hospital.

He didn't. He headed for home.

60

THE HOSPITAL WASN'T deserted, but there were very few people up and about after midnight. A few residents were scurrying from the call rooms down the hallway toward the ER. The night shift nurses were finishing up their hourly rounds and starting to congregate at the nurses' station. Family members were either long gone home or dutifully trying to catch a few minutes of sleep sitting straight up in uncomfortable plastic chairs.

No one thought twice about Dr. Carter walking through the hallway at this hour. She was a well-known fixture during midnight rounds. Usually, by now, she'd have changed into scrubs for the night. A few nurses made hushed comments about wearing high heels and no white coat after midnight.

Most of them hardly took notice of her.

Grayson didn't notice the small talk. She kept her head down and made her way through the maze of hallways as quickly as possible. She took the main elevators up to the bridge, then made her way across it and up another set of stairs. She used her badge to swipe into the main lobby and silently circled around several dark corners to the row of faculty offices on the back wall. She switched on the light on her cell phone so she could see the names printed on the placards soldered to each door.

Dr. Keefer. Dr. Reyes. Dr. Martin. Dr. Parker. Dr. Cain.

Bingo.

There was no light coming through the bottom of the office door or through the small side window. She'd called the hospital answering service on the drive over. Cain wasn't on call. There was no reason for him to be anywhere near the hospital tonight, but there was always the possibility that he'd be working late anyway.

Better to be safe than sorry.

She slipped her ID card off of the clip on the waistband of her pants and stuck it in between the door and the lock. Once or twice, she'd locked herself out of her dorm room in college, and this trick had come in handy. Thankfully, the internal medicine department was a bit behind the times and hadn't switched over to electronic door locks. They were due, but like every renovation in the hospital, it was perilously far behind schedule.

Grayson tried several times to get the lock to catch on the edge of the card, without any luck. Just to be sure, she tried her second badge. The edge was a little bit thicker. It didn't work either.

"Damn." She swore under her breath.

Well, short of calling up security to bring her the key…(and how exactly was she going to explain that?)…there was no getting into Dr. Cain's office tonight.

Shit.

She sat dejectedly on the floor for several moments, her head kicked back against the wall, trying to think of any possible way of manipulating the lock. She came up empty-handed and decided to get out of Dodge as quickly as possible before security came around on their nightly rounds and started asking questions.

As she wound her way back through the hallways, she mentally chastised herself.

Just what was this supposed to accomplish again?

She was going to break into Cain's office and then…find a detailed description of each crime, each target, sitting prettily for her on his desk? In a nice envelope with her name on it?

Right. I need sleep. I'm not thinking clearly.

Cain might have been a psychopath and a killer, but he was exceptionally intelligent and certainly wasn't sloppy. Even if he did have something written down, the chance it was being kept at the office were…basically zero.

Less than zero. Idiot.

Grayson found herself at the main department lobby door, standing in front of a large composite photograph hanging opposite the main reception desk. A copy was hung up in every department, on every patient floor, even in the cafeteria. It detailed each resident, their name, their department, and their year in training. It usually didn't serve much purpose, other than to occupy a wall, but as she took a moment to stop and look at it, an idea hit.

If she couldn't find a name written on a piece of paper on Cain's desk, maybe she could figure it out on her own. She could sit down and mark people off the list, one by one, until she had a small group of candidates. The last group was treachery, for heaven's sake. How many residents could really be labeled treacherous?

She stifled a yawn. *I can do that tomorrow. Well, later today. I really need to get some sleep.*

Grayson quietly made her way back to the main part of the hospital. She pulled her cell phone back out of her pocket and checked it. No messages, no calls. Either no one had woken up back at the department yet, or Gabriel had somehow been replaced with his twin who was calm, collected, and completely fine with her being at the hospital.

She eyed the clock in the hallway as she walked by it. It was just coming up on four o'clock in the morning. That gave her more than enough time to go home and get cleaned up before coming back for rounds.

She sighed as she approached the elevator bank.

I really don't want to wait.

Without a second thought, she ducked into a back stairwell and started lazily walking down the steps, holding onto the railing with her right hand for support. It was a stairwell she used all the time during the day, along with most of the residents who didn't feel like shoving themselves into elevators with sick patients and their families.

The faded mint-green walls mixed with a flickering light bulb or two didn't make it particularly inviting, but Grayson was too tired to care. As long as she made it to the bottom floor and out to her car, she'd be fine.

She'd just rounded the landing for the third floor when the hair on the back of her neck stood up. She slowed down. The only sound echoing up the stairwell was her heels connecting with the linoleum.

She was alone.

Grayson hesitantly put her right foot down on the first stair of the next flight.

Too late.

Two long arms wrapped around her, one around her arms and her midsection, the other up around her face. The hand at her face slammed a distinctly familiar-smelling cloth over her mouth and nose.

Grayson held her breath. She tried to squirm out of the hold, but whoever was holding her was too strong. Her arms were locked out straight by her sides. Her legs connected with air.

Despite all her attempts to flail around, her attacker's hold only grew stronger.

Her lungs were on fire. All she wanted to do was breathe. And it was the one thing she knew that she couldn't do if she wanted to get out alive. She struggled again and felt a sickening, warm breath inch up along the side of her neck.

Don't breathe. Don't breathe. Don't breathe!

"Deep breath, Beatrice."

Grayson's eyes went wide. She involuntarily gasped into the cloth that was pressed against her face. Almost instantly, her head began to swim and her vision blurred.

She could feel her body going limp. The more she tried to fight, the weaker she became. Before things completely went black, she heard a very familiar voice whisper again in her ear.

"You're mine now."

All she wanted to do was scream.

———

Glossary of Medical Terms
(listed alphabetically)

16s: A measurement of IV gauge or size

ABCs: From the ATLS protocol, abbreviation for Airway, Breathing, and Circulation, the first steps in the algorithm

ACL: Abbreviation for Anterior Cruciate Ligament

Amiodarone: An antiarrhythmic cardiac medication

Antecubs: A description of an IV placed in the elbow crease, or antecubital fossa

AP Pelvis: A front-to-back x-ray view of the pelvis

APC-III Pelvis: A severe injury to the pelvic ring resulting in instability

Art line: Arterial line

Articular: As in articular reduction, at the level of the joint

ASIS: Abbreviation for Anterior Superior Iliac Spine, a bony landmark of the pelvis

ATLS protocol: Abbreviation for Advanced Trauma Life Support protocol; the algorithm followed for acute management of life-threatening trauma injuries

Benzodiazepines: A class of medication used for its sedating effect

Bilateral: Both sides, left and right

Borderline hypotension: Blood pressure that is nearly too low

Bounding pulses: Easily palpable, strong pulses

Catheter: A flexible tube inserted to drain fluid, often in the bladder

Chronically: Opposite of acute; for a long period of time

Cirrhosis: A chronic liver disease marked by degeneration of the cells and inflammation, usually caused by alcohol use or hepatitis

CK: Creatine kinase, a muscle protein released during rhabdomyolysis, that contributes to kidney failure

Clavicle: The collarbone

Comminuted fracture: A break in the bone that is in multiple pieces

Compartment syndrome: An increase to intra-compartment pressures within muscular compartments which causes cessation of blood flow and muscle death

DIC: Abbreviation for Diffuse Intravascular Coagulation, a life-threatening change in the ability of the body to stop bleeding

Dilaudid: A strong narcotic pain medication

Displaced: Not properly aligned, as in fracture ends that no longer align with one another

Distal radius: The end portion of one of the forearm bones at the level of the wrist

Divert: To change course

Dressings: Surgical bandages

Dysphagia: Trouble swallowing

ED: Abbreviation for Emergency Department

Electrolytes: Ions, often measured in the blood

Embolization: The process of obstructing a blood vessel with a mass, whether naturally or artificially

Epi: Short for epinephrine

Etomidate: A short acting anesthetic used for induction

Ex-fix/external fixator: A combination of pins and bars outside of the skin that temporarily stabilizes a fractured extremity until definitive fixation can be performed

Exsanguination: A severe and rapid loss of blood

Fasciotomy: Operative release of the fascia tissue surrounding the muscle compartments of an extremity, performed to release pressure within the compartment and prevent tissue death

FAST exam: Acronym for an ultrasound examination looking at four particular intra-abdominal recesses for blood

Femoral nails: A metal rod that is placed inside the femur for fracture reduction and fixation

Femoral neck: A particular anatomic portion of the proximal femur; part of the hip joint complex

Fentanyl: A strong narcotic pain medication

FFP: Abbreviation for Fresh Frozen Plasma, a blood bank component used during trauma resuscitation

Four part intraarticular proximal humerus fracture: A fracture involving with shoulder joint with four separate fracture fragments

GCS 5: Glasgow coma scale score of 5, a sign of significant injury and neurologic impairment in a trauma patient

GI: Abbreviation for Gastrointestinal; pertaining to the gastrointestinal tract

H&P: Abbreviation for History and Physical paperwork, the initial paperwork performed for an admission to the hospital

Hemi: Short for hemiarthroplasty, a partial joint replacement, a common treatment for the hip following fracture of the femoral neck

Hemodynamically unstable: The combination of an abnormal blood pressure, heart rate, oxygenation, and respiratory rate indicating physiologic instability

Hemoglobin: A protein responsible for transporting oxygen in the blood

Hyoid bone: A bone in the anterior neck, often fractured when a person has been strangled

Hypertensive: High blood pressure

Hypotensive: A descriptor indicating low blood pressure

ICU: Abbreviation for Intensive Care Unit

IV PPI's: Abbreviation for Intravenous Proton Pump Inhibitors, medications used to prevent gastric ulcers

Intensivist: A subspecialty physician who works exclusively in the ICU

Interventional radiology: A subspecialty of radiology which specializes in invasive procedures, including embolization

Intra-abdominal injury: An injury to the organs and structures on the inside of the abdomen

Intra-operative fluoroscopy: Use of mobile x-ray during a surgical procedure, common in orthopaedic surgery

Ivy-League gunner: A tongue-in-cheek description of an ambitious, type A college student intent on a particular career goal

Lag screw/neutralization plate: A type of construct used to fix fractures utilizing a particular screw and plate combination

McBurney's point: A location on the right lower abdomen, pain at which may be related to appendicitis

ME: Abbreviation for Medical Examiner; a subspecialty trained pathologist dedicated to the examination of a deceased person in order to determine cause of death

Mercury Cyanide: An extremely toxic salt composed of mercury and hydrocyanic acid

Midline: In the middle; central

M&M: Abbreviation for Morbidity and Mortality
Conference; a medical conference examining the
patient cases involving death or suboptimal outcome

MVC: Abbreviation for Motor Vehicle Crash

Narcan: A medication used to reverse an overdose of
narcotics

Nasogastric tube: A tube inserted through the nose, down
the esophagus, and into the stomach, used to introduce
or remove fluid from the stomach

Nephrology: A subspecialty dedicated to the kidneys

Neurology: A subspecialty dedicated to the brain

New-onset arrhythmia: Newly diagnosed abnormal heart
rhythm

PACU: Acronym for Post-Anesthesia Care Unit; the
location where patients are transferred after surgery to
recover prior to returning to their assigned hospital
room

Palliative: Relieving pain without directing addressing the
root cause of the problem, as in palliative care consult
for a terminally ill patient

Palliative care fellow: A doctor who is undertaking
additional training in the care of the terminally ill and
actively dying patient

Pathologic fracture: A break in the bone secondary to
abnormally weak bone, commonly due to cancer and
metastatic disease

Pelvic binder: A device used to decrease intra-pelvic
volume following fracture of the pelvic ring

Pelvic ex-fix: An external fixator applied to the pelvis;
see ex-fix

Pelvic packing: A technique used to help decrease bleeding secondary to pelvic fractures which involves placing sterile towels along the pelvic rim inside the body

PGY2's/3's: Abbreviation for Post-Graduate Year; a particular year in residency training

Plate it: To place a plate and screw construct to stabilize a fracture

Platelets: Small, a-nuclear cells involved with blood clotting

Pneumo: See pneumothorax

Pneumothorax: A condition where air becomes trapped outside of the lung but inside the ribcage, causing collapse of the lung

Poly-extremity: Involving multiple limbs

Pressors: See vasopressors

Proximal humerus: The most cephalad portion of the upper arm bone, part of the shoulder complex

PT: Abbreviation for Physical Therapy

Pull traction: Use manual force to pull longitudinal traction on an extremity in order to lengthen and reduce a fracture or dislocation

Renal failure: Damage to the kidneys resulting in a lack of cell function and buildup of toxins in the bloodstream; kidney failure

Rhabdomyolysis: A serious syndrome resulting from muscle cell death and release of damaging proteins into the bloodstream, which can possibly lead to kidney failure

Rodding (as in a femur): Placement of a femoral nail

Sat's: Short for Saturation; intending to describe the level of oxygen in the blood

Sepsis: A state characterized by abnormal vital signs in the setting of infection

Septicemia: See sepsis

Stage-3 shock: A descriptor of vital signs and clinical findings describing a severe level of hemodynamic instability

STEMI: Acronym for ST-Elevation Myocardial Infarction, a type of heart attack

Stitch: Surgical suture

Stress steroids: A particular dosing protocol of intravenous steroid medication

Subclavian vein: A large vein underneath the collarbone that returns blood to the heart

Subspecialty: A particularly specific area of medicine, e.g. cardiology, neurosurgery, orthopaedic surgery

Succinylcholine: A synthetic compound used in anesthesia to induce paralysis for intubation

Syndesmosis: A ligamentous complex at the level of the ankle joint

Syphilis: An infectious disorder caused by a spirochete bacteria

T-waves: A marker on an EKG, or electrocardiogram, which can be normal or abnormal depending on its morphology

Tachycardia: An abnormally fast heart rate

TEG: Acronym for Thromboelastogram; an intricate method for analyzing blood clotting mechanisms in the bloodstream

Tibia: The shin bone, the larger of the two lower leg bones

Tibial plateau: The proximal portion of the tibia; part of the knee joint

Tubed and lined: A descriptor indicating that a patient has been intubated and has had central and peripheral IV access established

Turf it: Patient transfer to another service

Type-1 diabetic: Also called juvenile diabetes; an inability to produce insulin or a defect in the body's ability to use insulin to regulate blood sugar levels

V-fib: Abbreviation for Ventricular Fibrillation; a very dangerous heart rhythm

Vasopressors: Medications given to maintain appropriate blood pressure

VDRF: Abbreviation for Ventilator Dependent Respiratory Failure; a condition in which a patient has been unable to wean off of a mechanical ventilator machine because he/she cannot breathe well enough to maintain enough oxygen in the bloodstream on his/her own

Ventilator: A mechanical breathing machine

Versed: A strong benzodiazepine used for sedation

Weber B Bimal equivalent: A type of ankle fracture often requiring operative repair

Wide mediastinum: A description of the area in the chest containing the heart, bronchus, esophagus, and great vessels; a widened mediastinum can indicate severe injury

Widened pubic symphysis and gapping of the right posterior SI joint: A description of an particular injury pattern to the pelvic ring, including injury to the front and the back of the pelvic ring, indicating instability

Trademark Notice

The following trademarked items appear in *Descent*. The author acknowledges the trademarked status and the trademark owners of the following wordmarks mentioned in this work of fiction:

Barbie/Ken	Cold Stone
4Runner	Aleve
Kleenex	Blue Moon
Subaru	PowerPoint
New Belgium/Fat Tire	Calvin Klein
Super Mario Brothers	Morticia Addams
Mercedes	Vera Wang
Audi	Google
Yves Saint Laurent	Formica
Rolex	S. Godard
Rolodex	Adirondak
Jack Daniels	Wonder Woman
Styrofoam	Glinda the Good Witch
North Face	Subaru
Ray-Bans	BMW
Armani	Rice Krispies
McDonald's	Elie Saab

Any omissions in the above list are purely accidental.

1

LOGAN CHUCKLED TO himself in the backseat of the SUV. Thank God Blake was driving. They'd be dead by now if Gabriel had managed to get behind the wheel. They were headed south, the front fender pointing toward a now very familiar neighborhood.

Weren't we just here?, he mused sarcastically.

He and Blake had been able to hold Ryder captive at his desk until just after four o'clock in the afternoon. The young detective had been more than his usual pain-in-the-ass self, agitated and in a blatantly foul mood. He'd also spent the vast majority of the day staring at his cell phone, at one point begging the thing to chirp before he'd hurled it into the wall.

Nolan had taken it away from him, for the safety of the poor battered machine. Logan could see Gabriel staring at the bulge in Nolan's right pocket, actively devising a plan to get it back before they got to their destination.

"Would you stop staring at his pants, Ryder? It's getting a little awkward back here," Logan said with a chuckle.

"If he'd give me the damned phone back, I wouldn't have to," came the mumbled reply.

"Gabe, we're partners, but we're not that close. I know you're impressed, buddy, but stop staring," Nolan said, elbowing him in the ribs across the center console.

"Give me my fucking phone, Blake."

"When we stop."

"Fuck you."

Nolan shrugged and threw the right blinker on as they neared the traffic light. Gabriel sulked in the passenger seat until they pulled up outside the bungalow. Logan sighed and grabbed each of them by the shoulder.

"All right you two, kiss and make up. I don't need you trying to kill each other in there while lover-boy is trying to make nice."

Gabriel glared at him through the rearview mirror but kept quiet. Instead, he held his hand out for his phone, which Nolan palmed him without another word. Gabriel and Blake followed him up the front steps, each perching on the porch railing as Logan rang the doorbell.

Instantly there was movement behind it. Frantic movement. When the door creaked open, instead of the guilty blue eyes the trio expected to find, Noah Mason's worried face appeared. The deep lines in the young man's forehead instantly softened, and he let out a long breath he hadn't realized he'd been holding.

"Oh, thank God. You must have heard. Come in, come in," he said, ushering them inside.

Um, what?

What the hell does that mean?

What's wrong with him?

The three detectives glanced back and forth among themselves, each wondering what kind of news could possibly have Noah so agitated in the middle of the afternoon. They shuffled into the living room without a word.

Within seconds of the door closing, Barbara Parker came sprinting out of the kitchen, hot tea in hand, looking equally haggard.

Gabriel's blood froze. Something was very wrong here.

Where is Grayson?

Noah and Barbara sat huddled together on the couch, looking at the trio expectantly. Several awkward moments of silence passed with shoes scuffing nervously across the wooden floor and hands shoved deeply inside coat pockets. No one wanted to speak first. It didn't take long for Noah to decide he'd finally had enough and break the silence.

"Well?" he asked in an agitated tone. "Have you heard from her?"

The three detectives again looked at each other, confused.

Logan spoke first. "Have we heard from who, Mason?"

"So, you haven't heard from her either?"

Noah looked directly at Gabriel. The detective's face was like stone. No expression. No hint of life in his eyes. It was like he'd already disappeared inside his own head.

"From who?" Logan repeated.

"From Grayson, of course!" Babs shouted. "She didn't come home. She's not at work. Where is she?"

"She didn't come home?" Gabriel asked flatly.

Noah shivered at the blackness creeping into the young man's eyes.

"No, she didn't, genius," Barbara spat back. "No one's seen her since yesterday."

Noah laid a hand on her arm and tried desperately to keep the fear out of his own voice. "She didn't come home. She's not at work. Never showed up for rounds with her juniors or for the OR today. I parked next to her 4Runner this morning in the parking deck. We were holding out hope that she was with the three of you at the department somehow. We...we were trying to not panic..."

"Her car's in the deck? At the hospital?" Blake asked, eyebrows raised.

"Yeah. I checked on her badge with security. Gave them a song and dance about how she lost it and was too busy to come down and ask herself. It was last used to access the main building offices after midnight, then nothing."

"You haven't heard from her at all today?" Logan asked.

"No. And she's not picking up her phone. It goes straight to voicemail, like it's turned off. Have you?" Noah responded.

The three detectives shook their heads.

"Did you call the station?" Logan pressed.

"No," Noah said, shaking his head dejectedly. "She'd told me that she was going down to see you gents last night. I...I just figured she was with you and so I didn't worry. Seems rather stupid now..." He drifted off.

Gabriel took out his phone and looked at the screen again. No messages. No missed calls. Nothing.

"Something's wrong, guys," Blake whispered to the wall.

"Yeah, no shit," Logan said.

Gabriel walked to the front window, leaning against the frame for support. Four sets of worried eyes followed him. He didn't speak. He stayed silent.

"Try her again," Logan said, nodding at the pair on the couch.

Noah took out his cell phone and dialed. He lowered it a few seconds later, shaking his head.

"Nothing. It goes straight to voicemail."

"She's not going to answer," Gabriel mumbled. "He has her."

"What? Who has her?" Blake asked, craning his head around to look at this partner.

"Cain. He took her."

"Took her? Like, kidnapped her?"

He nodded.

"Aw, goddamn it, girlie," Blake groaned, pulling out his cell phone and stepping over to the door. He put the phone up to his ear and waited.

"Hey, captain? It's Nolan. Yeah, we've got a problem here. Grayson Carter is missing… That's right. We need to put a BOLO out on a guy named Douglas Cain and his car."

Harrison grabbed the phone from him. "And add on a search warrant for this piece of shit's apartment or wherever he lives… Yeah. Yes, captain, it's Logan… No, we're sure. She didn't show up this morning but her car is at the hospital… Sure, yeah, a warrant for the office would help, too. Thanks."

Harrison eyed Gabriel as he handed the phone back to Nolan. "Captain's getting us warrants for the house, the car, his office, and whatever we want. It's just going to take time."

"We don't have time," Ryder spat back, spinning away from the window and stalking toward the staircase. "He's taken her, and he's already at least a half day ahead of us."

He stormed up the stairs and to her room, nearly forcing the door off its hinges. It smelled of her. He could see her sleeping on her bed, curled up underneath her comforter. He closed his eyes. This was not supposed to happen.

What was she thinking? I should've gone after her last night. I knew I should have gone after her. I should have called this morning to make sure she'd stay at home.

He desperately looked around the room for any real sign of her. There wasn't one.

Goddamn it, Grayson…

The sound of a throat clearing by the door snapped him back into reality. Ryder found himself standing over her bed, her sheets fisted in his hands.

Noah Mason was leaning against the door jamb, looking at him. "You know, as sick as he is, Cain is right about one thing. She is precious, detective."

"I know."

"No, I don't think you do," he countered, pushing off the wall and walking into the room. "You've known her, what, maybe two months? You have no idea. You know nothing about her. You've seen her beaten up and pushed around and stalked like an animal. You've seen her weak."

"Weak? Are you fucking kidding me?" *I'm not in the mood for this, Mason.*

"No, I'm not. You have no..."

"Enough!" Ryder's eyes blazed. "It doesn't matter how I've seen her. It doesn't matter what or how much I know about her. Weak or not, that son of a bitch has her. I'm bringing her back. And for the fucking record, Grayson weak can put most men on their knees."

Noah nodded, stepping up to the bed beside him. "She's the best thing to come into my life, Ryder, and she's not here. She's got to be fecking scared out of her bloody mind."

Gabriel clenched and unclenched his fists in the fabric. He didn't respond.

Noah glanced out the window at the afternoon sky. "Find her, detective. You find her, and you bring her back to us. And then, when she's safe, you bring Cain to me."

Gabriel quirked his eye at the man to his left and chuckled. "What the hell for?"

"I'm going to kill him," Noah said bitterly.

There was no hint of mirth in the young doctor's eyes. Ryder could see that much. Mason had every intention of killing the man, and from the look on his face, he already knew exactly how he was going to do it.

Forget it, kid. You're not going to get the chance.

"No," Gabriel responded coolly.

"No what?"

"No, I'm not bringing Cain to you," he replied. "I'm going to kill the son of a bitch the second I lay eyes on him. Myself."

"Nobody's fucking killing anybody!" Blake hissed from the doorway. "I don't need my partner in fucking prison and Mason, you wouldn't last five minutes. Now, both of you get your asses downstairs. Noah, stay here in case she calls. Keep trying her cell. Gabriel. Car. Now."

Blake grabbed his partner by the collar and shoved him downstairs, not waiting for either of them to reply.

2

THE GRAY HAZE faded in and out, darker and lighter, deeper and shallower.

No matter how much she struggled against it, she kept slipping back into the darkness, then bubbling back up into the light. This wasn't like before, like the fog in the hospital after Greg Harlan had attacked her. She felt seasick, tossed about and manipulated by the new cocktail of drugs slinking through her veins. There was too much, then too little, then too much again. She desperately needed something to hold onto.

Grayson forced herself back up toward the waiting light. She was so close this time. She could feel the edges of the haze. They were just a fingerbreadth away.

Closer, closer...

She felt the weight of her head loll back onto something scratchy. Her eyelids each felt as if they weighed a hundred pounds, but she forced them open. The brightness of the overhead lights was blinding and painful, and she slammed them shut in protest. Then, hating the darkness even more, she forced them back open, focusing on whatever was directly on top of her.

Gray popcorn ceiling tiles met her gaze. She swung her head to the right. The scratchy thing grated against her cheek. Gray walls, the same color as the ceiling. She swung to the left. More gray walls, with gray pipes coming from the ceiling and passing uninterrupted into the floor. She pushed herself up as much as she could manage, which wasn't much, and looked forward.

More gray walls. And a gray door without windows, only a peephole. She tried to sit up, but something clamped down around her, stopping her.

Wait, why can't I sit up?

Grayson looked toward her right wrist, and her eyes widened. Her blood turned to ice. The hair on the back of her neck screamed as it shot straight on end in panic.

Beige fabric was wrapped around her wrist and lower forearm. It disappeared off the top corner of a rather small bed frame. She tugged gently and felt the sharp endpoint.

Restraints.

She twisted her head around to look at her left wrist. Same thing.

She strained as much as she could to get a look at her feet. Ditto and ditto. Same beige straps, each one snaking off the end of the well-worn mattress.

Her head swam as she dropped back on the scratchy pillow. Her eyes focused on her right arm. A line of bruises and small black circles tracked up her pale skin, all neatly in a row.

Track marks.

Holy shit, I'm strapped down in four-point restraints. Oh my God, oh my God...I've been drugged and restrained!

Her heart was racing up in her throat. She felt the thundering of blood in her ears and slammed her eyes closed again. A new wave of nausea roiled up in her stomach. She could taste the sour bile in the back of her throat.

It all came flooding back. The back stairway. The low voice. Something over her mouth. That voice...

Snap out of it!

Her own voice screamed inside her head, straining desperately to be heard over the roar of the blood rushing to her ears.

If you don't stay calm, you're never getting out of here! Now breathe...focus...

She complied, one long shaky breath in and out, eyes closed. *Again. Breathe.*

One more long shaky breath, in and out.

Grayson forced her eyes to open, then calmly and systematically took in her surroundings again. Four gray walls, one with piping. A ceiling with individual popcorn tiles, no air ducts. Two sets of power outlets that she could see. Desk lamps set on the floor with high wattage light bulbs. Cement floors. One door directly in front of her, another one directly behind her if she craned her head back far enough. No windows.

Okay, now me...

The restraints were obvious. She was still in her clothes from the day before. Her coat was gone. A blanket was draped haphazardly over her lower body. She looked over to the corner and noticed two stacks of fabric, one white and the other vaguely green.

Scrubs? And towels?

Her badge had disappeared from her hip, and she couldn't feel her cell phone in her back pocket.

Shit, shit! Where is it? Even if I figure out where the hell I am, I can't call for help...

The sound of keys jingling at the door lock in front of her snapped her out of her own head. Grayson craned her neck up as much as her positioning would allow and watched the door open.

Douglas Cain smiled down at her as he sauntered through the doorway, a tray full of food in his hands. He slid up to the side of the twin bed and set it down onto a small black card table in the corner, just out of his captive's peripheral vision. He looked her over from head to toe, drinking her in, and then sat down on the edge of the bed.

Grayson's abdominal muscles instantly clenched, desperate to keep away from his lecherous eyes.

"Well, well, my Beatrice, you're awake. How wonderful."

Cain casually started undoing her restraints, one at a time. The instant her right arm was free, Grayson swung at him, but she was too weak, too drugged, and at a suboptimal angle. The moment she pushed herself up, her head spun from the ether.

Cain caught her wrist in his hand to keep her from scraping against the wall and held onto it. She tried to pull away, but it took all of her strength just to keep her eyes open.

"Tsk, tsk," he scolded, looking down on her with a fire brewing in his eyes. "That's not very nice. You shouldn't do such nasty things. Keep that up, and I'll have to put these straps back on."

Grayson instantly stopped struggling against him. Being alone in a room with Douglas Cain was one thing. Being alone in a room with him while strapped down and helpless was much, much worse.

He waited a moment, poised over her cowering frame, watching her panicked face. She watched the confident smirk wash over his face when the fight left her straining muscles. He seemed to know that he had her exactly where he wanted her.

Cain let go of her wrist and turned on the bed, undoing the remaining restraints around her ankles. The sound of the Velcro ripping apart was the only sound in the room. When he was finished, Grayson instantly scooted away from him on the bed, rubbing her wrists while eyeing him warily.

Cain just sat patiently, staring at her like a starving man.

When she hit a particularly sore spot on her wrist, she

glanced down, gasping at the needle marks she found near her veins.

No wonder my head feels horrible. How many times did he shoot me up with something? And with what…?

"What…what do you want with me?" she squeaked out.

"I want to keep you safe." He shrugged. "Would you like something to eat? You must be hungry."

He stood and pulled the small card table over to the bed. Grayson immediately recognized the scuffed-up tray and the black foam plates from the hospital cafeteria. A small wave of curious relief washed over her face.

Wait, am I still at St. Joe's?

Still, she eyed the tray's contents suspiciously.

"Oh, come now, I know what you like. It's perfectly safe. You have to be hungry," he encouraged.

Grayson didn't move.

"All right, I understand. The food will keep," he said, smiling warmly at her. "I know these accommodations are not ideal, but it's necessary for now."

"Necessary? Why?" she croaked. Her voice was dry and weak.

"You are precious, my Beatrice. I must keep my precious things safe."

"Let me go, Dr. Cain."

He leaned over her and brushed the back of his hand on her cheek. Grayson tried desperately to move away from him, but the back of her head smacked into a concrete wall. She was at the edge of the bed and backed into the far wall. There was nowhere else to go.

"I just can't do that, Beatrice. Now, eat. The washroom is behind you. Get yourself cleaned up after you've eaten. There are clothes in the corner."

With that, he was gone, swiftly opening and closing the door behind him without a backward glance. She heard the deadbolt lock turn and the sound of his shoes retreating on concrete floors.

Grayson continued to rub the sore skin around her wrists as she shakily got up on her feet. She scowled at the tray in front or her. Eating was the last thing on her mind.

When she couldn't hear his footsteps any longer, she went to the door and tried the handle. It was locked, of course, but she twisted and pulled desperately, just to be sure. The view through the peephole was black. He'd put something over it.

She shuffled across the small room to the other door, which opened into a small washroom complete with stall shower, toilet, and vanity mirror. She wrinkled her nose.

What the hell? A prison cell with a halfway respectable on-call bathroom? What the hell is this place?

It was stocked with soap and shampoo and, sure enough, the two piles of fabric she'd seen before were bathroom towels and spare scrubs in her size. The edge of a small black form poking out from underneath the clean scrubs caught Grayson's attention, and she grabbed for it.

"Oh my God, it's my cell phone," she whispered.

She instantly turned it on and hit number one on speed dial, thrusting the box up to her ear. All she heard was light static. She looked at the screen and immediately saw why.

No signal. Not even a roaming signal.

Damn it!

She ended the call and looked at her battery. It still had more than an eighty-percent charge, but she knew it wouldn't last long if it kept searching for a cell signal. There was no Wi-Fi signal in range either. She sighed heavily and quickly shut it off. She'd save the battery just in case she ever got out of here…wherever here was.

Grayson stripped out of her clothes and steamed up the little bathroom with hot water from the shower. Naked and trembling, she stared into the fogged-up mirror.

I've been kidnapped. I have no idea where I am in the hospital. I can't call for help. I'm at the mercy of a delusional serial killer. What in the hell am I going to do?

She slid down the wall onto the unforgiving concrete floor, curled up by the side of the shower, and cried.

**Continue on with Grayson and Gabriel in Book Three of *The Inferno Trilogy*.
Ascent—Summer 2019**

He has her.

Kidnapped, drugged, and held against her will, Grayson is at the mercy of Dr. Douglas Cain. He feeds her. He clothes her. He keeps her locked away inside a grey cell with no windows, no fresh air, and no sense of time. Minutes tick by into hours, hours into days, and the longer she stays locked in her silent hell, the clearer one thing becomes:

No one is coming to save her.

As terrified as Grayson is now, nothing can prepare her for the horrors that she will face at the hands of her captor…or what she will lose when she tries to fight back.

About the Author

A. R. Nicole is a North American writer with a background in medicine and a fascination with the written word. Many lazy afternoons are spent either devouring the latest novel, her loyal pup sleeping beside the chair, or writing a new one.

Follow her at:
www.ARNicole.com

Trademark Notice

The following trademarked items appear in *Descent*. The author acknowledges the trademarked status and the trademark owners of the following wordmarks mentioned in this work of fiction:

Barbie/Ken	Cold Stone
4Runner	Aleve
Kleenex	Blue Moon
Subaru	PowerPoint
New Belgium/Fat Tire	Calvin Klein
Super Mario Brothers	Morticia Addams
Mercedes	Vera Wang
Audi	Google
Yves Saint Laurent	Formica
Rolex	S. Godard
Rolodex	Adirondak
Jack Daniels	Wonder Woman
Styrofoam	Glinda the Good Witch
North Face	Subaru
Ray-Bans	BMW
Armani	Rice Krispies
McDonald's	Elie Saab

Any omissions in the above list are purely accidental.